THE ACADIAN REVENGE

Book 3 of

The Saga of Terminus Mundus

Michael Mazzaro

SIGNALMAN PUBLISHING

The Acadian Revenge:
The Saga of Terminus Mundus
by Michael Mazzaro

Signalman Publishing
www.signalmanpublishing.com
email: info@signalmanpublishing.com
Kissimmee, Florida

Cover design by: Kate Danailov

ISBN: 978-1-940145-55-6 (paperback)
978-1-940145-56-3 (ebook)

Library of Congress Control Number: 2015949693

Printed in the United States of America

SIGNALMAN
PUBLISHING

To God, Family, and Country

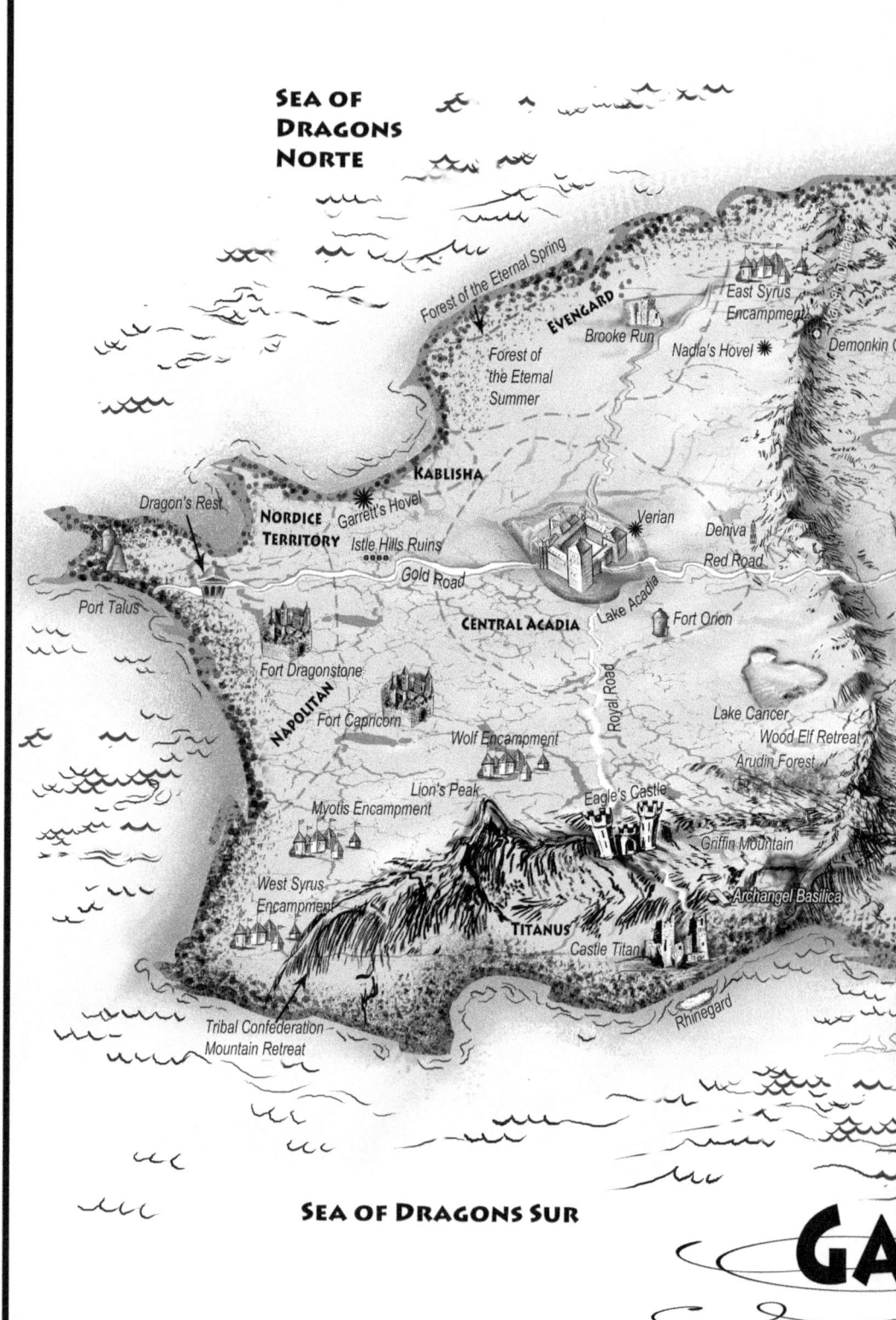

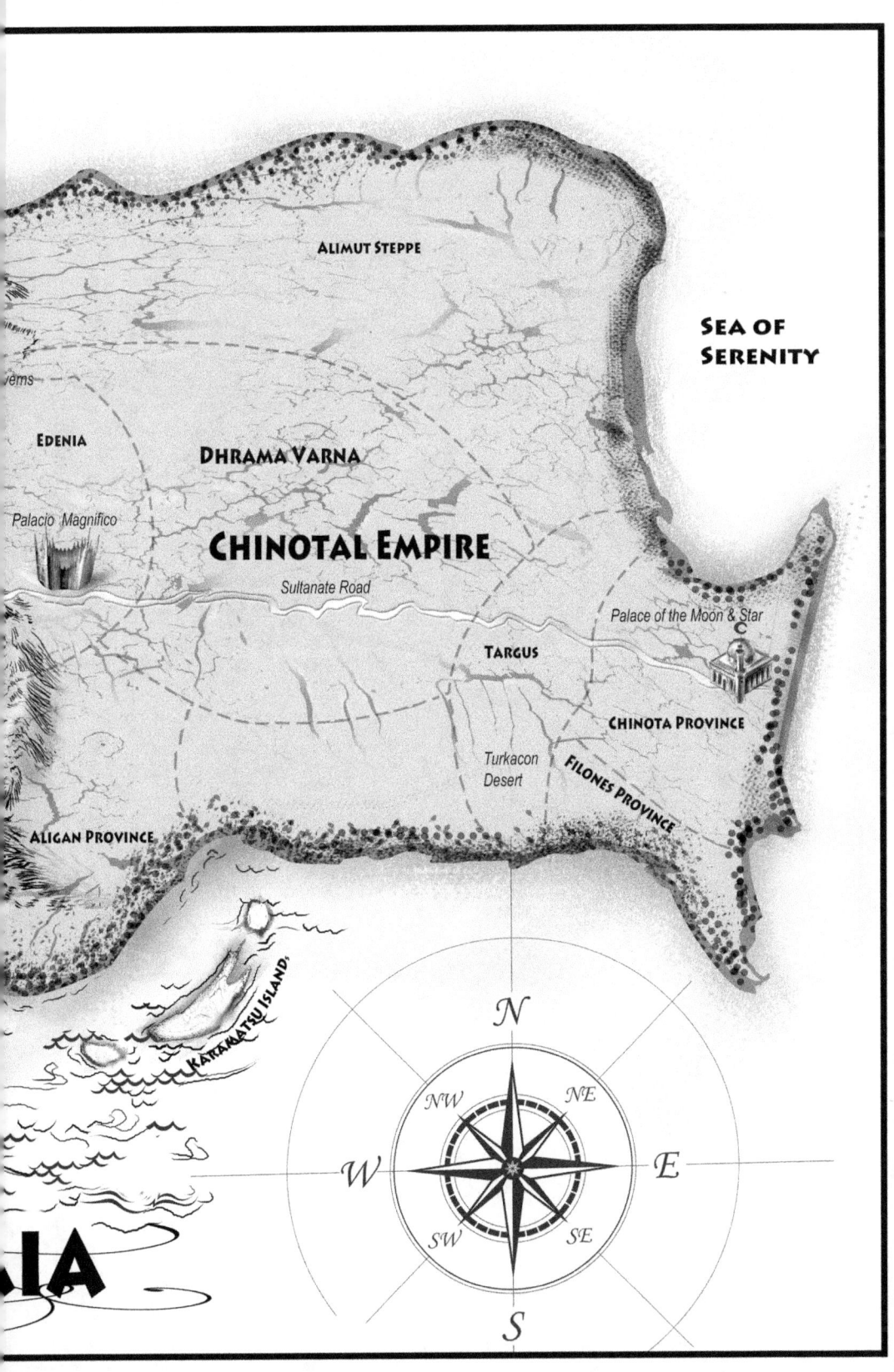

Also by Michael Mazzaro

The Legend of the Last Knight

The Denivan Exile

Then the fifth angel blew his trumpet and I saw a star that had fallen from the sky to the earth. It was given the key for the passage to the abyss. It opened the passage to the abyss and smoke came up out of the passage like smoke from a huge furnace. The sun and the air were darkened by the smoke from the passage. The great army of Locusts emerged from the abyss. They had as their king the Angel of the Abyss whose name is Abaddon.

Scriptures of the Christ, Book of the Gloria 9:1-7

Mapes Boarding House, Palacio Magnifico, Edenia, Nightfall

Echoing across the vast plains of Terminus Mundus, the *Legend of the Last Knight* resounds for all men and women of good will. In the 25th revolution of the reign of Stephen Acadia, King of Justice, Acadian conspirators lead by Count Maximilian Luminas succeeded in their bloody coup. Forging a diabolical alliance with a fallen angel named Abaddon, they exchanged the life of Stephen's daughter Cassandra for the crown. However, a group of elite warriors led by the three Marshals of the Alliance Army infiltrated the Castle in a daring rescue operation. After fighting their way through countless troops, Cedric Rhone rescued Cassandra and brought her to the only escape route out of the Castle. Trapped between the wrath of the Dark Angel and the dangers of the Royal Crypt, *La Morte Angelus* sacrificed himself to stave off Abaddon from his friends.

Yet the life of Terminus Mundus's greatest warrior would not come to end. His mentor, Wilhelm von Angelhardt, whisked him away to the safety of the Kablisha. Healed by the power of the Holy Grail, Prince Rhone remained in exile for five long revolutions as his friends established Cassandra as Queen in exile within the safety of the walls of the Margrave of Deniva. Biding his time, Abaddon plotted a simultaneous attack to destroy both the Kablisha and the royals in exile. These attacking forces met with overwhelming resistance and the armies of evil were dealt crippling defeats across the Acadian plains. As Cedric rejoined his companions, the brilliant Doctor Martha Heinrich developed a means of destroying the one defense her enemies had erected. But such a weapon needed time to operate and as such the royals saw to other tasks that must not be left incomplete.

Christian opened the door to the familiar boarding house garbed in his ranger disguise once more. Clearly annoyed by the light giggles behind him, the Titan spymaster found dealing with his new travel companion quite difficult. Cloaked in the robes of an imperial merchant, Valentine playfully flirted with a young girl. At first, DeVries believed Valentine would be less conspicuous then his normally massive companion. However, the penchant of the Napolitan spymaster for engaging every young girl in the city drew more attention than he had hoped. For his part, Valentine acted out his role magnificently. Studying the ways of imperial merchants for revolutions, the assassin knew every mannerism and habit of his mark. The excessive flirting was not uncommon of those in the trade and thus the incessant stares of DeVries didn't bother him.

The boarding house had a few rangers in the corner enjoying a brew and evening meal, yet it remained mostly deserted. Without a word, Mapes slipped a key down one end of the bar. Silently, Christian took the invitation and ascended the back stairs. Valentine stayed on the ground floor keeping his eyes and ears open. Leaving the remaining rangers in the room unnerved by his imperial disguise, the Napolitan national calmly took a place at the boarding house bar.

"How much for a drink?" asked Valentine.

"First drink is always on the house."

"I like your style, Mapes. You wouldn't happen to have any grappa, would you?"

"Ever since the trade with Napolitan stopped it has been difficult to obtain, but most patrons find that libation a little too strong."

Mapes reached under the bar and pulled out a green bottle. Valentine smiled as the clear liquid filled the short glass.

"Salud."

The spymaster downed it in one shot followed by a quick cough.

"Just like Papi used to make. Tastes like lighter fluid, but doesn't go down as easy. Join me for one?"

"Well-behaved for an imperial merchant, but I won't turn down a drink if you're buying."

Two more drinks were poured. As he brought the second shot of grappa to his lips, the sounds of a woman screaming caught the assassin's ear. Biting his lower lip, Valentine held his glass suspended for a moment. The second scream was undeniable, though no one but the assassin seemed to care.

"Where did that scream come from?"

"There's a brothel two blocks south from here that caters to the upper class clientele. They get a little too rough sometimes."

"Excuse me, Mapes. Thanks for the drink and your company."

Slugging down his final shot, Valentine dropped two gold coins on the bar before striding through the establishment door. Racing from the stairs above, Christian returned with a bag on his back. Diligently searching the room for his companion, an overwhelming feeling of dread gripped him.

"Mapes," queried Christian. "Where is the merchant who came in with me?"

"He seemed determined to investigate something at the brothel near here."

"Oh no…"

Christian dropped some more money on the bar as he sprinted through the door.

"Y'all come back now," playfully shouted Mapes as she picked up the coin.

As the disguised Titan agent moved from block to block, the sounds of women screaming gave way to the pathetic pleas of a man. The pleas would give way to blood curdling screams and Christian feared the worst. As he entered the brothel, the nervous woman working the desk pointed to a large room behind the staircase. Bleeding from his missing ear, bruised in the face, and deprived of three teeth, an Edenian noble crawled desperately away from his tormentor. Valentine was comforting a badly beaten young prostitute in the corner of the room. An incredulous stare from Christian was answered by a *what was I supposed to do* look from Valentine. The Napolitan agent handed the girl a card.

"If you're determined to remain in this profession, I'm not going to lecture you out of it," explained Valentine. "But if you want to be a lady of the night who is so feared that nothing like this will ever happen to you again, go to this address and work for me."

Leaving the girl with a slight kiss on the forehead, Valentine walked over the trail of blood back to Christian. The prostitute held her forehead for a second and smiled hungrily at her rescuer's offer.

"I didn't think it was possible, but a person of Colin's size and power is less conspicuous than traveling with you."

"DeVries, I think it's sweet you like to play house with a former elven princess. I can't do that. I prefer the company of these women and I will not tolerate anyone treating them as a training dummy. The girl is talented and she showed a lot of guts taking the beating she did."

"Do you have any idea who it was you beat the crap out of?"

"Based on his dress, probably some noble upset that the price of the services was above his pay grade…"

"That was the son of the Steward of Edenia!"

"Then that might be a problem."

Clanking armor and hurried steps echoed up the cobblestone streets. The two operatives exchanged a glance and fled up the stairs. Jumping out of the hall window, Christian and Valentine edged themselves across the building ledge until they could climb to the roof. Under a barrage of arrows from the streets below, the agents leapt from rooftop to rooftop to escape.

"Just once I would like to leave Palacio Magnifico without having to flee for my life."

Valentine laughed, elated by all the excitement around him.

"Well, DeVries, I must say you know how to show an old buddy a good time."

The Napolitan agent gave a loud whistle signaling two horses to trot to the end of the street. As they reached the last roof, the companions slid down a fire escape onto the backs of their waiting steeds. Turning their horses, they broke the city gate.

"Who's on duty tonight?" asked Valentine.

"Phil."

"He one of yours?"

"Thankfully, yes…"

Despite the shouts and commands of the closing guards behind the two operatives, the city gates remained open to allow the escape. Christian and Valentine made for the Kaiser Mountain Pass. They called for Calvary once more from above, and the eagle led the two riders swiftly through the pass. Not ready to risk breaking their necks at night, the Edenian pursuers ended the chase.

FC DENIVA STADIUM, DENIVA, CHRISTMAS DAY

The rivalry between Internationzale Talus and Aufgabe Rhinegard is worthy of lore. However, an equally important rivalry game is played every revolution at the height of the Kingdom of Titanus' holiday season. Football diplomacy may be one of Caesar Constantine's greatest legacies.

Excerpt from the journal of General Darius

"I know I have asked a lot of you," pleaded Cedric. "We're tired, we're hurting, and it just seems easier to give up. Those with experience have shouldered a heavy burden and we can't discount the contributions we received from those we didn't expect anything from. You've got to keep telling yourselves we're almost home. So dig down deep, reach for that something extra, and I promise you we will be victorious—"

"Hey Rhone!" screamed a voice from the distance.

Cedric, wearing a white and red football kit with red shorts and black boots, was setting up a free kick 22 meters from his opponent's goal. Behind him, Cagius set a defensive line at midfield with a back four of Hippolyte, Joshua, Colin, and a Wood Elf ranger on the left. Amuro wore a golden goalie shirt with her hair pulled back and gold gloves. The screaming man wore a black referee's uniform.

"Prince Rhone, it's been almost a minute, get your people in position for the free kick."

"All right," answered Cedric.

Cecilia and Cedric stood over the ball as Ethan and Cagius pushed up from their midfield positions into the box with Malcolm. Gerard hung on the far left side of the box. Walker and Robespierre wore blue kits on the opposing side representing the Knights of the Order of the Lion. A scoreboard showed no score under a banner reading the Christmas Cup and the stands were littered with soldiers, wood Elves, and Denivan residents. Amazingly the one building spared the destruction and chaos of the battle was the football stadium. In the front row, Cassandra, Saria, Rosa, Minerva, and Keiko were dressed in white cheerleader sweaters and red skirts. Blushing, the girls swung pom-poms and kicked their legs high in the air. Thomas was seated on the bench next to the girls. Cassandra kept bending over to him.

"So what's going on now?"

"Since Walker fouled Ethan, the referee awarded our team a free kick. We can put it directly on goal or pass it to one of our players."

"And what about this 'offsides'?"

"Offsides is when the attacker is behind the last defender before the ball is played to him."

"I don't understand."

"Don't worry, your Highness, based on his performance this morning, I don't think the referee does either."

Performing another kick, Cassandra shook her head and wondered what her friends saw in this game. She was getting uncomfortable with the leers of those in the stands at her tight outfit.

"Saria?" questioned Cassandra. "Don't you think these actions and uniforms are ridiculous?"

"I'm not sure, your Highness. I asked Cagius extensively about this ritual known as cheerleading and he said these were the appropriate outfits and actions."

"Of course Cagius would never seek to take advantage of your good nature," chimed Rosa sarcastically.

"I have no doubt my cavalier would never lie to me over something like this."

"Well, I don't know about you, but I never had so much fun in my life." Minerva screamed as she jumped in the air. "Go team!"

Winking at her brother, Cecilia stepped forward and bent a shot with her right foot around the right side of the Order's wall. The shot hit the post under the crossbar and bounced out harmlessly. The Vanadis kicked the dirt in disgust as the Order started their counter-attack. Five passes later, Walker launched a ball past Cagius' high defensive line allowing Robespierre to run free. Opting to hold her line, Amuro readied for a shot as Colin raced behind Robespierre. As he crossed the eighteen, Colin looked to slide tackle the ball away. However, the whistle of the referee called for a penalty and raised the ire of Cedric and his teammates.

"Come on, ref, that was terrible!" shouted Thomas.

"What's going on now?" questioned Cassandra once more.

"The ref just gave the Order a penalty shot and Colin had the ball."

"Is it like the one Cecilia took before?"

"No, the ref is going to place the ball on the nine box and Robespierre is going to shoot at Amuro."

"And Amuro's got to stop a shot from there? That's crazy, why would anyone ever want to play goalie?"

"That's what Mom keeps telling me."

Amuro put her hand up to Cedric in salute.

"I'd like to thank my good friend Cedric Rhone for putting me in this absolutely ridiculous situation."

"Hey, you were the one that volunteered to play when Christian had to leave on his mission. Just block the stupid shot, the Order's breaking the first commandment of Titan football."

"What's that?"

"Thou shalt not have the guy who was fouled take the penalty shot."

The cheerleaders locked their arms in solidarity as Robespierre calmly approached the ball. Without a stutter, he went for a power shot in the bottom left corner. However, Amuro guessed correctly and got a fingertip to the ball to barely knock it out of bounds. The psyched elven goalie got up cheering and pumping her fists, as the cheerleaders screamed her name. The ensuing corner came up short and Hippolyte brought it up the right side.

"Go, sis, go!" screamed Minerva as she shook her pom-poms.

Just beyond midfield, Hippolyte passed it to Cedric in the center. Two dribbles and skill move past Walker, he found his sister breaking down the right side. Cecilia took one touch and whipped a cross into the box. Timing it just right, Malcolm performed a perfect bicycle kick and ripped the ball into the bottom left corner of the net. Cassandra and the girls went nuts as the normally stoic Malcolm performed three backflips in a row landing a perfect dismount in celebration. After retreating to midfield, Amuro tackled her betrothed in celebration, kissing him over and over.

"Okay, Thomas, that's it, right? We won."

"You know, your Highness, I like it a lot better when you're teaching me. The ref is going to add about three minutes of extra time for goals and substitutions since the clock doesn't stop."

"I'm never going to understand this silly game."

"It's not silly, it's a beautiful game, your Highness."

Despite two good efforts to bring the ball up, it failed to materialize for the Order. As the referee sounded the final whistle, the royals mobbed each other on their side of the pitch. Goaded by her friends, Cassandra did two cartwheels and a flip in celebration. Ethan scooped up Thomas and put him on his shoulders. Walker put his hand out to Cedric.

"Well, this was fun, Cedric. I hope the Order filled in admirably for the officers of Napolitan."

"You guys played great. Of course, I didn't have my normal team from Titanus, either."

"I can't believe your two nations played this game every revolution. I guess we'll have to wait until next revolution for a rematch."

"No offense, Walker, but I really hope we're not playing here again."

"That goes for all of us."

Cassandra came up and kissed Cedric.

"Walker, I hope you didn't feel slighted that I was rooting for Cedric's team."

"Not at all, your Highness, it would have been odd to see you rooting against your fiancée and might have made most of us uncomfortable."

"You just wait for the surprise we have for you and your men tonight. You've earned it."

"We look forward to it eagerly."

Walker moved to congratulate the others. Disturbed by her earlier comment, Cedric turned his attention towards Cassie's outfit. She pirouetted for him once in it.

"My dear evil knight, do you see something you like?"

"I thought I'd take a second to admire all the work you put yourself through. Besides, you look very cute in it."

"Are there any other rituals attached to this cheerleading?"

"Just one little small one."

"What's that?"

"Normally the captain carries the head cheerleader off the field in celebration."

Cassandra stepped forward to participate but one whiff of Cedric from the game dissuaded her.

"No offense, my love, but you smell like a wet dog right now. I'll take a rain check."

The prim and proper Queen gracefully walked away from her disappointed fiancée. Cecilia came up to him with a bottle of lager in her hands and shot her brother another look. The two clinked the bottles and drank in celebration.

Castle Acadia, Central Acadia

The human body is an intricate assortment of biochemicals and salts that when mixed with water forms the person standing in front of you. There is nothing truly unique about this composition until we reduce it to the genetic level. Here in this intricate series of nucleotides and proteins, we have the blueprint of what makes the individual. After mapping this genome, it is my intent to learn all of the slight intricacies of the individual genes. For who knows what untold secrets I would discover by manipulating these codes.

The writings of Provost Virgus Tattenberg

Defiantly stationed in the circular foyers of the decaying Castle Acadia, Abaddon watched as slaves scrapped every piece of valuable metal and construction material from the formerly majestic walls. After news of the victory spread, King Luminas became obsessed with increasing the defensive capabilities of the outer Verian walls at the expense of his own castle. In his translucent state the dark angel gripped his hand tightly for the millionth time in five revolutions of disembodiment. This time was not the same—the flesh that formed on his right pinky had not decayed despite the failure of the remainder of his hand to regenerate. This morning Abaddon had trained Marie and a drop of her blood had fallen on this pinky area.

Could it be that her royal bloodline is the key to my salvation? he thought. *I dare not risk Cassandra, but this Marie could prove valuable. Damn Prince Rhone for doing this to me.*

20

Virgus cleared his throat.

"Did they find any of them?" asked Abaddon.

"Corpses piled as high as the eye can see and smoldering! Valadrim's head is marked with a warning in blood spelled out in the tongue of the ancients, Elf, and the unified. The Kablisha have grown a spine."

"Everywhere Rhone goes, he brings hope, courage, and virtue... when I failed to destroy him here, I handed my enemy the will to carry on."

"I know what you seek, my Lord."

"I thought I was the clever one when I oiled my blades with that hellish poison. However, the poison Cedric placed in my system with his dual blade was far worse. It does not allow me to recreate my physical manifestation. What good does this form do me? It's only a matter of time before that boy figures out some way to bind me and I dare not return empty-handed."

"What about the Prince?" Virgus asked.

"It took great effort on the part of the Prince to create a body for me the first time and he is not the type of Angel that will offer me a second chance. Thus, I need you to rely on all of your gifts to give me a new body."

"There may be a way...Cassandra..."

"The Prince requires her; she will be unblemished and unspoiled."

"I know that she doesn't possess Cassandra's gifts," Virgus said. "But maybe Princess Marie can provide you with what you need."

"I have discovered a certain regenerative power in her blood. At this point, even if she provided me a hulk of rotting flesh, it would be better than this."

"We can do better than that, my Lord... her magic has grown strong these revolutions. If her powers were increased to the proper level, then maybe that blood would be enough to create a full physical manifestation, but it would have to be a complete sacrifice."

"Unfortunately, Princess Marie has not outlived her usefulness. When Cedric and his allies come for us, her necromancy creations must reinforce our ranks."

"Of course, should she outlive her usefulness…"

"I didn't tell you that you shouldn't prepare."

"Of course, my Lord. I know that you are disappointed… would you like to see something that should make you very happy?"

"I could use some good news."

The dark angel followed his mad scientist from the foyer and down a set of circular stairs. Reaching the bowels of Castle Acadia, Abaddon witnessed Virgus' temple of iron and mechanization for the first time. His laboratory was filled with hundreds of massive vats containing light blue liquid. Abaddon could see appendages emerging from such liquid.

"I give you the cloning vats. I worked on them for revolutions in Titanus; I believe that Doctor Heinrich copied some of my work when she created Cedric and Cecilia. The light blue liquid you see contains the basic hydrocarbons and proteins necessary to create the genetic code for life."

"This will reinforce our armies?"

"No, my Master. I have created your army!"

Virgus brought Abaddon over to a lift. The two ascended over what appeared to be a huge training ground. The dark angel could see thousands of soldiers lined up and beginning their training. All of the soldiers were human; however, the officers appeared as if they were Julius Imperia's long lost twins. Each wave of infantry that passed the two began to look less and less like the late Napolitan prince. Abaddon smiled with delight.

"Since you could not actively bring your army into Creation, I forged you a new one."

"It's greater than I could have imagined," said Abaddon. "Julius Imperia… how is this possible?"

"After you killed him I had to work quickly. The genetic code and mental engrams do survive after physical death, but not for long. I extracted what I could and went about morphing it into a usable force. Since the code breaks down slightly after each clone, I did the officers first. The grunts have less in common with the original, but I've used other means to improve them. I've loaded them up with growth hormone and steroids, but manipulated the genetic code to make them subservient to orders."

"I'm not easily impressed, Virgus, but you've outdone yourself this time."

"As I've always said, you don't keep me around for my charming personality. We start with basic training. The Acadian Templars have ingenious methods of breaking the soldier down and building them back up again."

The two walked on to another section. Hundreds of orcs were working away at bellows and anvils. As they hammered and beat away at weapons, the more advanced members of the army were being fitted for their new armor. When their fitting was complete, they moved into the next area. In this area, mages were casting spells that enchanted the armor.

"I believe these methods will compensate for their obvious weakness to magic. The enchanted armor should protect against both elven magic and Dwarven craftsmanship. They won't be impervious, but it's the best we can do."

"What about the officers? We're running out of Nephilim."

"They are perfectly capable of commanding themselves."

They proceeded to the next area. A division of the troops were under the command of an officer. This officer wore a special helmet with fashioned golden dragon horns to distinguish him from the others under his command.

"I call them the Elite," Virgus explained. "These Elite were embedded with Julius Imperia's mental engrams, so they possess knowledge of his tactical skills. While maybe not a match for Cedric's genius, they'll hold their own."

"Very good," Abaddon said. "Let's see how Cedric and his friends do against one of their own. When can they be ready for battle?"

"They have the physical capability to fight now, but they haven't undergone enough training. Give me another lunar cycle or two before I dare send them out into battle."

"You'll have every moment as long as the barrier holds."

"Then I'd better hope the Titan scientists are slow in their discoveries. There is one more thing, Lord Abaddon."

Moving to the last location, the two came to a large and luxurious room.

"As I mentioned before, my Lord, the genetic code breaks down a bit after every use. Therefore you only get one shot to create what I call the perfect clone. May I present, Prince Julius Imperia of Napolitan."

As if he had seen a phantasm, Abaddon stood paralyzed and silent. The Napolitan prince thought dead had been recreated by the perverse science of Virgus Tattenberg. Rubbing his hands together, the wretched doppelganger bowed before his new Lord.

"What is your desire, my Lord Abaddon?" demanded the clone.

"Of course, I couldn't do anything about the soul. Even the Grand Lich couldn't bargain for it once he ascended into Heaven. However, I extracted enough memory to give him what we need. I cut out that whole nasty bit of the affair with Felicia and made him the perfect, devoted, chivalric hero in love with our Princess Marie."

"I'll have her completely under my control," offered the doppelganger. "I can't wait to get out there and do what my sire never could... best Cedric Rhone."

Abaddon laughed maniacally.

"I take it back, Virgus, you have exceeded my wildest expectations."

Raising his newly formed pinky in the air, the soldiers, orcs, and mages saluted their Dark Angel with cheers of victory.

CASTELLAN OF DENIVA

They were overjoyed at seeing the star, and on entering the house they saw the child with his Virgin Mother. They prostrated themselves and did him homage. They opened their treasures and offered him gifts of gold, frankincense and myrrh.

The Scriptures of the Christ, The Evengard Evangelist 2:10-11

Christmas decorations hung from the interior of the spire. While the Castle was not normally open to the public for Christmas celebrations, Dennis had issued a proclamation opening his halls for any citizen of Deniva who wished to attend. The receiving room had been set aside for the royals, wood Elves, Order of the Lion cuirassiers, and any imperial troops who remained in the city. Valentine and Christian, back from their daring Palacio Magnifico escape, took in the revelry as well. Tipsy and slightly rowdy, everyone was being entertained by Saria as she performed a mixture of classical and pop songs for those attending. When she finished the last line of her final pop song, she winked and raised her hand in the air. The Elf maiden got a standing ovation and catcalls from all over the room. Cagius just soaked it in and brushed it off.

"I thought you'd be more upset," teased Valentine.

"I'm used to it by now," retorted Cagius. "Besides, I'll whisk her away if anyone tries anything and then tear their little heads off."

Saria exited the stage and walked over to the royals table. After a long kiss with Cagius the events of before were quickly set aside.

"And all is right with the world once more," observed Valentine.

"What happened to you guys? You had half a kilogram of dust on your cloaks," commented Joshua.

"Well, let's just say there was a little incident with a girl in a brothel..." Christian started.

"Why does that not surprise me?" said Cagius condescendingly.

"I have a problem," joked Valentine.

"Yeah, no kidding!" Joshua mocked his mentor.

Playfully, the Napolitan prince hit his nephew on the back a few times. Joshua took it all in fun. Minerva munched happily on the Christmas cookies on the table.

"So which one is your favorite?" inquired Walker.

"I can't make up my mind. The flavors in all of these cookies just explode in my mouth."

"Minerva, is there anything the 'steel-bellies' make that you won't try?" asked Hippolyte.

"I can't help it, sis, everything they make sounds and tastes so delicious," responded Minerva as she spotted the nativity crèche in the corner of the room. "So even though we've done this over the past revolutions, I still don't get it! What exactly are we celebrating?"

"Christmas is the rotation that Christians celebrate the Birth of the Christ," offered Walker.

"And you give presents?"

"Well, that matter is open to some interpretation. In Central Acadia and Napolitan, we normally give our gifts on Christmas."

"However, the other kingdoms offer presents on the Rotation of the Three Kings," interjected Colin. "On that rotation, the Kings of Titanus and Edenia, along with the High Priest of the Kablisha Tribe, visited the Christ child and presented him with gifts of gold, frankincense, and myrrh."

Minerva was still scratching her head as Cagius shook an empty bottle.

"This isn't good...looks like we're going to need another bottle, Ethan."

"Another one? It's bad enough you wrecked half the city trying to save it, now you intend to drink us dry."

"Hey, we earned it!"

Ethan signaled to one of the servants who quickly brought over another bottle of Christmas Wine. The servant made her way around the table pouring everyone a glass. Cedric refused, preferring to stick to his brandy.

A message came to the table for Saria. She smiled and walked back up the makeshift stage.

"So what's this big secret performance all about?" asked Amuro.

"Don't ask me, Cassandra and my sister wouldn't give me any details," answered Cedric.

The catcalls were plenty as Saria adjusted her headset again.

"Thank you, boys, but don't be so raucous or my sister might fry you," Saria said, pouting. "Our final performance for this evening is going to be performed by our lovely Queen Cassandra and the equally lovely Vanadis, Princess Cecilia."

The appearance of the Queen and Vanadis from behind the stage curtain left the audience in a state of shock. Cecilia was dressed in a white gown with fake angel wings attached to her back. She complimented the outfit with her Valkyrie crown, white bracers, hose, and heels. Cassandra, on the other hand, wore a black and gold gown with fake bat-like wings and a spaded tail attached to the back. She wore a headband with ram's horns, black bracers, hose, and heels.

"Well, this was definitely my sister's idea!" breathed a shocked Cedric.

Adjusting their microphone headsets, the two stood still and background music played. They started singing in unison as they moved the opposite limb from one another in a carefully coordinated dance pattern. As they got into the first verse, the crowd was still too overwhelmed by what was happening in front of them to clap or cheer. Cassandra would sing first as Cecilia broke in with a verse of her own. The timing of their dance movements proved they had worked on the ballet for hours on end. By the time they reached the second chorus, almost everyone in the room was on their feet clapping and cheering along.

"Cedric, where has your sister been hiding all this time?" demanded Cagius. "She friggin' sings like an angel."

"I knew Cassandra had a voice like a bird, but your sister..." said an exasperated Amuro. "Whenever we were fooling around at the after-parties, she always put on a hardcore deep voice for the karaoke!"

"This is nothing, you should sit next to her in church," teased Cedric.

As they repeated the chorus for the last time the energy in the room was electric. The crowd screamed the name of both the Queen and the Vanadis, and the ladies played it up. They exaggerated the motions, and flaunted their assets before assuming the positions for their finale. Cassandra leaned against Cecilia's back with her arms down as the haughty Vanadis crossed her arms over her breasts. Both ladies turned to the audience with wide smiles on their faces. Embarrassed to catcall their Queen and fearful of the Titan princess's wrath, the Knights and guests awarded their performers with a loud and standing ovation. Only Cedric remained seated. Seeing Cassandra perform in her outfit hit a little too close to home for the Titan prince and his thoughts were haunted with Abaddon's actions once more. The performers happily skipped over to their companions, Cassandra putting herself next to Cedric and Cecilia throwing herself down on Ethan's lap.

"So what did you think?" demanded Cecilia.

"Awesome!" exclaimed Ethan. "Absolutely awesome."

"I knew you'd enjoy it."

"Who came up with the idea for the outfits?" questioned Amuro.

"It was Cecilia's idea," offered Cassandra. "Originally our roles were switched, but Cecilia just didn't look right dressed as a succubus. Well, Cedric, were you surprised?"

"Surprised is probably not strong enough. I would say flabbergasted."

"Oh boy, here comes my big brother, the killjoy," said Cecilia. "It was just a bit of fun."

"I know, but it brings up some traumatic experiences. I almost had my soul sucked out of me."

"No offense, darling, but I doubt you would have let me latch onto you if you didn't have a plan to get me off of you. I remember the taste of your soul… it was so delicious… like rich, molten, chocolate-covered…"

Embarrassed by the sudden and worried glares of her friends, Cassandra caught herself.

"Always chocolate with you Your Highness…" Walker added.

"Great, Abaddon made me a soul junkie!"

"I might be willing to try that, you make it sound so delicious," teased Minerva.

"As long as I'm now the Christmas curmudgeon, according to my sister," announced Cedric. "Whose turn is it to make the next toast?"

"It's mine, Cedric."

Standing teary-eyed, Cassandra held her wine glass high in the air. Everyone in the room stopped their conversation and focused on the Queen.

"It's wonderful that we're here together like this, and I want nothing more than to do this every revolution. I would never have been able to make it through these difficult times without the help of all my friends. Amuro, I didn't know what I was going to do that rotation we were forced to escape. I actually thought of killing myself for a few moments there, but you kept your composure and calmed me. Walker, you're my rock. I know that you always have that shield ready to protect me no matter what. I just don't have the words to say what the rest of you mean to me… especially best friend, fellow performer, and future sister-in-law, Cecilia."

Everyone laughed as Cecilia stood up and playfully acknowledged herself before letting the Queen return to her speech.

"I have a bargain to make with everyone in this room. In the revolution we retake Central Acadia, then God-willing, Cedric and I will marry on Christmas morning. In that, our love for one another will bring faith and hope to the entire West."

The room was filled with the clanking of glasses and cheers once more. As the music began to play again, the exiles returned to their seats. Cecilia toyed with a cocktail napkin.

"Time to sign the Napkin!" announced Cecilia.

"Sign the Napkin?" inquired Hippolyte.

"It's a very sacred Titan bar room tradition, and our dear Queen has just made quite the pronouncement. We pass around a cocktail napkin and we all witness it with our signature. Then I'll hold it for safekeeping to hold Cassandra to her word."

"I like it!" exclaimed Amuro. "Then again, knowing what you Titans consume in a bar, you probably would want a record of everything you said."

Amuro took the napkin and wrote out what Cassandra said on it. She handed it Cassandra who signed it. Passing it to Cedric, the Titan prince took a moment to read it.

"I would prefer to sign this in Abaddon's blood if I had some, but the pen is supposed to be mightier than the sword."

The napkin made its way around the table and was witnessed by everyone. Cecilia got it last and made her signature big next to Cedric's.

"That should just about do it. Dear brother, you do remember the formalities of the honor code as it relates to such a contract?"

"Such words coming from the woman who refuses to tell her own mother that she is married with a son."

"I'll tell her when we get home."

"That will be interesting. Where is the little rascal anyway?"

"I'm afraid it's a little too late for him tonight. Thomas likes to get to bed early."

"You know, I think I used up all my sleep when Abaddon knocked me out for that full rotation. I'm finding I'm not sleeping as much lately."

"Yeah, you've been downright grouchy since you got back here," interrupted Cagius. "I miss the old Marshal Cedric. Deniva provides some pretty good hospitality."

"My mind is occupied. What we did here in Deniva was a fantastic victory. We were at the brink. Had we lost here and at the City of Antiquity, I don't see how the West would have ever rallied against Abaddon and Luminas. In the grand scheme of things, however, it was only one battle."

"I certainly don't believe that any of us has put the cart before the horse here," said Malcolm. "Not after what we've seen and engaged."

"This war isn't over, Cedric, and every one of us sitting here is committed to victory!" added Walker. "You lead and we'll follow."

"I think that's something worth drinking to," interjected Colin.

Every one put up their glasses and took a drink. Despite the resolve of his friends, Cedric was still uneasy. Cassandra stood up and put her hand on his shoulder.

"Please, Cedric, dance with me."

"You're not going to try to guilt me by saying that it would break traditions, are you?"

"I know of no Denivan tradition that I can easily manipulate you with."

"All right, I'll dance with you just for your honesty alone. Which, of course, may just have been another form of manipulation all along."

Cedric wiped his mouth and stood up. He led Cassandra out to the dance floor for the foxtrot. Not to be left alone, Cecilia made Ethan take her up as well. Faced with the awkward and clumsy movements of her towering husband, the Vanadis wasn't as graceful as her usual self. Cedric, however, was sweeping Cassandra off her feet left and right

"You haven't missed a step," commented Cassandra.

"You've had first-hand experience with Florence Polazzi. She is just about the cutest cleric I ever did meet and her bedside manner is amazing."

"Stop trying to make me jealous! After what you did for me that night in Verian, I have no doubts about your commitment. My concerns for you are elsewhere."

"Really?"

"Cedric, it's not your responsibility to take on all of this alone."

"I intend to lean on all of you when I can. That being said, there are certain places where I have to go and you can't follow."

"Cecilia says that Titan women are prepared to stand to the last breath with the man they love," Cassandra said.

"When I took on the mantle of the Last Knight, I took on all of the rights and responsibilities with it."

"I thought you said the Kablisha told you that you didn't fulfill the prophecy."

"Only the Kablisha version of the prophecy," Cedric explained. "Believe it or not, there are three others. When you sat in Castle Acadia with me that evening, you suspected me to be the Last Knight in the Elf prophecy. Princess Cassandra dared to challenge a war hero to accept a nobler path. I am the warrior of faith, the Permaneo Eques Ordinaris, with the power to destroy evil. My firm belief is that in order to be granted a miracle, an act of true faith was required. Julius failed because he wanted to be the Last Knight, but I knew I needed the power to save you. Cassandra, if that moment of need comes once more, I will not hesitate to take on the mantle. Even the Kablisha believe that it has to be."

"You won't take that mantle on without me this time! I'm not running away again and leaving you to die."

Cedric pulled Cassandra close to his heart and embraced her tightly. The Queen believed in that moment that if her love could cry, he would. Kissing her gently on the top of her head, Cedric whispered to her.

"Cassie, I know you stand with me no matter what. I was gifted with a vision of both sides of your true nature. It didn't matter whether it was the succubus or the angel, they both balled with inconsolable sorrow at my wounds. Do you want to know what true charity is? It is the love of man and the desire to aid his fellow man without coercion or prodding. Cassandra, you are not the key to the gates that Abaddon and the Prince would have you believe. You were put here to make all of Mundus better by embracing the selfless examples of your charity. This was God's plan all along—I was put here for you!"

"For me?"

"Your father, Cerwin, and even Felicia, God rest their souls, all witnessed it and believed. Even Walker had the foresight to protect you. Time and time again, I pray I am worthy of the faith they had in me. I love you, Cassandra, but Abaddon is a different creature. Your magic is useless against him. Ragnarok is our only hope."

"I bow to the superior regarding war and tactics. Mark my words, Cedric, no one in this room is ever abandoning you again."

Cassandra kissed him on the lips before retiring to her room for the evening. Across the room, Rosa reclined in Christian's chest as they stared at the Queen and her fiancée. Rosa wept as Christian dried tears from his eyes as well.

"She'll never truly understand, will she?" wondered Rosa.

"Perhaps… in time…"

"Why her? She loves him with such strength and courage. Yet, he can only reward her love with more torment and pain."

"Everyone wants the hero that carries the banner above his head, gracefully performs his task, and rides off with his maiden never to be called on again. I've ridden twenty revolutions with the Prince now, Rosa, and Cedric's banner is a cross so heavy that a dozen boulders are crushing him every rotation. It's not just Cassie anymore, he's fighting for all of Terminus Mundus. Yet, I've never before seen this sadness that envelops his heart and eyes. His Excellency has realized the inevitable—he cannot defeat Abaddon in battle again. You speak of her love for him, well, Cedric will march into Hell itself to keep Cassandra safe from the Prince of Darkness' clutches."

"What can we do to help him, Christian?" Rosa pleaded. "I'll give anything."

"It's not just me or you, Rosa. Look around this table. You can multiply this number by every table in every home in every city in every country. That is the resolve we need if we are ever going to win this war. True charity, the ability of man to aid man… maybe if we can pull that strength together… maybe…"

Basilica of the Angels, Rhinegard, Two Weeks Later, Nearly Midnight

In our solemn hour, when the powers of darkness drown out the light from the land, the 'legions of light' shall seek refuge in the mournful eyes of the Bis Reginum. Her prayers and tears shall not go uncomforted, for in this hour the Divine Plan of the Father shall be revealed.

"The Hour of the Bis Reginum," Titan Scholar Cassiodorus

The interior of the Basilica was as opulent and magnificent as the outer structures. Five-story stained glass windows were dedicated to each of Jesus' apostles, the four evangelists, and the Sefiroth interspersed in the interior superstructure of steel and marble. The marble pathway to the altar was a quarter of a kilometer long covered with red carpet. Along the way, a marker post was established to show that every other church built on Terminus Mundus could fit within the Basilica. Candles blazed in front of the statues of the Saints at the ends of pews on both sides, and within the large chapel devoted to the Blessed Mother, separated by large wooden doors from the rest of the Basilica. In the far eastern corner of the room was a second private chapel where the synod of Bishops would say mass, pray for guidance, and congregate to either elect the next Archbishop of Terminus Mundus or make decisions on the doctrine of the faith. The arched ceilings above were painted with depictions of scenes from the Ancient Scriptures. The one ceiling panel at the direct center of the Basilica showed God the Father delivering "the Law" to the Prophet. A recreation of the stone tablets was placed in the back of the church. Upon entering the Basilica all eyes were drawn to its most prominent feature. A large mural depicted both the archangel Michael driving his spear into Lucifer during the Ragnarok, and Christ crucified with solid gold letters below it reading: *Deliverance from Evil and Sin.* In these late night hours, one light remained on in the back of the Basilica.

Tugging constantly at the nun's outfit she was forced to wear during her interment and tormented by the act of genuflecting on the padded kneelers, Nadia did her best to recite her prayers. Not fully saved yet, certain ones often produced a burning sensation on her tongue, and every time she tried to say the Lord's Prayer aloud it came out backwards. Alerted by the sound of the heavy wooden door opening at the back of the Basilica, the daughter watched Wilhelm bless himself as he entered. Nadia jumped from the pew and embraced him tightly. While unhappy with her actions, Wilhelm returned her affections.

"This is still a House of God, Nadia," whispered Wilhelm. "I had to call in every favor I had with Queen Civilia to get you to stay here at the least. Don't lose control and make Archbishop Langley kick you out."

"I'm sorry, Wilhelm. I was worried about you."

"Well, hindsight is twenty-twenty. You had nothing to fear. The Prince and I make a formidable tandem."

"That's not what I mean. I know that Garrett and Wulf have you wandering aimlessly along the plains in search of their mystery warrior. I knew you'd survive in City of Antiquity and Deniva."

"Oh really, I didn't know you'd become a psychic."

"I knew because Cedric was there to protect you."

Wilhelm tried to keep his laughter to a minimum.

"So you've joined that faction as well. My dearest, no man is more feared and revered in the whole of Terminus Mundus. Yet, only a fool would dare to go into battle without him if his Excellency would make himself available."

"Don't keep me in suspense. Did Cedric really win both battles half a continent away?"

"Believe it or not, it's completely accurate. We dealt with the situation in the City of Antiquity first. I find it amazing no one seems to criticize Cedric as a religious fanatic when he pulls a brilliant battle plan out of the Bible."

"And Deniva, I heard rumors that together you destroyed the entire Dark Elf Army."

"That's a little over the top. We were able to incapacitate them with the power of simultaneously cast Holy Wars!"

"He's learned the spell of the Sentinels!"

"Yes."

"Don't you know what that means, Wilhelm?"

"We shouldn't jump to any conclusions, Nadia."

"Now you're talking like one of the Kablisha! The mystery warrior they've been seeking is right under their noses."

"You weren't there Nadia. Before my Lord Camael accepted his divine task, he said to me: *By the will of our Father, we will meet again, old friend. When we do, we're not going to recognize one another, but we will both be overcome with joy when we finally do.* I've been around that boy for far too long...I'd know, Nadia. He's not Camael, he's what we need right now."

"But Wilhelm, Duke Camael is the only one who can rid you of that curse!" exclaimed a tearful Nadia.

The Sentinel shuddered in pain at the mere mention of the poison.

"Is it happening again?"

"Yes. The mere mention of it is starting to cause me pain."

Wilhelm bowed his head as Nadia used her magic to try to alleviate some of his suffering.

"How much more do you have to do? You've brought so many back from the throngs of sin and death. Look at me, a daughter of the Prince—you bargained to get me the free will I needed to make my case! You give out compassion as if giving alms to a beggar on the streets. When will it be enough?"

"It can take many lifetimes to understand the will of our Father and the plan that he has for all of us."

The two walked over to the stained glass window of Camael in his armor holding his fiery two-handed sword.

"Maybe it was destiny that prevented you from curing yourself," surmised Nadia. "If you had left with the others, I would have been trapped in Hell for all eternity. I have faith in Duke Camael's power. After all, he is the patron angel of those who love God."

"It was that love of God that allowed him to resist Lucifer's temptation. How are you being treated?"

"Many still look upon me with fear and hate," explained Nadia with a laugh. "While I don't blame them, it still hurts."

"Time will heal the wounds, Nadia."

"I pray every rotation it does, my love."

"Were you able to look into what I asked?"

"About the prophecies of the Permaneo Eques Ordinares? Specifically the ones written by the Titan scholars?"

"Yes, what do the texts say?"

"I didn't find anything about the Kablisha's precious 'Knight of God;' however, I did find something interesting. There was a lot of information surrounding the Bis Reginum."

"The Queen blessed twice," mused Wilhelm. "I haven't heard anyone speak of her since the early revolutions of Titanus. You know, a lot of people thought it was speaking about Marion and the events surrounding her son Gunther."

"Don't you find it interesting how divergent these prophecies are turning out? Especially when you consider they were translated by gifted scholars like Demetrius and Cassiodorus."

"I don't entirely grasp your meaning."

"The Elves predicted the coming of the Permaneo Eques Ordinaris, a warrior of indomitable faith who inherited divine power to destroy evil. The Kablisha speak of a 'Knight of God,' the ultimate agent of the Father in Creation. Yet the Titans talk at length of this Bis Reginum whose love and prayers will lead to divine revelations."

"Three separate prophecies, but one common thread?"

"I'd bet anything the Edenians have their own prophecy locked away in that Library of theirs," Nadia said. "Unfortunately, I've been banned from going there and you're not on the best terms with them, either."

"That's nothing I've ever heard of, but Garrett would be the one who I'd ask such a question. They respect him as a scholar, at least."

"If you ask me, Cedric already fulfilled the prophecy of the Last Knight. I think the Bishop and Garrett are wasting his time."

"Nadia, we need a Powers choir angel to bind Abaddon's soul. Do not dismiss the wisdom of the Kablisha so quickly. They want to see the fallen angel banished as much as we do."

"What about our daughter? How's she doing?"

"She's so beautiful, Nadia, and by the Father you taught her well. Obviously, she was elated to find Cedric was all right."

"You should have let me tell her!"

"I wanted to, Nadia, but at the time I couldn't risk the Bishop's wrath. The Kablisha are very particular about these things and he hadn't come around to seeing Cedric's point of view yet. Boy, did his Excellency change all of them for the better."

"All things being equal, they weren't the ones that had to dry her tears."

"You always had wanted the opportunity to do that."

"These past five revolutions were a blessing, Wilhelm! I was a sinner and I will accept any penance necessary for the absolution of those sins," Nadia said. "However, I was given the chance to finally be a mother to my beloved daughter. Maybe it's my imagination, but I think Cassandra may have realized it in the end. If I could only hear her just call me Mom once, well, I could endure anything."

"Stephen loved her with all his heart, but you're the only mother she ever had, Nadia."

"Yes, and that's why you need to tell Cedric the truth."

Wilhelm sighed. "Haven't I saddled him with enough burdens already?"

"You must, Wilhelm! You and I know that he is the only one who can protect our daughter. What we conceived was not done by an act of sin and the Lord gave us a beautiful gift. I can't imagine God would allow us to become the instrument that destroyed the temporal and eternal worlds."

"Cedric knows what he's fighting for. It is enough."

"Are you so embarrassed that you cannot face him?"

"Yes, I am. Pain, suffering, death—I brought these to Cedric Rhone through my sins. Yes, I became his mentor and I trained him how to fight and kill angels. What were my true ambitions, Nadia? I don't know anymore. Perhaps, I selfishly burdened my future King to atone for my own sins. I asked too much of him already, I cannot bear to ask for more."

Tears streaming down her face, Nadia pulled Wilhelm's eyes to her own.

"I resolved long ago that a warrior with your unconditional compassion and Teman's unbridled bravery was the only person who could save Cassandra from my father's dark designs. Confess to him, Wilhelm, he'll not think less of you. You're cut from the same mold."

"How could a creature born of Hell be so much wiser than an angel? Rest easy, my dearest one, when the time is right, I will tell Cedric everything."

Castle Deniva, Deniva, One Lunar Cycle Later

Go back to sleep, Cecilia. The monster in your closet is dead.

***Young Cedric to his frightened sister after
banging around her closet.***

Joshua, Thomas, and Cedric were gathered in a room within the walls of the Golden Spire. The younger offspring were a bit intimidated to be in the presence of such a great man and the sharp sternness within the Titan prince's face did not ease their tension.

"It's been nearly two lunar cycles since I made my return to Deniva," started Cedric. "However, I must apologize for not making myself available to either of you earlier."

"That's okay, Uncle Cedric. Mom always reminds me of how busy you are."

"That's still not an excuse, nephew. Rest assured, Thomas, Cecilia has spoken highly of your untapped potential and I've observed a fair share of it myself. I will be taking an interest in your career, but for the time being you're not going to be much assistance to me."

Thomas tried to flex his muscles in front of his Uncle, but it looked more like a skeleton wrapped in skin. The two Rhones shared a laugh before the sword master focused his full attention on Joshua.

"Can I pick them or can I pick them?" bragged Cedric.

"Your lessons and advice have served me well these past five revolutions," said Joshua. "Valentine certainly tried my patience at times."

"Valentine knows everyone's buttons and enjoys pushing them slowly. You probably have heard this a hundred times, but not from me: Your father would have been proud to see the man you've become."

"I thank you, Lord Cedric. However, there is something on my mind."

"What's that?"

"Why do you wear my father's gauntlets?"

The Titan prince let out a hearty laugh. "Right before I battled Abaddon, your Uncle Cagius handed me these gauntlets with the compliments of your fallen father. Julius recognized that even though I fought as a sword master, I had the heart and soul of a Paladin. His gift saved my life against Abaddon when I couldn't raise Ragnarok to defend myself. It's strangely comforting, in a way, to know that though he is gone, my friend still has my back in battle."

"You and my father remained friends?" Joshua asked.

"It seemed as if Julius and I were destined to be enemies. Boy, we had a couple of legendary donnybrooks. Even though our moral codes weren't exactly compatible, we shared the same goals—a legacy entrusted to you now that you bear his treasures."

"Yeah, so no pressure," teased Thomas.

Rapping on the door, Christian popped his head in the room.

"Cedric, we've got Andres incoming," announced Christian. "We're bringing him into the main conference room in ten."

"That condor is probably going to be the first raptor to be awarded the Titan Cross for the number of missions he completed. Go on ahead, Joshua, I need to speak to my nephew in private for a moment."

Joshua nodded and left the room with Christian as Cedric carefully pushed the door closed.

"What's this all about, Uncle?"

Cedric knelt down to meet his nephew in his eyes. "I don't want to give the impression that I favor Joshua over you. In the end, nothing is more important than family."

"I didn't assume…"

"You may be young, but Christian has agreed to let you shadow him. Succeed in this and I will assign you to greater tasks."

Thomas nodded and gave his uncle a hug before they left the room. In the spa section of the Castle, Cassandra, Cecilia, Amuro, Saria, and Rosa were enjoying a soak in the natural hot spring. Hair tied up to keep it out of the water, the Vanadis reclined in the corner with her arms spread out along the wall as Rosa and Amuro playfully annoyed her by flicking water at her. The Queen was moping with her lips almost resting upon the water. Watching the Titan princess' anger rising, Saria desperately tried to get her sister to stop.

"Amuro, if you don't stop it, I'm ripping your fingers off," ordered Cecilia.

"I can't help it, Cecilia, you just engorge me with jealousy when I see you like this. I always considered myself pretty endowed, but next to you I'm a washboard."

"What do they feed you girls in Titanus, anyway?" quipped Rosa. "I would have thought Cassandra being a succubus and all would be shapelier."

"Yeah, yet it's the more angelic one that's better endowed!"

"That's what this is about?" exclaimed an angry Cecilia.

With lightning quick reflexes, Cecilia whipped both her hands forward splashing the two Elf maidens back. Smiles all around, the battle was on. Even the prissy Saria giggled as she hit her sister and friends with water. Despite being hit from both sides, Cassandra remained in her depressed state. After a few moments, all of her friends took a good look at her.

"You know, Cassie, the number one cause of death in hot springs is drowning from depression," joked Amuro.

"One would think my brother returning would have put you in a better mood. You're bringing us all down seeing you like this."

Unable to elicit a response from their friend, Cecilia and Amuro tactically signaled the others. Acknowledging the order, Saria distracted Cassandra with a few stanzas as the Vanadis stalked her prey like a shark. Grabbing the Queen from behind, Rosa and Amuro attacked from the sides tickling her in the ribs. Snapped out of her stupor, the raven-haired maiden couldn't contain herself.

"Stop it!" shouted Cassandra amidst her forced laughter. "As Queen, I can have all of you executed!"

"Well, at least we got a response!" said Amuro.

"Are you going to be better company now since you dragged all of us out here?" asked Cecilia.

"I'm sorry… now stop it!"

The maidens ended their torture. Cassandra caught her breath and stared down her friends.

"You know I hate being tickled… but… well, I guess I understand why you did it."

"What's wrong, Cassandra?" asked Amuro.

"Cedric's changed!"

"I didn't expect you to be so blunt about it," commented Cecilia.

"You're his sister! Don't tell me you haven't seen it!"

"It's been five revolutions…"

"It's not just time, Cecilia. Part of him just isn't there anyone…"

Rosa remembered Christian's words from the Christmas dinner and couldn't hold back her tears. Amuro and Saria held onto each other as they looked over to Cecilia for some guidance. The Vanadis merely reclined in the corner of the tub again.

"My Queen, let me tell you a little story. When Cedric and I were very young, my mother was out on a campaign against the rebels that threatened her throne. I was prone to nightmares at that time in my life and often crawled into bed with my mom when I was scared. One night when the Queen was away, I had this horrible dream about demons and I was so scared I went to my brother's room. Oh, he was annoyed, but let me share the comfort of his bed only after I promised to let him sleep. I closed my eyes and thought of those demons again. I roused Cedric and asked him what I should do if the demons came for both of us. He turned his eyes to me and said with such harsh calm that I'll never forget it: 'You've got nothing to be afraid of, sis, I'll make the demons go away!'"

Beaming with pride at recanting the story, Cecilia noticed her friends' eyes were shining and watery.

"What?"

"I just have this enchanting vision in my head," stated Cassandra. "Did you have short-hair or pigtails?"

"Pigtails."

"Did you have a favorite stuffed animal for protection, too?" asked Amuro.

"Of course, there was Orson, but I don't see why—"

"A teddy bear?" further inquired Saria.

"No, he was a stuffed orca."

"An orca? You mean the whale that eats just about every living creature in the Sea?" exclaimed Rosa.

"That's another story I prefer not to go into at this point. Focus, ladies!"

"So, let me get this straight," recounted Cassandra. "Six-revolution-old, auburn-pigtailed Cecilia had terrible nightmare about demons. Her first instinct was to grip her favorite stuffed animal, Orson the Orca, tightly and seek out the protection of her older twin brother. She crawled into bed with him and he promised to make the demons away."

"Generally, yes, but I don't think you understand the point of this story…"

The maidens blushed and clutched their hands together tightly ignoring Cecilia's retorts. Cassandra hugged Cecilia.

"Thank you for this, Cecilia. I honestly believed that you didn't adhere to the stereotype. However, I know now that all younger sisters are cute and impertinent."

"That is the most adorable story I've ever heard," commented Amuro.

"I'd give anything to see a picture of her then," said Rosa. "I bet she was as cute as Vanessa at her age."

"I wish I had my own Orson the Orca," Saria moaned, pouting.

"I don't think so, sis. You see, they eat penguins."

"How could they eat them? They're so cute."

"Cecilia, thank you so much for recounting that story. You cheered me up more than you could ever imagine. I'll have to see if Cedric has any pictures of the two of you."

Water nearly steaming around her from anger, Cecilia grunted.

"This isn't about me…I can't believe I actually said that. The point is that since my brother was a young boy, he has always been driven to protect those around him and would do anything in his power to make the demons go away. The only reason why you think he's changed is that he hasn't figured this one out yet. Mark my words, when he does, he'll be back to his old self in no time!"

Cassandra looked at her blankly for a moment.

"But why the orca, Cecilia? It seems like an unusual choice for a young girl."

Cecilia screamed and lifted herself out of the spring covered in a towel. She took a soft robe from the chair and tied it up as her communicator went off.

"Please save me from my friends," answered Cecilia.

"What's happening now?" came Christian's voice over the communicator.

"You don't want to know. What's going on?"

"Andres just came in. Cedric wants everyone in the conference room immediately."

"If it's that important…" A wide smile crossed Cecilia's face as she turned to the other maidens getting out of the springs. "Ladies, I think we're going home!"

In another part of the castle, Walker, Cagius, and Colin moved quickly into the conference room.

"You know, I felt really good when I got up this morning," commented Cagius. "I just got a feeling."

"You always have a feeling," teased Walker. "It probably has something to do with what you ate last night."

"This is Cedric Rhone we're talking about. He wouldn't be calling all hands on deck if it wasn't good news."

"What if we're under attack again?" counted Walker.

"No, if we were under attack, we'd have to charge in and prevent Master Cedric from stopping the invasion single-handedly," interjected Colin.

Valentine, Joshua, Malcolm, Hippolyte, Minerva, Ethan, and Robespierre were waiting in the conference room as the three took their places. The bathing maidens arrived from the spa still dressed in their robes.

"Dressing a little informally for this meeting?" teased Valentine.

"Of course, the one rotation I agree to go for the spa treatment, my brother calls us out early," replied Cecilia.

"I hope this doesn't take too long, we've still got the kelp wrap and massage coming," argued Amuro.

Arriving last and with Andres in tow, Cedric and Christian took their positions at the head of the table. Ethan stood up and locked the door before the presentation began. Before starting the meeting, the Titan prince tossed a piece of meat up in the air for his condor companion to munch on.

"I apologize for interrupting your plans. However, Christian decoded a message from Andres and everyone who has suffered through this Denivan Exile has a right to hear it. Without further ado…"

Christian placed his computer on the center of the table. Plugging the chip from Andres in the drive, a hologram of Martha appeared before the Royalists. The recording spoke immediately on playback.

"Salutations, gang. While I'm sure you would just love to stare in rapture at the beautiful genius in your presence, I'll get right to the point. We were all very excited to hear Wilhelm's report to the Queen after the attack on Deniva. It's good to know that you're all safe. They're still celebrating in the streets here since everyone found out Cedric was alive. You have to admit the Queen is good at keeping a secret, but I digress. I've got great news for you. My scientists and I have come up with a way to take down the barrier. It's complicated, but here's the short, short version: The greatest genius on Terminus Mundus—me—has built a weapon that uses the pull of our three satellites to destroy the tachyon bonds. Execution of the plan will take place on the night of the equinox on the first rotation of the growing cycle. The Queen figured you'd use this as a heads up to come up with an extraction. You've been so patient and brave, but I'm begging you to just hold on a bit longer. Send Andres back with the details and we'll be ready for you. Good luck and God bless."

The transmission ended. There were cheers and fist pumps all around the room.

"Finally, we get to go home!" cheered Cagius.

"It's about a lunar cycle to the equinox, so we don't have a lot of time to get that extraction plan going," acknowledged Cedric. "In addition, our campaign strategy against Abaddon just hit a major setback."

"Why does this hurt the campaign?" asked Amuro. "No one has dared launched a winter offensive in the plains in over four hundred revolutions."

"I was counting on having some time this winter cycle to plan the siege and assault on Verian. Now, we're going to have to launch an immediate assault as soon as we get home."

"What's the rush?" inquired Joshua.

"Cedric and I have run some calculations," explained Christian. "The Kablisha victory at Gilgal was devastating to the Demonkin forces. Abaddon and the Acadians may be down to their last legs in terms of troops."

"According to the Kablisha, Abaddon's soul can only be imprisoned in Hell through the binding spell of an angel of the Powers' Choir," lectured Cedric. "While the fallen angel has no body, he is practically powerless against the likes of the Divikin. Thus, it is logical to assume Abaddon is consuming every resource left in Central Acadia right now to incarnate another body."

"The Wizards' Tower is a cache of many treasures, it's likely he could have found something already," injected Amuro. "Though if incarnate again, he'd certainly be breaking down the doors of Deniva."

"Which is why we have to strike quickly," responded Christian.

"You know, if you Titans keep hiding every piece of information from us, this Alliance isn't going to work."

"This information is strictly need-to-know and is to be held in great confidence," said Cecilia. "We don't want to lose morale within the Alliance before the battle begins."

"We are certainly not about to start broadcasting such information," assured Malcolm. "Five revolutions of being separated have not helped our countrymen."

"That's why we have to build a coalition and march on Verian fast," commanded Cedric. "We cast Abaddon out of Verian and then launch an all-out final assault on the Caverns of the Demonkin when they run."

"Your logic is sound, Cedric," countered Valentine. "However, this is a situation that must be handled delicately. The Alliance members will treat a massive buildup as Titan imperialism and interpret that you have taken Queen Cassandra as a hostage."

"This isn't about forging a government, it's about destroying evil. When this is over, we'll have plenty of time to debate government, philosophy and succession rights until the cows come home."

"I only attempt to remind you of the enemies that we will face within. I am certain there are already scores of people blaming Titanus for escalating this war."

"Then put the burden of justifying the war on me alone. I'll be the face and I'll pay the price. Let the historians decide whether to cast me as a hero or villain, but I am asking you as my friends to aid me in this hour."

"We don't have to put this to a vote, Cedric," stated Amuro. "For over a decade now we have fought and died together. Not one person seated at this table lacks the will for what must be done."

"All we're asking is that you cut us some slack with bringing the news to our people," concurred Cagius. "I don't even know what situation I'm going to find when I go home. I just hope my dad made it through my brother's death by now."

"As long as we're passing messages," interrupted Hippolyte. "Was there any further news on the Tribal Confederation?"

"The barrier is still limiting our intelligence network, so we get only bits and pieces at a time," offered Christian. "Her Highness feared sending a full delegation to your people's fall back point. The last thing they needed was to reopen old wounds. Our reports say that they're getting bored and itching for a fight."

Hippolyte and Minerva just laughed.

"Knowing your grandfather, I'm sure your defenses are appropriate."

"They might be, but I'm not disclosing that information at this time!"

"Very smart girl!" teased a proud Valentine. "You've learned quickly!"

"I think we'd better start working on that extraction plan," said Cagius. "Ethan, you'd better see to the defenses of Deniva. We've gotten so close now, I don't want anything to be screwed up."

"I doubt Abaddon would make the same mistake twice," responded Ethan. "He's tested our will and he knows it's strong. He's going somewhere else next time."

"Unless anybody has anything else to say, I'm about done here. Ladies, sorry I interrupted your spa treatment, please enjoy the rest of it with my compliments."

"Always the same Cedric Rhone!" joked Amuro.

As everyone got up to leave, Cassandra worked her way over to Cedric. Cecilia hung just behind her.

"Cedric, I wanted to… I wanted to apologize."

"For what?"

"I guess I haven't thought the same of you since you've been back."

"I was just teasing about Florence…"

"It's not that. Cecilia recounted to me a story of your childhood. I know where you're coming from, and what you want to do for all of us. If you want to be the face of this campaign, you've got my support."

"Thanks, Cassie." Cedric leaned in and kissed her. "So Cecilia told you about the time I put the bucket on my head and the broomstick in my hands to kill the monster in her closet?"

"What?" exclaimed Cassandra with an elated smile.

"No, Cedric, I actually told her the one about making the demons go away." Cecilia interjected.

"Oh boy, I just stepped in it…"

"No, I have to hear this story! A broomstick and a bucket?"

"Yeah, even in his younger revolutions, Cedric was always hell-bent on destroying evil. His methods have only improved slightly."

"Tell me, please!"

"Maybe over dinner, Cassie."

"Just one last thing. If we don't have the legendary angel, how are we going to bind Abaddon's soul once and for all?"

"Wilhelm thinks he has an idea, but it's in the preliminary stages for now. Let's focus on Verian and we'll move to phase two later."

"Come on, Cassie!" shouted Amuro. "If we don't get back down there, we'll lose out on the massage tables!"

The girls retreated down to the spa as Cedric slunk down in his seat.

"Don't worry, my friends, I finally have the power to make these demons go away."

CASTLE ACADIA, VERIAN, ONE LUNAR CYCLE LATER

Titanus is composed entirely of a citizen army. The reliance
on a smaller, more disciplined force causes the Titans to lean
on their vassal alliances for added manpower and resources
during wartime. It has been proposed by some of our leading
military minds that the best way to defeat Titanus is to first
get rid of their allies.

Personal Journal of Saladin, adviser to Sultan Khan

As storm clouds hovered over Lake Verian, King Luminas was
grateful for the opportunity to observe the work being done on
the outer walls. Parading with Sharon and Jonas along the formerly
pristine streets, the vampire actually felt sorrow for the once radiant
city. The King promised himself that once this mess was over, he
would rebuild it as a shrine to his own radiance. Once recalled from
the field, Gavin was charged with the outer defenses. Not knowing
if he had sufficient time, the Saint decided on building a new outer
wall first before reinforcing the remaining city walls. The non-stop
work by crews of Acadian and Demonkin alike put the project about
three-quarters done.

"Gavin!" cried Luminas.

Wiping the sweat from his brow, Gavin set another stone in place
before answering the summons of his King. The templar bowed before
him.

"What news of the wall?" asked Luminas.

"The Demonkin have dug out the last of our quarries, and considering what just happened with Deniva, they aren't in the mood for trading with us right now. We've been forced to cannibalize what materials we have left in the city."

"How long?"

"I can get it up by the growing cycle, barring any distractions or bad weather."

"Will the wall save us?" pleaded Sharon.

"I'm sorry, your Highness, but I don't have the appropriate information to give you a good answer. Titans haven't used siege weapons in over two hundred revolutions. Unless they found some way to let loose a prolonged barrage, we will be safe. Our best protection still lies in Virgus' barrier."

"I am very impressed with your work, Sir Gavin," commended Luminas. "Perhaps you should have taken up masonry instead of the sword."

"Actually, I come from a family of masons, but I can't take credit for this alone. The new Nephilim Commander Kaladra is really cracking the whip hard."

Pointing towards the southern wall of the city, Luminas and Sharon's gaze was filled with the hulking presence of one of the legendary giants. Roughly the size of a troll and wingless, muscles upon muscles spilled out of the frame of Kaladra. Copper skin covered in sweat, his blue eyes focused on the task of setting rocks on the wall and keeping his command in line. A sire of Basarabbas and a human girl, the giant was elected commander of the Nephilim who now numbered less than one hundred. Determined to avenge the loss of his comrades, Kaladra worked tirelessly.

"Glad he's on our side," commented Luminas.

"He's more than just bulk, Luminas!" exclaimed Abaddon, joining them. "Giants like him may be unholy sires of Nephilim and humans, but Kaladra is different. In addition to his brawn, he actually maintained his brains."

"To what do I owe the pleasure this time, Lord Abaddon?"

"Virgus has advanced far enough on his project that it has become necessary to test the combat efficiency of our new army."

"We don't need another army," interjected Jonas. "We have our wall, and the Templar Army will stand to the last to defend the motherland."

"I told you, Jonas, we can't defend ourselves against what is coming," corrected Luminas. "We number far too few on our own."

"Titanus will stand alone!" returned Jonas. "The other nations won't risk the raising our ire or the will and power of a Dark Angel. You actually expect them to die for that fanatic?"

"Perhaps, but that is not a chance we should willingly take," interceded Abaddon. "Once again, I must seek your counsel to determine an appropriate ally."

"If I may, Dark One, I have a target in mind," suggested Sharon. "Titanus fights by the vassal system. Our reports from Deniva tell that we damaged the power of the Wood Elves. Why not go after Lion's Peak next?"

"You want to attack the Dwarves?" asked Luminas.

"Every Elf knows that we handed control of the west over to the Titans when we allowed them to occupy the Dwarven stronghold. The tribe that was allowed to live provides all of the weapons that Titanus uses and sells to the other Kingdoms."

"I've studied the Dwarves extensively and seen them in action. They are tenacious fighters, but do tend to be reckless at times," recounted Jonas. "Lion's Peak is cut off from Titanus by the barrier—they would be unable to summon any allies."

"I think we've found our test subject," agreed Abaddon.

Overhearing the discussions, Kaladra dropped a heavy stone and prostrated himself before Abaddon.

"Please, Lord Abaddon, allow me to avenge the deaths of my brethren by leading your army into battle."

"There is no need, Kaladra, Virgus' army has their own commanders."

"I beg you, my Lord."

"You'll have plenty of enemies and battles to erase the stains of dishonor from your fallen brethren," Abaddon said, dismissing him. "I intend to only send a few divisions. Virgus can always make more troops but the training process is time consuming."

"Lord Abaddon, a few divisions will not be enough to destroy the Dwarves."

"Not if we use their own arrogance against them!" proclaimed Jonas. "The Dwarves will move to defend their treasures and resources at all costs. If we trap them in their mountain, they will have no escape."

"Excellent, we'll kill two birds with one stone," commented Luminas.

"In the meantime, I'll continue building the wall," said Gavin as he returned to his work.

"We've conscripted more help for the Templar Army in addition to our trained soldiers," boasted Jonas. "Still, preparations for the coming battle need to be made."

"Even you've accepted that the Titans are coming," countered Abaddon.

"I am first and foremost a soldier, Abaddon. I'll accept the fact that the Titan bastard will do anything that wench asks of him. That's why I never bothered with the code of chivalry."

"I see. I'll take my leave, Luminas. I have a battle to plan."

Abaddon hovered over to a position where Virgus and four divisions of his new army were armed and prepared for battle.

"What is the word, Lord Abaddon?" questioned Virgus

"Ready four divisions for an assault on Lion's Peak!"

"A worthy target! Why send out only a few divisions? We could easily crush the Dwarves by sending in more."

"I will not be so reckless again with my armies. We cannot risk underestimating the strength of the Royalists once more. The defeats at the City of Antiquity and Deniva were a crushing reminder of the resilience of these people. I don't want this mission to be considered a sacrifice, because what we learn here will serve us well later. However, if we are walking into a trap, I am not ready to commit the whole of our forces yet."

"Very logical," said Virgus, nodding. He turned to his Elite. The commander snapped to attention in Abaddon's presence.

"Lord Abaddon," hailed the Elite. "My troops are ready for your inspection."

"You command the first through fourth divisions?"

"Yes, my Lord. What are my orders?"

"March your army to Lion's Peak; the Dwarves there have proved to be a nuisance. Kill every last living thing in that mountain, steal whatever weapons you can find and let it be a warning to the Royalists that dare to oppose us."

"It will give me great pleasure to heed your word, my Lord. The mountain shall run red with their blood."

"When it is done, summon me. I wish to see this legendary ore for myself. Sir Esteridge and his personal escort will meet you on the main road. Remember, they are only there to observe. The command is yours."

"Yes, my Lord. DIVISIONS! FALL OUT!"

The named Divisions snapped to attention and followed the Elite outside the city walls. Once on the road they broke into a run. Astonished at their pace, Abaddon wondered at their actions.

"Will they have the strength to maintain that pace and still have the power to fight?" questioned Abaddon.

"Better strength and endurance were the first two traits I modified in their bodies," boasted Virgus. "Observers? I guess that's all an Acadian saint is good for anymore. That and killing defenseless women."

"Patience, my dear friend; this alliance is necessary towards both of our goals. Everything is coming to headwind."

"We seem to be giving more than we're taking."

"I know, but our final prize is the grandest of all. Can it be done?"

"She's compatible, but I was wrong about one thing. It would have never worked with Cassandra because Orpheus is the seed of Cain."

BISHOP'S RESIDENCE, CITY OF ANTIQUITY

The true treasure of the Dwarves lies in their ability to make high-quality weapons. All of the Legendary Weapons were forged in the bellows of Lion's Peak and many have attributed Titanus' military dominance to their exclusive use of Dwarven weapons. Thus, many enemies have sought the riches of the Dwarven mines.

Von Angelhardt's Twenty-Fifth Report

In a simple bed, Bishop Wulf lay asleep but not dreamless. Blood pouring from his palms and feet, the Kablisha leader's eyes twitched rapidly. In his mind's eye, Lion's Peak was engulfed in flames. Slaughtering their foes in perfect legion formation, Virgus' army trampled over the carcasses of tens of thousands of dead Dwarves and the crushed helmet of Lurac. Goblins and imps worked tirelessly at the forges of their former masters, and hundreds of carts of weapons and armor were dragged back to Central Acadia. Bellowing with laughter, the Fallen Angel stood behind the head of Lurac adorned on a sharp pike and twisted in terror. No longer able to contain his fear, the Bishop jumped out of bed and grabbed his staff. As if he anticipated Wulf's trouble, Argus dutifully hurried to the residence with Quinn and Mesmara in tow. When they arrived, they found Florence tending to the Bishop in his study.

"He's had the stigmata again," assessed Florence.

"That's not good news for any of us," observed Argus. "Bishop, tell me, what did you see?"

"It was horrible Argus. A genocide…"

"Of whom?"

"The Lord has revealed a terrible vision to me. The Dwarves of Lion's Peak are about to come under siege."

"Lurac and his band are sturdy fighters. If we could take the Demonkin, they shouldn't have any difficulty."

"It wasn't Demonkin, Argus. This army fought almost as if it was of the Napolitan Dragon Legions."

"No way. Wilhelm would have certainly sent word to us if Napolitan had thrown in with Central Acadia."

"I cannot comprehend the foul craft that mad scientist used, but this army has the potential to swallow the world. It wasn't just the genocide—the Demonkin took control of the mountain and all of its riches and forges."

"The Titans rely heavily on the Dwarves to build and repair their weapons. There is also the matter of the ore. My God, if there is any left and Abaddon gets his hands on a legendary weapon…"

"The Dark Angel knows this. He seeks to shatter the power of Titanus. He knows the Wood Elves were weakened by their sacrifice at Deniva and now he strikes at their other vassal. Abaddon is a sending a message to the west: Those that align themselves with the Titans will suffer unspeakable wrath and torment."

"He will be stopped!" exclaimed Quinn. "What can we do?"

"It looks like Cedric has rubbed off on your subordinates," Wulf said, giving a small smile. "Perhaps a little bit on you as well."

"We're talking about a smudge here, Bishop," joked Argus. "I just can't afford to stand here anymore and wait for the end." He grew serious again. "We must help them, though I fear our militia may not be enough."

"You and I both know only one person can win a battle against the worst odds imaginable."

"Then allow me to take Quinn, Mesmara, and some of our militia to Deniva. I'll go get Cedric and his comrades. I'm sure if we make a good case, they'll come with us."

"Thank you, Argus."

"All right! An actual mission," whispered Quinn to Mesmara.

"This will be slightly better than the last one," commented Mesmara. "Last time we were thrust into the middle of a war zone. At least this time, we'll have a few brief moments of peace."

"Don't worry, sweetheart, we'll be fine."

"Round up about a hundred of our best fighters," ordered Argus as he turned back to his troops. "We must leave swiftly."

"Yes, sir," Quinn said, saluting.

"My Bishop, your magic is going to have to see to the protection of our people while we're gone. I'll leave a capable commander with the rest of our militia."

"Concern yourselves with the battle ahead. Now that the barrier has been reinforced we are safe within these walls."

Kneeling before the Bishop, each of the warriors kissed his ring. Wulf laid his hands on the top of their heads and offered a blessing. "God watch over you, and may your Guardian angels keep you safe."

The warriors departed.

"What do you think, Florence? Will Cedric Rhone make me believe in him one more time?"

"With your permission, my Bishop... may I..."

"I couldn't hold you back if I tried. Hurry now."

Florence kissed the Bishop on his cheek and ran to her room to get ready for battle.

"Poor Florence, she's fighting a lost cause." Retiring to his personal chapel, Wulf went to pray.

Eagle's Gate, Titanus, Two Rotations before the Equinox

Members of the Board of Regents, it is with the most distinguished honors that I admit Martha Heinrich to Titan University. Despite the fact she is but a mere youth, her talent and potential exceeds the most qualified applicants twice her age. Her skills exhibit such potential that I will personally serve as her mentor professor. On the rotation of her graduation I assure you that she will be the greatest genius this planet has ever seen.

Provost Virgus Tattenberg on the admission of Martha Heinrich

Twenty divisions of cavalry patrolled the area outside of Eagle's Gate, as engineers and technicians unloaded Martha's weapon off of the hover train. The much larger version of the original cannon required thirty people to carry it. The Titan doctor directed them to a prepared location behind a raised stockade.

"A little to the left," directed Martha.

The carriers groaned and moved it over a just a smidge. The doctor nodded in approval and skipped over to her machine. Martha hooked two portable fusion generators into the cannon. Cannon computer online, Heinrich linked her personal laptop with the system. Unnerved as she heard the approach of the Queen, the relentless, nervous pacing of her sovereign annoyed her. Unable to contain his laugher, Horace puffed away at his cigar in the cold night air. Passing one to his son, Samuel enjoyed the chance to warm up.

"So, Dad, what odds do you want?"

"Five minutes and Martha snaps. Four rounds at stake."

"I'll take it!"

Transcribing her data meticulously, Martha looked oddly at a number. A nervous curl developing on her upper lip, the doctor laughed.

"Oops."

"Oops?" demanded Civilia. "What do you mean 'oops'? Is that bad?"

As she crossed out the numbers, Martha maintained her calm demeanor. "It's just that I forgot to carry the one here. I mean, this whole darn cannon might have blown up."

"Martha… I can't tell you how confident I feel in your abilities right now."

"Why, thank you, your Highness, it means a lot to me."

Still transcribing the numbers, Martha felt Civilia's warm breath as the Queen hung over her shoulder. Horace kept his eyes on the clock while Samuel smiled at his father's imminent defeat.

"How much longer will it take to get in place?" asked Civilia.

Unable to contain her patience any longer, Martha snapped. "About five minutes… AFTER YOU STOP ASKING ME HOW LONG IT'S GOING TO TAKE!"

Civilia drew back from the scream as Martha regained her composure. There was a lot of shock and even some laughter from the contingent standing around them. Horace slapped his son on the back. Though defeated, Samuel kept a smile on his face.

"Four rounds, son."

Suddenly remembering her place, Martha dropped to one knee in front of her blushing friend and sovereign.

"I must sincerely apologize, your Highness. My rudeness is unforgivable."

"No… I'm sorry… everyone is working so hard. The anticipation is getting to me as well."

"I'm under enough pressure without 'Mommy Eagle' scrutinizing every move I make! After five revolutions, if I blow one calculation or Virgus does something I don't expect, nobody is coming home."

"You're not a mother, Martha. You don't know what this pain has been like for me."

"No, I'm not, but I love Cedric and Cecilia, too. God willing, I'll work myself to the brink of death to make sure they get home. I will not fail you, your Highness."

"Martha, you never have to justify yourself to me."

Martha took a deep breath. "Then let me do my job, Civilia. Please."

Civilia nodded. "Maybe I'll review the troops again."

"When I said 'don't bother me,' that wasn't an excuse to go bother Horace."

"I am still the ruler of this proud country and one of my most important duties is troop review," replied a smiling Civilia.

Growing concern overtook Samuel's mannerisms as the Queen turned in their direction. Horace showed no emotion, but worked on his cigar.

"Damn, I hoped to avoid this."

"Dad, what are we going to do?" Samuel muttered. "This is the third inspection this last hour."

"Better get them ready, we're in for an earful."

"Can't she just leave us alone?"

"Don't ever tell your mother this, but Civilia's like a Golden Eagle, majestic, elegant…but if her chicks get lost, she'll tear everyone's head off just to get them back."

"I see. Where the hell is Duke Wilhelm? We need him to deflect this punishment."

"Oh he's here…either he's waiting to make his grand entrance or he's simply hiding from her. Then again, after what we just talked about, I don't blame him. Now get the army in order or else her wrath is going to be the least of your problems."

Turning to his troops, Samuel got them to snap to attention.

"Riders of the Armada, Her Majesty Civilia approaches."

"Long live the Queen!" answered the riders.

"Good evening, your Majesty," greeted Horace.

"Marshal, how is your evening?"

"A bit too chilly for my bones, but we make do. Troops ready for inspection."

Civilia observed them. "Have you received the news from Andres?"

"I certainly have. Ten Divisions will ride with me to the rendezvous point." Horace paused. "As per the instructions of his Excellency…"

"Do I detect a bit of tension, Horace?"

"I would have appreciated knowing that the Crown Prince was alive. It was a difficult time for all of us."

"I was sworn to secrecy, Marshal. I am sorry, but at the time it couldn't be helped."

"Wilhelm's orders?"

Civilia nodded and quickly sought to change the topic. "I'm charging you with a great responsibility. It is not only the twins; we have the duty to protect Queen Cassandra as well."

"When have I failed you, your Highness?"

"Never! That's why I selected you for the detail."

"Thank you. Your Highness, if this isn't out of line…may I make a suggestion?"

"What is it, Marshal?"

Horace took a quick puff and inhaled deeply. "Get some sleep! You've been up for three rotations supervising this operation. Will it do you any good if you've collapsed from exhaustion by the time they come back?"

Civilia closed her eyes. "Sometimes the Queen must accept the commands of her subjects."

"I did same thing when Samuel's company was overdue. But that was only for two rotations. You had to suffer for five revolutions, I understand your anxiety. But the best people in the world are working on this. Get some sleep!"

"Thank you. But I know you and Martha just want me out of your hair for the rest of the night. Don't worry, I understand."

Civilia summoned her horse and rode back to Eagle's Gates. Everyone in the area breathed a sigh of relief.

"And she's gone," sighed a relieved Samuel.

"All right, break out the booze, the scientists could use a break. Hey, Martha!"

"What is it, Horace?" replied Martha as she turned around.

"Take five!"

"Finally! I thought she'd never leave."

Bothered by her notes, Martha collapsed to the ground and went to look over her numbers again. Horace dismounted and broke open a few bottles of whiskey that the soldiers and scientists happily shared. Handing Martha a glass last, the doctor took it with a smile.

"So what's the real ETA?"

"Three more hours and everything will be set. We'll fire it in two moons and the barrier will come down…that is, if Virgus didn't change anything."

"You know him better than anyone else. Do you think he's discovered the flaw?"

"I don't think so, Horace. Virgus never shared my beliefs in trial, error, experiment, success, and trial again. He considered every experiment to be settled science."

"We can only pray he hasn't changed, and unfortunately you can't influence that."

"Try telling that to Civilia."

"If it comes to that, I'll handle Civilia for you. Besides, if you fail, Cedric will round up some mysterious ally who will grant him steel fists to shatter the barrier with his own hands."

"My confidence just shot up," joked a laughing Martha. "After all, he's just about done everything else these past revolutions—why not resort to science as well? Hey…how'd you get a bottle of Acadian whiskey, anyway?"

"I have my sources."

Approaching Fort Hawkeye, Civilia saw Wilhelm stationed as a lone rider in the valley between the forts. Startled by his appearance, Wilhelm's countenance placed a momentary fear in her heart.

"Duke Wilhelm, I did not summon you!"

"My Queen, I have a doubt."

"What do you mean? Martha's weapon won't work?"

"It's beyond that. I have received word from the Kablisha. Bishop Wulf had another stigmata. He sees the destruction of the Dwarves at Lion's Peak."

"Wilhelm, that's not a joke! We're at war, we cannot lose our strongest ally before it begins."

"The Kablisha are sending men. When the barrier falls, I would like your permission to take two divisions—"

"You can have five divisions. Twenty-five thousand will be at your disposal for any defense."

"Thank you, my Queen. Now, if in my insolence, I could beg one more favor from such a magnanimous ruler."

Civilia laughed heartily. "The nun's robes becoming a bit too much here?"

"Nadia's magic would be welcome in this fight, especially since I don't know what kind of enemy we could be going up against."

"You have my permission, Wilhelm. My division commander will make a report. If she serves with distinction, her interment will be considered over."

"Thank you, your Highness. Any plans for this evening?"

"My subjects are ordering me to get some rest."

"That is probably wise. Shall I arrange for some of my favorite libations to be brought to your quarters?"

"I've brought my own, thanks. Good luck. Oh, and when this incident at Lion's Peak is over, would Garrett Greensage be willing to align with Titanus once again?"

"He won't like it, nor will Bishop Wulf."

"The time for coyness and prudence is over. We are at war and will be damn sure to have all of the great minds leading us to victory."

"Yes, your Highness."

"Six revolutions ago on a chilly evening like this, Christian and Cedric came to me with a plan to end the Imperial encroachment by forcing the hand of our allies. I long for the times when Khan's ambition caused me sleepless nights. What frightful inevitability has befallen us."

CASTELLAN, DENIVA

While they have been vehemently opposed to undertaking wars of aggression, the Kablisha have shown in times of crisis their willingness to defend their brothers. The Kablisha offered Hayden Marisol the use of the Fortress City of Antiquity after Brooke Run had fallen to the Dwarves. That is why King Frederick Rhone was so badly hurt when his Kablisha brethren refused to come to his aid against the Imperial incursion.

Von Angelhardt's Eighth Report

A map of Deniva was enhanced to a three-dimensional image in the center of a long table. Cedric, Cecilia, and Christian hovered over the images. DeVries moved his right fingers along the board to zoom out, while his left hand traced a path south into the mountains.

"I believe this is our safest path to the mountains," suggested Christian. "While unlikely, we have to anticipate Abaddon may have a contingency for a full barrier collapse. The three of us should all be familiar with this terrain; we used this ridge to coordinate our quick strikes against the wild men."

"Horace knows that ridge well," added Cecilia. "The scant amount of raiders left in those passes aren't stupid enough to challenge Titan cavalry."

"Abaddon still may have another ally up his wings we don't know about yet. He did take down Central Acadia without me discovering his plot until the end."

"I still think that Wilhelm would have informed us of a problem. He hasn't lost his abilities to travel within the barrier."

"So now you trust him?"

"He saved our necks by bringing Cedric back. That's enough for me. You've been silent, brother, is anything wrong?"

Smiling, Cedric traced his fingers along the ridge to a point with a blinking red star.

"I'm sorry, I was just reliving some former moments of glory. The Valley of Mourning—no one besides members of Titanus knows of that mountain pass. The winter's snow will have been cleared and the pass is narrow enough so we'd be alerted to an impending attack. We cut through there and come out on the Titan side of the Vale, well in front of Eagle's Gate. From there it's a thousand meters to rendezvous points."

"With the snow cleared, the horses shouldn't have any trouble cutting through," interrupted Christian. "Which is good, because I'm concerned about those last thousand meters. I know we can sprint it, but what if Eagle's Gate is under siege?"

"Then we aren't going to worry about approaching the rendezvous point because there won't be one," joked Cecilia.

"It's not like there's a back gate we can sneak through, Cecilia," offered Christian.

"No, there is another path that Frederick used, but I dare not expose it to the enemy," retorted Cedric. "Cassandra, Walker, and her Order will have to remain behind in Titanus. We need to make sure our friends get back to their homes as quickly as possible. Evengard will be especially tricky, unless I can lean on some unlikely allies for help."

"What about the tribes?" asked Cecilia.

"I really don't know, Cecilia. Hippolyte has learned a lot from us, but I don't know how her people will react to us."

"While I'm dying to get there, part of me is really nervous about going home. After all, we're going to have to endure thousands of hugs and kisses Mom is going to give us."

"And wait until she finds out that you're married and you have a son. Don't worry, sis, I'll protect you."

Cecilia blushed. "Let's just worry about getting home first. Then we'll deal with what comes next."

"Get everyone in here, we'll discuss our final plans for the trek to the rendezvous point and then we can get to packing."

Alarms rang out throughout the room and castle. Christian immediately erased the board in front of them.

"Are we under assault again?" questioned Cecilia.

"Nothing surprises me anymore." Cedric sighed. "Let's check it out."

Perched on top of the main city gate with his mercenaries, Ethan stared at the approaching Kablisha militia. Hardened by the past experiences of the last five revolutions, the Denivan knight didn't exude fear, but was ready to verify these arrivals. Argus was at the head of the column with Quinn and Mesmara filling in behind him. At his right side was Florence dressed in her field uniform.

"I think that's the cleric from the battle," wondered Ethan. "Oh man, I hope she didn't sell us out."

Alerted to the sound of horses behind him, Ethan was relieved to see his brother-in-law and wife approach the gate.

"Husband, what's going on?

"A group of warriors are heading towards the city. They look human enough and that cleric is with them."

As if hit with a ton of bricks, Cedric dismounted and drew Ragnarok.

"I'm pretty sure they're friends," commented Cedric. "However, their intentions may be dubious. Open the gate, I'll meet them."

"How can you be sure?" demanded Ethan.

"They're of the Kablisha!"

Signaling to his men to open the gate, Ethan doubted the judgment of his brother-in-law. He slid down a rope and joined his wife.

Drawing their weapons, the couple locked hands as they walked behind the Titan prince. Argus held his army up as the sword master approached him.

"Peace be with you, Cedric," greeted Argus. "Your deeds in this fair city have reached us back in the City of Antiquity."

"Argus, if you brought an army with you to bring me back, I must warn you that I will not go of my own free will."

"We wouldn't dare."

"It's good to see you, Lord Cedric," announced Quinn.

"Though we wish we came to you under better circumstances," added Mesmara.

Blushing heavily, Florence titled her eyes down and shuffled her feet together. Cecilia rolled her eyes.

"Cedric, we're desperate," exclaimed Argus. "Is there somewhere I can address all of your allies?"

"Follow me! Ethan, I'm bringing these people into the city at my personal responsibility. Have everyone meet me in the strategy room in fifteen minutes."

"Right away."

"Cecilia, allow me to introduce my warden for the past five revolutions. Argus Kinkade, or…"

He leaned in and whispered something in her ear, and Cecilia's eyes shot out. She shook her head after taking another look at him and wound up face-palming herself. Composing herself once more, she sneered at the Kablisha commander.

"So you're the one who tried to keep my brother hidden away… how foolish!"

Attempting to intercede on behalf on her uncle, Mesmara curtsied before Cecilia.

"It is humbling to stand in your presence, mi'lady. Clearly the legends of the beauty and power of the Vanadis do you no justice."

"Finally, someone who gives me the recognition of the rank I deserve. I like you already."

In fifteen minutes all of the Royals had gathered in the strategy room. Senior officers of the Order of the Lion and the Wood Elves attended as well. Cagius was chuckling.

"We have a saying in Napolitan that ill news is an ill guest. I have a feeling that if the Kablisha had ventured outside of their borders, something has gone very wrong."

"I wish we sought your recognition under better circumstances, Prince Imperia, but these are dire times," explained Argus. "Bishop Wulf has had a vision of Lion's Peak under siege."

"Who'd be foolish enough to try that?" questioned Amuro.

"It was an army we'd never seen before, but they bore Abaddon's standards. It certainly wasn't Demonkin, but…"

"Titanus cannot dishonor a call to arms by an ally. Argus, what can we do to help them?"

"Your desire to save others still impresses me. Cedric, if you are to lead a successful attack against Verian, you will need the craftsmanship and resources of the Dwarves. Therefore, I need you to help me fight against this new army."

"It can't be easy for someone like you to ask me for help! However, there is a problem. Lion's Peak is within the barrier; we have no means reaching it."

"Cedric, there's a chance—a slight chance at that. Mesmara has certain mystical abilities that allow her to create and disrupt barriers. There's an ancient tunnel that will lead us straight to Lion's Peak. If Mesmara can break the barrier there at its weakest point, we can travel the tunnel into the mines under Lion's Peak undetected by the enemy."

"If not, I guess we'll have to wait for Martha to bring down the barrier," acknowledged Cecilia.

"We're not asking for miracle, Cecilia, we're just asking for a little help," joked Cedric.

"If Martha's theory on this barrier is correct, it may be weakest at this cycle," suggested Christian. "She might be able to break through."

"It is the belief of our Bishop that Abaddon is attempting to isolate Titanus," lectured Argus. "The attack on Deniva weakened the power of the Wood Elves, we suffered losses when we were attacked, and now he is turning his attention to the Dwarves. You must protect Lurac and his people if you ever expect to succeed against your enemies."

"This isn't another Crypt, right?" asked Walker. "This is a tunnel."

"No, this isn't anything like that. It's a clear shot, no enemies," replied Quinn. "That is unless the Dwarves fall before we get there."

"I hate to bring this up, but do we have an out strategy?" interrupted Valentine.

"The Kablisha will use recall spells to return us to the City of Antiquity if we are going to get overrun," offered Mesmara.

"Even if there isn't going to be an attack, Cecilia, Christian, Colin, and I must answer the call to honor the Alliance. Everyone here knows the value and importance of the weapons the Dwarves have developed for us. Despite all of their faults, the ingenuity and loyalty of their race cannot be denied. Everyone here has fought hard and far beyond the call of duty. I will not ask anyone to go further, but if you wish to volunteer for this desperate mission I would be honored to have you. Either way, I'll leave behind the safest route to get back to the rendezvous point."

"Cedric, do you honestly think after all this time that I am going to abandon you?" teased Amuro. "I want to go home, but I also want to beat Luminas. Elves and Dwarves may not get along, but I still respect Lurac."

"I'm going, too. For the death of my brother, I am not going to miss any opportunity at retribution. If I get chance to screw over Abaddon's plans, I'm willing to put my life on the line."

Cassandra lowered her eyes. Part of her wanted to volunteer to go, but she had a greater responsibility. As Queen of Central Acadia, her swift arrival in Titanus was necessary, if just to gain the support of Napolitan and Evengard. She felt the warm touch of Walker's hand on her right shoulder and Robespierre on her left.

"You have nothing to fear, your Majesty," announced Walker. "Robespierre and I will make sure that Central Acadia is well represented in the defense of Lion's Peak."

"Thank you, my brave soldiers. I had hoped to avoid another lecture from Cedric and Amuro over the dangers of my position, and as such I will sit this one out reluctantly."

Across the room were some nods. Slowly but surely, everyone stood and put their hands to the table.

"If DeVries goes, I go too!" exclaimed Rosa. "I am not letting him get out of his promise, even if I have to chase him all the way to hell to do it. We've suffered losses, but I can mesh some battalions together for battle."

"We waited five revolutions, what's one more adventure?" said Joshua.

Putting his arms over the shoulders of Joshua and Cagius, the smaller Valentine winked and licked his lips. Hippolyte and Minerva threw their hands in the air.

"It's been a while since we've had a good hunt," shouted Hippolyte. "My sister and I will bring the vengeance of the Tribal Confederation down on Abaddon."

"Not to mention the opportunity to pick up some new trophies!" bellowed Minerva.

As the remaining members of the room made their position known, Argus could only stare in wonder and held his head in shame.

"What's the matter, Argus?" inquired Ethan.

"I never believed Cedric when he said what kind of people you actually were. Each of you are a credit to your people. Perhaps together we do have what it takes to bring down Abaddon and save Central Acadia."

"I guess its settled then," determined Cedric. "Cassandra and Thomas will journey with the Order of Lion to the rendezvous point. Rosa, may I borrow some of your companies for the duty as well?"

"Of course, Lord Cedric, my people remain at your disposal. I'm sure Gerard will get them home safely."

"Into the Lion's Den once more," sighed Malcolm. "I just hope Lurac doesn't turn his weapons on us."

Saria gulped a little at the thought of the Dwarven prejudice. Sighing, Saria felt the strong hand of her sister on her shoulder. As she turned, the two smiled at one another.

"You don't have to do this if you don't want, Saria. There's no need to volunteer if you're not comfortable."

"It's my war too, Amuro. What was the point of training all of those long hard hours, if I run every time a battle comes?"

"Leave the fighting to the professionals, sister."

"Please Amuro. I never asked you for anything, but I always admired your bravery and courage. If this is going to be the start of the new era, let me be a part of it. I'm tired of being the doll. You left me behind once before and I was terrified. I want to stand with you this time around. I don't ever want to have to walk out on Maiden again. You didn't have to live with the look I saw in her eyes."

"I'm going to regret this, but there is no doubting your resolve. Just remember, my orders are law on the battlefield. Never try to be a heroine and don't do anything stupid."

"You can count on me, sis."

Amuro wrapped her sister in a warm hug, and Malcolm rolled his eyes at Amuro's decision. The Elf marshal threw her arms out with a resigned smile of defeat on her face.

"Okay, assemble in six hours. Pack appropriate food, water, and supplies," ordered Cedric. "Good luck!"

Ear to the door, Thomas jumped back as his parents exited the room first. Ethan scooped him up and put the boy on his shoulders as they walked to their room.

"So you're both going?" asked a depressed Thomas.

"There's no point beating around the bush," answered Cecilia. "Thomas, you were born a Titan and this is what happens. My mother was on campaigns all the time when I was young girl, and I'm afraid it's going to be the same way now."

"Queen Cassandra will take you back with her to Titanus," added Ethan. "Don't worry, you'll be in safe hands."

"Okay."

Cecilia took Thomas from Ethan and put him down. The Vanadis got on her knees before him.

"Your Grandmother is going to be a bit shocked by this revelation. I'm sorry I burdened you with this, but Cassie may do enough to soften the blow. Try not to do anything to aggravate her while we're gone. Keep up with your training and studies."

"Good luck, Mama."

"We make our own luck, Thomas. Just keep praying really, really, hard for us."

"And make sure Cassandra gets through okay," joked Ethan.

"You got it, Mom and Dad!" Thomas gave them two thumbs up. "Give those demons hell!"

"Where did you learn language like that?" probed Ethan.

Thomas looked at his mother, who stood with an innocent look on her face.

In a room on the other side of the hall, Cedric performed his pre-battle ritual. Kneeling with his eyes closed, he offered his final prayers before blessing himself. A slight knock on the door disrupted him as he stood. He found Cassandra standing there timidly, eyes focused on the ground.

"It's not what I'm used to, Cassie, but this is still my room."

"I promised I wouldn't fight you on coming any more. However, there is an Acadian tradition where the Ladies of the Court bid farewell to the Knights before battle."

"It's not appropriate for a Queen to dress a Marshal."

"I'm doing you a favor by not fighting you on the deployment. The Acadians do not have many of the fine and honorable traditions of the Titans. Allow me some dignity before you ride into uncertainty."

Unable to resist the pain in her face and voice, Cedric relented. Donning the chain first, the Queen delicately hooked it in place. Not missing an opportunity to, she kissed him on the back of the neck.

"Maybe it was the skull fracture, but I didn't notice how beautiful Florence really was."

"Yes, she is," murmured Cedric.

"It must have been torture for you. A beautiful noble before you, holy and pure, not cursed with a demon inside of her."

Cedric held his head down as he felt the tears of his betrothed rolling down his back. Grabbing the heavy plate, the sword master put it on himself, before moving to the remaining pieces.

"It's only you, Cassie…it's only ever been you…it will only ever be you."

Cassandra spun the Titan prince around and collapsed in his chest.

"How do you do it, Cedric? I felt all of the powers within you. You had the power to take Titanus and conquer every province in the west…perhaps all of Terminus Mundus if you desired it. When this is over, teach me! Teach me to destroy this thing inside of me."

"You can't destroy it, Cassie. I tried to tell you Christmas night, but you wouldn't listen. It's part of who you are. You have to draw strength from good and the bad, or else you're not really alive. To subjugate a world, sure, I have the power to do it, but I have no desire to watch countless innocents suffer because of it."

Cedric cupped Cassandra's face in his weathered hands.

"Reflect on what I told you about true charity, and you'll find all of the answers you'll ever need."

Feeling a little better, Cassandra removed the sash from her waist. She wrapped it around Cedric's battle kilt.

"Make sure you bring it back!" teased Cassandra. "Try not to get so much blood on it this time! The Denivans put a lot of effort in having this made especially for me."

"Make it back to Titanus safely and don't let my mother irritate you too much. I don't envy the position you're going to be in when Thomas arrives. That might be more difficult than the battle I'm fighting."

"I'll be waiting for your return."

Cassandra curtsied before Cedric as the final part of the ceremony. The sword master took her hand and drew her into a long kiss. As they pulled back ever so slightly, a flash of malice appeared in Cassandra's face. With a smile, she bid him farewell.

"Make them fear *La Morte Angelus*!"

"I gladly obey, your Highness."

Mountain Hall, Lion's Peak

The final battle of the war between the Elves and Dwarves took place at Emperor Dondarion's stronghold, Lion's Peak. The Titan King Ulysses Rhone drew the Dwarves out of their mountain by occupying the mineral rich Vale of the Gods Forge. There he was joined by the Elf King Hayden Marisol and the Elf Warrior Joab. The combined forces of the Elves and Titans killed Dondarion and ended the Dwarf Empire. Yet, some Dwarves willingly betrayed Dondarion before the battle and this tribe was allowed to live as vassals of Titanus, and their leader, Nurn son of Nery, became Lord of Lion's Peak.

History of the Elf-Dwarf War, Elf scholar Demetrius

The magnificence and opulence of the former stronghold of Dondarion had not faded through the ages. A massive, reinforced stone door guarded the entrance to the mountain. Marked with the Dwarven symbols of military might and ingenuity, it opened into the main reception hall. The massive stone floor was shrouded in a canopy of darkness due to its immense size. In this hall, the Elves led by Hayden and Joab finally dealt the deathblow to the ambitions of the Dwarf Emperor. It was kept intentionally barren to memorialize the final defeat. A labyrinth of stone chambers was supported by vaulted ceilings and gilded marble columns. Telling the tales of the Dwarves' rise to prominence and fall, they served as a chilling reminder to those who journeyed into the mountain that all glory was fleeting.

Deep in the mountain, the Dwarves had built an intricate mine car system. The three-layered track served to transport Dwarves, materials, and finished products from one workstation to the next. While most of the precious metals had been mined out long ago, Lion's Peak remained a key source of iron, silver, tin, and vanadium. Brave miners would spelunk deep into lightless caverns to gather the treasures from the mountain. Once collected, the train system would bring them to the great forges, where blacksmiths practiced their sacred and secretive craft. It was these forges that built the greatest weapons and armors of Terminus Mundus. The well-oiled assembly line from extraction to polish was a true marvel and it was easy to see how they could have created such a large and powerful Empire.

Three stones steps lead to an unoccupied golden throne which was large enough to seat a giant comfortably. Below these steps was the wooden bench where Lurac was seated. Towering behind him was the golden statue of the full-bearded and broad-shouldered Emperor Dondarion. Though they begged to tear it down, the Titan kings made Nurn swear to keep it standing and polished for all time. It was an omnipresent reminder to the conquered, that even the most powerful Dwarf was toppled by the mighty knights and Valkyries of the south. Lurac stroked his beard anxiously. The senior officers of the Dwarf army stood in full armor, holding their helmets underneath their arms. The pounding of boots against the floor made heads rise, as a Dwarven scout entered the room. Out of breath, he knelt before Lurac.

"Now what?" demanded Lurac. "I am tired of these daily reports on the situation involving this barrier blocking us in."

"I fear, my Lord, that the news is dire! Our scouts are reporting that a large army is heading this way from the North and Verian. They are making up distance rather quickly."

"So the traitors of Acadia come to steal the Dwarven treasures," bellowed Lurac as he lifted his axe high in the air. "Let them come!"

"They may be from Verian, but that's the end of it. These troops are well-armed with chain veils and closed helmets. They carry weapons crafted by goblins and imps."

"Clearly inferior to our own, but we best not take any chances. Close the main doors to the mountain and brace them. Arm all of our warriors and have them take up position on the stone pavement. Move the young and old into the Second Hall. We'll show these Acadian bastards what happens to those who dare invade our sanctuary."

"What about our Titan allies?" asked one the Dwarven generals.

"We'll try to send word to them, but with this blasted barrier up, I doubt it would do any good. By the time they get here, all they may be good for is to help us clean the blood we are about to spill in the defense of our home. If they do arrive in time, well, we'll try not to eat all of the treats at the party. FOR LION'S PEAK!"

Lurac stood and thrust his armored fist into the air. His warriors answered the salute and executed his orders. On the outskirts of the mountain, Sir Esteridge sat on his brown steed, witnessing the door being sealed. Known for his agility and speed rather than brawn, Esteridge favored the polearm as his primary weapon. In battle, he preferred to dismount and keep his opponents at a distance. The Elite stopped his troops five hundred meters from the mountain entrance.

"I didn't anticipate such a strong door in front of us," observed the Elite.

"Can you bring it down?" asked Esteridge.

"Certainly, Virgus provided us with a siege engine just for this purpose. However, it will take longer than anticipated."

"Well, bring it up, we'll foment a strategy while we wait."

A carriage was brought forward with two large metal hammers on each side. Mechanically set with a spring action, these hammers applied ten times the force on impact than an ordinary battering ram. When they struck in unison the first time, the whole mountain shook. As his army reached the stone pavement on the other side, Lurac knew without help, his people were doomed.

PLAINS OUTSIDE OF DENIVA

The tunnel system that flows under the Western Plains was first developed by the Edenians in conjunction with the Kablisha Tribe. While they knew their Titan cousins would fight to the last man, the Edenians and Kablisha prepared for the rotation where a massive evacuation may be needed to either Palacio Magnifico or the City of Antiquity. The tunnels would use the old Dwarf mines carved from Lion's Peak to funnel troops between these locations. However, the entrances to these tunnels were kept secret and known only to the Captain of the Watch of both the Kablisha and the Edenians.

Twenty-Seventh Report, Duke Wilhelm von Angelhardt

The makeshift army of Kablisha militia, Order of the Lion Knights, and Wood Elf rangers scoured the plains for the entrance to the supposed tunnel. Ahead of the column, Argus walked his horse forward, staring at the ground.

"These tunnels have secret entrances that can only be opened by the keys entrusted to the Edenians and the Kablisha."

Dismounting and bending down to the ground, the Kablisha Marshal swept the dirt away from an area near two stone circles. It revealed two marbles bases where keyholes had been engraved. Hidden underneath his armor, Argus withdrew both keys. Upon inserting and turning them in each hole, the ground shook underneath the army, unsettling the horses. Dirt was tossed in the air as a stone ramp fell from the ground above into the darkness below. The Kablisha Marshal entered the tunnel first holding a staff in his hand. Despite the darkness around him, Argus managed to find the grooves he was looking for beneath his feet. Inserting the staff into the ground, the tunnel erupted in an explosion of blue light. A perfect pathway was illuminated by soft, blue light by both the ground below and the torches flanking the road. Now deemed safe, Cedric descended into the tunnel, followed by the others. Knowing what lay ahead of them, the army traveled calmly for three kilometers before they saw the bane of their existence. The barrier had established the same roadblock in the tunnel as it did on the ground above. After receiving a hug of encouragement from Quinn, Mesmara took two deep breaths before approaching the barrier. The Kablisha maiden put her hand to the barrier and it discharged energy to push her back. She held her ground and chanted a spell in the ancient tongue. Circles of energy pulsed from Mesmara's hand and penetrated the barrier ever so slightly.

"Come on, Mesmara!" encouraged Quinn. "Just a bit more!"

She screamed in agony from the intensity of the spell. Amuro and Florence braced her, healing her with their magic so she could keep the cast going. Mesmara shouted once more. A break in the barrier, just large enough for a person on horseback to get through, was formed. Not wasting any time, Cedric charged through and ordered the rest of his army to follow. It took a good bit of time, but everyone made it through. As Mesmara passed through last, the barrier reformed behind her. Exhausted by the grueling spell, she fainted in Quinn's arms. A chilling inevitability was felt through the column as they knew they were behind enemy lines with no good means of escape.

"All right, Argus, how long is our journey?" questioned Cedric.

"It will take half a rotation to reach the Main Hall via the Mines," answered Argus. "The labyrinth that makes up the hall system should allow Lurac and his army to hold out for two rotations. If Martha brings the barrier down, Wilhelm could beat us there with luck. I suggest we travel three quarters of the distance before we rest and eat. That way we'll be prepared for the battle when we arrive."

"I don't like it."

"You know we have to do this, Cedric, just enough to recover our strength. We'll have traveled a long way."

"I'm upset that it's going to take us that long to get to that damn mine. Christian! Colin! Take the point with Argus! Robespierre, cover the rear with your guard. Columns of four through the tunnel!"

An affirmative "yes, Marshal" was heard throughout the column. Amuro brought Maiden over to Saria.

"I want you to ride Maiden, Saria."

"Sis, I can't do that."

"You can't ride side-saddle at the pace we're going to have to move at. Don't worry, I'll ride bareback on your horse."

"Okay, sis."

Bowing before Saria, Cagius lifted his love interest onto Maiden. The winged unicorn was getting used to having the little sister as a rider and happily accepted the slimmer of the two Jenitzens. The younger Elf princess bent down to the mare's ear and sang a cheery tune. Maiden nodded and readied herself to ride. After cutting the sidesaddle loose, Amuro took a running start and flipped herself onto Saria's ride. Quinn tied the resting Mesmara in her saddle before tying her horse to his.

"We're burning daylight!" ordered Cedric. "Ride now!"

Driving down the tunnel at pace, Christian and Colin flanked Argus. The soft blue light was mesmerizing as the horses passed the torches above. Filled with anxiety, Amuro and Malcolm questioned the tactics of those they were charged with defending.

"There is another issue. How do we know that the Dwarves are going to perform normal military maneuvers?" inquired Amuro.

"They're more likely to fight to the death rather than give ground." agreed Malcolm.

"Lurac is a better tactician than you might know." commented Cecilia. "He will fight by the correct strategy."

"The one thing I don't get is this," contemplated Walker. "You said you could whisk us out of Lion's Peak. Why can't you whisk us in as well?"

"The magic of teleportation is a very limited discipline," explained Florence. "In order to place a marker, you have to have physically traveled to that location before."

"Wilhelm can leave and enter places as he wishes," countered Christian. "He never mentioned anything about a physical visit."

"The powers of an angel are much more advanced; they are not bound by the limitations of time and space," argued Quinn. "It is the reason why Wilhelm and Abaddon can travel at will."

"Damn convenient!" muttered Cedric. "You had me trapped for five revolutions. Why didn't you teach me that?"

"If I knew how to do it, Lord Rhone, I'd use it myself!" countered a miffed Argus.

Pushing Myst closer to Jericho, Cedric could feel a worrisome aura coming off of his sister. The Vanadis clearly had something weighing on her mind.

"So how do you think Horace will take it?" asked a concerned Cecilia.

"I don't envy his position. Cassandra will at least give her some idea about what's going to happen."

"How do you think Mom is going to take the situation concerning my son?"

"You know her. She's probably driven half the Kingdom insane already waiting for this rotation. It's a surprise I don't think she's ready for."

"I think they should take a slow ride back."

"With luck, we may beat them home yet."

"You don't really believe that, do you, Cedric?"

"Pray for haste!"

Towards the rear guard, Minerva and Hippolyte rode side by side. Bubbling over as usual, Minerva recounted their mission.

"So, since we began this mission for Grandpa, we were sent to Verian, taken prisoner by the Acadians, rescued by Colin and Christian, fought for our lives through the Castle and Crypt, got trapped in Deniva, fought the Dark Elf Nation, met up with members of the Kablisha Tribe, and are now headed for the Dwarf mines. Isn't this the most fun you've ever had? By the time we get home, we'll be famous."

"It's been a wild adventure," said Hippolyte quietly.

"What's the matter, sis?"

"You're right, a lot has changed. When we get back, the fate of the Wolf Tribe is going to be in our hands."

"Seems as if you aren't too thrilled with that fact. The Confederation needs a strong leader and must be desperate for you come back and take over!"

"I knew Grandpa wasn't going to live forever, but I didn't think I was going to inherit a war, either."

"Don't worry, I'll be there for you, sis."

"I just hope Huskal is still alive. Reynard, Josephine, and others, too—we're going to need all of them to oppose Abaddon."

"Yeah. Hey, remember what I told you?"

"What?"

"Make sure you tell everyone back home that you stared the Prime Eagle in the eye and didn't blink."

The girls laughed and continued to ride.

"Or rather, I stared the raptor in the eye and nearly fell in love."

Eagle's Gate, Titanus

Ladies and Gentlemen, it would be easier for me to accept this position if you would cede me the undisputed fact that I am the greatest genius on Terminus Mundus.

Martha Heinrich on the acceptance of her position of Provost

Horace, Samuel, and his divisions were on horseback with weapons drawn. Not knowing what was going to happen if the barrier fell, Civilia took no chances and had Fort Hawkeye armed to the teeth with defenses. The center of attention was Martha, as she worked with her team of scientists, and began her final preparations. While they were all confident in their work and abilities, there was still a rush of anxiety among everyone. Civilia hovered all around in a daze. For the first time, she didn't know whether she should be armed for battle, pestering Martha, or locked away safely in Castle Titan.

"Doctor, everyone is in place for the experiment," offered Martha's chief scientist.

"Experiment... I guess in the end that's all this is," sighed Martha. "All right, I just wish I had time to check these again."

Martha took a quick look at her calculations, tapping a pencil against the paper. Licking her lips and moving her head back and forth, the good doctor frowned. Civilia's hand found Martha's shoulder.

"Calculations again, Martha? Aren't you the one who tells her students always to answer based on their first instincts?"

"I do say that… well, your Highness, this will either be the first salvo struck in the Final Battle against Abaddon, or a simple footnote in history."

"Perhaps a quick prayer would help," offered Civilia as she took a moment to bless herself.

"Make it a good one, your Majesty. Live or die, here we go."

Logging into her laptop, the rapid, precision movements of her fingers on the keyboard allowed the doctor to view flashing images at split-second intervals. Her feverish pace quickened as she worked deeper and deeper into the program. One more deep breath and Martha signaled to her team.

"Activate the generators now! Let's get this working up to thirty percent power and then ten percent increases on my marks."

As the team entered the sequences into the two generators, white flashing lights and a soft humming filled the immediate area. Along a green line, the number thirty percent was displayed. Kruger worked on the second generator, the youngest member of the team. After their first meeting, Doctor Heinrich had taken an interest in the young man's aptitude and unconventional thinking. As he worked diligently, Horace and Samuel both worked on their cigars.

"So, Wilhelm snuck out in the middle of the night?" asked Samuel.

"He's positioned his divisions in a mountain pass near Lion's Peak. They should be able to reach the mountain quickly if the barrier falls."

"What's with the extra contingents here?"

"If this is a clever trap, then all of the forces of Central Acadia could be waiting behind that barrier."

"Acadians lack the courage to perform such a trap! They probably still think they are safe within their walls."

"When you command this army, my son, you may command it as you see fit. I never leave anything to chance."

"Yes, sir."

Moving her right index finger in the air, Martha signaled to her team to increase the power levels. Even as the power reached sixty percent, it remained in the green zone.

"Initiate stage one," ordered Martha. "Fire particle burst towards the shield."

The scientists followed her orders. A concentrated beam of silver light flowed through the weapon to its front. Feeding more and more power into the cannon until a pulse was formed, the final blast left the cannon. The energy column was no more than a millimeter wide, but it had a definite effect upon impact. As it made contact with the barrier, small green hexagons flashed and tachyon bonds imploded.

"Does that mean it's working?" asked a confounded Civilia.

"So far so good," explained Martha. "The gravitational fields of our moons are counteracting the power of Virgus' generators."

"It looks like you've surpassed your teacher, Martha."

"It's not down yet, Civilia. This is only the first stage and I'm sure that Virgus has noticed something by now. On my mark, increase the power… three… two… one… eighty percent now!"

Kruger increased the power once more. The power display moved from green to yellow as it hit eighty. Bonds broke all around the outer portions of the barriers. Citizens in Evengard, Napolitan, and Deniva no longer could ignore what was going on. They went running for the barrier wondering what had caused the disturbance. As Martha worked, a video message popped up on her screen. Gulping nervously, she answered it and Virgus Tattenberg's face came up.

"My sweet Martha Heinrich, you've been a very naughty little girl!"

"Salutations, Doctor Tattenberg, it's been a long time."

"My instrumental panels indicate that you have invented a weapon capable of destroying my beautiful tachyon barrier. I've actually feared this moment for quite some time, but you are well ahead of my projected calculations. Well played, my dear!"

"I should be honored by such praise, but you always complimented me for handing in my assignments before they were due. So, I see you have a means of communication through the barrier."

"Actually, your weakening of it made this conversation possible. The gravitational force of the moons bend the tachyon bonds. It's hard to be angry when I'm so proud of you. Of course, my dear, you should know that I had a contingency ready for you."

"Uh oh!"

A spike appeared on the taskbar of Martha's laptop. Working at his own station, Virgus uploaded a virus onto Martha's computer. The generators reached critical and flashed with red lights. Despite the increase in power, the beam dissipated and the cannon was set to overload.

"What does 'uh oh' mean?" demanded Civilia.

"Nothing, your Majesty… I hope… well, actually, this is very bad. Virgus uploaded a virus into my laptop and reprogrammed the code for the cannon. If I don't fix it soon, it's going to explode."

Despite the distance between them, Martha and Virgus played a game of programming chess. Doctor Heinrich returned a spike at her mentor, which caused the mad scientist to frantically purge his data records. Frustrated at her inability to stop her mentor and worried the plan was going to literally blow up in her face, she stared at her invention and surprised everyone by giving it a swift kick.

"Come on, you stupid piece of junk! I didn't waste the last five revolutions of my life for you to fail me now! Work!"

Noticing the generator started to smoke due to her lack of professionalism. Martha's face fell and she immediately ran over to the generator. She applied some tender but swift repairs to the machine. When she was finished, she ran back to the cannon.

"All right, I'm sorry, you're not a stupid piece of junk. Don't tell the other inventions but I'm proudest of you."

As she regained her composure, a determined look crossed Martha's face.

"I'm sorry, Professor, but there's one thing they don't teach you at Titan Academy and that's how to deal with failure. Kruger, get a laptop ready and open the file I'm sending you."

"You got it, chief," answered Kruger.

"The rest of you on the generators, keep that power level at eighty percent and raise it all the way again on my mark. Kruger, you get that file?"

"It's open and ready, Doctor."

"Set the network mark five point seven point twenty-one point six five two. Now, Kruger!"

Martha could see Virgus's face turn sour as red lights blinked all over his lab.

"NO!" screamed Virgus. "This is impossible, even for a genius of your caliber!" Virgus worked frantically to save all of the systems in his lab. "You always cheated, Martha."

Letting loose a maniacal laugh in an extreme sense of self-satisfaction, Martha returned to her delicate work.

"Class dismissed, Professor Tattenburg. Stay clear, everybody, this baby is about to come down!"

The same shattering at the initial hit now occurred all throughout the field. Gaping holes emerged in the barrier all across the west. In a final, blinding flash of light, the tachyon particles escaped into the atmosphere and the shield was no more. After a moment of what seemed like endless silence, the sounds of cheers echoed across the plains. The prison was broken and the nations were free once again. Polonius and Darius led the Legions, as they bashed their swords against their shields in Dragonstone. At the borders of the Forest of the Eternal Spring, Sirius and the Elves bowed their heads in silent prayer offering a canticle to Yahweh for their deliverance. In the high mountains, Huskal and Josephine climbed a mountain plateau to get a better view of what happened. Holding each other tightly in an embrace, they gave thanks to the spirits as well. Not wasting any time, Wilhelm, Nadia, and Wilhelm's divisions rode immediately for the rear entrances of Lion's Peak, desperate to reach their allies in time.

At the Titan encampment, bottles were shaken and being sprayed everywhere among the scientists and soldiers. All participated save for Martha, who just stood their silently with tears running down her face. Privately she never thought this hour would come, that she could actually surpass the genius of the mentor she loved. A group of soldiers came up behind her and tossed her in the air in celebration. Her classic demeanor returning, Doctor Heinrich threw her arms out and laughed.

"Hallelujah!" screamed the flying doctor.

The hope that had begun when news spread that Cedric was alive had finally been fulfilled. The barrier was no more and even from his residence in the City of Antiquity, Bishop Wulf stared with a large smile on his face as he thought, *Our destiny is ours once more.*

As she was finally allowed to come back to the ground, Martha threw her arms in the air. "I am now officially the greatest genius on Terminus Mundus!"

"The greatest genius ever!" corrected her sovereign.

Smiling widely, Civilia grabbed Martha and kissed her. Shocked by her Queen's affection initially, the doctor embraced her friend tightly.

"Thank you, Martha."

"No, your Highness, thank you for having faith in me."

Breaking the embrace, Civilia's regal demeanor returned to her.

"Congratulations are deserved all around, but we have work to be done. Try our communication lines, see if we can raise the Dwarves or Deniva."

The scientists and technicians went to work.

"I'm sorry, your Highness, but we can reach anyone, there's still static," offered a technician.

"I was afraid of this." Martha explained. "Despite the fact the barrier is broken, those tachyons have ionized the atmosphere above us. It's going to be a few rotations before our communications are back online."

"Dammit. Horace, are you prepared?"

"Of course, your Highness. My men and I are willing to take the risk."

"Lead your contingent to the rendezvous point. The remainder of the army will remain here in case of an attack, though I doubt Luminas will be so eager for a fight."

"At once, your Highness. However, it is important we remain prudent. We don't know what Abaddon is planning."

"We're not going to make a move until my children and the others are safely home. I know that my son has a preliminary battle plan ready to go, and I won't act until I see it."

"That doesn't surprise me."

Horace raised his hand and a division of riders including Samuel rode off with him. Civilia and Martha stared at the Vale surrounding the Griffin Mountains. The once prosperous lands had turned brown. Even in the midst of the past winter, the land was dead.

"They've done nothing, Martha. I can't believe it!"

"I don't understand, your Majesty."

"Five revolutions and Luminas sat in his Castle. If I had the time they had to prepare, I would have been waiting for us. I would have stored provisions for a protracted siege and I would have built a labyrinth of defenses even the bravest soldier would fear to cross."

"That's why he was unfit to rule. You'll never forgive him for what he did."

"Never, but I can do nothing for Stephen anymore. For the sake of his daughter, we'll return life to his land."

"A fitting tribute, your Highness. I recommend we deploy soldiers to setup a stockade along the Vale. It will give us some extra time to prepare just in case."

"Martha, whatever recommendation you make today will be answered."

"In that case, I should ask for a pay raise."

The two laughed as Civilia gave orders to one of her knights. "Captain, take two divisions ahead with the mobile stockade unit and defensive siege weaponry. I want the Vale taken and defenses established in four hours. We must not let the Acadians get their hands on such valuable resources. I have a terrible feeling panic is going to set in and Luminas may get desperate."

"As you wish, your Highness!"

"The rest of you fall back behind Eagle's Gate and double the watch. This still may be part of larger plot and I will not be caught with my back to a door. Martha, I don't envy your cleanup job here. I'll leave some divisions to make sure you make it back through the Gate."

"Thank you, your Highness."

"Join me in my quarters when you're finished. I brought in my personal chef and staff to serve you tonight. Don't fight me on this—you've earned every bit of it. Besides, we have a lot of work to go over."

Martha laughed as Civilia rode away. The Doctor put her hands on Kruger's shoulder and mouthed a "thank you."

"You heard the Queen," ordered Martha. "Let's pack this baby up. Also, Kruger, when you get back to the Academy, pull up those files we have on the siege engines of the Empire. I have a feeling we're going to need a new trick or two to get into Verian."

Dwarven Courtyard, Lion's Peak

The Dwarves are tenacious in melee combat and very danger-ous over short distances. However, they possess a hot-blooded and ill-tempered nature that will allow us to gain an advantage over them in battle. We will achieve victory by performing an act that will make them go into battle stupidly. That's when victory will be ours.

King Ulysses Rhone to King Hayden Marisol

Spears and shields forward, the Dwarf army pushed their might into the reinforced door each time the siege hammer struck. Observing the cracks in the door and the rocks falling from the mountain, Lurac knew it wasn't going to hold.

"Fall back!" ordered Lurac. "Form the Dwarven Phalanx!"

Abandoning the door, the warriors entered a triangle formation. The tower shields interlocked with one another to form a second wall of iron. Despite the two hammers smashing through the door, the Dwarves still beat their weapons against their shields and hurled profane insults at their enemies. The sound of precision marching echoed in the walls, but Lurac and his men would not give any ground. The Elite led his troops into the mountain, ordering them into the Dragon Spear formation of the Napolitan Legions.

They look like Legions! thought Lurac. *Has Constantine betrayed us?* Lurac asked, "Any word from the Titans?"

"It's impossible to tell if a message got through," responded a general. "We're just getting static back and forth."

"Then we're on our own!"

The Elite stared at his enemies. Closing his eyes, he recalled his training and suddenly hundreds of pages of information flowed through his mind. He could see how the Dwarves fought in previous historical battles, their strengths, and more importantly, their weaknesses. Focusing his eyes on his enemies once more, he barked orders to his lieutenants.

"When we engage the Dwarves, be careful about being drawn too far into the melee, they'll want to surround us."

Acknowledging the orders, they passed the information onto their troops. Concerned over this preparation for battle, Lurac tried to goad his enemies into a mistake.

"As long as there are Dwarves in this Hall we will spill your blood! Don't waste our time and remain there any longer! COME GET SOME!"

Not willing to the take the bait, the army remained calm and waited for orders. Esteridge rode into the mountain with his command. Amazed at the precision and tactical superiority of his forces, he made diligent notes for his report.

"Spear Horde, advance!" ordered the Elite. "Sword Horde, close ranks!"

"This is it, Dwarves!" encouraged Lurac. "Kill all those who dare to the enter mountain!"

In a slow and methodical movement, the spear legions advanced. The Dwarves broke their shield and sprinted into an attack. Despite their small stature, the mountain defenders tossed their foes and beat their armor with mighty hammers. Lurac jumped on the back of a fallen soldier and leapt into the fray. The force of his hammer split the shield of another before finishing him off with an axe blow to the neck. As a second spearman engaged him, the Lord of Lion's Peak split his head open. However, many of his loyal and proud soldiers did not have the same fortune. Perfect strikes with axes and hammers were deflected by the enchanted armor.

"What treachery is this?" bellowed a Dwarf.

"They're protected by magic," yelled another.

"Is this Elf treachery?" wondered another aloud. "Are we betrayed by Evengard as well?"

Satisfied with his vanguard's attacks, the Elite waved his sword in the air.

"Retreat attack! Fall back to the entrance!"

The army closed ranks and backed away slowly, not allowing themselves to be flanked by the Dwarves. Shields and spears forward, the stragglers were easy pickings for the defenders. However, the protected formation kept their losses to a minimum. Unnerved by this new strategy, Lurac ordered his people to reform their ranks as well.

"Throw out the dead!" commanded the Dwarf Lord.

Lifting and tossing the bodies of the fallen forward, some warriors offered a final prayer. A new barrier was formed and the shields of the still standing were locked once more. The first round of combat brought out the rage and bloodlust of the Dwarves. Consumed by this frenzy, they were becoming difficult to control. Repositioned at the entrance to Lion's Peak, the Elite gave his next orders.

"Change tactics and position yourselves to break through their left flank."

The Dragon Spear shifted so that the right side of the formation gripped like the talon of a dragon. Convinced he was betrayed by Napolitan, Lurac tried to hold his army together.

"What is it?" questioned a Dwarf. "Why did Napolitan sell us out?"

"It's a clear attack on our left flank!" bellowed a general. "Cover the left side!"

"No, you fools!" commanded Lurac as he watched his army shift left. "Wait for them to move!"

"Tail strike now, attack pattern four point two!" ordered the smiling Elite. "Break ranks and charge!"

In the middle of resetting their lines, the Dwarves left themselves open on the right. The left side of the army swung wide like the tail of a dragon, flanking the Dwarves. Behind their lines now, the stout defenders were slaughtered on that side of the formation. In the center of the formation, Lurac bravely rallied his troops. The talon side of the dragon charged spear forward and the defenders found themselves caught in a pincher.

"Hold your ground!" bellowed Lurac.

Swinging wildly and arcing their attacks, Lurac and his phalanx managed to keep the army away from the center. Gathering his remaining forces, the Dwarves locked shields into an impenetrable phalanx. The stone pavement was lost and Lurac knew the battle would not be won here.

"Fall back to the Emperor's Gallery!"

Backing away slowly, the Dwarves left the stone pavement and retreated through the labyrinth. Initially worried that this was a trick, the Elite ordered his troops back to reorganize and finish off the stragglers. The stone pavement was littered with the bodies of fallen and dying Dwarves.

"I need a scout team to scour the path ahead," said the Elite. "Rest quickly, we mustn't give them the chance to recover!"

In the emperor's gallery, Lurac and his people closed the door. "The door won't hold long. We can't brace it," noted Lurac. "Reform the ranks and be more cautious with movements. This group is well trained."

The sound of armor and boots clanking against the floor behind them caused the Dwarves to jump and push their weapons forward. Instantly they were relieved as Wilhelm, Nadia, and twenty-five thousand knights and Valkyries of Titanus arrived.

"You're late, Wilhelm!" shouted an angry Lurac.

"We had to wait for Martha to bring the barrier down."

"It didn't seem to stop Napolitan and Evengard from betraying us!"

"I don't understand, Lurac. What are you talking about?"

"We're fighting an army that uses the tactics of Napolitan and they're carrying enchanted weapons and armors! What am I supposed to think?"

Wilhelm pondered this news. Taylor Yueh had no report of anything like this. Titanus could ill-afford to have lost their most skilled diplomat at this point. His musings were interrupted by a loud thud on the door. On the other side, the army brought forward a battering ram adorned by a hideous iron head with spawned teeth and spikes. Shouts of "put some muscle into it" could be heard in the King's Gallery.

"What are we up against, Lurac?" asked Wilhelm.

"The army they brought took us completely by surprise. They fight like the damn Legions of Napolitan and we got our asses kicked in the first engagement!"

"By Acadians?"

"This doesn't make any sense, Wilhelm," added Nadia. "Unless Virgus did something..."

"Excuse me, lass, but I don't think I ever remember seeing someone of your kind before," interrupted Lurac.

Nadia curtsied before Lurac. "My name is Nadia and I fight in Wilhelm's command."

"She's a fine woman, Wilhelm, and might pretty, too. Of course, a full beard would make her even more attractive. All right boys, we had a respite. Better get the ranks together."

"Agreed, Lurac," commented Wilhelm. "Abaddon's pulling out all the stops. Warriors of Titanus and Lion's Peak, we have to make our stand here. The only relief that's coming for us is a group of Kablisha warriors. No matter what, we have to hold this mountain or else we will fall to Abaddon's cruelty. Are you with me?"

Everyone in the room, including Nadia and Lurac, shouted in agreement.

"Defenders! On your feet!"

"Wilhelm, what about Civilia?" questioned Lurac. "We haven't been able to get any communications through to Fort Hawkeye."

"The communications are still dealing with residual static from the barrier coming down. We won't be able to get a message out in time."

"No matter! As long as one Dwarf breathes life, our defenses will hold!"

"I wish I had your confidence," added Nadia.

The sound of thumping on the door grew louder and louder. In its dead center, a red hot light melted away at the wood and iron.

"What mechanisms could they have that bend Dwarven craftsmanship so easily?"

"It must be some type of enchantment on the ram," guessed Nadia. "If I could see it, I might be able to place a counter spell on it."

"I have a feeling it won't be long before you get such an opportunity," estimated Wilhelm.

Weapons forward, Dwarf and Titan stood side by side. Turning from red hot to white hot, the door to the Emperor's Gallery melted away. Spears and sword pried the hinges off the door as Nadia unleashed a blast of hurricane winds from her staff. Crushing the first wave of attackers against mountains walls, Wilhelm ordered a charge of the defenders. Fearlessly rushing forward, they engaged their foes.

Castle Acadia

Cassandra came in from playing this morning. She walked over to the bookcase and pulled three from the shelf. She read them one after another and asked if she 'could please have some more.' Never before did I witness such behavior in the girl, nor such delicate politeness. Later that night, we received a report of a raid by slavers and Cassie cried a thousand tears as if the event touched her personally. I must continue to monitor this behavior as I fear a mental sickness has taken hold of my girl.

An excerpt from Queen Sharon's journal about twenty-one revolutions ago.

Panic and dismay raged like wildfire in Verian. The rebel Acadians were convinced the end was coming and with the collapse of the barrier uninvited guests would be arriving soon. King Maximilian held court in hopes to calm his people's fears.

"Send in the Doctor!" commanded the King.

Unfazed by the consternation and looks by the Acadians as he entered, Virgus strutted into the chamber as if he owned the place.

"You seem incredibly satisfied for a man whose invention was just made irrelevant," stated Sharon with scorn.

"This was a contingency we had planned for," lectured Virgus. "The barrier was always meant to be temporary. Gavin's progress on the wall has accelerated and we are testing my new army as we speak. With some luck, we may be getting our hands on new resources soon."

"Cassandra is now free from Deniva," explained Luminas. "There is no doubt she will return to Titanus to gather support."

"Then allow me to return to my work before Cedric Rhone returns at the head of an army."

Luminas was ready to launch himself from his throne and rip the jugular from this smug little man, but knew he could do nothing while Virgus still had the protection of Abaddon. Bowing before he left, the doctor closed the doors behind him. Leaning his left arm against the throne, Maximilian slumped his head.

"My husband, please do not think ill of me."

Shocked by the revelation, the vampire king shot up. "What did you do, Sharon?"

"As you know, Norville Warrington made his intentions clear that he seeks to flee to Napolitan."

"Indeed."

"I sent Roland out with a sealed royal parchment. He was to make clear to Senator Warrington that he should carry a notice to Caesar Constantine and Lord Camdem."

"To what purpose, my wife?"

"There are no negotiations with Titanus, but if Napolitan and Evengard refuse to march, well, it may be worth a few chests of gold."

"You honestly had me worried for a moment, Sharon. I should have known better."

"You're not alone in this. Due to her affections for Stephen, I have no doubt Civilia intends to string me up."

"True. I don't think Abaddon would object. After all, we have yet to deliver his prize to him."

"I would have never been able to believe it myself. My pasty, bookworm daughter is the key to all of this. It's a good thing we did kill Stephen; he would have fought with his last breath to save her."

"What about you? Are you not troubled by the revelations about your daughter?"

"I can't explain it, husband. When she was a little girl, Cassandra was fine enough, but there was that one rotation. Just watching her sit there reading book after book, I knew in my heart she wasn't my girl anymore. It's the strangest thing."

"Very strange. Well, it doesn't matter. You've done well, my dear, and maybe with luck, you might have given us an advantage."

In the bellows of Castle Verian, Marie diligently worked at her craft. Creating three black circles in front of her, Marie raised a skeleton warrior, a zombie warrior, and a hulking gargoyle. The three thralls knelt in obedience before their new Mistress. Excessively pleased at her recent performance, the princess ended the spell by striking each circle with her weapon. Once she broke the circle, the creatures disappeared.

"Very impressive, Marie," admired Abaddon as he appeared behind her.

"I feel my powers growing rapidly," offered Marie. "The only thing sending my children back to the other side now is when I choose to end the spell."

"Your progress has been nothing short of marvelous. Your aptitude for conjuration magic has exceeded my expectation."

"Thank you, Abaddon. To think the potential to raise such an army was locked away in my head all this time. Look at the rest of them now, they all thought my sister was the smart one and I was the doll. My poor sister locked away with that wretched madman all this time. I can't imagine the temptations and seductions he must have placed on her. To think she would consider marching on her own homeland. I won't allow it."

"You must remember how powerful and tactically sound Cedric Rhone is. He will be a difficult opponent."

"Indeed, especially with my sister at his side."

"Then, Marie, I beg you to try once more. You have the power now to do it. You can bring Julius back."

"I… I'm not sure I can."

Gripping her staff tightly, Marie opened the Libro Mortuem with her hand. Behind his back, Abaddon signaled to the Nephilim in the room to be ready. As she chanted away, Abaddon had them kill the lights in the room and set off smoke markers. A magic circle appeared in the center of the room, but as it had happened a hundred times before, Julius did not appear. As the princess closed her eyes in disgust, Abaddon made another signal and the perfect clone created by Virgus entered the room and took his position in front of the circle to create the illusion.

"Marie!" screamed the clone. "Don't give up! I'm almost back!"

Disbelieving the voice she heard, Marie opened her eyes and saw the clone reaching his hand for her. Overcome with joy, she completed the spell. Though the black circle faded away because the spell failed, the princess did not care. She ran into the arms of the man she believed to be her love and held him tightly. A smug look crossed Abaddon's face as he retired to leave the two alone. The girl would now be completely under his control.

"Julius… how can… all these revolutions… I worked so hard!" stammered Marie.

"Its fine now, darling," said the clone seductively. "It was so cold and lonely on the other side. However, I could hear your voice calling out to me and part of me would be sucked back into this world time and time again. I knew because of our love for one another you would find a way."

"I almost gave up, but part of me knew. You're so much warmer, warmer than you've ever been."

"There was so much to worry about then, Marie. I'm sorry, but it was a difficult time and I didn't know what I would do. However, this exile from you has given me time to think and I know what I must do."

"Julius, they say Cedric Rhone and my sister will come. The sword master is on a mad crusade to regain this land for Cassandra. I know my sister would never willingly destroy her home, so he must have her under some sort of spell."

"Well, Titanus will certainly be in for a surprise then. I offer you my sword and my life, Marie. With the power of our love and your magic we will beat back these invaders and destroy the hold Cedric has on your sister."

"Julius…"

The two kissed first and then the clone embraced Marie tightly. As he moved from her face to her shoulder, a terrible and devilish smile crossed the face of the clone.

Mountain Hall, Lion's Peak

Titans do not accept the concept of surrender; however, the word 'retreat' has a different meaning for us than most. The better term to use would be to 'regroup.' No Titan expects any soldier to hold onto a defense point that is clearly lost. However, a proper strategy drawn out before the battle would allow an ally to retreat to different points, thus allowing them to regain their strength so a counterattack can commence when opportune.

Cedric Rhone, The Titan Battle Manual

Having ceded both the Emperor's Gallery and the main quarters to the enemy, Wilhelm and Lurac regrouped their army in the antechamber of the mines entrance. Mining, transport, and crafting equipment were now being used as a makeshift barrier. As the enemy relentlessly pounded on the door with their special ram, the weary, injured, and downtrodden Dwarves awaited the inevitable. Armor, weapons, and clothes adorned in red blood, Wilhelm and Nadia shared a brief moment together.

"Best two out of three?" teased Nadia.

"I don't know what enchantment they have on that blasted ram, but your counter spell should have worked on it."

"Not to mention their high resistance to magic. I thought I was going to be some secret weapon and I'm turning out worthless in this first battle."

Tending to the wounds of his subordinates and kinsmen, Lurac clenched his fists with rage. Hanging his head in shame, the Dwarf Lord feared for this people.

"I'm getting worried, Wilhelm. No Dwarf has ever retreated from Lion's Peak, but I don't see how we are going last much longer under this condition. The mines lay behind us and there is no way we can fight in the darkness."

"We'll give it one more try! If not, you must retreat into the mines. Tunnels in those mines run deep into the mountains. We may be able to escape to Deniva or Titanus."

"I hate running away!"

"We don't have a choice."

"Start the elders and younglings into the mines. They'll need time to escape while we hold them," commanded Lurac.

As they witnessed before, the red hot doors gave way to the white hot burning.

"Ready yourselves—when the doors come down, attack!" ordered Wilhelm. "Hold them at the door as long as you can and fall back into formation."

Readying themselves for battle, the Dwarf and Titan army took position, but were interrupted by another Dwarf coming from the mines.

"Lord Lurac, a band of soldiers approaches from the mines!"

"Now what?" bellowed Lurac. "How many soldiers did the enemy send that they were able to lead them into the mines?"

"No, my Lord, it is an army I've never seen before. They are led by the senior officers of the Alliance Army."

"All right, Argus!" exclaimed Wilhelm as he pumped his fist. "Argus must have gone to Deniva to gather the exiles before coming here. I was wondering what took him so long!"

"Reinforcements… between the two of us, we may kill these things. Welcome them to Lion's Peak with the compliments of the Dwarf Lord!"

"But my Lord, they bring Elves with them!"

Doing their best to hide their laughter, Wilhelm and Nadia watched as Lurac blew his top.

"THE ELF WITCH, NO DOUBT!" Lurac fumed. "Forgive me, my ancestors, for letting that hussy into this hallowed ground. Only in our final hour would we have to turn to Elves to save the mountain. Well, I suppose we have no choice! Let them enter!"

Kablisha militia flooded forward from the mines. Taking kneeling positions, they drew their crossbows and positioned them on the door. Malcolm, Rosa, and Minerva commanded the Wood Elf rangers to fall in behind them with long bows. Organizing the Dwarves into a makeshift legion formation, Cagius compensated their losses by using the Order of the Lion Knights. It was the appearance of Cedric Rhone, however, that confounded the Dwarves. Believing a phantasm walked beside him, Lurac pondered his fate.

"This can't be... I didn't get a chance to fight... how can I be dead! Lord Cedric, have you come to take me to Valhalla?"

"Lurac, rumors of my demise have been greatly exaggerated."

Sprinting from warrior to warrior, Cedric assessed the situation. Cecilia retook her position among the Valkyries. As the Vanadis rejoined their ranks, the ladies swooned.

"Mistress Vanadis?" asked one of the Valkyries as she stared at Cecilia's hand. "Is that a wedding ring?"

"Indeed it is," answered Cecilia.

The trained soldiers screamed like a bunch of teenage girls. They shouted congratulations and showered their leader with praise.

"Girls, we can celebrate later," ordered Cecilia. "Right now, we've got business."

Finishing his command assessment, Cedric took position next to Wilhelm.

"We've got to stop meeting like this," joked Wilhelm.

"How come trouble always finds you?" teased Cedric.

"I'm just lucky I guess. Here I journey to Lion's Peak to determine if Bishop Wulf's stigmata was true and find myself in the middle of a battle. It's not going well."

"And you dragged poor Nadia into this?"

"Not without my full consent, Lord Cedric," interrupted Nadia. "It was either this or those uncomfortable nun's robes."

"My mom had you dressed like a nun?" said Cecilia, laughing. "I hope you took pictures, that's something I have to see."

"You just want revenge for dressing you in that ridiculous jumper I used to make you wear to court functions," fired Nadia right back. "Actually, your mom must have known this situation was really desperate; now that I think of it, she might have intended for me to be killed here."

"Enough fooling around," ordered Cedric. "What's the tactical Lurac?"

"They've taken the stone pavement, the Emperor's Gallery, and the quarters. We're running out of time and space. This army is like nothing I've ever fought before."

"What kind of army?" asked Cagius.

"Cagius, I don't know how to say this, but they fight like Dragon Legions. I'm afraid your kin have betrayed us."

"No way. They killed my brother, Lurac. Despite what madness may grip him, my dad would never make that alliance!"

"Well, if the situation is that bad, it looks like we've made it just in time," teased Amuro.

"If you think I'm going to accept help from an Elf witch, you are sadly mistaken!" roared Lurac.

"Looks like you don't have a choice, Dwarf! You can think of me more as a swashbuckler than a sorceress if it eases your mind!"

"You wretched hussy, if I see but one treasure missing from this hall, I'll have you tied to the side of the mountain!"

"You two better stop arguing and get your people into formation," interjected Argus. "Lord Lurac, I am Argus Kinkade of the

Kablisha. My subordinates are Quirinus Ophion and Mesmara Lorelei. I bring militia to aid you in your hour of need."

"Titans, Ancients, and Elves—our three enemies from the great war return to defend Lion's Peak. Emperor Dondarion, I offer my solemn forgiveness; he must be turning in his grave!"

The group watched as the door became molten and melted to the floor.

"What sorcery is this?" questioned Amuro.

"They're using an enchanted ram, none of my counter spells will work on it!" added Nadia.

Running to her younger sister to give her some last-second advice, Amuro took Saria's hand to stop them from shaking.

"Stay to the rear with the archers. Cast spells from there and don't try to be a heroine. Attack only when threatened. Let the professionals handle the melee until we know what we're up against. Do you understand?"

"I know, sister… I mean Marshal…I won't disobey your orders."

"That's my brave gal."

Stepping up with bow in hand, Rosa winked at Amuro. "Don't worry, Amuro, I'll take care of her."

Snapping themselves into formation, Cedric took position in the front. He rocked his head back and forth as if trying to figure something out.

"Cagius!" yelled Cedric. "They said they fight like Legions. How would you fight yourself?"

"Give me a second…" Cagius knelt down and drew pictures in the ground with his trident. Carefully working through various scenarios, the dragoon nodded a few times.

"This should do it… Cedric, we should let them come to us without making any commitments. I want the range to aim for the fifth out of every ten soldiers in the front lines. If we take them out, the entire line will have no command directions. After that, aim for the banner holders."

"All right ladies, gentlemen, Elves and Dwarves, you heard the man!" barked Cedric. "We've given enough ground, we fall back no further. No retreat!"

The command behind him screamed "No retreat!" in return.

The ram shattered the reminder of the door, allowing the exiles to get their first look at the armed attacked. Staff raised, Nadia chanted a spell.

"Nadia, I thought the counter spell didn't work on the ram," interjected Rosa.

"To hell with that, Lady Landon, I've hitting them with everything I've got."

"All right baby, let them have it!" Wilhelm encouraged her.

Thrusting her staff forward, Nadia shouted, "Fire Wall!" An inferno of fire and sulfur concentrated through the hole in the door, roasting the first soldiers through alive. Scattered by the initial attack, the army slowly moved into the hall. In moments, they were in formation. Cedric spiked Ragnarok in the ground and reached for his crossbow. Upon seeing the new weapon for the first time, Cecilia grew jealous.

"Cedric, what the hell is that?"

"A Kablisha automatic crossbow. They made it a portable size so I could fire it from horseback."

"God, I want one!"

Heeding Cagius' advice, Malcolm shot his first arrow through the neck of the fifth soldier in the group of ten. Falling dead on the ground, Cagius caught sight of the same whistle he used.

"Bring them all down!" yelled Cagius.

Reloading at speed, Malcolm shot down three more before the other archers even fired their first flight. The only difficulty was the space between the chainmail veil and plate armor was very narrow. It required an incredibly precise shot that few were able to match. The crossbows made up for this deficiency as the Kablisha's more powerful weapons could pierce the plate mail of their foes. Losing their unit commanders left and right sent the formerly disciplined army into chaos. They didn't know whether to push forward or retreat. A soldier went running into the previous room to confer with the Elite.

"Commander, reinforcements have arrived."

"From where?" asked the Elite.

"I don't know…. but I believe Cedric Rhone is leading them! Their archers are shattering our unit cohesion."

"Full attack! I want the head of Cedric Rhone before the rotation is out!"

"Yes, sir."

Overhearing the conversation, Esteridge pushed his horse forward. "Did he just say Cedric Rhone is here?"

"It's nothing we won't be able to handle," countered the Elite.

"That damn Titan prince is worse than a jinx. Wherever and whenever Abaddon seeks to destroy a Western nation, he is there!"

Passing the orders to the other soldiers from the Elite, the defenders watched the attackers push forward. Locking their shields together, Cagius forced his unit forward. The two units marched forward, forming a massive scrum in the center of the room. Using all of their muscle and might, both tried to gain ground. The attack left Abaddon's army in a tactical disadvantage. Cedric ordered his remaining warriors to flank the enemy. The Titan twins went back-to-back. Cedric sliced through two of enemies that came at them before turning back and allowing Cecilia to swing her spear in an arc motion taking out two more. The prince returned to the fray and sliced one upward killing him. Tagging off with her brother once more, the Vanadis thrust her spear through another. Suddenly, a massive hulking warrior descended on the twins. Winking at one another, they slashed the soldier in his shoulders and knees. Falling to the ground, brother and sister both stabbed him through the neck. As they removed their weapons, the soldier's helmet fell off. A similar attack performed by Cagius in the middle of the fray produced the same result.

"Julius!" said Cagius in disbelief. "What foul craft is this?"

Walker buried his shield into the neck of another soldier as arrows flew in around him. Valentine jumped in the air and buried his two daggers into another's neck. He pulled the dagger to his mouth and licked it.

"This is new," Valentine said. "This doesn't taste like Julius' blood, or any human blood I've ever tasted."

Enraged by the revelation that his father was being used against them, Joshua went into a frenzy. Bulling over soldiers with his shield and swinging wildly, he tried to destroy as many as these abominations as possible. Lost in the battle lines, a spearman got him in the back of the knee. Forced to the ground, Joshua continued to hold them off. Diving into the middle of the lines with no regards for his life, Valentine fought the soldiers back. Grabbing Joshua by the back of his armor, he dragged the boy to the safety of the rear lines where Florence rushed to treat him.

"I should beat you with a switch for that one, Joshua!"

"Don't you see those monstrosities out there?"

"Remember what I taught you! Don't fight angry and careless."

Broken by losses and not being able to take a true punch to the mouth, the attackers sounded the retreat. The Elite ordered them to return to the Emperor's Galley to devise a new strategy. Breathing heavily from the engagement, Hippolyte knelt to the ground for a moment.

"You guys sure know how to find the best hunting grounds."

"Yeah, it breeds for a whole new set of marks," added Minerva. "You know, these helmets might look good decorating a chief's tent."

"Agreed, we'll make sure we carry some home."

Lurac rallied his Dwarves. "We beat them back, boys! Now let's drive them from our mountain!"

As the Dwarves frenzied themselves into a charge, Cedric stopped them.

"Let's take the respite," ordered Cedric. "They want to draw us into battle back on their terms and I won't let them. Let them come to us."

"Cedric, what the hell is this?" demanded Cagius.

"Honestly, I have no idea, Cagius. Strip the helmets from the dead, I want to see what's going on here."

As the soldiers complied, they found that though they were not exact clones, each of the soldiers before them had some resemblance to Julius.

"They're sending our best against us now," commented Valentine. "It explains a lot, including how they fought like Legions and why Cagius was able to take them down. Julius was always more textbook than his brother."

Accepting the breather, Walker checked on Robespierre and his knights. "How are they doing?"

"A few scratches and bruises…these boys are finally learning how to fight. Combat is usually the best baptism for forming an army."

"Well, we've got a long way to go. Keep them up!"

"No problem, Lord Protector. Say, you're pretty good in a fight, and here I thought you were only good at protecting the chastity of beautiful young women."

Walker and Robespierre laughed at the salute. Wilhelm walked over to Cedric.

"We can't wait them out forever, Cedric."

"We've already exposed their weakness. They are completely reliant on command and control; without officers this army will break."

"Do you have a plan?"

"I'm working on one."

"THEY'RE COMING AGAIN!" shouted a Dwarf.

The warriors turned to see a vanguard charge through the door. They prepared for combat once more.

VALLEY OF MOURNING, GRIFFIN MOUNTAINS

Cedric Rhone's military career began the moment he stepped out of the Academy. He knew that Titanus demanded that a warrior prince gain a great victory before the Armada would truly accept him as their Prince Marshal. Cedric chose the 'wild men' of the mountains as his target, a nuisance to both the Western Kingdoms and the Tribes. Rather than allowing a large army to be trapped in tight passages, the prince divided the Armada into small patrols. When an enemy was spotted, four or five patrols would swarm their foes in a fierce ambush. After a revolution of fighting, the last of the organized resistance was crushed and it is common knowledge that no wild men remain.

Excerpt from Duke Wilhelm von Angelhardt's personal journal

Whipping through the ridges of the valley, the wind sounded like a lamentation for the fallen. As Horace and the Titans rode through the passes, he witnessed the handiwork of many revolutions ago. Markers still showed locations of mass graves from the campaign against the wild men. Confident their job was finished more than twenty revolutions ago, Horace was more at ease than his son. Still, the veterans took no chances, riding two-by-two with their weapons close. On the ridges above, light-armored cavalry scouted ahead.

"Are there still wild men in these mountains?" asked Samuel.

"Some would say that their ghosts still haunt these passages," responded Horace. "You were too young to remember when the Prince and I helped to rout them in this very Valley. They may still have some descendants here."

"Even they wouldn't be crazy enough to take on armed regulars, would they?"

"Desperate men resort to desperate measures…especially if they're starving, which I would suspect them to be."

Noticing his son reaching for his weapon, Horace punched him in the arm. "I'm just ribbing you, Samuel, but you passed the test. Only a fool would ride in here without some semblance of caution."

"I noticed you never talked about this campaign as much as some of the others you engaged in."

"It was a necessary evil, Samuel. The Titans weren't proud of what we had to do, but the wild men were the worst form of terrorists. They were killing people left and right. Hell, we witnessed firsthand the remnants of their handiwork with Colin's family. Still, we're not animals, and we don't kill without emotion."

"Are the tales true, Dad? Would you have followed his Excellency if he failed in this campaign?"

"It would have been difficult, but the campaign was so ambitious and so detailed it was difficult to imagine he knew how to fail. Give his Excellency and Christian enough time, and they might be able to win anything."

Hearing the approach of the larger, armored force, Gerard and his contingent breathed a sigh of relief. Cassandra and Thomas remained in the middle of the column under the heavy guard of some wounded members of the Order of the Lion. Cassandra had her arms around the shoulders of the young boy who loved the attention of the friendly, beautiful, and sweet Queen.

"Your Highness, the Titan escort is so loud they'd be hard to miss. You'll be heading home soon."

Cassandra rubbed Thomas on the back. "You hear that? You're going to be seeing your grandma for the first time."

Thomas didn't say anything, but stared straight ahead.

"Is something the matter, sweetheart?"

"I'm worried about Mom and Dad."

"Don't worry! Your Uncle Cedric is with them and he has been known to win the most difficult battles imaginable."

Despite her reassurances, Thomas wasn't convinced.

If I keep saying it enough even I may start to believe it, thought Cassandra.

Horace slowed his contingent when he spotted Gerard around the corner. Bringing his right hand up, he ordered the escort to stop.

"Those pointed ears suggest we're not dealing with wild men," stated Horace.

"Did Evengard send a unit that we didn't know about?" suggested Samuel. "Wait, those aren't high Elves, Dad. What are the wood Elves doing here?"

"My guess is that his Excellency recruited them for the escort."

"What about those Knights with them? Damned if I ever saw any unit bearing that banner before. Are they Denivan?"

"Lions are the symbols of Acadia and there were rumors Hector Reed was working on something in the east. Maybe this is the fruition of it."

Horace reached into his pocket for a cigar and lit it.

"I don't know if this is the best time for a smoke, Dad."

"For some reason, son, I've got a bad feeling about this."

"I see Cassandra, but I don't see anyone else. Is this a ransom?"

"I doubt it. If it was, they would be laying in ambush."

An apprehensive Gerard watched Horace and Samuel ride ahead of their escort.

"Of course it would have to be Horace Irvine." Gerard sighed. "I guess it could be worse, the Matriarch of Destruction could have come her herself. Are you ready, your Majesty?"

"I'm ready, Gerard, and thank you."

"It's been a privilege, your Majesty. We'll meet them together."

Gerard and Cassandra rode out to meet them. Exchanging a series of head nods instead of bows, everyone seemed relieved for a moment.

"Marshal Irvine, it's been a long time!" greeted Gerard.

"It's good to see you're still alive, Gerard," returned Horace. "How are your people?"

"We took some losses defending Deniva, but we've survived worse. And this is your second?"

"This is my son, Samuel, and yes, he is my second."

"Your father is a good man, Samuel, and a great soldier. You must have already learned a lot from him."

"I have. Your Highness, are you all right?"

"I've been a bit on edge actually." answered Cassandra. "However, I appreciate your concern, Vice-Marshal."

"My escort is thrilled to see you safe, your Majesty," started Horace. "However, I am concerned by your singular presence. Where is his Excellency and the others? Please, I don't need any bad news."

"Well, I've got some for you," interjected Gerard. "There's been an incident at Lion's Peak."

"So Wilhelm's suspicions were correct," deduced Horace. "He rode out with a full division for Lion's Peak."

"A man named Argus of the Kablisha Tribe arrived in Deniva a short time ago," explained the Queen. "He recruited Cedric and the others to fight with the Dwarves against Abaddon's new army."

"A new army?" questioned Samuel.

"I don't know the details," replied the Queen. "The point is they are there now."

"Leave it to his Excellency to rush into the eye of the storm," stated Horace. "If the Queen had only known, she would have sent more men to Lion's Peak."

"Can we radio back for help, Marshal?" inquired the Queen.

"Unfortunately, your Majesty, our communications are still fried," answered Samuel. "Martha's working her tail off to get them back up, but so far, we've had little success."

"Well, at least there's a possibility that both Wilhelm and Cedric have a division ready to aid the Dwarves in their battle," said the Queen.

"It would seem likely," agreed Samuel. "I doubt the enemy could have anticipated that coalition coming together."

"Well, that's bad news for me…and worse news for us all if they don't make it out of Lion's Peak alive," quipped Horace as he puffed away at his cigar. "Civilia is going to have my head if anything happens to those twins."

"Father, at least the Queen will be safely back on Alliance soil."

"It will be good to keep you safe from harm, your Majesty. We have many reasons for concern with a number of duco-matios about. You've become a very important target."

"If you only knew, Marshal. Abaddon will stop at nothing until I am in his grasp. If you saw the waves and waves of troops he sent after Deniva you would understand. I know I burdened you with many surprises this hour, but I fear I have a big one left for you."

Cassandra signaled for Thomas to come forward. An Order of the Lion knight brought up the young, scared Titan prince.

"Who's this?" inquired Horace.

"Allow me to introduce Thomas Rhone. Cecilia and Ethan De-Mily have married, and this is their son."

"Can my rotation get any worse?" Horace laughed. "Your Highness, I will give you the honor of presenting that information to the Queen. I have enough problems on my hands. Where is Lady Rosa?"

"She insists on fighting by DeVries side," said Gerard.

"As I expected… I'm sure we've got enough room for one more guest. Why not? Leave me to pick up all the pieces after they fall. Thank you, Gerard, for escorting them, but we'll ease your burden from here."

"It was my pleasure. Marshal, I look forward to fighting by your side when his Excellency gives the word."

"You want a piece of Abaddon, too?"

"We owe him for the suffering he brought our people at Deniva. Trust me, we're not the only ones. You guys are going to have a lot of allies when the time comes. I'm sorry, but when we let Prince Cedric Rhone loose on Central Acadia, Maximilian and the others better have said their prayers. Your Highness, I wish you the best."

"Thank you, Gerard."

The two put their foreheads together in a passing of Elf empathy from one to the other. The Order of the Lion rode away from their Wood Elf escort and joined Horace in the column.

Samuel looked to his father for guidance.

"What now?"

"We accomplish the mission and bring the Queen home safely as planned. Forgive my impudence, your Highness, but are you with child?"

"No… Cedric hasn't laid a hand on me."

"My apologies, but there is an issue. I'll take young Prince Rhone with me. As he is currently third in line for the throne of the Kingdom of Titanus, I am obliged to take him."

"I understand."

The Order of the Lion knight passed Thomas to Horace. He seemed at home on the larger steed.

"Your Highness, my name is Horace Irvine, I am War Master and Marshal of the Titan army. Allow me to officially welcome you to Titanus."

"You're just as Mom described you."

"I hope she only told you the good. This is my son, Samuel, he's serving as Vice-Marshal of our army now."

"Your Excellency."

"With your permission, Marshal Irvine, may I address your men?" requested Cassandra.

"Of course, your Highness."

Riding sidesaddle ahead of her knights, Cassandra placed herself in front of the Armada. They bowed their heads upon seeing her and the Queen reveled in the attention.

"Honorable Titans, my family has long disregarded your loyalty and your principles. My father tried to influence them to accept your great strengths and was killed for it. I have come to know you as nothing less than the bravest, most faithful, and strongest fighters in the world. I cannot think of safer hands to submit myself. Thank you, and know that from now on, true Acadians will never scorn you again."

Noticing a regal and commanding presence they had not seen in the betrothed of their prince before, the riders cheered.

"That's a nice speech, your Majesty," Horace said, thankful. "We've done our job, men, let's get home safely."

Both escorts retreated from the canyon.

Mountain Hall, Lion's Peak

He plays the battlefield like a riverboat gambler waiting
for an ace.

Marshal Hector Reed upon watching Cedric Rhone in battle

Feeling discipline had failed them against Cagius' tactics, the Elite sent wave after wave of his army in an attempt to overwhelm the reinforced Dwarf lines. On the other side, the alliance commanders feared they'd be able to achieve no more than a stalemate even though they had retaken all of the rooms up to the Emperor's Gallery. After finishing off another opponent, Mesmara found a spearman chasing her down. The Kablisha maiden ran up the steps to Dondarion's throne. When she reached the top, she vaulted off the top of the throne and thrust her blade into the spearman's neck. As a swordsman attacked her, Argus fired a bolt through his neck.

"I could have handled that, Uncle!" offered Mesmara.

"I promised your parents I would protect you," retorted her uncle. "Besides, there are plenty of demons for you to kill. Quinn, get a firing line going. We need to draw them back."

Quinn rallied the militia with their crossbows to clear some room for them, and Nadia drove her staff into the stone floor. The resulting blast leveled a company of troops into the surrounding walls. The Kablisha let loose a rapid-fire barrage to buy Cedric and the others some respite.

"Hey Cedric, you figure out a way to get to their leader yet?" inquired Christian.

"My guess is he's coordinating the attacks from the stone pavement now," figured Cedric. "If we don't clear a path, I'm not going to be able to get to him."

Spinning with devil slayer in his right hand, Wilhelm cut through another opponent.

"Aren't you thrilled to be back on the battlefield slaughtering evil again?" joked Nadia.

"Don't test me, Nadia, I'm not in the mood. Can we borrow your magic to clear a path for Cedric?"

"My magic well is pretty low right now, Wilhelm. I doubt I could cast anything strong enough again."

"We can't keep this pace up much longer!" exclaimed Cagius. "These clones don't run out of energy."

The cracking of a whip caught an enemy soldier around the neck. Saria pulled hard and slit the throat of her opponent with the knife at the end. As she retracted the whip, the enemy gargled to death.

"Cedric, let me help you!" offered Saria.

"Saria... I..." stammered Cedric as he felt the condescending stare of Amuro upon him.

"Saria, I told you not to be a heroine!" ordered Amuro. "You're doing great out here, but leave the planning to the professionals."

"I can help Cedric! I'm not joking, sis. My magic and powers are based on status effects! They may be resistant to destruction, but if they are based on Julius they're not Divikin."

"This isn't a game, Saria! This is real. You could get killed! Do you want to die?"

"I don't want to mess with your family affairs, but you have to let her do this!" demanded Cagius. "Saria is Cedric's only chance."

Knowing her comrades were right, the Elf maiden buried her stubborn pride. Putting her forehead to her sister's, the two passed the bond of Elf empathy. When she finished, she grabbed Cedric around the waist.

"You are a damned Riverboat Gambler!" screamed Amuro. "This is the biggest ante you ever laid, Cedric. You take care of my baby sister, because if anything happens to her, I'm going to tear you apart."

"No worries," offered Keiko as she fluttered in. "I'll stay with Lady Saria."

"All right troops, fall back and into formation!" commanded Cagius. "We've got to take care of these four! Malcolm, get the archers and lay in cover fire. The rest of you lock shields and form a wedge."

Following Cagius' orders, the troops got into position as Cedric whistled for Jericho. Startled by the arrival of the fierce beast, three enemies found themselves trampled to death. The sword master leapt on the back of his steed and pulled Saria up in front in him. Keiko slid in behind him. Eyes closed and praying, the Elf maiden started glowing in an otherworldly golden light.

"Lord Cedric, it was my greatest shame that we left you behind to die, and I only cared at that moment about saving my own life," prayed Saria. "My deepest apology can only be heard in this self-composed aria about your bravery."

Clearing her throat, Saria belted out a ballad:

In crumbling ruin, he held steadfast

The dark angel charged but could not pass

Our bravest knight, he held his line

The powers of hell would be denied

For the sake of love, he gave his life.

Carefully bending her inflections and manipulating tones, Saria created visible sound projections. Crashing against the ranks of enemy soldiers, they stood dumbfounded as the waves washed over them. Cedric reared Jericho and rode past his entranced foes knowing the Elf maiden's spell would be brief. Amuro threw her sword in the air and swung it.

"Cover them!" commanded the Marshal.

Cagius moved his troops slowly in the shield formation. Positioning themselves near the door to the gallery, they kept the attacking foes from chasing down Jericho. Amuro blew a kiss and winked at her baby sister.

"Stay safe, sis!"

On the stone pavement, the Elite and three guards could hear the approach of clopping hooves.

"What's this now?" asked Esteridge.

"I'm not sure," stated the Elite. "I have the feeling something isn't right."

The Elite pulled out a massive war hammer made of iron and enchanted with runes down the shaft of the weapon. On the bottom of shaft was a large spike that doubled as both a secondary weapon and a counterbalance for the massive hammer on the other end. The guards in front of him pulled their spears out. Witnessing Jericho's red eyes emerge first down the hall, the four were distracted as Saria jumped from the saddle and did a flip in the air before nailing the dismount. Thrusting her wings forward, Keiko temporarily blinded the troops with fairy dust. Ragnarok held high, Cedric did a sweep attack on the three guards as the Elite raised his weapon in defense. The sweep killed all three guards in the attack and the Elite staggered.

"Get to the side, Saria, and Keiko will keep you safe. The others should buy us the time we need to finish this. You have my thanks."

The Elite swung his hammer above his head to warm up before the battle as Saria and Keiko dashed for the cover of some fallen rock. She pulled her whip out at the ready. Even though he had heard the rumors of Cedric Rhone's return, Sir Esteridge was frozen in disbelief.

"So you must be the infamous Cedric Rhone," stated the Elite.

"Try to contain your excitement, but public enemy number one has entered the mountain," taunted Cedric.

Beckoning the Elite to fight him by waving his finger at him, the enemy was more than happy to comply.

"Lord Abaddon will reward me greatly for disposing of you."

"Well then, what are you waiting for? I've heard nothing but talk from all of his lackeys up until this point. Perhaps you will be the one worthy of killing me."

"The goblins choose to name this hammer Flesh-ripper, and that is exactly what I intend to use it for."

Cedric readied his blade as the Elite charged him. The Elite brought the hammer down with all his might, but the sword master still managed to block it with Ragnarok. Pushing into one another, the even battle soon gave way to the Titan prince's advantage. Bulling the enemy back with his strength, Cedric put his sword in the air and enchanted it with Saint Saber. Wildly swinging the heavy hammer, the Elite missed the sword master twice.

"You're too slow!"

Unleashing a powerful backswing from Ragnarok, the holy energy ripped at the Elite's armor and sent pieces of iron flying. Unable to defend himself, the enemy found Cedric thrusting through his right shoulder. Bone and sinew snapped and the Elite screamed in agony.

"Your plate is pretty tough, but you're no match for Ragnarok and saber techniques. Surrender now and I'll spare your life."

Refusing to comply with the Titan prince's demands, the Elite recovered and lifted his hammer. The enemy swung with all his might, but Cedric stepped back. The impact of the hammer made a four-inch crater in the stone pavement, but nothing more.

"Lurac is not going to be happy about that," joked Cedric. "Maybe it will give him an incentive to redecorate."

The Elite lifted his weapon again and swung wildly at Cedric. The sword master carefully parried his blows away. After a few swings, the enemy stopped to catch his breath. The wound Cedric had inflicted in his shoulder was starting to take a toll.

"The challenge of this battle will make it even sweeter when I rip the flesh from your body," taunted the Elite. "Then I'll take that sweet, little Elf and her little fae over there as treat. Don't worry, I'll be gentle when I rape her corpse."

"If you think your pathetic mind games are going to work on me you've got something else coming," laughed Cedric defiantly. "I'm getting tired, so let's get this over with!"

Screaming "Titanus," Cedric lifted Ragnarok in the air. He took two steps forward and unleashed a powerful upswing. The Elite's helmet rolled off and for the first time the prince saw a close replica of his late friend's face. Angered by this abomination, the Titan sliced at the Elite's legs. Circling around, the sword master took off and jumped in the air. As the larger Elite raised his hammer in defense, Saria and Keiko got a vision of the Titan prince bathed in light.

"It's as if *La Morte Angelus* truly has wings," commented Saria.

Bringing the full force of the enchanted blade against the Elite's hammer, Ragnarok annihilated the weapon and the Elite's plate mail was cut down the center.

"Impossible...a goblin weapon can't shatter like that," stammered the dumbfounded foe.

"You know, I count Julius Imperia as one of my best friends. You may look like him, but you sure as hell don't fight like him."

Spinning one-eighty, Cedric whipped Ragnarok around. A look of panic crossed the face of the Elite as blood dripped from his mouth.

"The sensation you're feeling right now is the gushing of blood. You see, with the arteries and veins cut, it can't reach your brain anymore," explained Cedric.

No longer able to control the nerves on his body, the Elite stammered as his head rolled to the ground. Sickened by the attack and the twitching body, Saria vomited.

"You were not worthy of that mantle," taunted Cedric. "As for you, Esteridge, you can skulk out of the shadows now!"

Fearful of what the prince might do, Esteridge obeyed. Thrusting his polearm forward, the Saint was prepared to defend himself.

"I dare you to try it, Esteridge!"

"No, Prince Rhone, not on this ground, not after what I witnessed."

"Then you have no fear of dying here. I need a good little messenger boy anyway. Go back to Abaddon and your false king and make the most thorough report you can. Tell your masters that there is no army on Mundus or in Hell that will stop me from marching on Verian. Queen Cassandra will take up her rightful throne and Abaddon will never have her."

Silently, Esteridge returned to his mount and rode his company away from the mountain. Once they reached the royal road, they picked up the pace back to Verian. Replacing Ragnarok behind him, the sword master walked over to the shaking and still sickly Saria.

"Lord Cedric, I must beg your pardon…"

"You have nothing to be sorry about, my dear."

The sound of armed troops raised the alert of the two. They both ducked behind the stone and went for their weapons as a disorganized retreat of the attackers occurred.

"I guess my sister and the others must have beat them back."

"It's all over now. I was thinking about what you said before. Saria, I want you to know that you shouldn't feel guilty over what happened. I ordered you to run and you took your orders like a good soldier. It was brave of you."

"But Cedric, how can I ever repay you for what you did for us?"

Kissing the Elf maiden on the forehead, the sword master offered a smile. Keiko pouted a bit at the attention Saria was getting.

"That's the beauty of it, sweetheart, you never have to."

"Get out of my hall" bellowed Lurac.

The Dwarves and their Lord killed and chased the remaining stragglers from Lion's Peak. Beaming with pride, Amuro took her position next to the Dwarf Lord.

"You know, Lurac, I believe a little gratitude is owed to the brave swashbuckling Elf who managed to save your home and your ass from the enemy invaders."

"We'll see who gets the last laugh, you no good hussy!"

Laughing at the insult, Amuro declared victory for the coalition of defenders.

"We've done well," commented Cecilia.

"Yeah, maybe this will finally be the signal to Abaddon to stop his attacks," added Ethan.

"That won't happen until we take them all down at Verian once and for all," countered Christian. "However, I don't think he'll dare assault another kingdom after this humiliation."

Piles of dead soldiers littered the halls of Lion's Peak. The Dwarves knelt before their fallen and said prayers to honor their dead. They had taken casualties, but the heart and soul of their people had survived the terrible ordeal. As Amuro hurried to the stone pavement, she spotted Cedric and Saria heading back.

"*La Morte Angelus*, you never cease to amaze me."

"I'll make a believer out of you yet, Amuro."

"Saria, are you all right?"

Embarrassed by her earlier actions, the younger sister hid her face from her sister.

"Cedric…what did you do to make my sister throw up?"

"How did you know?" questioned a puzzled Keiko.

"Because that is the look on her face whenever she vomited as a kid."

"Let's just say I had to resort to some gruesome tactics to take down their leader," explained Cedric. "He did say some horrible things about what he planned on doing with Saria, that may have rattled her as well."

"It's okay, you did great out there, sis, I mean it. I never thought you'd be able to handle yourself in battle the way you did. I am so proud of you."

"But Amuro… shouldn't… I mean, someone like you would never…"

"Trust me, a lot of people get sick to their stomach when they watch Cedric fight."

"Or eat, for that matter," added Mesmara from the other room. "Just don't ask him to go over his culinary expertise with you."

"Is that supposed to imply something about me?" inquired a disturbed Cedric. "Here I come, risking life and limb time and time again, and everybody just ribs me."

Amuro stuck her tongue out at him and walked off with her sister. Nadia slumped against one of the walls. Pouting, she was disgusted at the blood all over her body.

"How did it go?" asked a concerned Wilhelm.

"Look what those bastards did to my best costume… it's going to take forever to get the blood out of this. It might be better to just scrap it and make a new one."

"Still as prissy as a princess!" laughed Wilhelm.

"Next time I don't intend to be in such close combat."

"Oh? You intend to fight some more?"

"Yes. I decided to adopt the defiant daughter model, and dealing a blow to my father and his chief lieutenant is wonderful revenge for exiling me to this world. No offense."

"God help us all."

Christian walked over to Cedric. He gave him a high-five. "Nice job," praised Christian.

"Do I detect a sense of reservation in that comment?"

"We've got a new problem."

"You mean, if this is our enemy?"

"I was counting on going up against Acadians and the remaining Demonkin, with numbers we thought were significantly reduced. I didn't expect Abaddon to come up with something like this. We have to assume this is only a fraction of the number of soldiers that Virgus has created for him. We're going to be outnumbered in a direct assault."

"Christian's right, Cedric," added Walker. "This is a pure infantry army to match Napolitan, and the Templar Cuirassiers will complement them perfectly. If the Demonkin can muster even a few range soldiers, it's not going to be easy."

"Thank you for your observations. They are dead on," said Cedric. "I'll figure something out."

Hippolyte and Minerva were picking through the weapon and armor pieces of their foes. Holding open a burlap sack, the younger wolf princess picked through to the get the shiniest trinkets.

"This will make a great addition to the Leader's Hut," commented Minerva.

"Yeah, I'm sure it will trump anything they've brought in for a while," quipped Hippolyte. "Actually, don't I have to present some trinkets for the ceremony anyway?"

"That's right, I forgot all about it. They'll be decorating your chair with weapons and helms of the Acadian, Demonkin, Dark Elves, and this army. They'll be calling you Chief Hippolyte, slayer of steel-bellies."

Walker went over to Colin as he removed his mask, watching Minerva and Hippolyte perform their actions.

"I'm definitely worried about this," joked Colin.

"It's their way," remarked Walker.

"I don't know how they're going to accept me. A chief marrying one of their greatest enemy's servants is not going to go over well."

"I wouldn't think so. Then once they get to know you, it'll be even worse."

"You're pretty flippant about this, Walker. I've seen the way you've been looking at Minerva."

"Minerva is not a girl anymore, she's a woman. When I was younger, I used to think Cassandra was the most beautiful girl alive, but for some reason this one is making me think. I'm not sure if this ever could be meant to be. My duty is to my Queen. I can't see myself ever living out there among the tribes."

"Based on the way you spoke about your father, he seemed to love the ones outside of Verian politics more than those wrapped up in it. He had three sons, but he never lifted a finger for them the way he helped you."

"I don't know if it was out of some misplaced sense of duty or if he just appreciated my talents the most. Colin, I've got a lot of thinking to do."

"Trust me, Walker, I think she'd be more than happy to be with you. I wouldn't worry about the tribal way of life, either. Minerva is definitely a city girl from now on."

After the long and hard battle, Mesmara and Quinn found each other's warm embrace. The Kablisha warrior kissed his maiden on her cheek and lips.

"That's two battles now," noted Mesmara.

"There'll be more," agreed Quinn.

"Somehow I envisioned the world outside of our barrier to be much different."

"It's a shame we had to come at such a bad time."

"Deniva half reduced to rubble and Lion's Peak under assault... what next?"

"Maybe it will be better once we get to Titanus."

"Titanus? Uncle didn't say anything about going there."

"Well, providing them an armed escort home is the least we can do. After all, they did put their lives on the line to join us in battle."

"Yes. I guess now it's our war, too."

"Abaddon is never going to forgive the Kablisha for the insult we paid him. Your uncle set those bodies ablaze to send a message; the sins against the City of Antiquity will be atoned for in full."

Prayers and respects paid to the fallen, Lurac gathered all of his people at the entrance to Lion's Peak.

"Let Abaddon and Luminas know there are still Dwarves breathing in Lion's Peak," rallied Lurac. "Let them fear the hour the Dwarves march with *La Morte Angelus*. We will return the favor ten-fold!"

Screaming the name of their king and for the blood of the Acadians, Lurac left his people and extended his hand to Cedric. "You've done well, your Excellency. Thank you for being here."

"We need you and your people. Abaddon's cruelty knows no limits."

"We owe you a debt now, what can we do to repay you?"

"We're going to need your allegiance against Abaddon. I know you've suffered losses here, but the Wood Elves are sending forces as well."

"Aye! You can count on us. The Dwarf race will honor the Titan Alliance! Let no Elf march where a Dwarf dare not go first."

"Also, we're going to need new weapons and armor to use against these forces. I will provide you with raw materials and more than adequate compensation."

"For the fee as negotiated in our contacts and the vassalage agreement, we still have our principles."

"You drive a hard bargain, Lurac, but you have me over the barrel. I will pay whatever you deem fair."

"Come now, let us feast to commemorate this victory over darkness, honor our brave fallen, and renew the trust between the races of the west."

"Why, Lurac, that's wonderful," teased Amuro. "You've finally accepted the fact that you're helpless without the Elves."

"Did you say something, you beguiling witch?"

"Beguiling…oh, I didn't know you cared."

Amuro hugged Lurac tightly, and he fumed. Rosa couldn't contain her laughter, and even Malcolm managed a wide smirk.

"Cedric Rhone, you are a grand warrior, but you have far too many Elves in your party for my taste."

"Careful, Lurac, they're my friends."

"Well, not everyone has such good taste, but I'll bet I can drink you under the table tonight."

As the cheering Dwarves tapped large barrels behind the statue of Dondarion, Ethan put his arm around his wife.

"I guess we'll be delaying our trip home another rotation. Cedric is never going to drive home tonight."

"I just hope Mom doesn't march an army out here after us. I'm not sure if the Dwarves have enough mead."

"Gerard must have gotten the message through to Horace. I'm sure Cassandra and Thomas are just about there by now."

"Growing closer to the moment I dread, when Thomas and Cassandra try to explain the situation to Mom. I need a drink!"

"I think that makes two of us."

Despite the joyous mood around them, Valentine and Cagius found themselves kneeling on the stone pavement. The Napolitan prince stared at the head of the Elite and carefully removed it from the helmet.

"Cagius, I need to know what you're going to do with that?"

"See if you can muster up some brine, Valentine. I want to preserve this for the journey home."

"Then you suspect our enemy has lied to your father."

"I don't know what kind of reception I'm going to get when I come home, but this abomination must not be allowed to stand. How's my nephew?"

"He'll be fine. It's good for him to learn a lesson like that; the mental and physical pain will make him think twice next time. Do you remember what Cedric said in the Senate before he resigned? We backed him, but even we thought he was crazy talking about 'boogeymen.' Damn me for living to see the hour he was right."

"I remember something else he said, Valentine, and I believe it: You don't confront evil, you have to destroy it."

FORT HAWKEYE, TITANUS

Realizing turmoil would result from the death of her father, Civilia prepared well in advance for a succession war. She established a circle early that would eventually become her royal court. These great men and women included Horace Irvine, a prominent military officer to serve as her War Master; Martha Heinrich, a brilliant scientist with an appetite for politics; and, of course, myself. This ruthlessness in politics as well as the battlefield made her feared as the Matriarch of Destruction.

Von Angelhardt's Eighty-Seventh Report

Grasping her reigns tightly, a nervous Cassandra passed through the foreboding Eagle's Gate. Eight revolutions prior, when her father had taken her to formally propose a marriage to Cedric, the ride was filled with anticipation. Now the young Queen dreaded the information she had to pass on. Her only comfort was seeing Thomas happily ride in on Horace's horse. Catching a glimpse of his true home overwhelmed the boy. He badgered Horace with questions concerning Eagle's Gate and those defending it. The war veteran took it in stride and happily addressed the inquisitive nature of his young liege. The column expected to receive a lukewarm reception since only Cassandra had returned with them. However, there were smiles and celebrations going on around Fort Hawkeye and Eagle's Gate. As they rode up the hill to the fort, Horace spotted Martha with a contingent ready to greet them.

"Okay, Martha, what's with the celebration?" asked Horace

"Let's just say the greatest genius on Terminus Mundus managed to get our communications back online. We touched base with Lion's Peak. Cedric and Wilhelm got there in time, and they beat back the army the Acadians sent."

"Well, that's good news. What about casualties?"

"Just some minor injuries, but nothing fatal among the command staff. The Dwarves, unfortunately, got hit pretty hard. I wouldn't doubt their ability to make a speedy recovery."

"Are they on their way home?"

"Lurac insisted they spend the night commemorating the victory and would consider it a grave insult if anyone left. Civilia decided to let him have one."

"There'll be some mighty hangovers tomorrow, and knowing Cedric he'll have them out bright and early."

Martha watched Cassandra ride up. The doctor curtsied before her.

"I'm grateful for the good news," announced Cassandra. "Please accept my gracious thanks for your ingenuity in freeing us from the barrier prison. Your reputation was certainly not unfounded."

"Well, your Highness, aren't you just a darling. Such a polite and proper young lady; it doesn't surprise me that one of my finest experiments would choose such a beautiful woman!"

Cassandra blushed heavily.

"I apologize if I embarrassed you, but I have a habit of being blunt, your Highness. When your business is politics it comes naturally. The Queen is awaiting your arrival in the Courtyard. If you really want to thank me, please don't keep her waiting any longer."

"Thank you," stated Cassandra. "Come on, Thomas, I'll take you the rest of the way."

Horace passed Thomas to Cassandra's horse. The young prince could feel the hand of the Queen trembling and wondered why she was so afraid.

"Who's the kid?" asked Martha.

"That is Cecilia's son," Horace replied. "His name is Thomas."

"Today is going to be a grand rotation after all. Oh Cecilia, what have you done?"

As they approached the courtyard of Fort Hawkeye, a lump developed in Cassandra's throat. Directly in front of her, Civilia descended the steps of the Fort. Assisted in her dismount by the soldiers around her, she helped Thomas down.

"Cassandra!" greeted Civilia.

The Titan Queen took the Acadian Queen in her strong arms and embraced her like a daughter. Not expecting this reaction, Cassandra didn't know if protocol demanded that she curtsey or ask for a curtsey in return.

"Are you all right, my daughter?

"Begging your pardon, Civilia, but I am hardly your daughter yet."

"You're practically my daughter now, Cassandra, and you'll find I treat all of my family as family," explained Civilia as she let go.

Even your exiled brother, my Queen? thought Martha to herself.

"You look well, Cassandra... a little on the thin side, but still good," said Civilia.

"The food stores in Deniva have run low, and I've had a lot on my mind lately," clarified Cassandra.

"Poor Dennis. I'll see if we can do something to remedy that. I'm not surprised your mind is weary, my dear. I tire of all these surprises myself. Abaddon is the most ruthless and cunning enemy I have ever faced. No matter how many moves we anticipate, we always seem to fall one step behind him."

"I'm just glad we got the news from Lion's Peak. I don't think I would have made it through another night like this."

"You'll get used to it," expounded a laughing Civilia. "It is one of the responsibilities of being a proper Queen. It grows late. Come, Cassandra, I look forward to having a quiet dinner and long conversation with my future daughter-in-law."

"Civilia, I fear I must bring to your attention an important matter." Putting her hand on the young boy's shoulders, Cassandra moved Thomas to the forefront.

"Who's this?" inquired the Queen.

"Allow me to introduce Thomas Rhone, your grandson."

Properly bowing to his grandmother, Thomas never broke eye contact. Sensing her confusion, the prince tried to lighten the mood. "Hi, Grandma. I've heard a lot about you."

"Cassandra, is he yours?"

"No."

"That's impossible. Cedric would never take a child out of wedlock... how did this happen?"

"Thomas isn't Cedric's son. He's Cecilia's son."

"WHAT?" screamed the Titan Queen as her subjects scrambled for cover. "Cecilia's son? Who is his father?"

"My father is Sir Ethan de Milly of Deniva," offered Thomas.

"For five revolutions, Andres made trip after trip over the mountains, and yet in all this time, your mother never mentioned you were born."

Civilia cried. After a few moments, Thomas hugged her. Mood improved instantly, she embraced her young grandson back.

Ethan de Milly...the same man she knocked unconscious on the bar room floor. I told her to be an eagle...but I never anticipated anything like this, thought Civilia. "It would have been appropriate for your mother to inform me that she was married and I was a grandmother. However, I can tell that you're going to make a fine Titan."

"Thank you, Grandma."

"Now that I am a Grandmother, my first duty is to spoil you. Let's get you inside and find out the best way to do that."

Taking Thomas's hand, Civilia walked into the Fort with Thomas at her side. Laughing, Horace puffed on his cigar.

"We were lucky this time, Dad," observed Samuel.

"Let's get ourselves a drink," responded Horace. "It's late and I'm tired, but remember, you're buying the rounds."

"Happy to oblige, sir."

Mountain Hall, Lion's Peak

Contrary to popular belief, sentinels and acolytes are subject to the same temptations that influence those of creation. The most overwhelming of these is the unrelenting desire to con-summate our carnal desires. Lucifer knew how to exploit these when he sired his succubus daughters. The resulting offspring of such a union would have the powers of Heaven and Hell at their disposal. Thus the Prince will never rest until that child is thoroughly corrupted. For this reason, such carnal unions are frowned upon and must occur with the utmost discretion. However, the need for companionship can override the capacity for reason.

Excerpt from the journal of Duke Francesco Angelino

Preferring quiet solitude for meditation rather than the raucous celebration raging in the halls above, Wilhelm found solace in the mines. Seated on one of the steps, the sentinel muttered a prayer. Startled by the opening of the door to the mine, he turned to see Cedric enter and close the door behind him.

"You must be losing your touch. I expected you to have drunk three-quarters of the room under the table by now," teased Wilhelm.

"It's getting ugly up there. After I out-drank Lurac, Amuro grabbed a marker and started drawing pictures on his face."

"That won't be pretty when he gets up."

"No. Besides, they ran out of brandy." Cedric put two goblets on the stairs. Pouring two drinks, he passed one to his mentor. "I always

142

found that alcohol helps keep tensions from flaring up too much when a sensitive issue is discussed," reassured Cedric.

"So, you didn't come out here for a pleasant chat?"

"We've haven't had that luxury, old friend, since the rotation you told me Abaddon was coming for Cassandra."

"Yes, and I suspect you want me to tell you everything with nothing held back."

"My suspicions began when I saw what Abaddon was able to unleash within her. Then I got the vision when I was fighting for my life and it was confusing to say the least. Wilhelm, I'll fight to the death for her, but I need to know who I'm fighting for."

"As you would expect, it's complicated. I better tell it to you from the beginning," started Wilhelm as he took a drink. "King Joseph Acadia approached your grandfather and asked to marry Stephen to Civilia."

"That's when King Justin went to Mom and gave her the ultimatum to choose between the throne of Titanus or Acadia. She refused to give up the Rhone name and instead gave up the only man she ever loved."

"Exactly. So Stephen went to the Elves and asked for the hand of Gweyn Marisol. It would have been a grave insult to her Titan allies if the leader of Evengard would have taken the marriage that Civilia refused. Cerwin counseled her to say an outright 'no' but Camdem Jenitzen weaseled his way in and asked Stephen to take the only eligible maiden of royal blood in Evengard, Sharon Fenidor."

"Since Draconius had already promised Marguerite to Constantine, there was no other suitable candidate in the west."

"Yes. However, Sharon already had a reputation as a loose woman and even her uncle Alistair thought the marriage was a terrible idea. There were rumors that Stephen found her cheating on him before the Wedding Festival was over. After the incident, Stephen wouldn't bed Sharon; after ten revolutions without an heir, Acadian nobles finally decided to contract Virgus to create an heir from Sharon's ova and Stephen's sperm."

"Speaking as a product of genetic tampering, I've lost the moral high ground to be incensed by such a request."

"Virgus did so. However, he made sure that the child had extensive genetic manipulation. This was a chance to bring Elf and human DNA together and he wasn't going to waste it. Virgus didn't use the advance growth hormones you and your sister were fed, so the egg was implanted into Sharon's uterus. It appeased everyone because it gave the impression that Stephen had actually bedded her and the Acadians could have their wild celebration after the birth of the first heir. The child would have all the intelligence and magical abilities of an Elf along with the strength and endurance of a human. Stephen, however, made one request: that the child be a daughter, in case he had no son, so succession would be easily obeyed."

"The child was Cassandra."

"Yes and no. Physically and genetically Cassandra is the same as you see her now. However, early in life, the princess was quite susceptible to discipline and control because of the submissive nature of her manipulated DNA. Disturbed by the nature of the child, Cerwin Faulkner came to Verian and observed her. By a twist of fate, he was the girl's uncle by a marriage between his House and House Fenidor. We discussed at length the nature of Virgus' work and began an investigation to determine the motives of the mad doctor in this matter. All of our information gathering was for nothing, however. One rotation she was playing a game with two of the castle servants. She hid in one of the stables and they couldn't find her. A cow knocked over a lantern in the straw and the stable caught fire."

"What is it with cows and starting fires in stables, anyway," teased Cedric aloud as he drew conclusions from within.

"Cerwin Faulkner was brought in immediately by the terrified servants. He cast a spell that erased their memories of the incident completely. He pulled the princess out of that fire with third degree burns. She suffered severe smoke inhalation that caused massive brain damage and left her comatose. All of Virgus' plans literally had gone up in smoke."

"So, she died."

"Yes. The death of the heir to the throne would have been chaotic at the time. There was turmoil in Evengard; Acadia and Napolitan were up in arms over Tribal trade rights, and you were running your military operations against the wild men. We feared that the Empire would certainly take advantage of the chaos and send the Imperial Army to destroy us. Cerwin asked if there was any way to bring her back. I told him that once life was lost, nothing could be done to bring it back. I never saw such hurt in the face of an Elf before, and I thought of a second way."

Wilhelm rubbed his face. "When angels produce offspring, it's not the same as humans. A female can carry the life force—the soul, per se—in her for many cycles or even revolutions before coming to term. Nadia and I had conceived an offspring in love that we both knew couldn't enter this world. That union would have been sought by the agents of the Prince and manipulated to participate in their War against Heaven."

"You gave Cassandra a new soul."

Wilhelm smiled and held back his tears. "Yes. The damage to the physical body was easy to repair given the right healing magic, and Virgus' manipulation of the genetic code caused the cells to regenerate quickly. Nadia passed the soul living within her into the body of the princess. Even I didn't anticipate at the time how much more of my consort's own DNA would merge with the girl. Her intelligence skyrocketed and her beauty became beyond comparison. As such, though she bears Stephen's and Sharon's DNA, she is as much the child of Nadia and I."

"The *Bis Reginum*."

"I had Nadia look into such a thing."

"I half-believed the old legends of Titanus—a Queen who has been twice blessed. Yet before me, Cassandra has been blessed in both the wonders of Celestial and Temporal worlds." Cedric slugged the rest of his drink. Pouring another for both of them, he took another swig. "Don't make me drink alone, Wilhelm. I think you need this more than me."

"Thanks, your Excellency."

"So you blame yourself for this?"

"Though he sought Teman originally, my sin drew Abaddon to this world, Cedric. My foolish pride led me to believe by hiding the soul inside her body, everything would be all right."

"Well, it's not all right."

"Thanks."

"Do you want me to be honest? What can I say—you screwed up. You were right about one thing. Cassandra certainly got her looks from her mother's side, since you're so damn ugly."

"I can see this doesn't change your opinion on Cassandra."

"Are you kidding me? If anything, this is a plus, Wilhelm. I can honestly call her my angel from now on...or my little devil. Works either way for me."

"You know, I think you're only scared of one thing."

"He won't be careless twice, Wilhelm. I still don't have the means of binding him, so we're trapped."

"No. Cedric, what if I call someone in who may know of a way?"

"I would deem it invaluable, but would they come?"

"He owes me a favor, that's all I can say for now. It may take some convincing, but if there's a way to bind Abaddon, he'll know how to do it."

"All right, you've got my permission to call it in."

Alerted to the sound of a booted heel on the steps, the two turned their heads to see Nadia sweetly shuffling her arms and sashaying her body back and forth.

"I should have guessed you two would walk away from the party," joked Nadia.

"We had a lot to discuss," said Wilhelm.

"So, you finally worked up the courage to tell him." Nadia sat down next to Wilhelm and put her head on his shoulder. Reaching her hand out to Cedric, she caressed his face.

"You're not like the others, Cedric. You don't look at me the same way, and your body is as warm as a blacksmith's forge. It's like he bellows away right there in your heart."

"Maybe because I can see a part of you in Cassandra," replied Cedric.

Tears in her eyes, she hugged Cedric tightly. The sword master held her.

"I believe this world would take a turn for the worst without you. Live for my daughter!"

"In a situation so desperate, Nadia, it would be foolish to make such a promise. Take comfort only in the fact that as long as my soul remains ablaze, I will keep her from Lucifer."

Nadia pulled back and looked in the prince's eyes. Comforted by what she saw in them, she knew he spoke the truth. Letting her go, Cedric thought about what the succubus had said to him.

"What do you mean, 'the others'? My sister loves you!"

Nadia had a puzzled look on her face. "Surely you must be mistaken, Lord Cedric. I know we used to play a lot together when she was with you at Wilhelm's plantation. I think she made her opinion very clear to me."

"Don't be offended, but you creatures of Hell don't read people too well."

The door to the mines opened again and this time Cecilia entered. "Hey Cedric, we've got a problem. Amuro and Rosa have decided to defend the honor of every Elf maiden by wrestling two Dwarf professionals."

"All right, sis, I'll be right up. One thing first, Nadia is a little hurt over here. Would you please tell her that you love her?"

"You mean she thinks I hate her?"

"Well, don't you, Cecilia?"

"How could I hate you? You're the one who taught me how to sing, dance, flaunt my assets, wear pretty dresses, and come up with some of the most ingenious pranks in the history of Titanus."

"But the spear at my throat and the words you said to Ethan and Cassandra…"

"That was just bluster. It was the first rotations after the fall of Central Acadia, I couldn't be too careful. Do you realize the pressure I was under trying to hold that ragtag bunch together in Deniva? I willfully took on the role of the bad soldier in your situation so they would see the good in you and what you had to offer."

Cecilia walked down to Nadia and held her. "You were practically the crazy aunt to me all my life, and I love you very much. Besides, if what my brother says is true, well…you should be one proud Mama."

Cecilia kissed Nadia on the cheek. The succubus was delighted for the first time in a long time and Wilhelm mustered a smile as he stood and held her.

"It's nice you've had your little moment, sis," Cedric interrupted. "But focus! You said something about Amuro and Rosa."

"Oh shoot, I forgot! We've got to go!"

The twins raced back into the Emperor's Gallery where the slurred insults from the lips of Amuro and Rosa could be heard even in the mines below.

"Are you satisfied now?" asked Wilhelm.

"Wilhelm, was it right to place such a large burden on him?"

"Would you have anyone else?"

"No. He makes me want to believe like you make me believe."

CASTLE ACADIA, VERIAN

The Western Rite of the Temple of the Divine Saints differs from the Eastern Rites. The Eastern Rite as practiced in the Chinotal Empire does not have the hierarchy or military institutions that are so prominent in the Western Rite. The Templar Army consists of seventy-five thousand Halberdiers pulled from the elite ranks of the Acadian Army and twenty-five thousand Knights. All infantry are also skilled in the short bow. The Templars differ from most Acadian troops because they are well trained and conditioned to be fanatical. They are directly under the command of the Six Swords of the Saints. However, the Templar Army has only been tested in battle against the Tribes and there have been some concerns they will not match up against a professional army. Thus, I must create one.

Journal of Hector Reed

Riding at a break-neck pace, Esteridge and his retreating escort rode into the walled Verian. Gavin and Roland had seen his approach for kilometers and knew what was coming wasn't good. Upon his return, Luminas called his court together for a summit. Abaddon and his minions attended as well.

"I seem to remember sending out more soldiers to Lion's Peak," observed Abaddon.

"They were slaughtered. The few that remain have retreated to the Verian courtyard and Gavin sent them to work on the wall," reported Esteridge.

"I find it difficult to believe that the Dwarves would be able to repel this attack," countered Luminas.

"Not by themselves. The battle began well, and the Dwarves were driven into retreat after the first three charges. On the fourth charge, a group of warriors led by Prince Cedric Rhone appeared."

Anger rising at the mention of the name, Abaddon grabbed the wound on his chest. "How can he be everywhere at once?" he demanded.

"I don't know, but they weren't alone. A relief column arrived from Titanus and there was a third army as well. They were dressed in leather armor and had considerable skill in sword and crossbow."

"Sounds like the Kablisha have found a stomach for fighting battles," Abaddon said with a sneer.

"Perhaps there was another tunnel system we didn't know about," added Luminas.

"I'm certain of it."

"I would imagine we didn't do the damage to the Dwarves that we imagined and our cut of the spoils seems reduced to a minimum," deduced Virgus.

"We did some damage to the Dwarven army, but as for weapons and spoils we got nothing," said Esteridge, finishing his report.

"Maximilian, from your experience, how long does it take the Titan army to mobilize?"

"It took less than two rotations from the time that Stephen left Castle Titan for the Titan Armada to arrive at the Istle Hills. When they ride, they ride faster than any army known to the world."

"Perhaps a pre-emptive strike would be best!" suggested Jonas.

"Are you prepared, Commander, to move on Eagle's Gate itself?" taunted Sharon. "They'd shower you with arrows before you got within two kilometers."

"No! But I don't want to sit back here in this Castle and die!"

"Perhaps it's time we reinforced the defenses at Fort Orion," determined Luminas. "If Cedric is bringing his army north along the plains, they have to make an encampment somewhere."

"He'll have to strike Fort Orion first before he can launch an attack on Verian," deduced Celius. "It would have to be a protracted siege; if nothing else it would slow him down."

Abaddon turned and studied the map. "He won't be able to leave such a well defended Fort to his rear, he would risk an attack from behind."

"We have the Acadian Templar Army," offered Javos. "We dare not risk Lord Mormont on the defense but perhaps Sir Karstak would lead our forces."

"Just the Templars and I against the whole of Titanus?" countered Karstak. "Sounds like a suicide mission."

"You'd have all of the defenses of Fort Orion," said Jonas. "The last time I checked, horses cannot trample rock and steel. Besides, I could be there with a relief column in half a rotation when the fighting starts, and Orion will hold them off for much longer than that period of time."

"They won't trample it," said Karstak. "Okay, I'll hold the Fort with those men, the rest of you just better be close."

"Javos, can you guarantee that the Templar Army will fight for me as their King?" asked Luminas. "We're asking them to fight for a vampire after all."

"We've run short on coin at the Temple. I fear that if it comes to a choice between you and Cassandra, they may favor the Queen with a trove of Titan gold backing her."

"Well, then let it be heir against heir. Let them chose the true Acadian over the puppet controlled by the Titans. Abaddon, it's time."

"I believe so. Citizens of Central Acadia, I bid you welcome your new Queen. Maria Acadia, the first of her name. Long live the Queen!"

As the doors to the throne room opened, Sharon and Maximilian willingly stepped down from their thrones. Cloaked in a demonic smile and stare, the Necromancer Queen strode staff in hand. Unnerved and shocked by the appearance of this creature that once was a pure and sweet princess, the Acadian Court prostrated themselves hurriedly before her. As she seated herself on Maximilian's former throne, Marie stared adoringly at Abaddon, waiting for his command.

"And this throne belongs to me now?" inquired Marie.

"For now, in name and appearance only. Maximilian Luminas and his council will remain as the true rotation-to-rotation ruler of this Kingdom. However, if Cassandra has named herself Queen, we must be prepared to maintain the loyalty of your populace."

"I understand, Lord Abaddon. I will give them a Queen beautiful and terrifying; those that once dismissed me as a nothing more than my father's doll will feel the true power that flows through my body."

"Are you satisfied, Javos?" asked Luminas.

"Undoubtedly, my Lord," answered Javos. "Only the most disloyal of our subjects will not stand with Queen Marie Acadia. The Templars will be honored to fight and die for a true Acadian Queen against that half-elf, heathen, upstart."

"As per the formal declaration of war we received, the pretender Cassandra has chosen to commence the War of Two Queens. The usurper Cedric Rhone stands with my pretender sister against my loyal Acadian subjects," declared Marie. "Sir Karstak!"

Karstak clicked his heels together and bowed. "Yes, your Highness. I am at your service."

"Take our Templar army, reinforce them with whatever troops you may need! March them to Fort Orion and destroy the morale of the Titan army. Make it so even those fanatics will not fight!"

"Of course, my Queen!"

Karstak turned and walked out of the room. The sounds of armor clashing together in the courtyard could be heard.

"Now that we have seen to the outer defenses, we must look to our own protection. Sir Gavin, how goes the wall?"

"I need three more rotations, your Highness. We refitted the parapets and mounted them with catapults as well."

"Very good. Commander Mormont, since Sir Karstak has taken command of the Templar army, I want you to personally lead the army Virgus has created. I want them drilled and prepared to defend the city of Verian. This is my stronghold and I will not lose it to my sister."

"I'll see to it immediately, your Highness."

"Good. I have business to attend to, but I will return shortly. Count Luminas, please take over and see to our battle preparations."

As Marie walked back down the aisle and left the room, Virgus and Abaddon stared at one another and exchanged a smile. Waiting for her outside was the clone. Though he wore armor, it was nothing like the Paladin mail Julius bore. Over a layer of chain and padded mail was a solid black plate with a bloody skull as the insignia. The shoulder plates and gauntlets had spiked projectiles and the round shield slung over his back had a large dragon's talon in the center of it. The blade on his hip was tempered in black steel with a curved gold handle and split down the middle to give it four edges and good balance.

"I did as you said, my love," rejoiced Marie. "I'm sure they were quite surprised when flighty Princess Marie spoke of the necessary defensive preparations."

"Prince Rhone is a formidable enemy," responded the clone. "However, his greatest skills lie as a general on the battlefield. These fools don't have the slightest idea how to deal with someone of his skill."

"We can bide our time."

"The pawns will die first. The ninnies you have serving you at court will seek to dispose of you the second this threat is finished. You must be prepared for that."

"My Queen's Guard will be more than a match, and Abaddon has promised to combine the strength of his army with mine. I did not wish for such a bloody ascendance, but it was inevitable."

"It will not be so easy, Marie. Cedric always tries to be seven moves ahead of his enemy and he will anticipate the various maneuvers we are trying. Always remember the Titan prince has spies everywhere and the devil's luck."

"Then it's good that we have a decorated Marshal of our own on our side!"

"Until the end, my Queen!"

Marie ran to the clone's arms and he embraced her, but the devilish smile remained.

Eagle's Gate, Titanus

Home is where the heart is.

Old Elf Proverb

After five revolutions and two desperate battles, the triumphant exiles were on their final approach to Eagle's Gate. Already hearing the raucous cheers of thousands of soldiers and civilians, a sense of pride overwhelmed them—save for Amuro, who was still green in the face from the celebrations of the night before. She had Maiden pull over every few steps when a feeling of nausea overtook her. The source of her never-ending annoyance, Cagius, rode close by with Saria on his horse.

"I hate you!" seethed Amuro.

"What did I do?" retorted Cagius.

"You and your ability to get rid of alcohol fast. Here the great Marshal of the Elves, savior of Deniva, is waltzing into Eagle's Gate hung over!"

"I told you, it's one of my special techniques!"

"But you drank so much last night!" countered Malcolm.

"It doesn't matter."

"I wonder if I inherited some of that," added Joshua.

"You don't look too worse for wear. Though I don't remember my brother possessing any of my secret techniques! How's the leg?"

"It doesn't hurt as much as my pride. That and the verbal thrashing I got from Valentine after the battle."

"Damned right, you deserved it for your idiocy!" berated Valentine. "Besides, when it comes to you drinking, I'm sure it has much more to do with your tremendous height and weight."

As they approached the mighty stone eagles, a feeling of sorrow and foreboding overtook the Wolf Tribe princesses. Both grabbed the wolf talismans around their neck and prayed to the spirits.

"I never thought Eagle's Gate could look so beautiful," commented Christian.

"I hate it," shouted a scornful Hippolyte. "It's the sight of Apollo's charge."

"We prefer to refer to it as Apollo's massacre!" corrected Cecilia.

"Girt your loins, those of you with the blood of the Wolf. The enemy stands before you in a Fortress of Stone," recited Minerva. *"They will summon the bolts of lightning and the strength of their steel against you. We may fall but our actions shall be remembered forever."*

"Six hundred riders, half-frozen and half-mad, charged Eagle's Gate in a final move of desperation to grasp victory from defeat," continued Hippolyte.

"If my history is correct, Cecilia, Leto Rhone would have been King at the time," probed Cedric.

"Yes. The blood of the wolf stained the white poppies of Titanus. The Wolf Chief cursed his foe so that *all of the poppies of Titanus shall bleed.*"

Pointing to various fields of red poppies along Eagle's Gate, the Vanadis made her point to the tribal girls. Sighing and hanging her head, a few tears dripped down from her eyes.

"You honored our dead?" asked Hippolyte. "No one ever mentioned anything like that to us."

"Desperate men do desperate things, Hippolyte!" explained Cedric. "We do not believe in trophies in Titanus. We sent all the bodies back to the Chief."

"Yes, and King Leto officially adopted the red poppy as the flower of Titanus," expounded Cecilia. "True to the curse, there hasn't been a white poppy on Titanus soil since."

"Not one?" exclaimed Minerva. "How can that be?"

"Even Martha can't define it. White poppies are plentiful in all the other kingdoms," said Cedric. "However, there is another part to the legend: a Titan shall make amends with his fallen brothers and in that moment a white poppy shall bloom once more."

"But didn't you…with my grandfather… you were blood brothers," stammered Hippolyte.

"Perhaps I didn't do enough because I haven't seen a poppy bloom white yet. Then again, it is only a legend!"

"I didn't realize how interconnected your peoples are," remarked Walker as he rode up along Minerva. "All I ever studied was the viciousness of the battles between Titanus and the Wolf Tribe. I'm sure they never passed around the term 'honorable enemies.'"

"We never really have been able to tell who drew first blood," pondered Minerva. "That's the problem when you've been enemies for so long."

"At this point, my suspicions lie with Abaddon!" interjected Colin. "Well, we can hopefully leave that animosity behind us. We have far worse enemies to deal with now."

Rosa rode next to Christian. Letting his guard down for but a brief moment, the operative put his arm to the shoulder of his girl. Bringing a smile to her face, the high Elf ranger responded in kind.

"I can think of some more romantic places for a honeymoon," teased Rosa.

"Knowing my boss, I don't think we're going to be spending a lot of time here."

"You've got to learn to be less serious."

"When I'm not serious, people die. Hell, even when I am serious they still die."

"Always the same. Maybe that's why I love you."

It had been five revolutions since Amuro first noticed the promissory ring on Christian's hand. Eating away at her for some time, she couldn't figure out the connection between Christian and Rosa. As she furrowed away at it, Malcolm got concerned.

"Amuro, are you okay? You're not going to be sick again, are you?"

"Sorry, Malcolm. It's just something doesn't add up. Christian DeVries and Rosa Landon... it doesn't make sense."

"Why?"

"Rosa was a High Princess of Evengard, even higher than my family. I noticed that ring on his finger before. Now I'm sure it's the promissory ring of House Landon. Why would Rosa be betrothed to a half-elf operative in Titanus?"

"Makes you wonder, doesn't it, Amuro? What his other half is..."

"That stupid ring, if I could only examine it."

"I already did."

"Your eyesight is amazing, Malcolm. What did you see?"

"It's very old; however, it appears that a key piece of the ring has been removed."

"What piece?"

"Each Elf house of Evengard has a specific jewel to represent the house. It's clear in both of our rings. However, Christian's ring is missing such a stone."

"Do you think they deliberately pried it out?"

"I wouldn't doubt it. However, I wouldn't concern myself so much with their love life."

Waiting for them at Eagle's Gate was Civilia and Cassandra. The exiles got off their horses and walked them the short distance remaining to their destination. The Titan Queen embraced both of her children in the same warm hug.

"My brave boy and girl, I never expected anything like this to happen to you," started the crying Queen. "It's not that I stopped believing, it's just now that I can physically hold you both again I believe you really are all right."

"Mom, the care packages were amazing," said Cedric.

"I'm so sorry for everything I put you through…I just couldn't do it by bird," apologized Cecilia.

"Cedric, go see your betrothed."

Laughing, Cedric lifted Cassandra up in the air before bringing her in for a kiss.

"As for you, young lady!" started Civilia again. "You should be commended for holding them together all this time."

"I just followed your model." Cecilia said.

"You could have had the decency to tell me that you got married."

"I'm sorry, but I felt it needed to be done in person."

"It's my fault. I never worried about you. I only worried about your brother doing something like this."

"What does that mean?"

"Don't take that condescending tone with me, my daughter. I'm not saying you disgraced our family. I blame myself for pressuring you so that when it happened, you felt obligated."

"Ethan and I were married before Thomas was born!"

"I'm sure it was a beautiful wedding. How I so wanted to be there when my only daughter got married," Civilia sobbed harder. "You must have been a beautiful bride… tell me you have pictures at least."

"Of course, Mom, you've got to get yourself under control. If you keep crying, then Cassandra's going to start crying and we're never going to get her to stop."

"Where's my new son-in-law?"

"Your Highness," announced Ethan as he bowed before the Queen. "Please accept my humble apologies for not making a proper announcement. Cecilia is the best thing that ever happened to me and for that I am nothing but grateful."

"You're family now, I expect you to call me Mom," corrected Civilia as she embraced him. "You've already given me one grandchild." She turned to Cecilia. "Your father's prowess is legendary. I hope Thomas will only be the start."

"Mother!" screamed Cecilia. "How could you say such a thing? Where is Thomas, anyway?"

"Sorry. Horace was teaching him how to spar. The little rascal has already imprinted himself on just about everyone here."

Civilia signaled behind her, and Thomas came running up. He jumped into the arms of his mother and father, who rewarded him with many hugs and kisses. Wilhelm took the time to approach the Titan Queen and salute her.

"Your Excellency, Lurac and his people have survived the assault of the army that attacked them," reported Wilhelm. "They have suffered significant casualties and thus, like our Wood Elf allies, their contributions will be reduced."

"They knew exactly how and where to hit us," reasoned the Queen. "What about the capacity of their smith and crafting operations?"

"It suffered little because most of the battles took place elsewhere," continued Wilhelm. "Though Lurac is not giving us a discount."

"Nor should I have expected anything less," Civilia said, laughing. "Your heroics and ingenuity should be rewarded, Wilhelm. As such, I release Nadia to your custody, and you may travel with her anywhere in Titanus as you wish without fear or scorn."

"I thank you, your Highness, and I'm sure she will as well. The nun's outfit was really getting to her."

Civilia went individually to each of the exiles, including the Wolf Tribe girls, and offered them welcome. When she approached the Kablisha command staff, Cedric intervened.

"Allow me to introduce Argus Kinkade, Marshal of the Kablisha militia, and his subordinates Quirinus Ophion and Mesmara Lorelei."

"So this is the infamous Argus Kinkade, the gentleman responsible for holding my son captive for five revolutions!"

"At the time we believed certain steps needed to be taken to ensure his safety," apologized Argus. "Fortunately, we did have the foresight to see the importance of your son to all of Mundus."

"It takes a strong man to admit that. I accept your apology and note that any prior ill-will I held to you is over."

"Your son is literally amazing, and I can see where he got a lot of it from."

"Thank you." Civilia saluted as she spoke to the group again. "You've had a long journey and I'm sure you long to reach the safety of your countries. We will provide you the use of our hover trains if you wish so you can reach your destinations quicker. However, I would offer the opportunity for each of you to join us for brunch."

"Well, that depends, your Highness," joked Cagius. "Did you happen to bring some prime Titan beef with you to Fort Hawkeye?"

"I assure you, Prince Cagius, there is nothing but the best food prepared by my personal staff."

"What kind of cavalier would I be if I turned down a free steak dinner from a beautiful lady? Your Highness, we accept."

"Your Highness, I can't thank you enough," offered Amuro. "I just hope I can get a few hard-boiled eggs for this hangover."

As the group headed to Fort Hawkeye, a nervous Colin approached Cedric. The assassin was holding Hippolyte's hand.

"Master Cedric, with your permission, I would like to accompany Hippolyte and Minerva back to the Tribal Camp. I believe I could help make your case."

"Nice try, Colin, but I think Hippolyte is the one that's going to have to decide what the Tribes intend to do. You have my permission to ride. Go ahead, but don't get killed."

"He'll be fine as long as he's under my flag. We'll treat him as if he's going to become the Chief's consort."

"You know what, sis," reasoned Minerva. "I've been thinking about something. We've been assuming all this time that Huskal is still alive and Reynard has kept things at bay. We could be in for a nasty reception if anything's changed."

"That's beautiful," teased Cecilia. "Minerva, you have been hanging out with us too long. Sorry, Hippolyte, she's definitely one of us now."

Hippolyte grimaced.

"What's that look?" asked Colin. "I thought you said this wouldn't be a problem."

"Don't worry about it… I hope."

As they prepared to enter the Fort dining room, a smiling Horace embraced the twins.

"I see my survival training actually paid off," quipped Horace. "Tales of your victory in Deniva reach far."

"Why, thank you, Horace," said Cecilia. "Though I'm sure they left out some details."

"Unfortunately, the myth of the invincibility of the Heavenly Twins is over," stated Cedric.

"Oh, so you both finally got some nasty scars!" teased Horace. "Whose are bigger?"

"Mine, of course," boasted Cecilia. "Multiple arrow wounds, including one right in the gut, but I had a whole company on me."

"Sorry, sis, I've got that one beat. I took three from an angel, one right in the center of my chest."

Raucous laughter filled the courtyard as the twins continued to argue over their wounds.

Mountain Retreat, The Tribal Encampment, Two Rotations Later

The Tribal Confederation was formed by the four great tribes of the West when they deemed it was no longer advantageous to stand against the Kingdoms by themselves. During this first Confederation there was the naming of a special 'general' who would lead the Tribes into war. This position was called the 'Ogle Tanka Un' or 'Skin-wearer' in the unified tongue. The first of these Ogle Tanka Uns was named Ares and he did success-fully lead the Tribes in a victory against the combined armies of Central Acadia and Napolitan. However, the position has been sparsely used since as the Chiefs of the Tribes have relied on the Alpha of the Wolf tribe to lead troops into battle.

"On the ways of the Tribes," General James Darius

The first horn was sounded from the cliffs of the far western Griffin Mountains. Horn blowers stationed throughout the bluffs picked up the call. The pleasing sounds of the tribal horns were music to Hippolyte's ears as she entered the pass with her sister, wolf, and Colin. The assassin was surprised to see such a heavily armored pass, including a full stockade for the tented city. However, it was apparent that as a result of Abaddon's treachery, no nation in the west would leave anything to chance. As the gate opened, the travelers witnessed the cheering throngs of all four tribes. In celebration of the Chief's safe return, they sang and danced as a large bonfire raged high and hard in the center of the encampment. Disbelieving the horns at first, Huskal ran out of his tent. A large smile crossed the old warrior's face as the granddaughters of Aramas returned.

"Hippolyte!" exclaimed Huskal. "Thank the spirits!"

Alerted to the new presence, Josephine and Reynard left their tent as well. Though overjoyed to see the girls, Josephine couldn't help her sense of foreboding at the presence of Colin Wilkins.

"Chief Reynard? Is that not Colin Wilkins?"

"I believe it is, Josephine. Did the Prime Eagle send him as her escort?"

"While, I do believe that few would dare to challenge a warrior with his reputation, I wonder if it's prudent to let an assassin into this encampment."

"Keep your weapons close."

Breathing a sigh of relief at the sight of her grandfather's most loyal allies, Hippolyte dismounted. As her sister jumped down next to her, the two embraced.

"Well, at least Huskal and Josephine are still alive," commented Hippolyte.

"We don't have to worry about an overthrow then," added Minerva. "Between them and Colin Wilkins no one should object to your rise to power."

"Maybe Adnar?" countered Hippolyte. "I see a few merchants, but where are the rest of the Vikings?"

"They're well defended in their own lands, sis. They probably were able to sail here and back without much difficulty. They know the rivers and channels into the mountains well."

"It's so good to be home. Colin, if you don't mind, let me take the lead here."

"Hippolyte, don't worry. I have no intention of whipping out Deathbringer and demanding to be made leader. Besides, I think I've got a dozen arrows trained on me right now."

"Oh boy, that's something we're going to have to remedy."

As she reached the central fire, Huskal rushed to Hippolyte and lifted her up in a tight embrace. On cue, Stryker let loose a loud howl. The other wolves in the encampment joined in unison to announce her return.

"Hippolyte, thank the spirits you've come back to us," cried Huskal. He set her down. Kneeling in front of her with his palms up, the Alpha remembered his place. As her grandfather had done many times before, Hippolyte placed her palms upon his.

"Forgive me, Great Chief of the Wolf Tribe, and rightful leader of the Tribal Confederation."

Irritated at all the attention paid to sister, Minerva cleared her throat. As she had aged significantly since they last saw her, many in the tribe did not recognize the mature version of the spunky little sister that left.

"Minerva?" inquired Huskal.

"In the flesh."

"How could I forget that smile and attitude? Welcome home." Huskal stood, grabbed Minerva, and embraced her. Flailing to break the embrace, the younger wolf tribe princess caught her breath as the old warrior let go.

"It's good to know some things never change," commented Minerva. "Those hugs still hurt."

Arrows still trained on him, Colin signaled Hippolyte to move the introductions along. Blushing in embarrassment at hanging her love interest out to dry, she stepped back and took his arm.

"My people, I present to you the man I have chosen to be my consort, Colin Wilkins."

To say that the announcement was met with a lukewarm response would be the understatement of the revolution. Many tribal members were simply waiting for the punch line. Colin seemed undeterred and stood there with all of his pride. Breaking the ice, Huskal approached him and extended his hand.

"So it is you. Are you not the assassin of the Prime Eagle, the one they call the Lunar Falcon?"

"I am his Excellency's Master Assassin," Colin said, nodding, as he took Huskal's hand.

At first, Huskal tried to outgrip Colin at the handshake. However, it was a mere seconds before the old warrior knew it was impossible with the young assassin's overpowering strength. Returning his eyes to the new chief, the Alpha sought guidance.

"And you love him, Great Chief?"

"With all my heart, and I declare it before the spirits and the fire."

"Then by Tribal Law we cannot refuse the right of the Chief to choose her consort. Welcome to the Tribe, Colin Wilkins!"

No longer silent, the tribal people let loose another cheer at the choosing of their chief's consort. All of the traditions of the tribes had been fulfilled and no one would dare question the will and heart of their leader if she was willing to make a declaration by the fire.

"I wish I came here bearing joyous news but I'm afraid we have much more serious issues to discuss," said Colin. "I was sent here for a reason."

"And that would be?" interrupted Josephine as she stepped forward to challenge Wilkins. "Despite my happiness for my chief, I worry about the motives of the Prime Eagle."

"Prince Cedric Rhone is preparing to launch an assault on the City of Verian. He is calling for all warriors of good will to join him in the largest battle ever fought on Terminus Mundus."

"Another treaty, Lunar Falcon?" continued Josephine. "We've seen what happens when we attempt to abide by the written words of your people."

"Not this time, Josephine. No promises, no treaties, no armistice—Master Cedric is simply calling on the Tribes to help him destroy evil."

"You expect us to trust the man who is the most reviled in the all of the Tribes?" attacked Josephine once more.

"It is your choice, but I'm sure you are aware of the price the Syrus Clan has already had to pay."

Posha was standing there with her fellow tribesmen. The mere mention of that slaughter caused her to break out in tears and kneel to the ground in prayer.

"Yes," answered Huskal. "Honor compels us to demand vengeance for their loss, once more at the hands of Acadian swords."

"It's not only the Syrus Clan," added Hippolyte. "These same enemies in Verian were responsible for the death of my Grandfather."

"We know this, Great Chief. The Acadians cannot be trusted."

"These eyes have seen more than you can imagine, Huskal. No matter what safety or sanctuary I sought with my friends over these past five revolutions, unspeakable evils have followed and tried to destroy us. The Acadians are advised by a creature known as Abaddon. Colin can inform you more about his kind. Maximilian Luminas has been following his orders this entire time. He slaughtered my Grandfather and the fellow members of our tribe. We must call the Tribal Confederation together and answer the call of the Prime Eagle to march to war."

"War is a last resort among our people, and many will not understand your motives," said Huskal. "However, you are the Chief of this Tribe now, and by right, the Chief of Chiefs in the Tribal Confederation. If this is your will I will not question it."

"Fear not, Hippolyte," interrupted Josephine. "The Myotis Clan will add you as well. I will send the longboats from the Viking merchants here to call on Adnar for aid."

"The Syrus Clan will aid you as well as we can," said Posha. "The blood of our pacifist kin demands it."

"Good," said a gracious Hippolyte. "Obviously I've been gone a long time. Chief Reynard, there is much we need to discuss."

"You may join me in my tent for now," offered Reynard. "I'm sure we will have many volunteers to set up a new Chief of Chiefs tent immediately."

"I thank you. Captain Huskal, I need to be briefed on anything that happened."

"Briefed? Chief Hippolyte, what does that mean?"

"Sorry, I've been around steel-bellies too long. I just want to know everything that went on while I was gone these past revolutions. We have much to do and very little time to do it."

"Of course, my Chief."

As Hippolyte and Colin joined Reynard in the tent, Minerva got a devious smile on her face. Surrounded by an army of tribal children demanding to hear stories of her adventures, Minerva pulled three bags off of her saddle.

"Who wants to see something amazing?" asked Minerva rhetorically.

Pulling out the desiccated head of one of the Jacobin Legions from her battle in the Crypt five revolutions ago caused the crowd to draw back in speechless awe.

"There we were, five long revolutions ago..." recounted Minerva as she finally had the full attention of everyone in the tribe.

Inside Reynard's tent, the three stood over a wooden table. Colin noticed a small map on the table showing the area.

"Please allow an old man to make a few observations, Hippolyte," begged Reynard. "Your Grandfather's vision and teachings were not in vain. I can see he lives on in you."

"Yes Reynard. I didn't understand why he sent us to Verian at first, but now I know. He wanted me to discover whom I could trust and whom I couldn't. Living among them was the only way, and I have a new respect for them and their leader, Queen Cassandra Acadia."

"But she is still an Acadian."

"She is not like the other Acadians because of the Elf blood that flows in her. Besides, Cedric Rhone trusts her and he sees things in people others cannot. We can only avenge the evil brought upon us if we stand with the power of these two great leaders."

"The Titans are honorable foes. King Frederick Rhone once called upon us to fight with them and we answered. For risking his life to protect you and Minerva, we owe the Prime Eagle the courtesy of listening to his offer. We will ready our armies to march. Now, there is one more matter to discuss. No Chief has every married an outsider before. Though they dare not speak publicly now, I am sure that many will object."

"It is not against our ways, Reynard. Many have steel-belly husbands or wives."

"If he is to be your choice, I offer no objection. However, it will not be appropriate for the Chief and her consort to ride separately in battle."

"I have already contemplated this. Colin Wilkins will be named Ogle Tanka Un."

"Such an honor has not been bestowed upon a member of the Tribal Confederation in revolutions. Yet, you would have an outsider wear the skin?"

"Pardon me for my ignorance of your ways, but what exactly is the Ogle Tanka Un?" asked Colin.

"He is the one chosen by the tribe to wear the wolf skin cape into battle as a leader in war," explained Huskal. "It's a mantle appropriate for the consort of the Chief of Chiefs."

"If we are to join this battle, we must fight under one commander," injected Hippolyte. "I have faced the armies of our enemy in combat already and they are formidable. We must stand as one. Colin has tactical knowledge of our foes we don't possess."

"Even though many in our tribe will not admit it, a Titan would be suitable to lead in times of war. I am happy with your choice, Chief Hippolyte. We will initiate him into our ways."

Reynard took out a sharp dagger. Colin put his hand up.

"I've been circumcised already if this has anything to do with that. Wow, I didn't know you guys did that also."

"I do not know of what you speak, Ogle Tanka Un Wilkins. I am simply going to carve a wolf head into your chest to mark you as one of us."

"Can I get drunk first?"

"Come now, the skin-wearer must be tougher than that."

"He's pulling your leg, Colin," teased Hippolyte. "The knife is just for show. We'll use the same magic that placed the tattoo on Prince Cedric's hand."

"Good, because that would have been a real problem if I wasn't allowed to get drunk!"

"Don't be so serious, sweetheart!"

"Actually, I'm impressed, Ogle Tanka Un," countered Reynard. "Most run out of the room when I brandish the knife. No one has ever asked for a drink before. Now come, we feast tonight, for our Chief has returned to us."

Port Talus, Napolitan, Three Rotations Later

It is traditional that when a son of Napolitan returns to Port Talus that the Captains of the Watch take up the call. However, such a call often has to do with the manner of his return.

General James Darius

While he didn't expect cheering throngs and a chariot for a hero's return, Cagius did not expect the silence of a graveyard as he entered the city of his birth. As he passed under the Dragon holding the RPQN engraving, the Captain of the Watch spotted him, but did not take up the call to arms.

"The last time I entered the city the Captain took up the call," said Cagius.

"What do you expect, my Lord?" commented Valentine. "No one in this city is going to consider you victorious!"

"After the personal hell I've gone through these past five revolutions, Valentine?"

"This isn't Dragonstone, Cagius! Sure, they gave us a wild celebration, but you do not command the same respect in this city as you do with the Legions. Besides, did you notice the armor on the Captain of the Watch?"

"Yeah, it was Praetorian black. A Legionnaire is supposed to be the Captain of the Watch so he serves as the last warning to any Legion who dare enter the city."

"Very strange."

As his uncle and mentor argued over their arrival, Joshua soaked in the sights and sounds of his home for the first time. Passing civilians in the streets, many of the populace looked at him with a certain degree of awkwardness. They wondered who exactly was this giant carrying the Sacred Shield and Excalibur. The rumors of Julius' son had reached Port Talus long ago and this appeared to be the fulfillment of those whispers. The six foot seven Paladin wished he had somewhere to hide.

"Hail Prince Cagius!" screamed a familiar voice.

Turning his head to the Senate steps, the Napolitan prince saw Marcus Polonius and group of Senators racing toward him. The former legionnaire grabbed him by both of his wrists as was the traditional greeting, causing a smile finally to cross Cagius' face.

"Marcus, it's good to see a familiar face."

"It's been five long revolutions, but finally you've come home. I just knew that you were still alive out there."

"It's been desperate, and I nearly lost my head a bunch of times. What's going on, Marcus? What's with all of the extra Praetorian throughout the city?"

"We needed you desperately. Your brother's former squire has been made head of the Praetorian! Vincenzo has made many changes to the lists and uses his guard as a personal army."

"Has my father lost his mind? The son of the snake as his bodyguard! Has he learned nothing of the mistakes of King Stephen?"

"I fear your father does not learn much these rotations. Judge Gravius handles most of the duties of running Napolitan these dark rotations."

"What of my mother?"

"She is doing her best to keep up a sense of normalcy at the Palace. Your father believed for a long time that he had lost both of his sons. You can't understand what that does to a man, especially an old soldier."

Marcus broke his hold on Cagius and performed a similar greeting on Valentine. Finally he reached Joshua.

"I thought all of the giants of legend were dead," joked Marcus. "What have you been feeding this one?"

Joshua smiled at the ribbing, but didn't say a word.

"I believe you have your suspicions," suggested Valentine. "However, I think it's best we keep them unspoken for now."

"Agreed, Valentine," responded Polonius.

"Take me to my brother's tomb." commanded Cagius.

Polonius nodded and led the three on a short walk. As they ascended the hill, Marcus droned on about certain political changes he had been trying to fight, but Cagius was too focused on his task to hear. At the top, two Praetorian guards stood watch over the site and the carvings in the stone tomb bore the name and crest of Julius Imperia.

"Open it!" ordered the Napolitan prince.

"My Prince, have you gone mad?" asked the first guard.

"Even if we could obey your orders, it's been five revolutions. The stench would be overwhelming!" reasoned the other guard.

"The prince of Napolitan just gave you a direct order," seethed Valentine. "Now open the damn tomb unless you want to find out how long you can swim in the Sea of Serenity while wearing full armor!"

Intimidated by the men and the silent Joshua cracking his knuckles, the Praetorian joined Cagius and the others in removing the stone from the top of the tomb.

"Prince Cagius, I know you've been gone for a while, but I sure would like to know what you're doing," wondered Polonius.

"Just call it a soldier's hunch!"

Lifting the slab, they dropped it to the side. No stench left the tomb, and the Praetorians present were shocked to see the interred Julius in same condition as the rotation they had laid him in the tomb five revolutions ago.

"Why is there no decomposition?" pondered the first guard aloud.

"Because this isn't my brother!" exclaimed Cagius with an edge in his voice.

Reaching into his brother's jaw, Cagius ripped the mandible clear off. As he felt the composition in his hand, the Napolitan prince knew it to be nothing more than wax and sawdust. Angrily smashing it into the ground, Cagius stood at the edge of the mausoleum and let out a large cry.

"I don't know what foul science or craft that Virgus and the others are using, but these sins are unforgivable! It was bad enough when I thought it was a sample...but they..."

"They hacked his body to pieces," reiterated Valentine with the same edge as his prince. "To have the audacity to send this mannequin back as well..."

Frustrated, Joshua lifted the stone slab and destroyed it against the ground. Taking a few breaths to cool himself down, expecting Valentine to bite his head off again, the massive Paladin was shocked to see a thumbs up flashed at him.

"Bring my father here!" Cagius ordered the Praetorian. "Tell him that I am desecrating my brother's tomb and your task will be less difficult."

More frightened by the Prince than the Caesar at this point, the guards did as Cagius commanded. Waiting in front of the tomb with focused eyes, Cagius crossed his arms.

"Listen, Joshua, Constantine is probably still devastated over the loss of your father," advised Valentine. "He lived in self-denial over the fact that Julius never had an affair with your mother. So I would not further antagonize him by bringing up your lineage."

"Don't worry, Valentine. The strong, silent type seems to be working out pretty well so far."

"Very good, son. Just let me do all the talking. Hey Marcus, you might want to get out of here before the explosions."

"Are you kidding me? This is the most spine anyone has dared to show around here in five revolutions. This is going to be worth the price of admission."

Even from the mausoleum, the call to muster was heard. A lone chariot tore through the city streets and up the hill. When it stopped, the elderly James raced from his escort as if his youth returned to him. Unused to seeing his mentor blubbering, Cagius accepted the hearty welcome by the old legionnaire.

"I didn't know what to expect when they made the report at the palace," started James. "I just knew…I just knew that you were still alive, that a son of Imperia would still be with us." Strained from the ride, the retired Legate pulled out a handkerchief and coughed hard. Cagius noticed blood.

"What happened?" inquired a shocked Cagius.

"It's cancer, inoperable and incurable."

"How long have you had it, Legate?"

"I should have been dead a revolution ago according to the doctors. However, something inside me wouldn't let me die until I knew one of you had come home."

"I'm going to miss you, old man."

"Hey, I'm not gone yet! We've got one more battle to fight. You left me in a very bad way at the palace when I heard reports of someone desecrating your brother's tomb. I figured I'd better come out here first and either kill the imposter or talk some sense into him before the raging dragon that is your father gets here."

"It was the best way to get his attention. My father must be made to listen to reason. My brother is not in that mausoleum."

"That can't be true. Why would the Acadians send a fake back to us? It would only enrage your father."

"The enemy is using our tactics, James!" Cagius said as he handed James the wax and sawdust mandible. "They cut his body to pieces. They're using his genes to create an army of soldiers and they're using his mind to engrain our tactics into them."

The old legionnaire stared at the mandible and wept.

"I guess a part of me knew that…the body was too perfect… someone engaged in a desperate battle should have been more wounded…I am sorry for not seeing through the defeat. If they've done this with your brother—"

Noticing Joshua standing next to Valentine for the first time caused James to stop midsentence. "This is not one of them, is it?" reasoned James. "No, this is Julius' son, I can tell. Valentine, how could you? How did you know to train him as a Paladin?"

"I was able to adapt your training methods. Based on our circumstances, it became necessary to strengthen our ranks. Excalibur is Joshua's legacy and as such he deserves the class before you. The boy may be a bit rash and he's got a monster of a temper like his father; however, I am proud to stand alongside someone as brave and passionate as him in battle."

"That's a fitting testament coming from a man like Valentine. Joshua Imperia, whether you want it or not, you carry the legendary weapon and armor of your father, a true Paladin and tribune of Napolitan. You'd do best to use them wisely."

"Yes, Legate. Every rotation, I stride to carry on the fight against the atrocities brought forth by this darkness."

The approach of Praetorian boots against the cobblestone city roads was unmistakable. James assumed his place next to Marcus. The former legionnaires conspired to stop Constantine in case he tried to take any drastic actions against Cagius. Upon seeing his father in his chariot for the first time in five revolutions, the Napolitan prince couldn't believe how frail and weak he looked. There was still a commanding presence in his green eyes, but he appeared to have aged a hundred revolutions in the short time. Decorated in the most expensive and flamboyant black Praetorian armor, the man

Cagius once knew as a boy approached. Vincenzo Gravius removed his golden helmet with a black plume and smirked at the prince.

"So, the runaway finally decided to come home," taunted Vincenzo.

"Yeah, well I didn't see you volunteering to stay behind and carry on the fight," remarked Cagius.

"Don't take my actions for cowardice. Your brother ordered me away when I was desperate to help."

"I see you've done pretty well for yourself."

"The Caesar knows the men he can trust."

"You know, Vincenzo, I liked you a lot better when you were falling over drunk."

Unhappy at the comment, he cleared the way for Constantine and Marguerite to approach their son.

"Cagius!" screamed Marguerite. Unable to contain her joy and forgetting her station, mother embraced son with hugs, kisses, and many tears.

"I couldn't bear the thought of losing the two of you. Julius was hard enough, but if I had lost both my sons…"

Joshua shielded his face and eyes from the Caesar and his wife to save his uncle from further agony and rage. Constantine allowed Marguerite her precious moments.

"Very well, Marguerite," ordered Constantine. "You've had your moment. Now I prefer to know what madness has overtaken my son."

"Do you think my mind has truly failed me, Father? I feel that I've seen things more clearly than ever before."

"I didn't realize grave robbing was in your nature, or is it mutilation!"

"The only mutilation that happened to your beloved son was done by his captors, not me."

"The Acadians assured me they left the body unspoiled save for the treasures you robbed from him."

"Very well father, I am not offended that you value the trustworthiness of the Acadians over your own flesh and blood. Come gaze upon your son. Perhaps then I will relieve the sickness that has infested my country these past five revolutions."

Horrified at his son's defiant tone, Constantine considered leaving him where he stood or taking a spear from one the Praetorians and running him through. His curiosity got the better of him; he never remembered his second son being so sure of anything before. As he set his eyes on the body inside, Constantine could not believe no deterioration had taken place. Only the slightly melted wax and sawdust from the missing mandible blemished the perfection. He fell back slightly, and Valentine caught his Caesar out of fear he was having a heart attack.

"Martha Heinrich was incredibly specific in her description," explained Cagius. "Virgus needed the raw materials at his genetic level and information locked in his brain on how to lead and command an army. So they ripped it out and experimented on it. Most likely they melted his body down into some genetic soup. Now, get ready Dad, because this is the ultimate haymaker to the jaw: they created an army cloning that genetic material, which they intend to send against us."

Cagius reached into his saddlebag and pulled out the preserved head of the fallen Elite. It was as if his son was taken away from him again. Despite his desire to scream, nothing came out of Constantine's mouth. After a few moments, the weakness and frailty that consumed him left the Caesar. Shoving Valentine away, Constantine stood tall with tears in his eyes. He walked to Cagius and took both of his forearms in the same traditional greeting of a legionnaire. The Caesar pulled his son tight to his chest in an embrace he had never felt before. No one standing there could believe their eyes.

"I haven't always had you close to my heart," Constantine said with regret. "I hated you because I saw myself in you. We were two wretched Legion grunts that rose to command, while your brother was the tall and graceful Paladin. I thought that was what Napolitan needed, a Caesar who could separate himself from the Legion to never be associated with that damned coup against Draconius again. It was only to the darkness or to your mother alone that I ever made mention of the pride I had in you. It took five revolutions and the believed loss of both my precious sons to realize that."

"Father, I never sought recognition and I never would have done anything to insult my brother. It was embarrassing to believe that my father was disappointed in me because I was born."

"That is no more, because we can no longer afford it. You are my only son now, and the last in line to carry on as heir. Since you stopped by Titanus first, I assume you know that Taylor Yueh has been traveling here regularly."

"Even if I hadn't heard it from her lips, I wouldn't have put it past Civilia."

"I know Cedric Rhone is alive and part me held out hope that your brother might have been alive and well."

"There's no hope on that, Dad. He literally died in my arms and I took his armor and weapons to prevent them from falling into the hands of the enemy. I would have taken the body as well, but I couldn't risk carrying it through the Acadian crypt. With my whole being, I wish I had."

"What does Cedric Rhone need of Napolitan? I'll give him anything he asks."

"Cedric wants us to prepare the Legions to march. However, we aren't to do anything until he gives us a sign."

"A sign?" offered James with a hearty laugh. "If I know anything about *La Morte Angelus*, his sign will be the stuff of legends."

"Very well, Cagius, you've been promoted," commanded Constantine. "As our Legate Maximus, you will serve as the commander of five legions in the coming battle. Tomorrow you will ride to Fort Dragonstone and make preparations. I will join in the coming rotations with the rest of the battle escort."

"I had hoped our son would be able to spend a little more time at home," countered Marguerite.

"We don't have the time, my dear wife. I'm sorry. Fear not, we shall slaughter the finest of the stocks tonight to have a hero's feast for my son. After five revolutions away from Dragon's Rest, he surely deserves it. Come, join your father on his chariot and ride with me." Constantine put his arm around his son.

"Father, please, there is someone in my company I need you to meet, but I want it to be done privately. I beg this one boon of you."

The Caesar nodded, dismissing the Praetorian. Only James, Marcus, and Marguerite stayed behind.

"Cagius, I don't understand all of this attention for Valentine."

"It's not Valentine, Father." Cagius went over to Joshua. For the first time, the massive Paladin dared to lift his eyes. Marguerite brought her hands to mouth without having to be told. Constantine took a few deep breaths.

"May I present Joshua, the son of Julius and Felicia of House Yannis of Evengard."

"I thought you said she was Cassandra's handmaiden," retorted Constantine.

"We all thought a lot of things Caesar," added Valentine. "It is apparent that no Kingdom in the Alliance trusted the Acadians. Felicia was to serve as a deep cover bodyguard for Cassandra from her own people."

"This is worse than I could have possibly imagined," reasoned Constantine as he hung his head. "Let him stand in battle with the legacy of his father, I owe my son that much. However, we must publicly disown him."

"Constantine!" exclaimed his wife. "Do you dare take your grudge against that woman so far?"

"Can you imagine the chaos that would arise if all of Evengard were to learn of my son's actions? Camdem Jenitzen would never allow Saria anywhere near Cagius if he learned of Julius' shame. We can't have Evengard at our throat if this alliance is to succeed."

"This seems cowardly, Father."

"If he is Julius' son, I'm sure he can take it. My son had the heart of a dragon, so to the world you will be known as Joshua Dragonheart, an unacknowledged bastard. Perhaps some rotation we can correct this horrendous abomination of justice I've placed upon you."

Constantine and Marguerite approached Joshua. They embraced him at the same time, but the Caesar could not look him in the eyes. It was not only the shame weighing on his heart, but also the ghost of his own son.

As the tearful reunion took place at the mausoleum, Judge Matthias Gravius was working at his desk. Two Praetorian guards escorted Norville Warrington in the room. Cleaned up and dressed in his noble clothing again, the Senate President leader felt at home once more.

"Judge Gravius, I must thank you for your hospitality. It's been quite a while since I had running water, let alone hot water. The clothes are a nice fit as well."

"Enslaved on a communal farm is a cruel fate for anyone," said Judge Gravius.

"I expected the interrogations I received from the Legion, but I thought I'd get a warmer reception here. Surely you don't think I'm a traitor?"

"President Warrington, I don't know what to believe. The last thing Napolitan needs is for two hundred nobles to show up claiming to be Central Acadia refugees. Titanus is clamoring for a war that might decide the fate of all those who dare to wrest power away from absolute monarchs. So, yes, I find the situation a little too convenient that Luminas just let you go."

"Luminas is gathering anyone loyal to him for the upcoming battle. Individuals like our little group don't see things his way. We replaced a king that listened to the concerns of nobles and the Senate with a ruthless insane autocrat. His court is a scene of debauchery and he has surrounded himself with foul creatures to defend his false crown."

"All that aside, I am cursed with Caesar so outraged at the death of his first-born son that he has allowed a nation of fanatics to convince him to participate in what should be a personal crusade. That being said, you mentioned a deal."

"Before we left, I was forced to carry a sealed message to Napolitan. Knowing the close-mindedness of the Caesar and his militarist advisor, I felt you would be the best one to open it."

"That was wise, at least. Let's take a look, shall we?" Matthias opened the seal and read the document. After a few lines he passed it to Norville Warrington, who examined it as well.

"So he'd willingly cede power?" pondered Norville.

"I doubt it," reasoned Matthias. "Perhaps he'd cede the throne to Marie, but probably in name only for now."

"There is a problem. Stephen declared publicly that Marie would be his heir, but when he was dying he made the same declaration for Cassandra."

"Another war of succession," said Matthias. "You'd think after five revolutions we'd have moved beyond this. It does present an opportunity, if a strong case could be made."

"I didn't become Senate President by pencil-pushing. I was also known as a master debater. It will be tough sell, but I might be able to make the case that this is not a crusade, but simply a succession dispute between two selfish young women."

"Publicly I must save face and stand at the side of my Caesar. However, I will dispatch messengers to my friends here and in Evengard to back your play."

"What goes on with the Elves?" Norville asked. "I've heard rumors of a power play."

"Some say that Camdem Jenitzen has gone drunk with power since the death of Cerwin Faulkner. Of course, these are only rumors, but it wouldn't take much for Camdem to turn his back on Cedric Rhone. He never liked him, even before he began his relationship with Cassandra."

"Well, Judge, I have a lot of preparation ahead of me. I'm going against Cedric Rhone, after all, and he will enflame passions throughout the alliance. Once again, thank you for your hospitality." Norville paused. "The Praetorian, however, make me nervous."

"The only person who should be nervous around the Praetorian is the Caesar himself. Once I willed my son into the position of their leader, I bought and paid for most of the replacements on the list. They answer to him and to me now. One word of warning though, Norville, Valentine is back, so if there is a girl around, don't say a word or do anything. He will be watching."

"I understand."

BROOKE RUN, EVENGARD

According to the Ancient Scriptures, the borders of Evengard were defined by the Divine Father. Brooke Run was the central fortress built when Saulides was anointed as King of Evengard. It was lost to the Dwarves in the final defeat of Saulides, but was retaken by Hayden Marisol. During Hayden's reign, it was abandoned at the time of the Dragon Rider's Rebellion. This has led to the jinx that no Elf can successfully lead a defense. Twice sacked but never razed, the Holy Temple dedicated to the Divine Father is prophesized to last for all eternity.

Cerwin Faulkner

Nervously riding Maiden through the Forest of the Eternal Spring, Amuro could feel the presence of eyes all around her. Saria rode close to her sister and Malcolm held his bow in his hand.

"Never before have I felt so many pairs of eyes on me," commented Amuro. "It's a shame, really. I spent all that time and effort over the revolutions dolling myself up for royal balls and I draw the most attention in my battle clothes."

"They could always be staring at your sister," teased Malcolm.

"I wish we never tried to develop your sense of humor, Malcolm. Let me have at least one moment of triumph before it crumbles to reality."

The stone walls of Brooke Run sprouted up among the thousand-revolution-old trees still bearing the scars from the two sackings. Roaring behind the walled city were two massive waterfalls flowing into two streams. This barrier served as a natural moat around the walls. At break-neck speed, the three witnessed Captain Sirius and a troop of Elf lancers on hard approach. Not knowing if they were friend or foe, Amuro drew Enhancer and readied for battle. Submissively putting his hands up to indicate parlay, the albino Elf captain pulled his troop up short.

"Lady Amuro, we don't have much time," said an exasperated Sirius. "Your father Camdem had Lord Alistair and other nobles placed under house arrest."

"Sirius, I had a long ride. I know we've had our differences, but you're going too far."

"I wish I had lost my mental faculties, Marshal. I've got to get Lord Malcolm out of here or I else I fear what your father might due to him."

Malcolm studied Sirius. He was never fond of the conspiracy theories and musings that brewed in his talented subordinate's mind. Yet, the panic in the captain's face and his utter concern for the ranger's safety was undeniable.

"Amuro, I think I'll play along with the Captain's game for now. Sirius may be a little crazy, but he's loyal."

"Your loss, but don't worry, I'll scout the situation out for you and clean this whole mess up," said a determined Amuro. "Just be careful, especially around the Captain."

A quick wink to Sirius defused the tense situation. As Amuro and her sister pressed on, Malcolm and Sirius rode the opposite way.

"So my father is imprisoned?"

"I'm sorry, Malcolm. I did my best to warn him and the others ahead of time, but no one listened to me. I'm afraid my reputation preceded me and most determined it to be another one of my conspiracy theories."

A full camp had been set up away from the city. At this point, Malcolm reasoned that Sirius might not be crazy. A large number of soldiers, mages, nobles, rangers, and priests occupied the surrounding area.

"How long has this been going on?" asked Malcolm.

"About two revolutions ago, news leaked to us that Cerwin Faulkner was dead. I assume since he's not traveling with you the rumors are true."

"He got killed nearly five revolutions ago in our escape from Verian. Jacob Acadia's Revenant stabbed him clear through his heart and he called on his meteor spell to bury the undead Jacobin Legions alive in the Royal Crypt."

"I was afraid of that. After we received the news, Camdem took up the throne in Hayden's palace. He claimed in the absence of a prophet and with the death of the Judge of the Change the most powerful noble in Evengard was rightfully King. When the Chief Priest objected he had him arrested and installed a puppet, who in turn willed the crown to him. He used an ancient law to have your father imprisoned for sedition due to his blood ties to Sharon Fenidor."

"My father never spoke to his cousin, even before she married Stephen."

"You'll find details like that matter not to Camdem," Sirius said. "I figured that he might attempt to use you as a bargaining chip or shoot you on sight, so it was best to separate you from the girls. Camdem is obsessed with one of his daughters becoming Queen, so the girls should be safe for now. Besides, Amuro needs to see her father's lust for power with her own eyes."

"We can't just stay here. Cedric is going to march on Verian, and soon."

"I follow the will of the Divine Father and I have prayed long and hard, Malcolm. It has been revealed to me that I must not siege Brooke Run. Thus, I have developed a second plan. Come with me."

The Elves dismounted and entered Sirius' tent. The Elf ranger stared at a nexus of clippings, strings, notes, and pictures. Shaking his head at the bizarre rantings and conclusions of the loyal captain,

Malcolm wondered if he had made the right decision following Sirius.

"There are many things that the Elves once knew, but have forgotten. I can lead troops in battle, but I lack the charisma and discipline to be a true leader. These people need you, Malcolm. It is fortunate that you have returned to us."

"I appreciate that, Sirius. However, I am not marching against Amuro."

"I never wanted you to. Did you know that I was the ward of Cerwin Faulkner? My appearance had made me an outcast. I was known as the 'Snow Elf' for so long I spent too many rotations wallowing in my own self-pity rather than devoting myself to my true calling. Cerwin took me into his home and he taught me. The more knowledge I assimilated, the more I craved. A wretched addiction, I must admit, but a necessary evil. Trust what is told to you, Malcolm, but always verify, for absolute truth is only known through the Divine Father. My life's work has led me to conclude that Gweyn Marisol's murderer was indeed Camdem Jenitzen."

Sighing, Malcolm regretted following Sirius. He knew Sirius was giving him another lecture on history rather than dealing with the important issues. As he moved to leave the tent, Sirius grabbed his arm.

"Camdem's advances were spurned by Gweyn time and time again. His true desire was not her but rather Hayden's legacy. When he found she had taken another love and been impregnated, Camdem became insanely jealous. Lord Jenitzen would no longer accept the Father's will, but would make his own path to power. As she lay defenseless in childbirth, her powerful magic suppressed by many excessive enchantments to protect the child, he stabbed her repeatedly in the belly to kill her and the child."

"Every Elf knows that legend, and we also know the legend that the child survived."

"The child did survive, Malcolm. Cerwin Faulkner was brought in and performed an emergency procedure at the behest of the dying Queen. He saved the child's life and succeeded in whisking him away to a foreign land so the infant would escape Camdem's treachery. Now that you have come back to protect and lead these people, I ride to the Kingdom of Titanus to consult with Lord Wilhelm von Angelhardt, who knows the exact location of the Elf."

"What good is all this now at a time of war?"

"This Elf is the only one who can draw Lord Jenitzen out and expose him for traitor and murderer that he is. This is the will of the Divine Father and the only way that the she-elf we both love can ascend to the throne."

"Why is your goal to make Amuro Queen, Sirius? Why not ascend this Elf instead? It is his birthright."

"There are some secrets that must stay silent, Lord Malcolm, but have faith that I serve the will of the Divine Father, even before my own."

The two left the tent. A fresh horse and ten Elf lancers joined Captain Sirius. Leaping to mount his horse, the Captain grabbed Malcolm's hand once more before he left.

"Cedric is calling for 'all those of good will' to look for his signal," explained Malcolm. "When this happens, I will lead these people from here and follow him."

"I expect nothing less of you, my Lord," said Sirius. "Lord Cedric is a holy man and will destroy the evil that threatens all of Terminus Mundus. However, if we cannot defeat the enemy within first, all will be lost."

The Elf lancer escort broke hard from the camp and rode away into the forest. One of the lancers flanking Sirius spoke to his commander.

"Sir, why did you not tell Malcolm the name of the Elf we seek?"

"There are many reasons," expounded Sirius. "It is best for him to maintain an aspect of plausible deniability when we break the news. Besides, if I told him that the Elf I seek is Christian DeVries, I doubt he would have believed me, anyway."

Despite the events around them, Amuro and Saria slowly approached the stone gates of Evengard. The surrounding battlement parapets of the city were adorned with statues of the Patriarchs, the Great Prophet, the General, the Judges, and Hayden Marisol. The Elf Marshal could feel something was wrong just by looking at the soldiers on the wall. They didn't look like her kinsman at all, rather members of her father's personal army. As the gates opened, the soft grass and bubbling streams gave way to a line of blooming trees. The serene feel calmed the fears of the she-elf momentarily as did her approaching father.

"Amuro!" screamed her father. "Saria! I see you are both unharmed. When we heard what had happened in Castle Acadia, we feared the worst."

As the maidens dismounted, Camdem embraced both of them.

"We've paid for it with many lives," explained Amuro.

"So the rumors were true," reasoned Camdem. "The old man is finally dead."

"Father, please, Cerwin died saving all of us! He should be honored for his heroism!"

"Amuro, you are so naïve. Cerwin Faulkner was the only thing standing in the way of our claims, he and his so-called visions he received from the Divine Father. Setting himself up as 'Judge of the Change' to transition from the Marisol line! The old wizard was simply trying to regain his former glory. Well, the matter has finally been settled. Where is the ranger? Was he killed, too?"

Thinking carefully for a moment, the Elf Marshal pondered her next step. Overcome by a viciousness she had never seen in her father before, Saria found herself reaching for her whip, determined to use it if necessary.

"Malcolm fell in the Battle of Deniva," mentioned Amuro, changing the inflection in her voice to sorrow. "He was killed defending my sister and I from many foes."

As if on cue, Saria turned on the tears to back up her sister's claims.

"Pity. I suppose it doesn't matter. I have to find suitable husbands for the both of you, anyway. How can we trust a family who produced a wretched traitor like Sharon?"

"Father, Cedric Rhone is marching on Verian..."

"Of course he is. Well, I can't afford to have either of you gallivanting off into meaningless battles anymore, not when the mantle of leadership has fallen onto our great family."

"Meaningless? How can a confrontation against the forces of evil be anything but our duty?"

"It has never been our duty! The foolish Alliance that Hayden Marisol dragged us into with Titanus has cost us too much in blood and treasure over the revolutions. If the Titans continue to play Sentinel on Terminus Mundus, let it be their war. We Elves make our own destiny from this point on, independent of the old ways."

"Father, Titanus is calling on all nations for aid in this war. They will demand we honor our commitments."

"I owe the Titan prince an explanation, and for his bravery it will be done in person so that all will know the meaning of my actions. I have been informed of this so-called sign that Prince Rhone will give us. When that event comes, we will meet and I will render my Final Judgment."

"What judgment will that be?" asked Amuro.

"Our period of interaction with the lesser races of this world is over. Our mages will seal the barrier to the Forest, and our people will be forever protected."

"That is not my wish!" exclaimed an angry Amuro. "If that was the wish of the people of Evengard, where are the other lords and priests? Why does your personal army hold the garrison?"

"In the start of everything new, certain unpopular actions must be taken that can only be understood later on. These so-called swashbuckling adventures you were determined to have all of your life are over. You're the heir to your people now," Camdem shouted. "ACT LIKE ONE!"

In disgust, Camdem left his two daughters without another word. The heavy stone door was sealed behind them and Amuro knew she had no escape. The tears of her sister were loudly dripping behind her. Taking the younger maiden in her arms, the two sisters had a good cry.

"If we do this… I'll never see…" stammered Saria. "I'll never see Cagius again."

"This isn't over yet. Malcolm's out there. I can't believe Sirius was right about all of this, but I just don't understood why Father would do this. Divine Father, Family, Country—they have always guided me well. No, we mustn't forsake our family yet, Saria. When he sees everyone together, he'll see the truth."

CASTLE TITAN, TITANUS, SEVEN ROTATIONS AFTER THE RETURN

It is no surprise that on Terminus Mundus, the most dazzling of all of the military parades is the Titan Call of the Cavalry to Arms. Since the time of Ulysses Rhone, the Call has been a union of the three things valued most by the Titan Rider: God, Country, and Family. Pipers blast the challenge from the top of the parapets to the borders of the Realm. All Riders who hear the Call come to answer the challenge fit only for warriors. These warriors are granted the favor of God because no one else would ever grant them such a blessing.

Titan Battle Manual, Prince Cedric Rhone

Deep in the bowels of Castle Titan, the pinnacle of their technology, the Titan War Room bustled with activity. Unlike the smaller version adapted to serve the embassy in Verian, one hundred uniformed technicians and twenty supervisors worked in front of monitors and listening devices; they were connected to every event happening on the planet. Large screens around the room showed maps of each country. Thermal heat imaging showed concentrations of troops on the borders of Evengard and at Fort Dragonstone. Fully armored for battle, Cedric, Cecilia, and DeVries worked the room. Examining various reports coming in, the three moved to a large circular table in the middle of the room. Christian called up the three dimensional image of Central Acadia as the Titan prince set his Rising Moon Helmet down on the table.

"While our reports of gathering troops at the borders of Napolitan, Evengard, and along the Griffin Mountains have been encouraging, I'm afraid a new problem has emerged," described Christian. Shifting the map so it followed the path of the royal road, the Titan operative brought up the rendering of Fort Orion. The same thermal images showed the fort to be well occupied.

"Our crux is Fort Orion," continued Christian. "Our spies report that Sir Karstak stands at the head of the Templar Army and they have reinforced the garrison at the Fort. We dare not go around such an important structure and lay siege to Verian. If we do not deal with Fort Orion, they will be at our rear."

"I fear your assessment is accurate," agreed Cedric.

"Cedric, if we lay siege to Fort Orion, too many cycles will pass. Even the outnumbered Templars could hold that structure easily. You must abandon your plans to launch an abrupt attack on Central Acadia and call on our allies to lay provisions for the siege of Fort Orion."

"The plan will go off unaltered," ordered a smiling Cedric. "Well, except for one little wrinkle that you wouldn't have been aware of until now."

"All right, do you care to let me in on your little secret?" retorted Christian.

"I'm surprised a smart Elf like you didn't figure it out. Then again, some family secrets are best kept in the family. Care to do the honors, sis?"

"My pleasure, Cedric. Bring up the design and technical schematics on Fort Orion." Signaling the technicians to upload the files onto the center table, Cecilia showed Christian a maze of tunnels running underneath the Fort.

"The Acadians had no experience with building forts," explained Cecilia. "They contracted Titanus to do the work for them on Fort Orion. Of course, we secretly retained all of the building plans and put in a few surprises just in case the Acadians ever thought to betray us some rotation. However, I don't think my ancestors saw this one coming."

Pointing his finger, Cedric drew Christian's attention to a location ten kilometers southeast of the fort, where the sewer system constructed underneath Orion emptied into a nearby stream.

"Christian, I would have brought this to your attention sooner, but I had to confirm the schematics with my own eyes. You learn a lot when you're stuck in exile, reading for revolutions. You are going to lead your commandos and our wood Elf allies down the waterway, into the underbelly of the Fort, and come up via the bailey. When you do, you will head to the southeast corner parapet where Cassandra will use her explosion spell to take out the cornerstone."

"Cedric, you're going to send the Queen with me? That's a lot of responsibility."

"There are no better hands to trust her life in. Besides, she and Rosa have bonded. You've got a mighty great gal there and she's vowed to stay with her."

"Wouldn't Nadia be a more expendable target?"

"Nadia is afraid Abaddon may be able to track her movements," added Cecilia. "So she prefers to remain near Wilhelm, who can mask her signal."

"I though the Order of the Lion was set up to guard the Queen, so why the wood Elves?" asked Christian.

"The Order of the Lion are brave knights who pledged their lives and honor to Cassandra, but they are much better suited to charge on a battlefield. If we put them in the sewers it might be the equivalent of shooting fish in a barrel."

"This is a lot of troop movement," wondered Christian out loud. "As silent as I can keep my men, I'm sure it won't be long before we're discovered."

"Don't think you're going in there alone, Christian," interrupted Cecilia. "We've timed it so a distraction will take place around the Fort to keep the Templars occupied. The biggest danger you'll have is if we've underestimated the ability of their commanding officer.

If he's either sealed the sewers or has guards on the waterway, you get out of there and we'll revise the plan."

"I wouldn't speak highly of Karstak's command ability," said Christian. "However, he is ruthless and won't give up Orion without a fight. That we can be sure of."

"Karstak?" pondered Cedric. "He always travels with a scribe or two; Christian, I think I can guarantee you won't have a problem."

"I'm sorry I'm going to miss this," Christian said regretfully as he rubbed his chin. "Do me a favor and preserve it for the records, it will make for some interesting entertainment later."

"It's time, Cedric," Cecilia said as she stared at the clock on the wall.

"Right," answered Cedric as he closed his pocket watch. "Ladies and gentlemen, you will remain our eyes and ears as we begin the final stages of this desperate campaign. When the fighting starts keep your shifts short and your senses alert. For God, Country, and Family—let's send this Dark Angel crawling back to Hell."

Standing and saluting the Sword Master and Vanadis, the technicians and supervisors clapped, cheered, and yelled words of encouragement to their commanding officers. The twins took the time to shake hands with the people nearest to them on their way out of the room. Making their way out of the castle, the three journeyed into Saint Michael's Chapel in the castle courtyard. Most would consider the chapel to be a good-sized church, but it was dwarfed by the Basilica. The main feature in the stone chapel was a large stain glass window behind the altar showing the deathblow to Lucifer. The remaining panes featured warrior Saints of Terminus Mundus. As they were the last to arrive, the twins joined their mother in the front row. Cassandra was happily seated next to Nadia on the other side, joined by Wilhelm, Walker, and Robespierre. In the pews behind these front rows sat Horace, Samuel, Ethan, Rosa, Christian and Martha. Finally, there were the four noble banner men and women of Civilia Rhone. These four houses represented the last of the proud Divikin noble blood in Titanus. Lord Stillwell and Lord Johnstone were heavy armored knights in silver plate mail bearing shields and mace. Lady Flynn was a light-armored knight in her chain with sword and bow. Lady Gerhardt was a Valkyrie and Cecilia's second-in-command. Everyone was armed in battle mail save for the removed helmets. Nadia had placed a black lace veil over her head. Laying his hands over the congregation Bishop Arthur preached at the altar and offered his final blessing.

> God of power and mercy, maker and lover of peace, to know you is to live,
>
> and to serve you is to reign. Through the intercession of St. Michael, the archangel,
>
> be our protection in battle against all evil. Help us to overcome war and violence,
>
> and to establish your law of love and justice. Grant this through Christ our Lord.

When he was finished he distributed communion to all of the warriors. Reaching Nadia she simply crossed her arms across her chest and bowed her head. Arthur returned to the altar.

"May the Hand of God be with you, may He act as your shield when surrounded by foes. Go forth in His Name. In nomine Patri, Filia, Et Spiritus Sanctus!"

Removing his bishop vestment, Arthur donned his mail and knelt before the standard of House Rhone behind the altar. Reverently, he took the banner and led the procession from the chapel. A lone piper stood at the Chapel entrance waiting for orders.

"Call the Cavalry to Arms!" ordered Cedric.

Acknowledging the order, the piper moved to the elevator on the east parapet and rode the lift up. Black and red capes blowing in the wind, the Scarlet Riders trotted their steeds on the stone courtyard. Joining them, the Order of the Lion Knights rode out in full regalia with white and blue banners flying. Martha Heinrich had her team loading up a hover train with giant boxes of heavy equipment.

"What's your status, Martha?" asked Cedric.

"We're just about ready here, your Excellency. I don't know if my new trebuchets are going to work, but they certainly are heavy."

"What about your other passengers? Have they arrived yet?"

"They finally arrived from the Shtetl a few minutes ago."

Cedric turned to see a man in black robes with red trim leading four other men dressed the same way. Two wooden poles on either side allowed these four men to carry a large silver-plated box with two seraphim facing each other on top of it. The leader had a long white beard and curls hanging down from the locks of his hair. Christian's face had dropped completely as if he had seen a ghost. Cecilia was there to steady him.

"Easy there, before you fall off your horse," teased Cecilia.

"The Ark of the Covenant…but how… I thought it was lost when Brooke Run was sacked the second time," stammered Christian.

"As a wedding present, an Edenian Prince asked King Marisol if the Ark could be kept in Palacio Magnifico in order to spread the legacy and religion of the Elves throughout all of Terminus Mundus. However, when the Chinota Turks laid siege to Edenia, the religious community there feared for the Ark's safety. It was brought to Titanus during the reign of King Frederick and the community living in Rhinegard chose to keep it out of sight ever since. Knowing what we're facing here, even the Rabbi knows we're going to need some divine intervention."

Cedric greeted the leader at the head of the Ark.

"Chief Rabbi, I am pleased you have honored my request."

"I never thought a heathen Titan king would ever have use for our sacred treasure," joked the laughing Rabbi. "But I tease, your Excellency, we are honored to bear our treasure at the head of your train."

"Warfare can be won on many fronts. I intend to introduce psychological warfare into this battle. Even Templars fear the power of this weapon!"

"I understand. But know that if Dulles Marisol did not ride with you, I would not have honored your request."

"That is your prerogative and your right. I would not have dared to force the chosen of God. It comforts me to see you here with this, for if God is with us, who can be against us?"

The bearers and the Chief Rabbi boarded the hover train as Cedric returned to the main contingent. Mounting Jericho, the Titan prince looked back at his determined group of warriors.

"This rotation has been a long time in the making," started Cedric. "This is merely the first step on a long journey, but it's better than sitting in exile separated from family and friends. I vowed to banish this dark angel and restore light to the darkness that covers Terminus Mundus. I am elated that I do not go forward alone."

There were tears and laughter as Cassandra strode her horse forward. She was seated sidesaddle as usual, but this time Keiko was seated behind her. The sylph held the Queen tightly, who wasn't bothered in the least by Keiko's actions. The first blow from the piper was sounded on the east parapet. The bells of the Basilica rang first, but every other church in Rhinegard picked up the chorus quickly. As the incessant gonging rang throughout the city, every citizen stopped what they were doing and ran to sidewalks along the main road. All traffic was cleared between Castle Titan and the main city gate. The first piper was joined by eleven others on each of the parapets. Their tune echoed across the land thanks to Martha's enhanced sound system installed on the castle walls.

"Take us out, Marshal!" said Cassandra encouragingly.

"Cassandra, you're about to become a part of one of the great wonders of Terminus Mundus. The Titan Cavalry shall come to arms. For God! For Country! For your Families!"

As his riders echoed the last call, Cedric raised his hand. Rearing Jericho, he dropped his hand and the Scarlet Riders and the Order of the Lion rode from Castle Titan into Rhinegard. The Queen stared in wonder as she saw the populace of the city locked in arms cheering and singing the final chorus of the Titan national anthem:

We will defend our land and families

Until the time when all of man is free

God grant us strength so we may heed your call

Faith, Love, and Honor grant us one and all.

As they passed, the citizens cried, blessed, saluted, and threw red poppies at the riders. Cassandra couldn't believe the contrast with her own country. The Acadian nobility were the only ones present at a parade review and usually only came out of duty or bribery. Titanus was special—the nation was united behind their leaders who understood the terrible chance they were taking in this battle. From every corner and alley of the city, members of the Armada began to join the column. Noticing their capes were only black and not two-toned, the Acadians assumed that the regulars were joining the march. Even as they exited Rhinegard, people in the fields, towns, and bishoprics carried the cheers and cries of support. More and more members of the Armada joined the column as they passed through the twelve provinces of the two distinct regions of Titanus. The Titan heartlands, a region of seemingly endless fields of grains, fruit, and livestock made Titanus self-sustainable. The Titan highlands were hilly terrain serving as the source of mining, mineral production, and heavy industry. Still donning war paint and kilts, the highlanders stood in stark contrast to the modern stoic heartland warrior. Despite the contrast in these two separate worlds, knights and Valkyries joined the column and Cassandra understood it to be the ultimate form of propaganda. It didn't matter what station one held in life or what region one was from in Titanus. All were called to defend the crown and those that served were greatly rewarded. It seemed like every single soul in the populace of Titanus made an effort to salute the Armada as it passed. By mid-rotation, the riders finally reached their destination, Fort Hawkeye. With a mere signal from Horace, the column split perfectly into two units and rode to either Fort. The nobility remained together at the west fort since it had the more luxurious quarters. Shaken by the events and her participation in it, Cassandra needed help from Walker to get down from her horse.

"Are you all right, your Majesty?" asked a concerned Walker.

"I heard rumors… but do they truly do this every time?" elicited a shocked Cassandra.

"I've heard so, your Majesty. We should get you inside."

"Get a quick meal and get right to bed," commanded Cedric through a microphone. We have to reach rendezvous point Alpha before dawn tomorrow."

The Riders dismounted their horses as apprentices and servants rushed to take the horses into their corrals. A servant walked over to Wilhelm and whispered something to the angel. He gave a quick nod and found Cedric.

"He's here," said Wilhelm.

"Okay," acknowledged Cedric as he took a deep breath.

The two walked towards a lone tower at the west end of the fort. Cassandra caught up with Cedric.

"Hey, aren't you going to grab something to eat with the rest of us?" asked Cassandra.

"I'll be around later, Cassie. Don't worry, Cecilia will take good care of you and show you to your quarters."

As she approached, Cecilia shoved a book into her twin brother's arm with a pen and a smile on her face. Before leaving with Wilhelm, Cedric gave Cassandra a goodnight kiss. The Vanadis put her arms around the Queen.

"Come on, Cassie. I've got a nice room ready for you. My mother and I want to have nice quiet dinner with you."

"Do you know where they're going, Cecilia?"

"Yes, but its high-level security stuff. Though if he doesn't get that damn autograph for me, I'll never forgive him! This way, your Highness."

The girls entered the aristocrat wing. In the west tower, Cedric and Wilhelm entered a private room sealed off from the rest of the fort. Serenaded by their guest, the two heard a voice singing a form of music completely foreign to them. At first Cedric and Wilhelm drew comfort from the lyrics, but as their guest continued, they became horrified by what they heard.

"What is the heck is he singing?" questioned Cedric. "I've got chills up my spine."

"He's a bit eccentric," warned Wilhelm. "He's always telling me how he considers this the greatest song ever written."

Standing from a chair was a man smaller and less built than Wilhelm. Removing the headphones from his ears, he combed his fingers through his light brown hair. Brown eyes focused on Cedric and Wilhelm; they seemed much older and weary than his youthful features betrayed. Dressed in a white shirt and coif with black pants and boots, the man wore a long red military coat and held a long ivory cane in his right hand. The Titan prince determined his guest to be a clear contradiction with forces beyond his control pulling him in all different directions and yet he had an oddly comforting presence about him.

"Prince Cedric Rhone, may I have the pleasure of introducing Teman, of the Second Triad, Dominion Choir, or as those in creation call them, the Guardian Angels," announced Wilhelm.

Friendly and amiable, Teman stepped forward and shook Cedric's hand. "If you don't mind, I prefer to use the name I use in creation, Francesco Angelino, Duke of the Kingdom of Prester John."

"You're not from around here, are you?" joked Cedric.

"My realm and charges are far from here, but I pop up on Terminus Mundus every so often when a great crisis occurs that threatens Heaven and the rightful order of things. A lot has changed here since I rudely dropped in the last time. But we did a hot time in the old town, didn't we, Wilhelm?"

"That's why I half-doubted the wisdom of Prince Cedric when he told me he needed to consult with an expert," teased Wilhelm. "Then again, no one knows more about the savagery of Hell than you."

"Maybe the girls have a little more insight. How's Nadia?"

"She's getting closer every rotation. I can feel it. What about Eva?"

"I practically had to lie, cheat, and steal to keep her from coming with me. She insisted on some payback for what Abaddon did to her in Hell. I didn't think it was prudent; Eva still has a strong connection to her father and his mind control can be dangerous. Besides, if we both left, only my protégé would be able to defend the realm."

"I thought I had problems," quipped Cedric. "Well, I'm not one to stand on ceremony, let's have a drink."

Opening a decanter on the table, Cedric poured three glasses. Each individual took one as the Titan prince offered his traditional toast. "To the heroes of the past and the soldiers of the future, God bless the warriors, for sure as hell no one else will."

"Amen, brother. I wished to arrive a day ago…let me catch myself now…a rotation ago, but crossing this barrier is a delicate process and I did not want to alert the enemy to my presence." Francis took another sip of his drink. "Your brandy is much better than what I'm used to in my realm. You guys have to give me a bottle or two to bring back. Aidan would enjoy this."

"I'm glad you were able to answer my summons," said Cedric as the three took a seat.

"All the action is on Terminus Mundus right now, and I figured that all the remaining Sentinels needed to gather here for this final battle against the best of the Acolytes."

"How many more can we count on?" asked Cedric.

"Didn't Wilhelm tell you?"

Wilhelm cleared his throat. "Francis and I are all of the divine assistance that the Sentinels are going to be able to muster…because we're all that's left," he stammered.

"I figured as much. Well, Francis, can you help us with our Camael problem?"

"I'm registering power levels from five creatures on this planet that belong in the Celestial rather than the temporal realm. It accounts for myself, Wilhelm, Nadia, Abaddon, and unfortunately, Cassandra. I'm sorry."

"I thought so. You have to forgive me, but my sister and I grew up on Wilhelm's stories of your heroism. In some ways you could say that you're my idol."

"I appreciate your praise. However, I wouldn't exactly call what I did heroic, I mean, compared to the deeds of my brothers and sisters that came down from Heaven. The Holy Spirit ordered me into Hell to complete a desperate mission. Circle after circle of horror and torture, by God it could change anyone...even a Guardian Angel isn't immune. The despair was the worst of it, when I close my eyes at night I still see the lost souls tearing at one another. I wanted to pull them all out, but they all believed that God was separated from them and the Prince was the only Lord they served now. Then I reached the bottom and poor Eva was there. Chained to a wall, more animal than daughter at that point. You know, the first thing she did when I released her was bite me in the neck. Talk about gratitude—it was probably the closest I came in my existence to believing God wasn't omniscient. I'm sorry if I'm rambling...but you, Cedric Rhone, you are someone more deserving of praise than me. A Divikin who risked everything to fight an incarnated angel to save the woman he loves. In some ways, you're my idol."

"Then let's drink to the idols, and those like Wilhelm von Angelhardt who are willing to put everything on the line to train and aid them," pronounced Cedric.

"Damn right we'll drink to that!" exclaimed Wilhelm.

The three took another drink.

"Absent Camael, is there any other way I can get Abaddon out of the temporal realm permanently?"

"I am honor-bound to tell you there is a way, Cedric," started Francis. "While I am capable with a blade, my powers lie in the realm of sorcery. There is a ritual, if I could perform it, that would bind Abaddon's soul back to Hell where it belongs."

"You made the night for me, Francis!" exclaimed a jubilant Cedric. "What do you need to perform this ritual? We'll get it immediately."

"Cedric, please listen to me," explained a melancholy Francis. "I used the conditional on purpose. There is only one catalyst I need for the ritual. It can be of two forms. The first form is an incarnation of divine being. Wilhelm is eliminated because of the poison coursing through his veins and wings. Nadia can't be used either because she is more of a creature of hell than heaven. Cassandra has the same problem because she's practically split down the middle. Since I'm performing the ritual and have duties back in my realm, I'm eliminated as well."

"Well, I guess we're stuck with the second form, then."

"The second form for the catalyst would require a Divikin, but not just any one of that race. They would have had to master the ancient art of the spell holy war, which eliminates everyone on Terminus Mundus except for you, Cedric."

"If we only have to sell one more life to defeat Abaddon, I'll gladly give mine."

"You're brave, but you don't understand what I'm saying. You're not an angel, you're body and soul like all of creation. Therefore you don't have an incarnate existence to sacrifice. The price for you serving as the catalyst for the ritual is not your life, it's your immortal soul itself."

For the first time in his life, Wilhelm saw fear in the face of Cedric Rhone. Never before had there been a moment's hesitation in his brown eyes, but the Titan prince was finally beaten in battle.

"My immortal soul?" questioned a nervous Cedric. "Do you mean I'd be damned to Hell?"

"Those damned to Hell have to despair. I highly doubt that state would ever overtake a Divikin as faithful as you. I speak of oblivion. Your essence would be wiped from the history of creation as if you never were created. I can't even begin to explain it, because it has never happened to any soul in the eternity that is God."

Brandy glass still shaking, Cedric set it down to prevent it from spilling.

"Prince Rhone, you must understand, magic like this was forbidden for a reason. There were rules that had to be set so the Acolytes and the Sentinels would not abuse their power influencing the free will of creation. You can't break or bend this rule. The only way absent a servant of the Powers choir appearing on Terminus Mundus to banish Abaddon is for you to give up literally everything. As a Guardian Angel, I don't think I could perform the ritual even if you begged me."

"No, Francis, I understand…. I… I thank you for your honesty…"

Cedric took a drink to steady himself and then downed another one. After regaining some semblance of his composure, he continued. "I'm afraid I can't give you a command in my army. Outside of an inner circle that would understand, I prefer you assume the identity of a Kablisha mercenary warlord."

"That'll be fine, I just want to do my part. I'd prefer to serve under Wilhelm if that's possible."

"I'll be glad to take him, your Excellency."

"Good, I'll leave you two to catch up."

"Angels don't need sleep, your Highness, but Divikin do," chided Wilhelm. "Rest up."

"I find I haven't been sleeping much these past revolutions."

"Nightmares?"

"No, I just seem to be functioning perfectly with less sleep. Oh, there is one last thing you can do for me, Francis." Cedric pulled out the book Cecilia gave to him. "My twin sister wants you to sign her autograph book."

"No problem. What's her name?"

"Cecilia."

"Lovely name. In my realm, there was a wonderful saint named Cecilia, and it's also the title of one of my favorite songs, but you don't get what I'm talking about."

"My sister has always fancied herself of more of a war goddess than a saint. Though she wouldn't mind listening to a song with her namesake."

"I don't know. It's depends what kind of gal she is."

The three laughed as evening crept over the Fort. In the hours before dawn, pipers on top of the fort made call for reverie. Groggy and grumpy, two columns of fully armed riders poured out of the twin forts to Eagle's Gate. The technicians opened the Gate on either side by entering a special coded sequence. Passing underneath the giant stone eagles signaling them to war, Cedric went to the head of the column. Exhausted from lack of sleep, Cassandra yawned as the Titan prince signaled to come forward. In addition to her personal knights, the Titan riders numbered a quarter of a million. Putting his arm around Cassandra, Cedric whispered into her ear.

"I ask only that you put that sweet smile across your face. These men and women deserve to see the radiance of who they're fighting for."

Obeying the order, the young Queen noticed every rider bow their head to her as she turned to them. Overwhelmed by their act of loyalty, she couldn't contain herself. "I thank you for your service in reclaiming my Kingdom. Let the Eagle and the Lion be joined forever."

The last yells and cheers of night came forth as horses stomped their hooves against the dirt in salute. Cecilia joined her brother up front. Immediately she sensed something was off.

"Hey, Cedric, are you okay?"

"Just a little jittery, we haven't done something this big in a while. We'll ride through the night in alert columns."

"That will get us to the rendezvous point before dawn. I hope you've worked out that crazy plan of yours."

"I have a showing of pomp and circumstance the likes of which these Templars have never seen."

"Then we'd better get moving!" retorted a smiling Cecilia. "Lead them out, brother, or should I say, Marshal Commandant!"

"Haven't heard that in a long time! Forward!"

It took some time for the massive amount of riders to filter through the narrow Gate, but when they broke through the army went into columns of one hundred across and twenty deep. Valkyries were on the edges with Lord Knights protecting the front and back. The light cavalry hung to the middle. The Order of the Lion Knights rode in a column between Cedric's lead group and the middle Titan riders. Relying once again on the Fae to aid him, mystical creatures lit the path for the columns to pass the Vale in the night quickly and without fear of injury to rider or horse.

Fort Orion, Central Acadia

As the horns blew, the people began to shout. When they heard the signal horn, they raised a tremendous shout. The wall fell, and the host stormed the city in a frontal attack and took it.

The Ancient Scriptures, The Book of the General 6:20

The skeleton night watch patrolled the walls of Fort Orion as the Acadian Templar army tried to get some rest. Two soldiers at one of the parapets were drawn to a large pillar of fire in the distance. Squinting to discern the light time and time again, they lost sight of anything else happening around them. In the control room below, a sleepy Karstak entered. Templar personnel were frantically working the computers around them.

"What's so damn important that you need to wake me at this hour?" bellowed Karstak.

"I'm sorry, sir," answered his subordinate. "But we've had a situation in the control room. About two hours ago there was a quick power surge and all systems have been functioning at quarter power since then."

Karstak rubbed his unshaved chin. "That sounds too weird. Refresh my memory, did Titanus offer a formal declaration of war?"

"I believe such a document was received, Sir Karstak."

"I wouldn't put it past that tech-savvy bitch to have done something ahead of an attack. Rustle everyone up and get them on the wall, even the guards at the bailey. I'm not taking any chances."

"Right away, sir."

Alarms and sirens roused the Acadian Templars throughout the Fort. Donning armor and grabbing their weapons, they mustered to their positions on the wall. Ten kilometers away, two light cavalry scouts rode back to the main column, binoculars in hand. Waiting for them was the combined forces of the Titan Armada and a column of Wood Elves lead by Gerard. Gerard had his soldiers smear black war paint across their faces and don black cloaks for the operation. They saluted Cedric.

"Lord Cedric, the Templars have finally mustered to the wall."

"It's about time!" exclaimed Cecilia. "We've been waiting almost two hours."

"Open it up!" commanded Cedric.

In the river below them was a large stone sewer with a black grating in front of it. Using the back ends of their spears, two Valkyries prodded the black grating loose. Christian stepped forward and put his finger to his glasses. Red lights emerged from them and created a three dimensional map of the path from the sewer entrance to the bailey. Cedric aided Cassandra down from her mount.

"Wish me luck," said Cassandra with a hint of apprehension.

"You'll be fine, Cassie. You're in good hands."

Walker started to strip off parts of his armor to join the assault team, but Horace put a hand to his shoulder.

"Where are you going, Walker?" asked Horace.

"I have to see to the Queen," replied Walker. "It's why I'm here."

"The Marshal needs you with your Knights to aid us in the assault."

"But the Queen?"

"Robespierre's good, but he doesn't have the field experience to lead your men into war. It's time to become more than a simple protector, Walker. You're a leader of men and you're going to make your Knights prove their worth."

"I understand."

Wood Elves and Titan operatives raced into the sewer with bows drawn on point. With no one in sight, they gave the signal for everyone to move up. Christian returned to Cedric for final orders.

"It should take you until two hours past dawn to reach the bailey of the Fort," explained Cedric. "Don't worry, I'll have all of the eyes of the Fort drawn on us at that point. Use my channel to signal me when everything is ready."

"You just keep them off my team or all this cloak and dagger is for nothing. What I wouldn't give to have Colin here right now."

"There is an Alliance that needs to be secure."

"Of course, I know that. Two hours—we'd better hustle. Don't worry about the Queen. She's in good hands."

Rosa strutted past the two and took her place next to Cassandra.

"Just stay with me, your Highness, and we'll be fine," teased Rosa. "Please don't attack anyone with counter magic activated this time. My body isn't built to handle that force of power again."

"I'll be careful," promised a laughing Cassandra.

"Good luck, Christian and Godspeed," Cedric bid them.

"Thanks, buddy. All right, Commando unit, move out!"

As the commando unit entered the sewer, the teams broke into two. Each unit covered the stone walkway on either side of the flowing water. Wood Elves were on point with their keen eyesight ahead of the column. Every time they reached a turn, four archers would dart out prepared to cover fire so the remaining column could pass. Christian continued to follow his path at a quick, but prudent pace. The whole time, Rosa was right with Cassandra as she funneled the precious cargo along.

Reorganizing his troops outside, Prince Rhone ordered the hover train to be brought up. To further distract the Acadians, he made them bring it in nice and loud. Wearing a conductor's outfit, Martha stood in the engineer's booth happily tooting the steam whistle with a smile on her face.

"I always wanted to do this," rejoiced Martha happily.

The sound of the train further alerted the now-shaved Karstak to an imminent attack.

"The Titan son of a bitch is actually going to try it. Here's going to find out that the Acadian Templar army does not lose a fort as easily as the Imperials."

Loading up their horses first, the Armada hopped on the hover train to cover the next eight kilometers. Cedric and Cecilia entered the car carrying Chief Rabbi Levi and his fellow scholars.

"I hope your trip was uneventful," asked Cedric.

"It was, except for the snoring of Martha Heinrich!" quipped Levi.

"Well, she needs her beauty sleep!" teased Cecilia.

"I heard that!" exclaimed Martha from the next car. "You'd better watch your manners, Princess Cecilia, or this genius conductor will start asking for tickets."

"Are you sick, Cedric?" inquired Cecilia. "You haven't been yourself since the ride last night."

"I'm fine, sis. It's all right."

"I guess I would be anxious, too. You do realize this plan is completely crazy?"

"I did my thesis on treating the Ancient Scriptures as a military history. It worked then, it will work now."

"My interpretation of scripture may not be as scholarly as yours, brother, but if I'm not mistaken the Lord God took down the Walls of Jericho."

"Allow me to explain, sis. If you read the Book of the General like a military manual instead of pure scripture, it says the walls fell. We know the General sent spies into the city so its reasonable to deduce..."

"Other agents might have been present in the city as well. They could have opened the Gates for a frontal attack and the walls fell. That's why you sent Christian and the others inside."

"It's worth a shot. Walker, we're ready for you now."

"Ready for the status report?" queried Walker as he entered the room.

"You mentioned the Templar Army consists mostly of Lord Knights and Halberdiers," recounted Cecilia. "What are their missile capabilities?"

"The short bow, with a maximum range of one hundred-twenty meters and armor-piercing capability. Technology trumps the skill of the archer in this situation."

"We'll stay at two hundred meters to be safe," deduced Cedric as he pulled out his pocket. "Two kilometers to go. Martha, stop the train and let's get them up."

"Right away, your Excellency," announced Martha as she turned on the intercom. "All right, ladies and gentleman, Fort Orion will be the last stop on this train. All must disembark."

Stepping outside, the sword master looked to the sky and saw the early morning orange and red rays painting the purple sky. He smiled. "Let's take it nice and slow, we want to give Christian plenty of time."

Disembarking the train, the horses went right to their riders. As the ranks were reformed, the Chief Rabbi and his followers moved the head of the column with the Ark, followed by Cedric and his command staff. Without a word, the Armada moved slow and steady towards Fort Orion. As first rays of light crept over the defensive structure, the Templars' worst fears were confirmed. Staring out at the approaching army, Karstak called for his binoculars. Three other Templars raised their visual tools as well to take additional marks.

"I've got no sign of siege weapons," observed Karstak. "What about you?"

"Nothing, sir, it's just horseman and something else...I don't know," affirmed one of the scouts.

"Cedric Rhone, you will have gone quite mad indeed if you think you can siege this Fort with merely horsemen," taunted Karstak. "Raise Verian and tell Jonas we may need that relief column he promised. Archers to the wall. I want flights armed and ready."

Obeying the orders of their officer, Templar bowmen took to the front walls. Drawing their bows, they prepared to fire on the coming column.

"Don't waste your arrows," ordered Karstak. "I want them right on top of us."

Tensions were high as they saw Cedric turn his column two hundred meters from the Fort. The Armada still moved at a very slow and deliberate pace in columns of twenty. Knowing the riders were out of range, Karstak had his troops lower their bows. Deliberately parading around the whole of Fort Orion, the Ark led the way. Confusion and terror reigned across the walls and parapets.

"Hey, Rhone, what are you doing?" pondered Karstak.

As if he was staring at the grim reaper, Karstak tried to read the eyes of Cedric Rhone through the Rising Moon Helmet. However, all he could make out was that dreaded smile filled with malice.

"That's it, just keep watching the train," taunted Cedric. "Even that puny brain of yours can figure it out, Karstak!"

"His archers can't hit us from here and there's been no word of movement from Evengard," wondered Karstak out loud. "I just wish I knew what that damned totem at the head of the Armada was. Get me an Acolyte versed in the religions of other cultures!"

As the drama took place above, Christian and his team moved silently and efficiently through the sewers. Reaching the bailey, the teams were shocked to find it undefended.

"He left the bailey undefended!" exclaimed Christian. "I know Cedric had something big planned but that's just crazy. All right, Alpha team, go!"

A first team of twenty Wood Elves took positions along the walls of the bailey keeping a lookout for any soldiers approaching. A second team of twenty Titan operatives ran forward with crossbows drawn. One of them took out a computer to bypass the code on a door. The bailey door opened to a series of new corridors. Gerard and Rosa emerged with Cassandra. She had a team of Elite Wood Elf rangers guarding her. Breathing heavy, the Queen was rattling from her boots to head.

"Are you all right, your Highness?" asked Christian.

"More nervous than tired," explained Cassandra. "I'm afraid, Christian, but if I'm ever going to get my kingdom back, I'm going to have to start taking some chances. Just point me in the right direction, I'll do the rest."

Christian handed a second pair of his glasses to Rosa. She took a look through them and determined the path. The two smiled at one another and shared a kiss.

"The corridor that you're looking for is directly east," described Christian. "On the third tunnel, you'll reach the area with the foundation point of the east wall."

"Wait a second!" squealed Cassandra. "You're not coming with me?"

"I'm afraid I need this army to take the Fort Command Center. It controls the outer defenses and I can't allow them to be used against Cedric and the others. Don't worry, Rosa and her elites will take good care of you."

"Nothing to worry about, your Highness," assured Rosa. "Christian's going to draw all their fire, anyway."

"The way is clear, your Highness," observed Gerard.

"Then we must hurry," determined Cassandra.

A hundred of the Wood Elf rangers lead Cassandra, Rosa, and Gerard down the corridors and stairs to the cornerstone. The remaining assault team gathered around Christian.

"This is what we've trained for. We have to take the Command Room without arousing enemy suspicion! On my mark, let's move out."

Christian led his unit down one of the hallways. They moved up the stairs from the underbelly of the Fort in the opposite direction of the Queen's unit. Using his glasses to see around the corners, his team performed the same cornering maneuvers as they used through the sewers. They proceeded as planned to a huge double door that had computer encryptions on both sides. Two Templars stood guard at the entrance. DeVries signaled to two archers. The Wood Elves drew and fired silently. The two Templars made no noise from death as the arrows caught them in the throat. Two team members with bypass computers raced to the encrypted panels covered by archers. The operatives hacked into the computer and waited for Christian's mark.

Cassandra's team followed similar protocols making their way to the basement. They stopped at one corner as a Templar guard passed their position. Gerard jumped him from behind and slit his throat.

"All clear," determined Gerard.

Rosa ran out with her bow as Cassandra stayed on her heels. As they reached the stone wall, the Queen moved her hand up and down searching for the cornerstone. A smile crossed her face as she found the correct brick. The remaining members of her team formed three firing lines to cover her position. Cassandra reached into her cloak and pulled out a watch. There was countdown clock ticking towards zero.

While this happened below, a pudgy Acolyte raced up the stairs to the walls of Fort Orion. Tripping over his long brown robes a few times, he bowed to Karstak. His patience wearing thin, he grabbed the Acolyte by the neck and showed him the parading army. The eyes of the Acolyte widened.

"Saints preserve us!" cried the Acolyte.

"What's going on?"

"They're trying to bring down the walls of the Fort!"

"They're parading around this Fort in order to bring it down?" said Karstak, laughing irritably.

"There is a precedent in one of the Scriptures…apparently the Elves performed a similar action in the Demonkin stronghold of Jericho. They paraded around the city seven times, blew their horns, and the walls came crumbling down."

"How many times have they walked around?" demanded Karstak.

"I counted six, sir," replied a soldier.

"I don't believe in fairy tales, but I do believe that Titan has an ace up his sleeve. Don't move your eyes off that army."

The officers on the wall acknowledged the order and passed the orders around to the other soldiers. Karstak and the Acolyte didn't take their eyes off of Cedric. Twin brother and sister laughed from their mounts as they witnessed the panic.

"This is it sis! Here are your final orders for the battle."

"Right, brother."

"We're about to make our seventh and final pass. The timers I gave to Christian and Cassandra are about to go off. When the east wall comes down all hell is going to break loose, so I'm going to need your help to keep everyone organized. We're going with lines of twenty. I'll take the first wave, Horace will have the second, and you'll lead the third. There will be three walls remaining on the Fort if my plan succeeds, and we'll each need to secure one of them to corral the frightened defenders. I'm counting on you, sis."

"Don't worry, just save some for my team."

"There'll be plenty of Templars for everyone."

Cedric winked at his sister who dropped back to her team. A communication began to come through to him. The sword master grabbed the side of his helmet.

"Talk to me, Christian."

"Both of my commando teams are in position, we're ready when you are," came in Christian over the radio.

"Stick to the countdown as planned! Over and out!"

"Yes, sir. Over and out!"

Lifting his arm in the air, Cedric brought the Armada to a halt. Riding to the front of the column was Cedric's personal standard. In a single motion, the entire Armada turned in one swift motion to face the eastern wall. Karstak remained on the north wall, but shifted his eyes.

"Are they going to charge the eastern wall?" wondered Karstak. "What happened after the parade?"

"There was the sound of horns and the walls came crumbling down," murmured the Acolyte. "This is, of course, only a legend."

"NOT THIS FORT!" taunted Karstak loudly toward the invading army. "YOUR PATHETIC FAITH WON'T SAVE YOU NOW, YOU TITAN BASTARD!"

Smiling, the Titan prince signaled to the Titan Drill Core. Readying their pipes and drums, Cedric, Cassandra, and Christian all waited for the countdown clocks to reach zero. As the numbers hit, the Queen chanted her spell. A brown light shined from her orb, and her protectors save Rosa dropped back to the stairs. Driving the staff into the ground, Cassandra yelled, "quake," so the magical aura from the staff hit the pre-determined cornerstone. Cracks appeared in the wall immediately and rumbling was felt by the operatives. Underestimating her own powers once more, the Queen looked nervously at Rosa.

"Time to run!"

At break-neck speed and no longer worried about guards, the operatives raced up the stairs. When they reached the bailey, they took refuge at an open space on the western wall. The first shakes were the signal Christian needed to give his team. The technical operatives hacked the security system at Fort Orion's Control Room. The doors opened and a flurry of arrows and bolts overwhelmed the desperate technicians and guards in the room. Caught unprepared for battle, they were slaughtered before they could even turn around let alone defend themselves. Christian was pointing his daggers towards the members of his team.

"On the terminals! Get those outer defenses offline!"

Clearing the dead bodies from their terminal stations, the operatives shut down Martha's virus first and proceeded to use Titan computer programs to override the systems. The shakes reached the walls of Orion. Overcome with terror, the Templar defense force panicked.

"It's impossible!" shouted Karstak. "It was a children's story!"

"The legends are true!" exclaimed the Acolyte. "The walls are going to come down!"

"Get off the walls to the center of the courtyard!" ordered Karstak. "Defensive positions!"

Cedric smiled as he watched the bricks falling out of the Eastern Wall. The Armada had already aligned themselves into attack columns. Dressed in light silver plate underneath a white cloak with red trim, Francis took his position in Cedric's command. Holding a long silver staff marked with a blue orb in one hand and a long katana blade in the other hand, he saluted Wilhelm's Devil Slayer with his own blade. The angelic Duke winked back and smiled. The Templars on the eastern wall were trapped by the spell. Some jumped to their doom, others were crushed to death as the rubble buried them. Fearing for his command, Karstak got on his communicator.

"Raise Orion's defenses! Fire everything!"

"I'm sorry, but the number you have reached is no longer in service," replied a voice.

"Who's down there? FIRE!"

"If that's what you want," replied the voice.

A temporary relief was achieved as the sound of the automated defenses coming online penetrated the Fort. The relief turned to horror, however, when the weapons fired on the Templar defensive positions.

"What's happening?" demanded Karstak. "This is madness!"

As Ragnarok was raised in the air, the Armada screamed and cheered "TITANUS!"

"INTO THE BREACH!" ordered Cedric.

The banners of the eagles were unfurled and flew through the air as the first column tore into the former position known as the eastern wall of Orion. Ten meters behind them were Horace's column leading the second wave, with Cecilia's column ten meters behind them. Skillfully leaping over the rubble like a trained equestrian mount, Jericho led the other armored horses through. Seeing the Armada emerge through the death and dust around them overwhelmed the Templars. Frantically rallying his men, Karstak ordered them into defensive positions.

"Fear not, Templars!" screamed Karstak. "Believe the Saints will preserve us!"

His words fell on deaf ears; the shaken troops believed they were not only fighting the greatest military force in the world, but a divine power as well. Riding his column right for the western wall, Cedric took an opportunity to strike at Karstak and two officers with him. The Saint raised his axe in defense. Bringing Ragnarok down upon them, Karstak staggered back, but successfully blocked it. The two officers flanking him fell over dead, their long swords lying broken on the ground.

"They're too fast!" said Karstak.

Horace and his column rode to the northern wall while Cecilia took her riders to the southern wall. The Templars found themselves corralled in the middle of the Fort surrounded by Knights and Valkyries on horseback. Civilia brought her light cavalry to the fallen wall. Firing a barrage of arrows at the wings of the Templar defense force, they kept them penned in. A wolf pack mentally emerged as each of the commanding officers sent their riders through the column. Not stopping to attack, they slashed and trampled the enemy forces into the ground from all sides. Refusing to risk an attack, disorganized and terrified soldiers were killed at will. Cedric had the Armada repeat this action ten times. Both human life and morale were annihilated until Karstak's numbers shrank to a fraction of his original force. A few brave Templars tried to reach the manual overrides on the Fort automated defenses to turn the tide, yet they found themselves shot to death by the scorpions and arrow launchers. Realizing they were done for, Karstak put his axe in the air.

"ALL RIGHT, CEDRIC RHONE! I'll die a soldier before I die like prey! I'll fight any one of you! If I die the fort is yours. If not, get the hell out for one full rotation! What do you say, boy? Are you man enough to accept the challenge?"

Willing to reward them for their bravery and vows to Cassandra, the sword master looked to the Order of the Lion. While a number of them were ready to volunteer, Robespierre seethed with anticipation.

"Your Excellency, if it is your will, I welcome the honor!"

"All right, Robespierre, you've got carte blanche!"

"Thank you, my Lord."

Dismounting, Robespierre took out his shield and longsword. Karstak ordered his men back to the safety of the wall. While they remained under the watchful eye of the Armada, none of Cedric's command made a move. Karstak twirled his axe around to warm up before the fight. Recognizing his opponent brought a smile to the Saint's face.

"I remember you, boy. Jean-Luc Robespierre. You had the make of a good Templar Knight, maybe even a Saint, but you suddenly disappeared."

"I couldn't stomach defending a lie anymore, Sir Karstak."

"And what emblem do you wear now?"

"The Order of the Lion, the defenders of Queen Cassandra Acadia, the rightful ruler of Central Acadia, to whom we have sworn our lives and sacred honor."

Laughing, Karstak watched the young Queen and her team enter the courtyard. Nervously grasping her heart, she wondered what had possessed Robespierre and Cedric to give Karstak what he wanted.

"The rightful ruler!" taunted Karstak. "You and your precious order. Do realize that you are following nothing but a usurper!"

"A usurper? What claim of right did Maximilian Luminas have to the throne of Central Acadia?"

"I'm not talking about Count Luminas. The normal order of succession has taken place. Queen Marie Acadia as by her right of succession now rules Central Acadia. You, Robespierre, are following the usurper."

Shocked by the news, tears fell from the eyes of the Queen. How could the enemy engage in such treachery by putting her sister on the throne as a puppet Queen? A stern look crossed Cedric's face, as if he had not anticipated this turn of events.

"How can I trust that Marie is simply not being used by Luminas and Abaddon to fulfill their nefarious purposes?" questioned a defiant Robespierre. "Besides, we all know that Stephen declared Cassandra the heir before your commander executed him."

"Do you honestly believe that the Titan isn't manipulating Cassandra? This is simply part of his master imperial plan! I thought you were smart enough to figure that one out."

"I have stared into the face of evil firsthand, Karstak! I know where I stand and I know that God stands with us!"

"Then be prepared to become the first martyr of the War of Two Queens."

Karstak charged at Robespierre with his axe. Robespierre countered by bringing up his shield. The larger saint pressed into him but the skilled knight used his strength to keep him far enough away. Robespierre turned his shield to block him, and he tried a sword strike but Karstak blocked it with the handle of his axe. Both men recovered and took a step back from one another.

As they sized up one another, they walked in a circle stalking each other. Karstak took another aggressive charge swinging his axe wildly and widely at Robespierre. The Knight of the Order stepped back on each attack until he chopped with his sword and came down on the Saint's axe, deflecting it towards the ground. The larger warrior swung up and knocked the order's leader on his back.

"It's going to be fun killing you, Jean-Luc. It's a shame your fearless leader didn't have the courage to face me himself. He'd rather watch you throw your life away recklessly!"

Robespierre only moved to place his sword and shield back into a guard position. Karstak shook his head and positioned himself for another attack. As he was about to move, the Order Knight moved first with a jumping attack. The Saint used the handle of his axe to deflect the attack. His smile disappeared fast when in a second motion Robespierre batted down on him with his shield. Karstak dropped his guard and Robespierre sliced upwards at him underneath his armpit between the link and chainmail. Staggering back two steps, the brutal saint reached underneath the wound. When his gauntlet came back covered in blood, the frightened warrior tried to get his axe back into a defensive position. When he failed Robespierre took advantage of the situation. Shield charging into the saint, the order commander stabbed with his longsword and found another vital point between the sections of his torso and leg armor. Probing deeper with the tip of his longsword, Robespierre slipped the blade into his larger opponent's stomach. Karstak gasped and coughed up blood as he felt his insides being torn to pieces. The brutal saint felt his own mortality catching up to him.

"Who trained you, Jean-Luc?"

"The greatest warrior Central Acadia never appreciated, Hector Reed."

Karstak took a moment to stare at Walker. Recognizing the legacy of the old commander in him, he accepted his fate.

"He always said... he would get us... damn me for thinking we were no longer threatened when he died. Hey, Walker, maybe you traitors can pull this off...finish it!"

Robespierre ripped his sword out rapidly from Karstak's underbelly. The so-called enforcer fell backwards to the ground choking on his own blood in agony. It was a fitting final punishment for a saint who performed nothing but cruelty in his lifetime. The remaining Templars stared with hate and tried to raise their weapons, but knew it was helpless against the numbers they faced. The sound of steel and iron hitting against the ground was a welcome sound to the Titans. Cedric smiled as he watched the remaining Templars kneel on the ground and surrender to him.

"Horace, have three divisions see to the prisoners," ordered Cedric. "Martha's engineers have already begun work on a mobile stockade where they will be held before they can be safely transported to Storm's Diadem."

The mere mention of the name caused one of the Templars to jump up.

"NO! WE'RE PRISONERS OF WAR...YOU CAN'T SEND US THERE!"

"Storm's Diadem is where Titanus sends all of our terrorists and insurrectionists. You'll fit in well there."

"It is a death sentence! There's no escape!"

"Then I suggest you live the rest of your life in repentance for the sins you and your army have committed against your brothers! I'm done with all of you!"

Horace directed a few companies to see that the prisoners were secured. Martha Heinrich walked into the Fort and immediately examined the Eastern Wall. Cecilia rode up to her.

"Well?" queried Cecilia.

"No problem, my engineers can have this repaired in no time," assured Martha.

"Good, because we're on a tight clock. Christian is going to send word out to the Kingdoms and the Tribes to come to Fort Orion."

"We'll be done well before that time comes."

"Don't be so sure..." Cecilia pointed out in the distance. Captain Sirius and his men came riding towards Fort Orion.

"Elves... looks like a scouting party," observed Martha.

"I don't think so, Martha. That's Captain Sirius and a company of lancers. If he's traveling ahead of the Elves with a royal guard, this can't be good."

Approaching the gaping hole in the Fort, Sirius slowed his horse. Engineers were already staking out the land for suitable locations for the Titan barracks and blacksmith. Though maintaining his stoic

Elven countenance, the Captain stared around him as if trying to determine how the battle could be already over.

"Hey, Sirius!" greeted Cecilia. "You lost?"

"Forgive my intrusion, Lady Cecilia," apologized Sirius. "A desperate situation has risen in Evengard and I must speak with you and your brother immediately."

"And here I thought you wanted to speak with Christian first."

"It will come to that, my Lady. However, some ground rules need to be set first to handle this delicately."

Intrigued by the Elf's tone and politeness, Cecilia nodded her head. "I think my brother was heading for the command center to oversee communications to the other kingdoms, but if you come with me I'll grab him."

"Thank you."

The two rode off into the Fort as Martha got her people working on the replacement wall.

FORT DRAGONSTONE, NAPOLITAN

Napolitan has relied on a single principle to train its soldiers and that is discipline. Every aspect of battle is controlled from formation to combat to division of spoils. The Legions are divided into five forty-thousand-man units, each carrying the standard of one of the five classes of dragon: the Golden Dragon, which is commanded by the Legion General, the Wyvern, the Fire Drake, the Ice Drake, and the Tidal Dragon.

The Titan Battle Manual, Cedric Rhone

Neither aesthetic nor large, the simple stone stockade of Fort Dragonstone served its purpose well. The fort had highly defensible walls impossible to scale, and ten sentries walked the length of the wall. The entrance to Dragonstone was marked by the five dragon heads of the Legion's namesake, the Golden Dragon, the Wyvern, the Fire Drake, the Ice Drake, and the Tidal. Dragonstone also bore the distinction of being the only building left in Napolitan to use the SPQN rather than RPQN on the entrance to the building. The mark served as the final act of defiance of the Legionnaires who did not agree with Draconius seizing power.

A raucous crowd of publicans and plebeians filled the gallery around the Fort cheering and showering flower petals on the Legion soldiers. For the first time in many generations all two hundred thousand Legionnaires had gathered in the center of Dragonstone, each group standing behind the five standards. In the center, Cagius stood proudly with his helmet off in front of the golden dragon standard with Marcus Polonius serving as his Centurion. Behind the Legions, Joshua found himself in a group of Napolitan horseman.

Entering the Fort from the front gate, Constantine came dressed in his old Legion armor, his head adorned with an olive leaf crown symbolizing his office as Caesar. Marguerite was also dressed in a traditional green toga with golden sash to see off the Legion. Saving all the strength he had left for battle, Darius rode in a cart behind them but wore his armor as well. In the Caesar's right hand was an ivory baton with a gold dragon head on top of it. Valentine took his position next to Cagius and playfully bumped him. A smile crossed the face of the dragoon as he waited for his father.

"Brave citizens of Napolitan, we received news. Prince Cedric Rhone of Titanus has successfully taken Fort Orion from the Acadian Templar army," announced Constantine. "As per our alliance, Napolitan will join them for an assault on Verian and their false king Maximilian Luminas."

Deafening cheers overwhelmed the Fort as screams of "Victory" came off the lips of every citizen.

"Cagius Imperia, son of the Caesar and Napolitan, you are granted the honor of leading the Legions into battle," continued the Caesar.

"Hail Caesar!" answered Cagius.

"Your exceptional talents and the respect you have garnered among the Legionnaires has led to an unprecedented decision on my part. While I have every intention of fighting this battle with you, I do so as your subordinate."

Constantine's decision was shocking to everyone but his closest commanders and confidants. The old Caesar knew his son would do a better job leading the Legions and the glory for their victory would rightly fall on Cagius' shoulders instead of his. Putting his fist to his heart, Cagius took the baton from his father and gave him a strong embrace. Turning to her son, Marguerite hugged him tightly before she stepped back. She took a favor in her hand and placed it within Cagius' armor.

"Return this favor of Napolitan to me, General. The hearts and prayers of this country are with you," said his mother.

"Thank you, Mother."

Cagius returned to his Legions, and the troops proudly beat their spears into their shields as they screamed in unison, "All Hail Legate Cagius!" Swooning women in the crowd threw flowers of every kind at the dragoon, but two men in particular were not happy by the events surrounding them. Standing at the entrance of the Fort, Judge Gravius and Vincenzo stood with the Praetorian. Cagius' popularity among the Legions and people was something that was going to have to be dealt with. Both men privately wished an accident would befall the Legate in the coming battle. Holding the baton high in the air, Cagius gave the order for the troops to fall out.

The sound of drums could be heard in the background as the Legions marched in perfect step and order. As usual, a nice, slow cadence was preferred by the Legate. Joshua and the Paladins around him took to guarding James' cart. General Darius choked blood into a towel as they started to leave.

"General Darius, would you not prefer the comfort of a bed to this?" asked Joshua.

"You know, you're the only who has even dared ask that question," responded Darius. "It gives me hope, that even in my last rotations, I was able to meet you. However, I won't die having my guts ripped out and doped up to the point I don't recognize my own family. It's one last battle, perhaps for our very souls. Please, Joshua, promise me you won't repeat the mistakes of your father."

"I promise."

"Good boy. One last thing, take care of your uncle," said Darius as he stared at the scheming Gravius above. "He's going to need brave and faithful men like you."

Fort Orion, Central Acadia

Sirius, it is not your responsibility to single-handedly determine the fate of the Evengard. Trust in the Father and the fact
that very powerful people know what happened that fateful
rotation. There will come a time when you need to use this
sensitive information I am about to give you, and that is why I
entrust it to you.

Cerwin Faulkner to Sirius

Overseeing the actions of the operation technicians, Christian
stood in Orion's command center. Synchronization with the
War Room in Titanus had been established and messages had been
sent out to all of the allies. He noticed one of the technicians having
a difficult time with his communication. Christian stepped in and
took his terminal.

"Amuro, is everything okay?" asked Christian.

There was dead silence for a few moments.

"I hate to press you," assured Christian. "However, Cedric is
running a tight clock here and we need some confirmation that your
armies are on the way."

"Christian, the armies of the Elves stand apart."

"What are you talking about?"

"I have no command authority over a vast majority of the armies of Evengard anymore. A large percentage of it has fled the forest and gone rogue."

"Wait, Amuro. What the hell is going on?"

"My father considers Cedric an honorable man and as such believes he owes him an explanation. I am riding with him. As to what the other Elves choose to do, I have no control. Over and out."

Dumbfounded by the conversation and the lack of the Elf marshal's cheery disposition, Christian threw the headset down. Banging his hands into the desk for a few seconds, the operative finally regained his composure. As he moved to the entrance of the control room, Sirius stood there waiting for him. DeVries wore a disappointed look on his face.

"So an Elf has already come. I thought our operations were well concealed."

"Sir Christian, I need to speak with you…in private, please."

Christian saw the seriousness in his eyes and bent down to his technician. "Hold the Fort for me! This may take a while," ordered Christian.

The two stepped into the hallway and proceeded to a private room. Christian took a few moments to scan and secure the location. Satisfied, he allowed Sirius to proceed.

"Where are the Elves of Evengard, Sirius? Why does Amuro no longer command them?"

Sirius threw himself down at Christian's feet. Though irritated by the Captain's actions, the operative pondered what had brought this sudden change in demeanor over the normally hardened Sirius.

"My true King Dulles Marisol, I bring ill tidings in this hour."

"I asked you never to call me that and to forget about that dream."

"I promised Cerwin my obedience and I've kept silent my entire life, but I cannot do so in good conscience anymore. My Lord, Evengard is in turmoil. Camdem Jenitzen has seized power and he's imprisoned the other great lords. He believes that Cerwin's death has forfeited all rights of the Judge of the Change. He wants the crown for himself."

"Camdem has no authority to do so. He would need the blessings of a prophet!"

"He does not embrace the Will of the Father! I know of the sins of Saulides well, as I am descended from the Great Warrior Joab. I will not sit idly and watch my country die. Thankfully I reached Malcolm and Amuro before they returned to Evengard. It must have pained him greatly, but the ranger believed me. Malcolm is marching the Elf army of Evengard here in secret. They stand in conflict with Jenitzen's personal army with Amuro at their head."

"We can't withstand an Elven civil war in the midst of Abaddon's cruelty. Camdem would dare not oppose all of Evengard unless he had a second plan."

"Camdem wants to seal off the Forest! He intends to use his daughters as bargaining chips to keep other families loyal to him. Jenitzen believes that Cedric has brought this war upon the West, but let's deal with reality. Camdem has been driven mad over the past thirty revolutions and was always looking for a way out of the Alliance. This fracture gives him the perfect excuse. He even has the gall to tell Lord Cedric to his face."

"What about Amuro? She's popular with the army and her people, surely they would…"

"It is true that all of Evengard loves Lady Amuro and a prophet would rise up to grant her the mantle of leadership, but she will not stand against the wrongdoing of her father. Amuro believes in her family strongly and her blind love for him leaves her ignorant to his true motives. Her overwhelming desire to please her father at all costs is her weakness."

Tears in his eyes, Christian could only imagine the sorrow Amuro was experiencing. How could anyone go against their own father?

"Without Evengard… we're sunk," acknowledged Christian.

"There is another way, my King."

"You ask me to walk a path I cannot."

"Surely there is still a part of you that loves Evengard! A part that honors the beauty and Majesty of your mother."

"It is because of that love that I cannot walk that path. My mother's dying wish was that her son would not succumb to the same forces that destroyed her."

"I do not ask you to come back as ruler; that time is over. I would not dare insult the memories and will of her Highness. We both understand what must be now! Amuro needs help and you're the only one who can expose her to the truth. Make her put country before family! Besides, you don't know the whole story."

A gentle rapping took place on the door before Cedric and Cecilia entered. Angry at the emergence of his friend, Christian turned his back on Cedric.

"And you dare to eavesdrop on this!" retorted Christian.

"It was not difficult to ascertain what this conversation was about when Captain Sirius shows up with a company of Royal Elf Lancers at a newly taken Fort," countered Cedric.

"Please, Christian, for all our sakes, you have to listen to my brother," pleaded Cecilia.

"Why from his lips, Sirius?" questioned Christian.

"Because the Father truly favors Cedric Rhone and some of our people do see him as a great prophet, or perhaps the second coming of the General or one of the Judges. Most of all, you should listen to him because he is your friend."

"Let's just say I've been privy to information over the revolutions," suggested Cedric. "Information I kept secret out of friendship."

"I thank you for that. It would have been easier for you to place me on the throne of Evengard to achieve your goals."

"Are you ready to know the truth of the circumstances of your birth?"

"What truth? My mother fell in love with an Edenian Ranger. It's easy enough fact to accept."

"Do you know who Anton DeVries really was? He was more than a mere Edenian Ranger, he served as the shield-bearer to Prince Richard Archibald. He wasn't always a pusillanimous wimp, you know. He was once a handsome and courageous young Divikin who was quite taken with the beautiful Queen of Evengard."

"The young Prince spent a full holiday in Brooke Run," revealed Sirius. "He revisited the Kingdom many times."

"Are you saying that my father was Richard Archibald?"

"When your mother was murdered, the Empire and Titanus were at war," explained Cedric. "Prince Archibald felt that tensions would rise if he formally adopted you and brought you to Palacio Magnifico. It would have given both the Empire a claim in the West and Titanus a reason for marching their armies into Imperial territory. Thus, he sent his most trusted bodyguard to extract his son from Evengard."

"Naturally the child was brought to Titanus. It was easy because of the widespread persecution of Christians at the time," interjected Sirius. "Cerwin arranged it with Wilhelm so there would be no investigation."

"That loser!" exclaimed Christian as he fell back into a chair and covered his head. "That was his response to the situation! Leave my mother to die and abandon his son to Titanus. I should have let Colin kill them all! How did you learn of this, Cedric?"

"I had my connections, but I confirmed everything with Argus Kinkade. He's Gustav Archibald, Richard's brother and your uncle. You're not the only person who was disappointed in your father."

"Who murdered my mother?"

"It was Camdem Jenitzen," revealed Sirius. "He knew when to strike. When an Elf woman is carrying a child she must suppress her magical powers or risk a spontaneous abortion. Your mother needed to wear a tremendous amount of charms to suppress her substantial magical powers. Those around Gweyn trusted him and it was easy for him to get close to her with a dagger and do the deed. Despite the wound, she used all of her strength to make sure you were born alive."

"Gweyn knew that you could never sit on that throne," added Cecilia. "Camdem, along with his agents, would do anything to destroy you. That is why Cerwin pretended you died before you were delivered."

"And now, Sirius, you want me to take revenge on your enemies?" queried Christian. "Plan your own assassination."

"Camdem's death gains the country I love nothing!" shouted Sirius. "Expose this heathen for who he really is, free our Lords and inspire Amuro to do what is right."

"Do you know why I have this scar on the right side of my face?" asked Christian.

"No, my Lord Dulles."

"This is where his dagger touched me. That's how deep that animal cut my mother. Wilhelm begged me to have it fixed, but I refused. I wanted to stare at it in the mirror every morning to remind me of what I left behind and what remains for me in the nation of my birth. I am not the King called by the Father to come and rescue you...for that I'm sorry."

"My Lord, I will honor your decision and abide by it," offered Sirius as he bowed his head in respect. "I thank you for your time and I will do everything possible to keep Malcolm and the rebel army safe."

When the Elf captain left, the twins remained behind. Shaken slightly, Christian accepted the hand of both of them. Smiles were all around, despite the harsh nature of the conversation.

"I know what you would have me do, in that way I have failed you, your Excellency," said Christian regretfully. "I know now that I do not have the courage or the resolve to follow the path you would choose."

"I've never asked anyone to follow me where I must go. We both have duties to attend to. I will say nothing more of this. Your fate concerning Evengard is your own."

Mountain Retreat, Western Griffin Mountains

The Ogle Tanka Un is leader of the Tribal Confederation and as such must be acknowledged by each of the four tribes. This is done by the granting of certain totems that serve as both a symbol of leadership and spiritual protection.

On the Tribes, General James Darius

Deep in the mountain retreat, representatives from all of the tribes gathered around the great fire. Though not garbed in war paint, nor frenzying themselves for coming battle, the Tribes had heeded Colin's advice and prepared to advance for Fort Orion. Hippolyte, Reynard, Posha, and Adnar stood before each of their people and their standards. Colin stood alone by the fire in his armor, sword staked in the ground in front of him. Stepping forward with incense in her hand, Posha chanted in the ancient tribal tongue. All of the other chiefs would interject at different points in chorus. Foreign to everything that was happening, Colin simply soaked it in. When she finished, Hippolyte came forward.

"Colin Wilkins," started Hippolyte. "You stand before the four Chiefs of the Tribal Confederation. Each tribe must name you Ogle Tanka Un, skin-wearer, to lead us in the coming battle."

Adnar came forward brandishing a hatchet. Wilkins felt a bit uneasy with the boorish Viking sizing him up. After a few tense moments, he presented the hatchet.

"The axe is the symbol of power for the Nordice Vikings. We name you Ogle Tanka Un out of respect for your size and power."

"The amulet of our forefathers, the sacred symbol of wisdom of the Syrus Clan," added Posha. "We name thee Ogle Tanka Un to avenge our fallen brothers and sisters."

Posha placed the amulet around his neck as Reynard stepped forward holding a paint horse by the reins.

"From the Myotis Tribe, we present the Ogle Tanka Un the finest horse of our stocks. Bred for centuries in the ancient ways of our clan, it will serve you faithfully and courageously in battle. This horse is a true companion worthy of what is best in you."

Colin put his hands out to the horse's nose. The beast nodded twice to acknowledge Wilkins as his master. Finally Minerva walked over to Hippolyte and presented her with a cape made of gray wolf fur.

"In this matte of skin is the bravest of our fallen battle wolves," presented Hippolyte. "Only those who distinguished themselves in life have been granted this honor in death. They serve as the penultimate guardians as their pack carries on the tradition."

As Hippolyte started to dress him, Colin put his hand to hers.

"A cape?" questioned Colin nervously. "You didn't say anything about a cape!"

"All of your steel-belly friends wear cloaks! I didn't think this would be a problem."

"I just don't like the idea of something hanging behind on me. What if it gets snagged and I wind up breaking my neck?"

"How neurotic you are!" teased a laughing Hippolyte. "I thought someone who wore armor made of bones wouldn't care for aesthetics."

"It's only designed to look like bones, Hippolyte."

Hippolyte tied the cloak along his shoulders so that the ceremony could be completed.

"Four tribes have named you Ogle Tanka Un, War Leader of the Tribal Confederation," said Posha in blessing. "Very few throughout our proud history have ever been granted such an honor. May you lead us to victory in the coming battles."

Posha waved the branch around Colin to complete the blessing. All of trial warriors bowed their heads toward Colin, who felt quite uncomfortable with all the attention. He knew, however, what needed to be done.

"Brave Warriors of the Tribal Confederation, we march for Fort Orion to join forces with the Alliance of the Western Kingdoms," announced Hippolyte. "I know that many of you are uneasy with joining our forces together, but I have witnessed firsthand the enemy we face. It is for that reason that I had my chosen consort Colin Wilkins named as Ogle Tanka Un. He will represent our armies before the steel-bellies because he respects the Tribes. We are on the brink of a New Age for our people and this change will be difficult. However, we will have no future if we do not make our stand against the darkness. We owe Prince Rhone of Titanus and the others the opportunity to make their case to us."

The tribes cheered this statement on.

"Now, we will all follow you!" said Hippolyte to Colin.

"Then I will lead you to Prince Cedric Rhone at Fort Orion."

Hippolyte, Colin, Minerva, and Huskal went to their horses as Adnar and Josephine joined their formations. The tribes marched out of the Mountain retreat and towards Fort Orion. As they journeyed, a contingent of Dwarves led by Lurac joined the protection of the train. Titanus had taken the first step, but what remained to be seen was if a coalition of willing would be formed.

GARRET'S HOME, EVENGARD

The First Alliance consisted of the Kingdoms of Titanus and Evengard, the city-state Verian, the Napolitan Trade Federation, and various tribes from the West. Though fundamentally different, fear of being swallowed by the unstoppable Empire brought them together.

Garrett on the forming the First Alliance

S eated on his porch with pipe in one hand and tankard in the other, Garrett listened to a rumbling on the road. A smile crept across his face as the sound of horses grew louder and louder. Argus, Quinn, and Mesmara rode at the head of a column of Kablisha militia. Behind them was a carriage carrying both Bishop Wulf and Taylor Yueh of Titanus. Stopping outside of Garrett's fence, Argus dismounted and assisted the Bishop from his carriage.

"Peter Wulf," reasoned Garrett. "It's been far too long. May I have your blessing?"

The Bishop performed the necessary rites of greeting. After laying his hands on the kobold's head, the two laughed and embraced one another.

"It's been five revolutions since I was visited by exiled royalty—Prince Dulles Marisol and Prince Gustav Archibald—and if I were a mercenary I would have made quite a bit of money."

"Are you prepared?" asked Argus. "I fear our time is short."

"That depends on if you brought what I asked," demanded Garrett.

Reaching into her saddlebag, Mesmara pulled up a glass case. Inside the case was an old book, bound in leather with gold-trimmed pages. Taylor Yueh carried a newer book in his hands as well, bound in more traditional methods.

"This book from the Library of the City of Antiquity contains information on the *Permaneo Eques Ordinares*, at least the version the Kablisha have been told for centuries," explained Mesmara.

"While the Queen dare not part with the original, we have a copy of the Titan legend as well," said Taylor. "We both assumed you still have the Elven copy."

"Indeed," affirmed Garrett. "And Argus, what of the Edenian legend?"

"The only known written version is in the Library of Edenia," expounded Argus. "It cannot be removed and can only be viewed under the care of a librarian."

"Very well," said a resigned Garrett. "I had planned on such a contingency."

"Why the newfound interest in the prophecies?" inquired Quinn.

"The prophecies don't fit with one another," lectured Garrett. "We know from the scriptures that no writers will ever write from the same perspective; however, there are pieces missing in each of the prophecies. The Elves speak of a Last Knight, the Kablisha a Knight of God, and the Titans the Twice-Blessed Queen."

"What about your visions?" asked the Bishop.

"My visions have been clouded as of late. There is no illuminated path to the future. We must rely on faith, hope, and charity."

"Then there is no word on Camael," said a dejected Argus.

"I hope to find my answers when I study the prophecies."

"It may be too late for that," offered Argus. "Cedric is marching on Verian as we speak. If Abaddon can take physical form again…"

"Then we must rely on the faith and judgment of Cedric Rhone and the prophecies."

"Why Cedric alone?" demanded Argus. "All will march…"

"Will they? The Alliance that was brought together is maintained only because they fear and revere the Prince of Titanus. Even so, there are fractures. Camdem Jenitzen is going to try to force the Queen's hand. Constantine for all his strength has been slipping these past revolutions and surrounds himself with vultures. Will the Tribes so easily trust the same foes that murdered their people? No, Argus, that is why my own personal quest must be delayed. I must come to Fort Orion with you and prod the Alliance once again."

A bag was packed next to the kobold. Reaching down with his cane, he caught the strap of the bag and tossed it to Quinn. A hearty laugh was shared.

"Argus, do you believe in Cedric Rhone?" inquired Garrett.

"I don't understand the question. Cedric Rhone is a great warrior who will die to save those he loves. He proved how far he willing to go when the Nephilim invaded the City of Antiquity."

"Do you believe that he can do the impossible? Do you believe that he can succeed when no one else can?"

"Yes," replied Argus after closing his eyes for a moment. "I think he can change fate."

"Argus, inside my drawing room you will find a potted plant that is yet to bloom. I want you to take that plant to Fort Orion for me. Handle it with extreme care, it's quite fragile."

"As you wish, Garrett."

Entering and emerging from the home in but a few moments, Argus carried the plant back outside. Garrett closed and locked the door behind him.

"I'm no botanist," offered Argus as he stared at the plant. "This flower seems familiar, but I don't know what it is."

"It's a poppy plant," observed Taylor. "Based on its leaves, I'd say that Garrett probably had it cultivated in the Titan Heartlands."

"You have sharp eye, Minister Yueh," complimented Garrett. "With that damned barrier up, I never thought it would make it in time, but here we are."

"Well, then there's no mystery involved," joked Quinn. "The poppy will be red when it blooms. Cedric and Cecilia explained that to us."

"So you have said," commented Garrett. "Let us go to Fort Orion, the Alliance awaits."

Wulf and Taylor assisted Garrett into the carriage. Following orders, Argus mounted and took great care to maintain the potted plant. When all was secured, the Kablisha made their way to the gold road and Fort Orion.

Castle Acadia, Central Acadia

It's the end of the world...

Last transmission from Fort Orion

Gavin was sitting in one of the rooms with his face buried in his hands. Wet drops on the table and floor showed that he had been crying. On his desk was a formal declaration of war bearing the mark of Titanus and signed in the large cursive script of Prince Cedric Rhone. Roland entered the room.

"So you've heard..." offered Roland.

Gavin looked up with red eyes, visibly shaken. "THE WHOLE ARMY, ROLAND! THE WHOLE DAMN TEMPLAR ARMY! Seventy-five thousand of our finest Knights and soldiers lasted mere hours against the Titan Armada."

"Karstak dead—it's unimaginable."

"How can we fight something like this, Roland?" questioned Gavin rhetorically. "How do we fight an army bred from birth for this Crusade?"

"We still have Commander Mormont and Abaddon's army."

"And what else? Do you truly believe in this cretin army that mad scientist has created?"

"I follow the Queen."

"Don't mince words with me, my friend. You and I both know that the Queen is completely under the sway of Abaddon! This isn't about Central Acadia anymore, and you know it."

"I still trust her judgment. You saw the commanding presence she had when she first took up her throne. There's power behind it. Surely you can believe in her if nothing else."

"I don't know if I can anymore."

"Gavin, there's so few of us left now."

"I'll be there when the fighting starts…but…I don't know, I guess I still talk too much."

Jonas Marimon walked to the door. Gavin and Roland snapped to attention. Though bearing a sorrowful countenance unused to his face, the Saint Commander was boiling over with rage.

"Gavin, Roland, we're having a briefing in twenty. We need to prepare a battle plan for the coming invasion. We've confirmed that Fort Orion now flies the flag of Titanus. Armies are on approach from the four corners of the west."

Both replied with an affirmative. Jonas turned to leave, but stopped for a moment. He turned back to face his subordinates once more. They almost spotted a tear in his eyes.

"After the meeting, we'll remember Karstak. I know he wasn't the best of us, but still…those Titan bastards are going to learn that no one takes down one of our own."

Gavin and Roland both nodded as Jonas walked down the hall. Gavin walked over to a bottle he had on the desk. He poured a drink for himself and Roland.

"For our fallen brother…" toasted Roland.

"Karstak was a cruel soldier, but he knew how a battle needed to be won," Gavin said with a salute. "I'm not surprised how he died… he did everything he could to save his command. We're going to need more men like him for what is coming."

The two finished their drinks quickly and left the room. In one of the upper rooms, Abaddon stood staring out at the remains of the city through glass windows. The massive renovations to the outer walls and defenses were completed and Verian was now a Fortress city. Almost breathing a sigh of relief at their newfound defenses, the dark angel heard Virgus enter the room.

"Is it true?" asked Abaddon.

"Seventy-five thousand killed or captured…their commander dead…Fort Orion sits in the control of the Titans," explained Virgus.

"And?"

"I'm tracking movement from all over the west. They are moving towards Fort Orion."

"It will be a matter of rotations now. What about the walls? Did you spray them with the reinforcement compound that you promised me?"

"You have to give me one more rotation. I really need two but I can push it to one. Kaladra and the others are at their limits. They need about two rotations of rest to be battle-ready."

"Would you prefer to have the Alliance Army gaining easy access to the city?"

"I can only do so much…"

"The odds are that they would not move so quickly. Cedric still has to convince many hearts and minds of his plan." Abaddon could feel his wound acting up.

"The wound again, my Lord?"

"Don't worry about it. Are the remaining preparations taken care of?"

"Yes, though I'm not certain how it's going to work."

"Just handle your clone, I'll take care of the rest. This is it for all of us. I can't go back empty-handed, Virgus!" Abaddon said, becoming tense. "Do you understand that I CANNOT GO BACK!"

Virgus swallowed hard at the edge in Abaddon's voice. "My technology will be the least of our worries."

"Good. What is the status of your cloning vats?"

"I've run out of genetic material. Yet, based on the rates that it takes to clone the soldier and have them up and ready for battle, this was going to be the last batch, anyway."

"I've never believed in quantity of forces until I meet the quality and discipline of these Western Alliance troops. The army must be prepared and ready to go against the coming forces."

"It will be."

"I know Jonas is meeting with his Saints. When it is complete, we need to gather everyone to discuss our battle plan. We must present a united front, for surely the alliance will as well."

Virgus nodded and left. Abaddon stared at the distance.

"He is close now, and another power...something I haven't felt in a long time...what are you doing here, Guardian?"

FORT ORION, CENTRAL ACADIA

You would march into a massacre, Frederick, if you attempted to tackle this Imperial army alone. You must seek out those of goodwill, those that have the courage and heart to fight against tyranny and oppression. You must seek your allies among your brothers in the West. If you plead your case to them and speak with a righteous heart, all will follow you.

Garrett Greensage to King Frederick Rhone on the forming of the First Alliance

It had been a good five revolutions, but the Alliance army was not completely out of practice. On one side of Fort Orion, the nine-square encampment was established with each of the Kingdoms assuming their normal positions. On the other side of the Fort, thousands of war tents were established for the Tribal Confederation. A great raging fire had been started in the center of the war encampment, and, under Colin's advice, they dug in a stockade at their position as well. Unlike their superiors and leaders, the aura of tension seemed to not exist among the professional soldiers. Rather, they calmly spoke to one another, shared a few laughs, and even traded armor and tokens.

Inside the Fort, a silence overwhelmed all other emotions. It was tense all morning, especially after the arrival of Camdem Jenitzen. It took almost everything his two daughters had to keep him at Fort Orion, once he noticed Malcolm stationed there with his Elf deserter army. Still coming to terms with the information presented to him, Christian stared out the window of his quarters. Alerted to a gently rap on his door, the operative opened it to see Rosa standing there. Not draped in her usual forest camouflage or her ranger's gear, the Elf maiden truly looked like a princess in a gown of green with gold trim. A silver circlet with a sapphire stone held her fiery red hair in place. Rosa smiled.

"I can see you're surprised."

"Rosa... you look... you..."

"It's been a long time since I wore one of these. I really must thank Cecilia, she thought of everything. Oh...I haven't twirled in such a long time! Watch!" Rosa pirouetted in a circle, absolutely enjoying the sound the frilly dress made. "So, how do I look?"

"You look magnificent, Rosa."

"I can live with that. Given the importance of the coming conference, I deemed it appropriate to look like the leader of one of the armies. Now the three warrior maidens of Cassandra, Cecilia, and Amuro can add a fourth in Rosa Landon."

Putting her head to his heart, Rosa squeezed Christian around his waist. "Are you still haunted by what was said to you?" asked a concerned Rosa.

"Of course. It's just that I tried to believe in something for such a long time. However, I fear I don't know who I am."

Rosa didn't answer but continued to stare at him.

"I have always lived a double life. Am I Christian DeVries, Colonel of Titanus, or Dulles Marisol, Prince of Evengard? Two lives... one I love, and the other I have loathed since the rotation I was born. Yet, the only thing that ever converged in my two lives was my love for you."

"Well, you can't beat that, Christian. Would you care for an honest assessment of your situation?"

"Perhaps a she-elf perspective might be best."

"My dreams of being married to an Elf prince ended when I was very young. From the rotation I first met you, I knew you could never ascend to the throne of Evengard. The thought of it repulsed you. You are what our people traditionally described as the shield-bearer of Cedric Rhone. You are his finest warrior, confidant, friend, and servant. You are not afraid to tell him what he needs to hear, but can still give him the information he wants. You are Christian DeVries."

"I'm glad you understand."

"You are also your mother's son. Gweyn Marisol was loved by our people and there were those that thought of her as a radiant Queen of Light. When the heathen Camdem Jenitzen killed your mother, a piece of Evengard's soul died with her. My father, mother, and Captain Sirius have given everything to restore that piece of soul. Evengard is crying out for a savior. Yet, Dulles Marisol can't save his people anymore. Amuro is the only one who can. She's the leader they've been dying for and Malcolm is her perfect consort. He will provide the temperance and understanding that has been missing in Evengard for revolutions. I looked into Amuro's eyes and saw hesitation. With her father's overwhelming presence, she fears for any child that he doesn't deem worthy of a throne."

"That's why Sirius came to me…he knows I have an extraordinary opportunity—that I've got not only an Elf maiden at my back, but also the most feared warrior on Terminus Mundus."

"I don't care what Sirius says. No one has the right to demand that you do this. No matter what path you trod, you will not stand alone."

"Maybe that's what I really needed to hear…"

"Always happy to oblige, my dearest one."

The two could hear the chimes coming from the four parapets of the fort. Both took a deep breath and smiled.

"I think he's getting anxious," observed Christian.

"You know how Cedric hates for anyone to be late."

The Grand Conference room in Fort Orion usually featured an intimate gathering of no more than twenty. Yet, for the first time in history, it hosted a vast delegation of the leadership and senior offi-cers of the four kingdoms, four tribes, the Kablisha, Deniva, and the Titan vassals.

At the northern end of the room, four thrones were stationed for each of the leaders of the four kingdoms. Civilia, Cassandra, Constantine, and Camdem occupied each of them. The senior staff and advisors of all twelve nations were each allotted a long round table facing the four thrones. The remaining politicians, advisors, and officers were in chairs on the sides of the room. It wasn't enough that vitriol existed between the kingdoms and tribes in the room. Yet, each individual kingdom seemed to be undergoing their own problems as well. Norville Warrington was upset that Jonathan Walker was given a higher place of honor at their table. Amuro and Malcolm sat with their heads down as Elves on either side of them hurled insults back and forth at one another. Before a single word was said, Gravius and Darius were already fighting with one anoth-er. As Christian and Rosa entered the room, a pain formed in both of their stomachs. Parting with a kiss, the Elf maiden took her position at the wood Elf delegation with Gerard and his kin. DeVries scanned the Titan delegation for Cedric, but instead found him just outside the main room with Wilhelm, Francis, and Nadia. The Titan sword master leaned against the wall with his arms folded across his chest and eyes closed.

"Cedric, do you hear what's going on in there?" demanded Christian.

"It's annoying that an event like this must take place in order to destroy an evil that desires only to consume us all," pronounced Cedric.

"Isn't giving them the illusion of a choice better than none at all?" asked Christian.

"No," interrupted Francis. "It may not be my place to speak. This is your world and I am but a guest. However, I have tried so many times to array a similar alliance and most have resulted in epic failures."

"You have to forgive Francis' bluntness," commented Wilhelm. "However, he does speak the truth. It's been so many revolutions, and we have watched history repeat itself again and again. It's so tiring."

Christian didn't know what was worse: Wilhelm resigned to the fact this meeting was going to fail or Francis' abject panic and crestfallen face. But as Cedric opened his eyes, the Titan operative sensed an aura of calm that reassured him. He went to speak another word, but could hear the sound of Taylor Yueh banging a staff against the floor signaling silence and the beginning of the Conference.

"Lord and Ladies of the West at behest of the sovereign of Titanus, Queen Civilia Rhone, may I humbly present Queen Cassandra Acadia of Central Acadia," announced Taylor.

Dressed in her finest gown, the Queen stood from her throne. Though her companions had been used to this for some time, many in this room had not yet witnessed the radiance and majesty of the beautiful young Queen.

"I extend my fondest greetings and salutations to some of my oldest and newest friends," pronounced Cassandra. "I welcome all of you, Kingdom, Tribe, Nation, Human, Elf, Divikin, and Dwarf. A great crisis surrounds our beloved plains and it is imperative that we act to remove this blight from our land."

"Let us thank the Saints for allowing us to gather," appealed Constantine.

"And the spirits who have brought our people together," said Posha.

"And by the Grace of God, we will stop the evil plaguing our lands," prayed Bishop Wulf.

"Before we begin, I do believe that the Queen of Titanus wishes to address a formality," added Cassandra.

"It is necessary that the three Wards of the Realm officially recognize the new ruler of Central Acadia as steward of our Alliance," started Civilia after standing from her throne. "Titanus fully accepts Cassandra Acadia as the new Queen of Central Acadia. In doing so we are severing any allegiance to Queen Marie Acadia. I ask my brethren from Napolitan and Evengard to address this issue now."

"Napolitan recognizes that Queen Cassandra Acadia is the lawful ruler of Central Acadia by their own laws of succession," agreed Constantine. "We will never support that harlot that deceived me and allowed my son to die."

"She may only be half-blood, but Cassandra remains kin to the Elves," explained Camdem. "We support her fully for the position of stewardship and disavow Marie Acadia."

"Since all three Wardens are in agreement, Queen Cassandra Acadia is officially recognized as the ruler of Central Acadia and as such will receive the position of Steward over the Western Alliance," pronounced Civilia. "In doing so, all nations shall disavow Maria Acadia as Queen of Central Acadia and thus anyone found supporting her ascension will be subject to the Alliance punishment for treason."

"I am humbled by your judgment and will do everything in my power to keep your trust," said Cassandra, nodding. "It pains me greatly that my sister has cast her lot with these forces of evil and we must do whatever is necessary to break those bonds. For now, we must turn to the matter at hand, the planned invasion of Central Acadia and the siege of Verian. I now cede the floor to Prince Marshal Cedric Rhone of Titanus."

Cedric pushed off the wall with his back foot. In one motion, he fixed his jacket and swung his cape back behind his shoulders. The room became silent as they stared at the hardened warrior.

"Let me take the time to reintroduce myself! I am Cedric Rhone, Prince of Titanus, Marshal of the Alliance Army, known as *La Morte Angelus* or *Prime Eagle* depending on the tongue you prefer. My cause is simple, I want to see the evil that has penetrated and corrupted Verian to be purified in fire. As many of you know, I've had five long revolutions to contemplate how and why this needs to be done. Some of you have come here expecting a long-winded speech followed by the necessary concessions and promises to forge an alliance to march on Verian. I'm sorry to disappoint those of you."

Many in the room were stunned by such impertinence, but his closest friends and allies knew the Divikin for what he was. There was no difference in this Cedric than the one that defied Stephen at the Inquisition. Though Christian had no idea how this was going to help their cause, Wilhelm's hand to his shoulder reassured him.

"On the third morning, I will march with the armies of Titanus on Verian. Our allies the Dwarves and the Wood Elves have honored the pledge to join us in battle. The Kablisha, Denivan Mercenaries and the Order of the Lion of Central Acadia have also made similar pledges. I welcome all others willing to join us. These terms are non-negotiable. If you wish to join us, I ask you to decide quickly, for there are many preparations to make."

Cedric walked back to the pillar he was leaning against. Wilhelm leaned over towards Cedric.

"Is that all you have?"

"No matter how long I continue my diatribe, it won't do us any good unless they are willing to make the first step. Using my powers would make it easy, but it won't do us any good in the long run. This isn't about one battle, Wilhelm, I'm in it for the long road. It's time that Cassie makes use of the tremendous power she yields."

When the murmurings over Cedric's opening speech finally settled down, Cassandra stood from her throne once more.

"It was the dream of my father that all of us should live in peace. Yet there is something stopping that dream. Count Luminas is determined to destroy my father's legacy. I know that there have been many rumors spreading about myself and my nature. It is with great shame that I must affirm some of them to be true. In spite of this, I know that I must lead my nation and stand with Titanus in the effort to dispose of Luminas and the traitors. I now open the forum to all nations. I ask only that you act in proper respect towards one another."

"As Chief, I speak for all of my people," volunteered Hippolyte as she stood. "It is not easy for my tribe to enter the Fort that became the symbol of our oppression. For revolutions, we suffered under the tyranny and threats of war from the Kingdoms. Nowhere was this oppression worse than from Central Acadia and its wretched self-centered bureaucrats. I have come to know Cedric Rhone as a knight of true honor, but I cannot say such words of the rest of those

gathered here. The Tribal Confederation must have guarantees before we take up arms at your side."

"It would be foolish to assume that the Tribes could wage their
own war against Verian," retorted Constantine. "If you couldn't
even match the power of our combined forces in battle, what could
you do against the armies of Luminas?"

"You would find, Caesar Constantine, that our warriors are
worth just as much as yours," countered Reynard. "We were presented with an Armistice by King Stephen and your late son Julius
made certain promises to us! We want a similar treaty enforced if we
are to join this war."

"The time of war between Kingdom and Tribe needs to end,"
offered a conciliatory Posha. "The murder of one another has only
brought us misery. There were so many needless lives lost when our
Northern tribes were murdered by Luminas and his men. We hold no
ill-will toward your people for this, we just wish you to understand
our suffering."

"We have all suffered at the hands of Abaddon!" exclaimed Civilia, clearly disconcerted with the stubbornness and pride of the
Tribes.

"Please, your Majesty," interrupted Camdem "But how much
longer must we endure the old wives' tales and legends of Titanus?"

"The Dark Angel walks in this world!" proclaimed Bishop Wulf.
"His greatest strength is the denial of his existence by those in this
room."

"Excuse me, sir," inquired Huskal politely. "I have not had the
privilege, who are you?"

"I am Bishop Peter Wulf, leader of the Kablisha."

"The Ancients are here?" exasperated Josephine. "I thought
when the Istle Hills were abandoned, you left this world."

"It is true, Josephine of the Myotis Clan, that the Kablisha felt
that if we simply retired from the world and sealed ourselves off our
worries would end. Yet, the dark angel Abaddon seeks to destroy all
of those that would oppose him and he will not discriminate between

us. He invaded our Kingdom and only through the heroics of Cedric Rhone were our people able to defeat him. We cannot hide ourselves away any longer. If we don't stop Abaddon and Luminas, all life on Terminus Mundus, and perhaps creation, will be wiped out."

"If the Ancients have come, then there must be a terrible danger among us," reasoned Posha. "We knew that one as strong as Chieftain Aramas could not be slain by an ordinary warrior, but a creature of evil…"

"Yes," shouted Ethan as he stood next to his father. "It is hard to believe all of this at first, but Deniva has suffered catastrophic loss at the hands of this dark angel. Abaddon used the Dark Elves like puppets to attack and destroy our Margrave. Fortunately, thanks to the brave sacrifices of those sitting in this room and the timely arrival of Cedric Rhone and Wilhelm von Angelhardt, we were able to fight off such an attack."

"Abaddon has a new army that invaded the sanctity of my halls and killed some of my finest warriors," bellowed Lurac in support of Ethan. "This army can overrun us all individually; a single nation attacking—it would be suicide. If the Dwarves couldn't hold them without aid, no one can."

Despite the sighs at the Dwarf's boasts, the people in the room did find truth in some aspects of his speech.

"I'm still wondering why we have to fight with the Kingdoms!" screamed an angry Adnar. "They will only betray us as they have before. Your oaths are meaningless to the Tribes! How many times have you stabbed us in the back?"

"The words we gave you were spoken in honor!" exclaimed Constantine. "How dare you insult the memory of my late son with these slanders? The attacks against your chief had nothing to do with him!"

Wilhelm threw up his arms. Noticing he was about to lose it, Nadia grabbed his arm to calm him down.

"Wilhelm, it's all right," offered Nadia. "These things take time, it's bound to—"

"No, Nadia. I'm going to say something. I can't hold back any longer."

"But they…"

"It'll be all right."

Francis flashed him a thumbs up as Wilhelm took the middle of the floor.

"I'm getting too old for all of this," stated Wilhelm. "I grow tired of the lack of will to fight these battles. Your petty differences are irrelevant in the eyes of the Prince of Darkness and his Acolytes. We are no longer talking about the survival of Terminus Mundus as a planet, we are talking about the end of Creation!"

"Sir Wilhelm, you do not have the right to question us here!" explained Constantine.

"Right? I am the only one in this room that was present the last time a true Alliance was formed. Despite the overwhelming threat presented to the Western peoples, King Frederick Rhone practically had to get down on his knees and beg everyone to fight the single most important war in this planet's history. What happened when it was over? What happened when a ragtag confederation of those with the goodwill to fight turned back the largest army ever marched anywhere? I'll tell you! Two generations later, King Justin called for aid and all of you refused him, preferring to fight each other over petty plots of land or trade rights. You turned your back on everything King Frederick Rhone gave you, the freedom to build your own kingdoms and the lands for the tribes to prosper."

Wilhelm shook his head. Everyone's attention was focused directly on him and a sense of shame fell upon them.

"I am tired. You can do whatever you want from this point on because it doesn't matter. I know the Divikin I love and respect is going to do what is right and I am going to be standing with him—may the Final Judgment take us both. However, I leave you this warning: either we join together or die together, there can be no quarter with Abaddon."

The Duke retreated into the warm embrace of his paramour as the remainder of the room sat in silence and pondered the ranting. Seizing an opportunity, Norville Warrington stood.

"Duke Wilhelm is a soldier whose word is important. He has forgotten more over his lifetime than many of us will ever know. When he speaks of Abaddon's cruelty, I can testify that I have experienced such events firsthand. We were exiled to a distant part of Central Acadia, left to fend for ourselves while our provisions were stolen by the crown. While I have no love for any of them, Marie Acadia has ascended to the throne. As such, she has charged me with presenting terms."

Audible groans and screams of "traitor" were shouted, but many were curious as to what Norville had to say.

"Central Acadia shall be stripped of all territory save for a five-kilometer radius around the city of Verian," continued Norville. "Napolitan, Evengard, and Titanus shall take all disputed territories. In the east, sanctuary territories will be ceded to the Tribal Confederation. A lump sum of reparations along with an annual payment of reparations will be allotted to each nation for the next ten revolutions. Cassandra Acadia will assume the title of Queen of Central Acadia and Marie Acadia shall remain crowned Queen of Verian. The only concession they ask for is a ten-revolution armistice."

The terms threw the crowd up in arms. Every nation wondered if it would be better to make peace rather than invite a full-scale war. Sensing the change in the mood of the audience, Cedric pushed off the pillar once more.

"King Stephen Acadia, the King of Justice, was murdered by Count Luminas on his own throne," began Cedric. "He died because he dared to break the power of the nobles that had a stranglehold on his power base. Prince Julius Imperia was killed by Abaddon in battle. He had the courage and fortitude to mount a rescue of Stephen's daughters. Cerwin Faulkner, an Elf mage, sacrificed his life allowing a group of nobles to escape the wrath of the undead. Selim Ataturk, Pasha of the Turk Guard in Deniva, died when a building collapsed on him. Despite the fact he had no stake in our war, he still chose to remain behind in Deniva and was killed saving Cassandra's life. Ask yourselves: will you dishonor the lives of these men?"

"There is no dishonor, Prince Marshal Rhone, in seeking peace," argued Norville. "We have the means of avoiding the loss of blood and treasure in a senseless crusade. Come now, even Titanus has expended an inordinate amount of money in getting this far. Your efforts here at Fort Orion should be praised. You have given the Alliance the leverage we needed to end this war at a conference table."

"I stand before you as Marshal of the Alliance Army no longer. It is a post I have long surrendered," Cedric reminded Norville. "I come before this audience as the *Permaneo Eques Ordinares.*"

Garrett's smile confirmed the resolve of the Titan prince. It was no longer a matter of pretense; to defeat Abaddon the Alliance needed a hero, and who better to lead them then that penultimate legendary warrior.

"You expect us to believe that you fulfill an old children's story?" retorted Camdem.

"We stand here not as separate nations, but as a single entity. All of us have come to know firsthand the intolerable suffering and cruelty wrought upon us by Luminas and Abaddon. Now, they have the audacity to ask us to negotiate a truce!"

Cedric removed his cape, jacket, and shirt. The room stared at the three large scars on his body.

"Look at what Abaddon did to me. In the end, this is mere damage to the flesh, but I was able to stand against this evil and I destroyed it. The faith to enter the struggle, the hope that we will win, and the charity to stand as one people of goodwill against the demons of nightmares—this is what we can accomplish together."

"I do not doubt the boasts of Prince Rhone, for he is what he claims to be," began Garrett as he rose from his seat. "I know we have many differences to mend but look at what we've achieved. I was the one who advised King Frederick to gather all of the nations in this room together in the First Alliance. It should be that we face a darker and more formidable enemy than the Empire to bring it back together."

Eyes glued to the kobold with reverence, the mood of the room shifted from Norville back to Cedric as he dressed himself. Hippolyte took the opportunity to stand once more.

"Prince Rhone, you called my grandfather your blood brother. I would know the reasons as to why the ceremony was completed."

Hoping to avoid the conversation, Cedric closed his eyes. Christian would not let his friend fail and took it upon himself to join the conversation.

"There was a battle on the Terrace River, Chief Hippolyte. Jonas Marimon had cut down the undermanned force of Aegis, son of Aramas. Not satisfied with this victory, he ordered Karstak and his Templar vanguard into the village. Lord Cedric had learned of this treachery, but arrived too late to save the village populace, save for two young girls."

Tears forming in Hippolyte's eyes, the face of her rescuer was finally fresh in her mind. As she found the comforting hand of her tearful sister on her back, the Wolf Tribe Chief looked adoringly at Cedric.

"You've always been there for me in my time of need," said a gracious Hippolyte. "On the Terrace River, before the Senate, and even that fateful night before the Crypt! Your Excellency, please do not find me impertinent, but in good conscience I must dissolve any armistice formerly negotiated by my grandfather. The Tribal Confederation needs no further guarantees. I have chosen my consort and the Tribes have elected Colin Wilkins as Ogle Tanka Un. We swear no Alliance to any nation here, but our tribal standards and armies are sworn to Prince Cedric Rhone alone."

"Perhaps that is what we have forgotten in observing the proper protocols of this meeting," announced Cassandra. "I will testify that Cedric Rhone not only sacrificed his life for me, but did indeed bring me back from the brink of Hell itself."

"The Castellan of Deniva was lost until Prince Cedric Rhone magically appeared to lead a charge to save us," testified Ethan. "I am proud to call him my brother and would gladly march with him to Verian."

"The only reason I grace this room with my presence today is because Cedric Rhone managed to come to our aid," bellowed Lurac. "Our axes and hammers are with him!"

Not to be outdone, one person after another stood up to give testimony to the deeds of Cedric Rhone. Not even the Titan prince imagined that he touched so many lives. The modicum of fear that followed him evaporated among his friends and allies. Laughing, Cagius stood with his arms up.

"I think we can make this pretty easy. Cedric Rhone, everyone in this room owes you. Not once have you ever called in a marker on any of us. I dare anyone in this room to make the case that we should not follow the Titan prince into battle."

"He is indeed a master of oratory as well as arms," countered Camdem sarcastically. "The High Elves of Evengard have a different opinion of this scenario."

"Please note, Prince Rhone, that the opinions of Camdem Jenitzen do not speak for all of the High Elves of Evengard," interrupted Malcolm.

The statement being out of character for him, Amuro stared at her love. It was as if she saw passion awaken in his eyes for the first time. Burning a cold stare at Camdem, Malcolm would not allow this tragedy of justice to go forward, nor would he let the Elf maiden he loved suffer because of it.

"I was not the one who declared myself rogue, Lord Malcolm," continued Camdem. "But I digress, while it appears that many of the nations sitting in this room agree with the path that Titanus would lead us down. It is in the best interests of our nation to decline this invitation to war."

"Lord Camdem, I beg that you reconsider," pleaded Cassandra.

"The unity between the High Elves and the lesser races is over. We will use our magic to seal the borders of Evengard once and for all. Never again will we endure these foolish escapades that have sullied our noble people."

"The only excrement that covers the people of Evengard is from your corruption alone!" screamed a defiant Christian DeVries. No longer able to hold back and watch this happen, Christian stepped to the front of the chamber.

Insulted, Camdem refused to back down. "You should be ashamed of your insolence. Do you, Cedric Rhone, endorse these insults from your subordinate?"

"I have always found the counsel of Christian DeVries to be wise and that every word he speaks has meaning. I have his back."

"Cedric, this is dangerous conversation," argued Amuro as she stood. "While I do not endorse my father's position, I can't allow Christian to use such words."

"Lords and ladies of the nations of the West, I stand before you ashamed of my country," added Malcolm. "I stand with Christian DeVries in open defiance of this pretender."

Sirius and his supporters surrounded Malcolm and screamed "Marisol" again and again. Amuro was prepared to draw Enhancer, but Wilhelm's hand came down upon her shoulder.

"I remember the rotation well when the Elf warrior Joab and Cerwin Faulkner journeyed to Rhinegard as an emissary of Hayden Marisol. He told us that Hayden had holed up in the City of Antiquity with his army and a handful of Kablisha militia. He was defending all of the Elves who had survived the Siege of Brooke Run. Embarrassed and disgraced that he would have to beg for help, I never saw such relief in one Elf's face when Rhone willingly offered everything he had to aid him. What you do when this is over is your decision, Camdem. Would you not at least reciprocate what was done for you in your people's time of need?"

"My decision is final!" exclaimed Camdem. "Evengard is mine now and my daughters' lives are far too valuable to waste in this desperate folly."

"Saulides might have fallen because of the sin of pride, but even he never deserted his allies," argued Wilhelm. "Yet, you are but a tin god who never lets a crisis go to waste. Tell me, did you have the courage to plunge the knife yourself or did you hire someone to do it for you?"

Amuro threw Wilhelm's hand from her shoulder. Drawing Enhancer, she turned it on Wilhelm as the room gasped. Everyone around them went from their weapons, but the Sentinel merely put out his hands to stop them.

"Wilhelm!" cried Amuro with tears streaming down her face. "How could you say such a thing? You would dare insinuate that my father had anything to do with such a murder?"

"Because every word he says is true!" offered Christian DeVries. "I'm so sorry, Amuro, but I've been living a lie my whole life. Before you I stand, Prince Dulles Marisol of Evengard."

"Really!" evoked an out of control Amuro. "What evidence do you have to back up such an audacious claim?"

"As my mother lay in bed, she was adorned with many magical suppression amulets and charms, so weak she didn't have the ability to move. It was easy for your father to plunge an ornihalcum dagger into her. The scar on my face bears the mark of that."

"CEDRIC!" exclaimed the enraged Elf marshal. "You're my friend and you can't believe that rabble! He's my father…he's not capable of doing such a thing!"

"Open your eyes, Amuro! You've questioned how easy it was for an assassin to bring down a sorceress as powerful as Gweyn, and you certainly don't believe that she simply died in childbirth!"

"Maybe they are right about you! You'll do and say anything to achieve your goals. You don't care who you hurt!"

Christian reached for the hair around his ears and brushed it back to reveal the ears of an Elf. Removing the glove on his right hand, the Titan operative revealed a magic circle birthmark. Camdem clutched his throne's arms tightly and moved to skulk away. Civilia grabbed him by his shoulder and shoved him down into his seat.

"So, Camdem Jenitzen, I see you recognize the magic circle mark of the Marisol line, given to us when Hayden was anointed by the Father's prophet. In addition to the written testimonies of Cerwin Faulkner, I can also present the spoken testimonies of Captain Sirius and Lady Rosa Landon."

Rosa and Sirius proudly raced behind Christian DeVries.

"Father!" pleaded Amuro on the verge of a nervous breakdown. "Retort him, please! Tell me he's not Dulles Marisol and that you had nothing to do with this!"

"I thought I saw a stillborn babe," recollected Camdem as he felt Civilia applying more and more pressure to the back of his neck. "Yet, I knew I was chasing a phantom all my life. Hidden in plain sight, I never gave that old fool of a wizard enough credit."

Inconsolable, Amuro tore her uniform top and shirt as Enhancer fell to the ground listlessly. Everyone in the room was heartbroken as the Elf maiden dropped to her knees in front of Christian. As Saria tried to comfort her, her older sister pushed her away. Solemnly, Malcolm raised his hate-filled eyes at Camdem.

"Sirius, arrest this traitor and have him incarcerated in the deepest dungeon in Brooke Run for the rest of his miserable existence."

"With pleasure, Lord Malcolm."

"It is only my love for your daughter that prevents me from slitting your throat in front of this congregation!"

"Malcolm, don't be hasty!" pleaded Camdem. "We can still make a deal here!"

"You would have sold us to the devil to satisfy your own greed."

"Gwendolyn was going to be the death of our nation. She destroyed the bloodline and needed to die for that. Amuro, help me!"

Still crying on her knees, Amuro was deaf to her father's voice. Christian got down on the floor across from her with tears in his eyes as well.

"Amuro, please look at me. We need you! Your nation needs you. The emotion you're showing now is why you're so important."

"No, not after the suffering you and Rosa have been forced to endure. Prince Marisol, nothing I will ever do can pay you back for the loss of your mother at my family's hand. I offer my resignation as Marshal of the Alliance Army and will accept whatever punishment you deem fit. However, I beg that you spare my sister from this fate."

Christian held Amuro tightly to him.

"Amuro, you are destined for greater things and I will not allow you to shame yourself by your resignation. Cedric would never forgive me if I cost him his best field marshal before our most desperate battle. The sins of your father are not your own!"

"That's right, sister!" confirmed Saria. "I don't understand why you're burdening yourself with this. It isn't like you. You're the one that taught me not to carry the weight of events I couldn't control and yet you're doing it now!"

Sucking her tears up, Amuro looked to both Christian and Saria. Overwhelmed by their compassion, she found her courage to stand once more.

"My Lord Dulles Marisol," said Amuro as she curtsied before him.

"No, Lady Jenitzen," answered Christian as he stepped back and knelt before her. "The fate of Evengard must be in your hands. The Promised Land needs a ruler with the faith of Hayden and grace of my mother."

"Cerwin Faulkner believed in you, that is why despite everything he knew Camdem had done, he still wanted you on the throne," added Sirius.

Amuro felt the arms of Malcolm drape over her shoulders. He kissed her and held her in a tender embrace. "Go get them, baby!" he whispered.

"In the absence of a prophet, my blessing will have to do," said Christian. "In this time of war and distress, Evengard needs a strong ruler. I can think of no other than the Elf that finally broke the siege jinx."

Breaking the embrace, Amuro laughed to the relief of her sister and comrades. "I had more than a little help," suggested Amuro.

"Queen Cassandra Acadia, would you help me out here and officially recognize Princess Amuro as the new leader of Evengard?" requested Christian.

"It would give me the greatest pleasure," said a smiling Cassandra. "Since I was a former follower of the worship of the Divine Father, I am fully aware that certain leaders were appointed as Judges in time of war. Would you accept such a title temporarily?"

"Yes, your Highness," answered Amuro.

As if a dark cloud was finally lifted from the Evengard, the normally stoic Elves broke out in celebration. Sirius mouthed a personal prayer and thank you to Cerwin. Saria found Cagius and kissed him. Meanwhile, Rosa treaded softly behind Christian and held him.

"Christian, your mother would be so proud of you."

"Are you upset, Rosa?"

"I hold no animosity against that she-elf. Seeing her as she was, it seems her father enjoyed torturing his own daughter as much as others."

Seeking to restore order, Civilia shooed everyone back to their seats. "I don't want to play timekeeper in a tender moment, but there is much to be done," pronounced Civilia. "I'm hoping this is the end of the theatrics of this meeting."

"Sorry, your Majesty," apologized Cagius. "For some of us, this was the only thing keeping it interesting."

"I believe it's time for the Alliance to render their final decision," announced Cassandra. "Central Acadia so swears their standards and armies to Cedric Rhone."

"Napolitan swears its standards to Cedric Rhone as well. I will have vengeance for the death of my boy."

"Evengard so affirms!" exclaimed Amuro. "We are with you, Cedric."

"So when faced with survival once more, the course of history repeats itself," recounted Wilhelm. "I am proud to have lived to see this rotation. Let the whole of the West challenge the evil before us!"

Walking to the north end of the room, Cedric found himself saluted by everyone there as he passed. Even the rulers of the nations of the Alliance submitted before him. Turning to face the whole audience, the Titan prince maintained his humility.

"I offer you my sincerest thanks for your sacrifice of blood and treasure. I know what we face will tax the limits of our faith and reason, but it must be done to save the lands we cherish. The Acadian Rebels dare to call this the War of Two Queens, but for those of goodwill it is more than that. For us, this is emotional—this is our Acadian Revenge!"

Spreading his arms wide, a fire exploded inside of the sword master. The aura he gave off quickly infected everyone in the room.

"Stand up if you wish to avenge our fallen brothers and sisters. Stand up if you wish to make Luminas and his cohorts pay for his sins. Stand up if you want this Dark Angel and his minions banished from our world."

It took time for the crescendo to build, but with every word the passion ignited every soul in the room. Each time he called them to stand, the cheering and shouting grew louder.

"Stand up, because we are created beings of free will and we have the right to determine our own destiny—a destiny that shall not be shattered by the mad ambitions of the Prince of Darkness and his malevolent servants! STAND UP, KINGDOM AND TRIBE, ALL RACES, CREEDS, AND CLASSES, TO HONOR OUR ALLIANCE AND DRIVE THE DEMONS FROM VERIAN!"

An explosion of cheers and chants echoed throughout the chamber. Cedric had successfully riled them up so shouts of "death to Abaddon," "death to Luminas," and "take Verian back" was being screamed all around. In full regalia, Cassandra turned to face Cedric and curtsied before him.

"Your Highness, Cassandra Acadia, first of your name, my great-great grandfather formed what was known as the First Alliance because the coalition of nations he brought together was the first of its kind. Today I stand at the head of what shall be known as the Final Alliance. It is an Alliance consisting of 'beings of goodwill' who will no longer suffer at the hands of what plagues our beloved homelands. Is the word given?"

"Prince Cedric Rhone, you resigned your post as Marshal of the Alliance Army," stated Cassandra. "As steward of this Final Alliance, I now appoint you to the office of Supreme Commander of the Alliance Forces, which has been vacant since the death of Hector Reed."

"Your Highness, I must request that I be given the opportunity to name my command staff."

"It is granted. I believe you are much better suited to the task than I."

"I name Duke Wilhelm von Angelhardt my Brigadier Marshal to serve directly under me. Princess Amuro Jenitzen, I hereby promote to Field Marshal of the Final Alliance, which places her third in command. Princess Cecilia Rhone, you will serve as Cavalry Marshal. Prince Cagius Imperia, you will serve as my Infantry Marshal. Prince Malcolm Fenidor, you will serve as my Ranged Marshal. Since he has been promoted to Ogle Tanka Un, Colin Wilkins will serve as Tribal Marshal."

Each of the named individuals stepped forward and offered their fealty to their Supreme Commander.

"Commander Rhone, the floor is yours," announced Cassandra.

"Alert your forces to the coming battle. In the early morning hours of the third rotation, the Final Alliance marches for Verian and the defeat of the usurpers. All Marshals and Senior Officers of the Kingdoms, Tribes, and Vassals will report to their assigned rooms for individual tactical meetings. Any tactical or command suggestions should be directed to my chief strategist, Vice-Marshal DeVries."

Accepting the orders and ready to fight, everyone in the room shouted, "Long live Queen Cassandra! Death to Luminas! Death to Abaddon! Acadian Revenge!" As everyone shuffled away to their individual meetings, Christian approached Cedric.

"Really, Cedric?" quipped Christian. "Vice-Marshal! You know I damn well can't stand a command title."

"You can resign from the army when this is over, Christian. With what we're up against, I need an ordered command structure with those I can trust."

"That's why you promoted Wilhelm. It's not going to be easy getting some of the officers to accept that decision. There are many that consider him a fossil long forgotten."

"I can't think of anyone better to serve an executive officer in a battle against the forces of Hell."

"What about this other one you're traveling with, this Francis? What's with the aura of secrecy around him? I asked to use the device he plays his music on to get a better sense of who he was. I listened to three songs he said were three of the best ever written. I couldn't make it through the second song, Cedric, it freaked me out!"

"He's a private individual. Trust me, Christian, we need him."

Interrupting the conversation between them, Cecilia threw her arms around both of them.

"Well, that was fun!" teased Cecilia.

"Fine time for you to go silent, sis. I could have used the back-up."

"Please, brother, you wouldn't have wanted to see me angry. I figured the best thing I could do for your case was to bite my tongue. Hey, we got everything we needed, so I guess I was right again."

"You are simply amazing, Cecilia," offered Christian.

"Thank you, Christian, or should I call you Dulles from now on? No, I like Christian better."

Playfully kissing the operative on the cheek, she and the others noticed Garrett approaching.

"Perfect, the two nestlings right where I want them," greeted Garrett. "By God, your mother must be so proud of you both. I would have never imagined when I first laid eyes on the two of you what you would become."

"Why do you always start off a conversation like that when you're going to give me bad news?" retorted Cedric.

"There are matters of grave importance that must be tended to. I am about to go on a journey to Edenia."

"I hear it's lovely this time of the revolution," offered Cecilia sarcastically.

"It's not about pleasure, Princess Cecilia. Rather, I have business in its Grand Library. Apparently the Edenians keep their version of the Legend of the Last Knight in the Inner Sanctuary of the Library."

"What do you mean 'their version'?" inquired Cecilia.

"I have discovered three separate versions of the Legend of the Last Knight among the Kablisha, Titans, and Elves. For the first time in history, I have managed to secure a copy of all three. I must see the one in Edenia as well."

"So what does that have to do with us?" Cecilia pushed further.

"There is much on your mind and the fate of this battle is in God's hands. Yet, I want to ease one of your burdens. Allow me to take your son with me to Edenia. In light of recent events, Prince Thomas Rhone could freely pass through the gate in Chinotal territory without question. King Archibald was very upset at Sultan Khan's decision and would gladly wage his proxy war against the Empire by allowing a foreign dignitary to be treated to all the wonders and comforts of Edenia."

"Are you sure about this, Garrett? Thomas is at that age where he is very impulsive and has a highly inquisitive nature. I just can't see him locked up in library for that many hours."

"Come now, your Highness, I know mother eagles better than this. In lieu of our situation, Edenia may be the safest refuge for him, well, for now, at least."

"Well, I guess you read me correctly, then. I'm not happy about this."

"I realize it is much to ask, but it would ease my burden as well. Do not concern yourself if the young Divikin asks many questions. I feel that sometimes it is better to see things through the perspective and heart of a child to gain true wisdom."

"Cedric, I'm not asking, I'm telling. You'd better be able to spare very good soldiers for an escort to Edenia!"

"Absolutely, sis."

"Just like that? You commit my son's well-being to this blind kobold?"

"I have to admit that I'm curious why four legends exist. Besides, it will give the boy something to do rather than simply worry if you're alive or dead."

"Dear brother, I don't know what I'm going to do with you," sighed Cecilia as she put her hand to her forehead. "I will allow this, Garrett, only because of your reputation with counsel towards my family."

"Thank you, my Lady."

"Christian, I demand good men on that escort. I want my son delivered safely."

"You'll have some of my finest. After all, there is very little intelligence can tell us at this point."

"When are you leaving, Garrett?" questioned Cedric.

"As quickly as possible, our time is precious."

Kneeling down to Garrett, Cecilia embraced him. "You may be blind but I know you aren't deaf," whispered Cecilia. "Reputation aside, nothing had better happen to my son or else you'll have to deal with me."

"You have nothing to worry about, Princess. We're going to have a great time."

Garrett walked away. Cecilia stared at her brother. "And you're sure this is safe?"

"Safer than the Hell we're marching into. Gather the officers of the heavy armor cavalry, I need my strategy reports tonight so we can appropriate the proper tactics."

Playfully, Cecilia stuck her tongue out at her brother before heading to her group. Cedric looked up and opened his arms. "God, I am begging you, I just need a little help…that's all!"

As if he needed another distraction, Cassandra jumped him from behind. "Thank you," offered the gracious Queen.

"Thank me after we retake the city. This is just a brief prologue, the story is far from over."

"It will be a fine read. I was wondering to whom I should report."

"You should join with Malcolm's group. He's in charge of the range and I believe our sorceresses are best suited in that unit."

"I know you're busy so I won't take any more of your time." She kissed him on the cheek before heading off.

Suddenly finding his only companion in the conference room was Francis, the Titan prince was greeted with the sound of applause.

"They have taken the first step towards something greater than themselves, Prince Rhone. You should be elated, but I sense apprehension. How may I ease your mind?"

"Francis, you know the fallen angels better than anyone. Explain to me why Marie Acadia became their puppet Queen."

CITY OF VERIAN

Verian will become the Palacio Magnifico of the West. We will not concern ourselves with turning it into a Fortress like Rhinegard but rather the epicenter of the cultural elite and necessary bureaucracy. My predecessors, who sit on this throne, shall never desecrate its beauty for the cause of war.

Henri Acadia, third King of Central Acadia

The rotations of the aesthetic beauty and luxury of Verian were over. With every piece of stone and material that could be cannibalized, a mighty wall now protected the city. As the three satellites in the evening sky entered their new moon phase, the outer defenses gave the impression of a harbinger of doom to all who dared enter. The walls had been outfitted with spikes, pigeon holes, and cauldrons. The canals around the city had become moats filled with acid and spiked traps. Orc catapults had been built and stationed on the city wall parapets. It was truly a tribute to the ingenuity and hard work of Gavin and Kaladra that Verian had come so far. It was duty of Jonas Marimon to inspect the work of his subordinate.

"What's our status?" asked Jonas.

"The walls have been reinforced and we've built two posterns to funnel our troops in and out of the city," explained Gavin. "The gate has been reinforced and barricaded as good as we can. I've laid some traps at points where I think sappers would mostly likely tunnel under the wall."

"It's not enough, get more wood and stone," ordered Jonas.

"We've used it all, Commander."

"What about the castle furniture? Portraits? Pots? Caskets?"

"We've already taken all of that. I'm sorry, there just isn't any more."

"Dammit! What about provisions?"

"We've raided all of the outlying fields and our supporters contributed everything they had. We can hold out for more than a revolution if necessary."

"I know Cedric Rhone too well. We're not going to need supplies for that long. One of our sides will break long before then. Still, our soldiers need to stay feed and hydrated."

Jonas pointed out a series of positions across the plains. As the cool wind blew across the grass, only the sound of mating insects could be heard.

"I figure they'll set up picket lines first to prevent us from charging out and catching them off guard. They'll put down some siege lines next and barrage the walls with arrows and bolts."

"What about siege weapons, Commander?"

"There's no intelligence on that yet. As far as we know, Gavin, they used sappers on the walls of Fort Orion and not siege weapons. Fortunately, we've got a couple of catapults that will buy us some range. Did you tar the fields and the walls?"

"Of course."

"I'm sorry, Gavin. I know you and, let's face it, we don't like one another. It's just the death of Karstak and this overwhelming sense of doom hanging over us. I don't mean to question every single thing you've done here, because no one else in Verian could have done this."

"I am still a son of Acadia and I'll fight for my freedom, but I won't die for Abaddon. When this is over, if you remain in league with that demon, then you'd better just kill me." Gavin stormed away as Esteridge approached his angry commander.

"Commander Marimon, you're wanted at the Castle," reported Esteridge. "They want an update on the defenses."

Devoid of furniture, art, and any other luxury items, the rotations of opulence and depravity that had defined the court of Maximilian Luminas were over. Marie reclined on the floor for lack of a seat, with the clone of Julius squatted down next to her. The court of Central Acadia presented themselves to their Queen along with Abaddon and his subordinates.

"I remembered this room being full," recollected Marie.

"As per your orders, everything has gone to the defense of the city," Luminas informed her.

"It is a pity," observed a saddened Marie. "When this conflict reaches its resolution we'll have to seek out the talented to replace what was lost. It seems cowardly building walls and hiding out here. Why not match them in the field?"

"Your Majesty, if the rumors that are swirling are true, then Cedric is attempting to hold together the largest coalition of nations every attempted on Terminus Mundus," reported the clone. "Twelve nations with twelve different interests—Titanus will never surrender, but the wills of the other nations are not as strong. We have to make it so those nations can no longer stomach this war."

"You don't sound confident in such a strategy," offered Abaddon.

"That is because Cedric will have anticipated this…that is why he sought to move so quickly to war against us," noted the clone. "He's got something planned that I missed."

Realizing the prospect of their worst fears, those present were thankful Jonas entered. The welcome arrival of the hardened commander alleviated some of the fear.

"Your Highness, preparations for the defense are complete! There isn't time or material to do any more."

"Thank you, Commander Marimon."

"With everyone's permission, I wish to barrack the soldiers in the ruins of the old embassies because of their proximity to the Main Gate. Whether it be one hour, one rotation, or longer, we do not know the hour of Cedric's arrival."

"That would be reasonable," concurred the clone.

"I don't need military advice from you," retorted a sneering Jonas. "I will conduct this defense as I see fit."

"I suggest you take it seriously. After all, I know Cedric," countered the clone.

"This is not the time for infighting," said Abaddon attempting to ease the tension. "We are at the dawn of a great battle and everyone has to be on the same page. Jonas is charged with defending the walls and gates. He shall act as he sees fit!"

"I intend to, Lord Abaddon. We'll thrash them so hard, the usurpers will kneel before the Saints."

Jonas and his staff left the room. However, he took a long hard look at Luminas before he left as if sensing some sort of betrayal. Luminas dismissed the remaining members of the Acadian Court before he spoke with Queen Marie.

"Your Highness, what if the first wave of defenses fail?"

"You should not concern yourself with such details," dismissed the clone.

"I will provide for the second wave if necessary, dear Count," pronounced a haughty Marie.

"As I expected, your Majesty."

"I hate this calm before the storm," argued Marie. "We know they're coming. Why don't they just come?"

"It's all part of Cedric's plan to make us nervous," suggested the clone. "Rest assured he's designated an exact time to launch his attack."

"When they do finally attack, even with this preparation it will take us by surprise," determined Abaddon.

Enraged more by the anticipation of what was coming, the darkness in Marie's body and eyes grew stronger and everyone in the room could feel it. Suddenly bursting into the room, an exasperated soldier held up a translated message.

"My Queen, we've received a second formal declaration of war," recounted the soldier.

"Didn't they cover that formality already?" exclaimed Celius. "Seems like a waste."

"The first message was signed only by Prince Cedric Rhone of Titanus. This second declaration has the signatures of the leaders of each of the three kingdoms, four tribes, the two Titan vassals, the Kablisha, the Margrave of Deniva, and the Queen's sister. They call themselves the Final Alliance."

"Why is it always twelve?" bellowed Abaddon at the irony. "So the little bastard actually built his coalition."

"Your Majesty, I'm afraid you're not going to have to wait much longer," suggested Julius' clone.

"I can't believe it!" exclaimed Marie. "How far under the sway of that monster Prince Rhone is my dear sister that she actually signed the document to lay siege to her own home? The time for pretense is over. Order all of the soldiers into defensive positions on the wall."

The soldiers in the room rushed to obey their liege's orders.

Grand Library, Edenia, the Second Rotation after the Conference

If a book exists, it is found in the Library of Edenia.

Elf Scholar Demetrius

Thomas stared twenty-five stories up from the hexagon-shaped atrium. The marble floor underneath him shined with the light of the stained glass windows above the young Titan prince. The stacks and rows of books in the rooms around Thomas formed tunnels and corridors. Reassured by the kobold's hand on his shoulder, he waited with Garrett at the center lobby desk. Three of Christian DeVries' best operatives guarded the two.

"Thomas, you stand in the Grand Library of Edenia, designated as one of the great man-made wonders of Terminus Mundus. The First Edition, or a copy of it, of every great work ever published on this planet is in this library."

"Is Uncle Cedric's book here?"

Garrett burst out in laughter as a humming noise came from the direction of the delegation. The source of the hum was a circular platform, surrounded by a railing, hovering over the floor of the library. An attractive young woman operated the device. The librarian's brunette hair was pulled back in a tight bun, held in place by two sticks. Her green eyes were partially shielded by a pair of thin gold-rimmed glasses. Garbed in a professorial black robe over her normal outfit, only her black flats were visible. Stopping the platform near them, she disembarked with a hop.

"It is a great honor to have you in this Library, Prince Thomas Rhone, and you as well, Sage Garrett Greensage. My name is Sophia, I am an associate librarian and have been assigned to your party."

"Is Richard Archibald afraid we'd steal something?" teased Garrett.

"All scholars who request to see the ancient works are required to have a Librarian escort them," stated Sophia. "I must say that when such a famous dignitary made this request, I jumped at the chance."

"Well, considering that the works in those halls are priceless, I do not begrudge you your duty," continued Garrett. "Time is precious to us."

"Of course, Lord Greensage. If you please step onto the platform, I will take you to the lower levels."

Sophia stepped up first and lowered the platform as close to the ground as possible. The three operatives carefully lifted Garrett onto the platform.

"Thomas, don't forget the plant," chided Garrett.

Moving over to the bags they brought, Thomas sighed and searched for the pot Garrett had given to Argus. With the plant, which had become the bane of his existence, Thomas jumped on the platform. Two operatives joined them, while the third remained in the atrium with the equipment.

"I don't know why you're having me lug this heavy plant around," complained Thomas.

"I heard talk of a poppy that was a late bloomer, so I requested the horticulturalist preserve the flower and send it to me. I have a theory."

"Red poppies are a dime a dozen in Titanus. I don't know why you'd waste your time and money. I could have plucked one from Eagle's Gate if you wanted it so badly."

"Just humor an old blind kobold, young prince."

"Please hold onto the handrails and be aware that I may have to make sudden stops," Sophia announced.

Thomas helped Garrett and then grabbed the rail himself. Working the controls without looking, Sophia took them down the northwest corridor. The platform ascended over stacks of books, and the passengers looked down at the people reading below. Directly in front of them, librarians funneled knowledge seekers from one part of the library to another. Reaching a circular room in the back of the library, Thomas noticed two portraits. The first was the Elf scholar Demetrius. The wizened old Elf had deep blue eyes that appeared to stare directly into the young prince. The picture on the other end of the room was that of the Titan scholar Cassiodorus, in his brown and white monk's robes.

"This is the entrance to the historical wing of the Library," explained Sophia. "Our people feared oppression by barbarians, so like our catacombs we buried our great library treasures as well."

The librarian pressed two buttons on the platform and the floor opened below them. Lights came on in sequence as the platform nestled itself into the grooves of the tunnel. Acting like an elevator, the group descended into the library catacombs ten stories below. In a short time, a brightly lit and climate-controlled room awaited them. The party walked off of the platform and moved to a table that had been carefully prepared for them. The two operatives did a quick sweep of the room and found no trouble. Assisted to his seat at the table by Thomas, the blind kobold felt for the satchel on his shoulder. Finding the three books with his fingers, he placed each of them on the table.

"What books are those?"

"This is how we accomplish what even Demetrius failed to do, Thomas. Each of these books contains a different version of the *Permaneo Eques Ordinares*: the Evengard legend describing the coming of the warrior, the Titan legend of the *Bis Reginum,* and the

Kablisha legend of the *Deus Eques Ordinares*. The Edenians have their own legend, and my theory is that once we bring the four of them together we'll discover the way to beat Abaddon."

Getting very close to Garrett, Thomas was confused and concerned. "But Uncle Cedric is already marching on Verian. Besides, her Highness and my mom told me that he already fulfilled the legend."

"Maybe, Thomas…or perhaps Prince Cedric only fulfilled part of it."

"Ok."

"You don't get it, do you?"

"Hey, I'm new at this! You're supposed to be the great expert, and you can't decide what one book said."

Garrett laughed heartily at the ribbings of the young Prince. Sophia retuned with a hand-bound book with a red cover and gold lettering. The librarian grinned from ear to ear at the opportunity to present such a rare book to a living legend.

"Lord Greensage, here is the bound copy of the scroll that you have requested, *The Permaneo Eques Ordinares*."

Placing the book on the table, the librarian stepped back and folded her arms behind her. Expecting more of a reaction to this treasure, Sophia was worried when Garrett didn't move. "Lord Greensage, is this not what you requested?" asked the nervous librarian.

"It is, but because of my blindness I can't read it, and frankly, I didn't hear you put it down so I have no idea where it is."

"I'm terribly sorry," apologized the embarrassed Sophia.

Garrett, Thomas, and Sophia got comfortable as the librarian opened the book. Before she began, Thomas let out a yawn. Garrett gently whacked Thomas on his side with his cane.

"What was that for?" demanded Thomas.

"Listen and pay close attention to where this legend compares to the other three. I don't want to miss anything, and often a second perspective is just what I need."

War Room, Fort Orion, the Morning of the Third Rotation

The Ten Commandments were handed down by the Divine Father to the Great Prophet on the Mountain. When the Christ came to Terminus Mundus, he bestowed on his listeners an Eleventh Commandment to 'love one another as I have loved you.' Well, I believe there is one more commandment that we as Titans must obey. We have the duty to destroy all agents of the Prince of Darkness who threaten the sovereignty of humanity.

King Justin Rhone to his grandchildren

As the sunrise stole the last bastion of darkness from the morning sky, the sound of reverie was announced throughout the encampment and Fort Orion. Five hover trains had pulled into the center station waiting for the passengers. A sense of angry anticipation overwhelmed the soldiers as a whole. Not used to being around so many different comrades before deployment, they tended to their final preparations. Jumpy horses were settled by their owners and attending servants. The largest coalition of troops in the history of Terminus Mundus started to take shape rather quickly. The infantry unit consisted of the Five Legions of Napolitan, Dwarven skirmishers, Denivan mercenaries, Tribal infantry, and

Kablisha militia. The heavy horse unit was compromised of the Titan Armada and the Order of the Lion Knights. The ranged unit featured Battlemages and two species of Elf Rangers. Lastly, the light horse unit loaded up with Wolf Tribe cavalry and battle wolves. Forming a column on either side, they awaited the arrival of the senior officers for the assault. Reporters from the Alliance News Organization and other stations set up their crews as well. Some of them were dressed in military armor and helmets.

The command staff and military officers had gathered one last time in the conference room in Fort Orion to go over the battle plans. Heavily armored and weapon-ready, it was the safest place to be for anyone on Terminus Mundus. Sensing the trepidation of those gathered, Cedric moved quickly to display the hologram of Verian for his audience.

"Before I give out the final instructions, I just wanted to take a moment and thank all of you for your courage and sacrifice in these dark times," announced Cedric. "It's been a long five revolutions for all of us building up to this morning. Please indulge me when I say I have never been more proud of my fellow Westerners and it is my honor to fight with you."

"I think I speak for all of us, Commander, when I say that you are the only person we would follow into this final battle," shouted Amuro amidst the deafening applause. "We have the utmost confidence that you will find a way to lead us to victory."

"Thank you, Marshal Jenitzen," said Cedric as he switched to a slide of four pennants. "As we have laid out over the past three rotations, we are using a pennant system to coordinate the attacks. I have chosen to mark the pennants with animals to represent the different forces. The dragon will be used for infantry, the eagle for heavy horse, the unicorn for range, and the wolf for light horse. The terrain surrounding our objective is about as flat as it comes, so we're not going to be able to aid ourselves with any tricks to disguise our arrival. Doctor Martha Heinrich believes she might be able to mask the appearance of one of our trains. Therefore the light horse group will travel to a location opposite of the remaining forces. However, I can't guarantee that they will go undetected. Vice-Marshal DeVries will continue the briefing."

Turning the floor over to Christian, the newly made Vice-Marshal manipulated the screens further until a full three-dimensional projection of Verian and the surrounding plains was seen by all.

"Our spies and scouts report that Verian has been heavily fortified by our enemies," assessed Christian. "Their strategy appears to be one of outlasting our attack to steal away our will to fight. We are not going to give them such comfort. I do not believe that Verian suspects our use of siege weapons. Our trebuchets will unleash a barrage on the eastern wall of the city. That way their defenders will not only have to fight our weapons but nature as well. We'll keep the sun in their eyes and at our backs for some time. It is our belief that when the pounding starts, Jonas Marimon will take the bait and empty his army onto the fields. We'll be outnumbered so we're relying on surprise, skill, and strategy to beat them on their terms—that is, if all goes according to the plan; if not, we'll have to adjust in the first five minutes of the battle."

Everyone grimaced but they still managed a few chuckles. Many of the officers crossed their fingers as if asking for some luck.

"We've gone over this battle plan a hundred times and everyone has commented on it. There is no need to go through it in detail again. Lord Commander, the final words are yours."

Christian ceded the floor back to Cedric. As the Titan prince closed his eyes for a moment, he held the rapt attention of everyone. Flicking a button on the screen, Christian allowed Cedric to project to the soldiers in the encampment below. The sword master finally raised his eyes and spoke.

"My grandfather, Justin, took my sister and I onto his lap at the last moment of his proud life. Believe me, trying to tell anything to two rambunctious children at five revolutions of age was difficult. However, he made certain to drive one point home to the two of us. He spoke of what he called the Twelfth Commandment, the duty of all Titans to destroy the evil that poisoned this planet in the form of the Nephilim and Demonkin. For a long time, I felt I carried that burden alone, but no longer. There are those among us who continue to criticize me for this war and my detractors have asked me to justify the actions that we take this morning. To those individuals I say this: battles have been fought over power, over land, over greed, and even over love. Five revolutions ago, Abaddon destroyed Verian and killed kin we loved; this morning we take the first step together towards our Acadian Revenge!"

Frenzied by the call of battle, an echoing horror filled the plains of Central Acadia. The warriors at Fort Orion had accepted the call and reasons of their Commander, and they knew Cedric would not allow them to fail.

"Revenge for the murder of the King of Justice, Stephen Acadia! Revenge for the fall of the great city of the West! Revenge for the thousands that had to flee their homes in fear! Revenge for those whose greed caused them to conspire with the agents of the Devil! Even revenge for the madness that had beset the false Queen who dared to sit on throne of Central Acadia! The hour has longed passed for us to say God is on our side, for there is truly only one side God is on; it is our duty as individuals of goodwill to get on His side. REPORT TO YOUR DETAILS! GOD BLESS ALL OF YOU AND GOD PROTECT THE RIGHT OF THE PEOPLE OF TERMINUS MUNDUS TO THEIR OWN DESTINY!"

The sound of weapons being drawn to salute their Commander reverberated throughout the Fort. The senior officers left the room to get to their command units. As she slung two quivers worth of arrows over her shoulders, Minerva felt Walker grab her arm.

"Jon, come to bid thy Maiden farewell before battle," flirted Minerva.

"Cecilia's right, you're definitely one of us now. Here we stand on the dawn of battle and I can't believe the girl I first escorted through the Castle is not only a soldier, but a beautiful woman as well."

The wolf tribe archer grabbed him tightly. "Why didn't you come see me sooner? I was thinking you didn't care anymore."

"In case you hadn't noticed, things have been a little hectic around here lately and we're in different units."

"It's still no excuse, but I'm glad you did come see me before this started."

"I actually had an ulterior motive to find you. I wanted to give you something to keep you safe before this battle begins."

"A present for me? You shouldn't have, Jon."

"Please don't be offended if you were expecting jewelry. It's something a little more practical than a mere trinket."

From behind his back, he presented Minerva a silver longbow coated with amber runes.

"The Dwarves always make sister weapons for each of the legendary weapons," explained Walker. "Malcolm carries the Bow of Artemis, and this is the Bow of Apollo. I noticed it first when we defended Lion's Peak. Since we're going up against Demonkin and other legions of hell, the silver will provide for more powerful shots. It's rumored that the string is made from the hair of a unicorn mane and can't break, but I'd still rub some guts on it no matter what. Just be careful with it; this bow is priceless and Lurac charged me a pretty penny for it."

Minerva took the bow with sheer delight and held it tightly to her chest. It glowed in her hands for a moment as it accepted her as its new Mistress. Feeling a newfound rush of power burning inside her heart, she screamed at the top of her lungs. "SISTER, I'M GETTING MARRIED!"

"Wait a second, Minerva," interrupted a shocked Walker.

"Oh Jon, I can't imagine a more wonderful betrothal present. I can't believe you learned so much about our culture so quickly."

"This has nothing to do with a wedding. This is a desperate battle, Minerva, and you need extra pop…"

Ignoring Walker completely, Minerva hummed the bridal march as she swayed back and forth. "When I first saw you in the Castle I knew you were the one," recollected Minerva. "The bow is the most treasured possession of any archer, and to think you presented me with one as beautiful and powerful as this. You're right, who needs a silly ring when I have this? I can't wait to tell everyone. Don't worry about my sister—I'll fight her to death if she dares object to this union."

As she ran off, Walker stood dumbfounded. Colin had not informed him of any tradition like this taking place. It was only then that he remembered the line Cassandra had used on Cedric a thousand times: "I guess among the Wolf Tribe there are ancient customs and traditions that maidens use to justify anything."

A smile crossed his face as he knew there were worse things in life that could happen to him. Of course, now the Lord Commander would have to survive the battle for fear of Minerva chasing him into the afterlife. Meanwhile, dressed in chainmail that didn't fit her at all, Martha was overseeing the loading of her precious trebuchets onto one of the hover trains. Having tested them a few times while they were at Orion, the good doctor was satisfied they were battle ready.

"Come on, we're on a deadline here!" ordered Martha. "I need those trebuchets packed and ready for transport five minutes ago. Let's pick it up!"

Hearing the sounds of shouting behind her, Martha saw Florence tending to James. The old legionnaire had fallen and was hacking up blood.

"Oh Jesus…" prayed Martha.

Florence attempted to help the General to his feet. Dressed in her starched uniform, the Kablisha cleric was heading up the Triage unit traveling with the army.

"I told you, Florence. I'm fine. Leave me be."

"You're not fine, General," assessed Florence. "You should return to your bed."

"I think the cleric has got you beat on this one," added Martha. "Need I remind you that besides being an engineer I'm also a medical doctor. You're doing yourself no good out here."

"I haven't lived with this cancer for five revolutions to lie in bed during the greatest battle in the history of this planet." James said as he stopped coughing. He wiped the blood from his lips with a towel.

"Martha Heinrich, I do not pretend to understand the Titans and their belief in God. However, I do believe that each man comes to the end of his life in his own way. I intend to die in the way that best fits me and that is on the battlefield. Now if you would please allow this beautiful young maiden to aid those more befitting her talents and help me to the hover train, I would be most grateful."

"Doctor Heinrich, James Darius is a great man," said Florence with admiration. "But I can't in good conscience clear him for battle in this condition."

"I'm asking you, Lady Heinrich, please don't force an old man to beg."

"Florence, this man is my responsibility and I'm overruling you as chief medical officer. I will see to the General."

Crying, Florence silently returned to her duties as Martha aided James. Overcome with grief as well, the doctor's blood boiled. "You stupid moron, are you happy now?"

"Thank you, Martha, for granting me my final dignity."

As the officers gathered their equipment, Amuro plucked a braeburn apple from her bag. Feeding Maiden, she gently stroked the winged horse's neck and kissed her.

"That's a good girl; I need you one more time." Playfully stroking the unicorn's mane, Amuro laughed as Maiden acknowledged her orders.

"Marshal," called Sirius.

Turning her attention behind her, Amuro saw a different look in the Captain's eyes.

"A change, Captain?"

"Permission to speak freely…"

"I know I'm definitely going to regret this. Granted."

"My loyalty still lies where it always has with Cerwin Faulkner and his judgment. Forgive a fool who did not believe his master when he spoke of your humility. My Lady…no…your Highness, you committed no sin in this matter."

"Christian had always been such a good friend. I know he is Cedric's best soldier, but part of me always felt he watched over me too. I guess the revelation of everything I've always partly suspected was just too much for me in there."

"Take comfort in that you have my life, fortune, and sacred honor at your banner. I hail thee, Judge Amuro Jenitzen, Marshal of the Final Alliance."

Sirius clicked his heels together and bowed to Amuro in full salute. Not knowing whether to cry or hug the Elf captain, she simply answered his salute.

"Get to the head of the column and make sure our boys and gals get on the right train," quipped Amuro.

Entering the center of the column, Cassandra felt underdressed compared to the armor worn by the Order of the Lion Knights around her. Holding her wizard staff at her side, a sense of overwhelming sorrow overtook the young Queen as she stared out at all of the soldiers around her.

"Is something wrong, your Majesty?" inquired Robespierre.

"I'm sorry," apologized Cassandra. "I'm just simply coming to grips with what I'll tell the parents, wives, husbands, and children of those who will die for my crown."

"Even when fought for the most righteous cause, war is a hell that should be avoided at all costs. Sometimes, however, we must fight for what we believe in," recited Walker.

"That's beautiful, Walker. Did your father teach you that?" asked Cassandra.

"Actually, your Majesty, I read it in the Titan Battle Manual."

Appreciating the levity of the moment, Cassandra marched calmly down the column to cheers and adoration of those around her. One by one the senior officers paraded to the same cheers and adulations. Linked arm and arm, Colin, Cecilia, Cagius, and Malcolm choose to stride together as the four unit commanders. It was appreciated by all as a sign the individual units were prepared to fight as one. A reporter from the Alliance News Organization and her crew stood to the side of the gauntlet.

"We are reporting live this morning from Fort Orion," the reporter said. "The largest coalition ever put together in Terminus Mundus has assembled outside of this Fort for their march on the city of Verian. We have been granted special permission by the command staff to embed our reporters within various units to broadcast firsthand what is shaping up to be the defining battle in the history of the west. Queen Cassandra Acadia has already made her appearance and now we are waiting the arrival of the Supreme Allied Commander Prince Cedric Rhone of Titanus."

Standing before the column, an armed Civilia waited for her son to arrive. When Cedric reached her, she held him tightly.

"No son has ever made their mother prouder. God protect you and go with your mother's love."

"Thank you, and please stay safe. Cecilia will take good care of you."

After kissing his mother on the forehead, Cedric mounted Jericho for the final parade. Wilhelm and Francis took up flanking positions on either side of him. It was oddly reassuring to have an angel watching over each of his shoulders. Amuro awaited him on Maiden.

"Ready to get this show on the road, Cedric?" teased Amuro. "Tell me, how did it ever come to this?"

"Keep your head up, sister!" quipped Cedric right back. "Ladies first."

"Yes, sir. Make way for Prince Commander Rhone!"

Trotting slowly through the gauntlet of soldiers, Cedric took the time to go over to many of his soldiers. He took the hands of those he could and tried to make eye contact with everyone. Argus stood at the end of the column and took his approach in.

"The Legend of the Last Knight," murmured Argus aloud. "We were all waiting for a prophecy...for a sign. He didn't wait, he saw evil and he knew what he had to do."

As he reached the end, Argus put his hand out to Cedric. The Titan prince didn't discriminate and gripped it tightly. Command staff waiting for him, Cedric dismounted and hugged each and every one of them. When he reached Cassandra, the two embraced tightly and kissed each other.

"For luck!" joked Cassandra.

"Keep it coming, Cassie, we're going to need a lot of it."

They interlocked their hands and raised them high in the air. The remaining senior staff interlocked their arms together in unity as well. Even Nadia found Civilia interlocked with her on one side. The two smiled and laughed through their tears. Bishop Arthur staked the standard made for Cedric Rhone's host in the ground. It featured a winged knight holding a fiery sword standing atop a pile of dead demons.

"I realize that many of you do not believe in the traditional ritual I am about to perform, but I'm sure that no one will object to a blessing before this battle," offered Arthur as he held his hands out.

Posha and Peter Wulf joined him as everyone unstrapped their helmets, hoods and circlets. Bowing their uncovered heads in reverence, they waited on the Bishop.

"Let us pray… In nomine Patri, Fillia, Et Spiritus Sanctus. O God, I beseech You, watch over those exposed to the horror of war, and the spiritual dangers of a soldier's life. Give them such a strong faith that no human respect may ever lead them to deny it, nor fear ever to practice it. By Your grace, O God, fortify them against the contagion of bad example, that being preserved from vice, and serving You faithfully, they may be ready to meet you face to face when they are so called through Christ our Lord."

Everyone responded, "Amen."

"Sacred Heart, inspire them with sorrow for sin, and grant them pardon. Mother of God, be with them on the battlefield during life and at the hour of death, and grant that they may live and die in the grace of thy Son. Saint Joseph, pray for them. May their Guardian Angel protect them!"

Everyone responded "amen" once more. Francis shouted out in a loud voice, "Saint Michael the Archangel, defend us in battle, and be our protection against the wickedness and snares of the devil. May God rebuke them, we humbly pray, and do thou O Prince of the Heavenly Host by the power of God cast into Hell Satan and all evil spirits who prowl about the world seeking the ruin of souls. Amen."

"In nomine Patri, Fillia, Et Spiritus Sanctus," prayed Arthur as he finished the blessing and took the standard once more.

"LOAD THEM UP!" commanded Cedric.

The sound of drums, trumpets, and pipes could be heard along the massive column. The soldiers cheered and marched forward with a tapestry of banners and emblems. Loading the trains based on their unit divisions, every last detail was accounted for. Syrus Clan Priests blessed the warriors with incense while Titan Priests threw holy water upon them. Cedric wore a determined look on his face before boarding the engineer car of a train himself. Blasting his train's whistle long and hard, he stared north.

"Abaddon, I'm coming for you."

Fusion engines firing, the trains were boarded and chugged full speed on their invisible tracks to Verian and the decisive war.

VERIAN, CENTRAL ACADIA

A battle plan should be viewed as a rough sketch and not a series of concrete orders. A general should remain flexible, so his
plan can be adapted to the situation before him. However, the
best commander is the one who can manipulate his enemy to do
exactly what he wants them to do.

The Titan Battle Manual, Prince Cedric Rhone

Like a prisoner in his own homeland, Gavin paced the walls
of Verian. Staring to the east in the early morning hours, he
squinted to keep the sun from his eyes. As the new watch replaced
the night watch on the walls, soldiers shielded their eyes. Rousing
himself from his short sleep against the wall, Roland jumped to
attention when he saw Gavin standing there.

"Why did you let me sleep?" asked Roland.

"There was no need to wake you...not yet, at least," replied
Gavin.

"It's the third morning since they took Fort Orion."

"Yes it is."

"It's been my experience to note that the Titans take certain
numbers very seriously. We don't have any good intelligence."

"We know he's coming, it's just a matter—"

Gavin cut himself off mid-sentence and listened carefully. In a matter of seconds, Roland picked up the same sound.

"You hear that light humming as well?" questioned Roland.

"It's a hover train, sounds like two or three of them. You're right, the Titans love their threes. Get them up! This is it!"

Roland and Gavin sounded the alert, rousing the soldiers to their stations. While the overwhelming majority were created in Virgus' laboratory, each of the remaining Saints still had their personal troops with them. Spearman and archers took to the walls, while swordsman braced the main gate. Breathing heavily, Jonas ascended the steps to the top of wall. Sir Esteridge and Sir Pytor carrying his two swords had joined Gavin and Roland.

"Talk to me, Gavin," ordered Jonas.

"Do you hear that hum, Commander?" asked Gavin. "There's no doubt about it, fusion trains are on approach."

"We've got contact," shouted Esteridge behind a pair of binoculars. "Four fusion trains on approach!"

"At ease!" commanded Jonas. "Move the soldiers in the courtyard to the sapper holes on the walls. I'm not going to get caught with my pants down if Cedric performs his little march again."

Slowing to a halt, the infantry train disembarked first. Cagius snapped the legions into a shield formation to protect the range units disembarking the second train. Malcolm positioned them quickly and the archers readied themselves for the first volley. Cedric rode Jericho to the front lines to keep the focus of the rebels off of the rear. Martha and her engineers were working diligently unpacking the twenty-five trebuchets and their payloads. To buy more time, the Titan prince rode ahead of the column. Even underneath the Rising Moon Helmet, Jonas and his Saints could make out a grin filled with malice. Activating a microphone on his transmitter, his voice carried to the walls of Verian.

"Jonas Marimon! Long time, no see!"

"It's a shame, really," Jonas bantered back using his own loud-speaker. "I really hoped that you had died five revolutions ago. I assume you want a pre-battle parlay."

"We gave you a chance to parlay the rotation the barrier came down. You made the choice to double down on defending yourselves instead and that's fine. You got my declaration of war and now my Final Alliance demands that you and your vampire master pay for your sins against Central Acadia and the Alliance."

"I'm not easily goaded into a fight, especially when I'm stand-ing on the high ground. If you want Verian, you've going to have to come in here and take it!"

Jonas leaned over to Gavin, who was working on calculations with his engineers.

"Do they have a mark on him yet?" questioned Jonas.

"Keep him talking!" responded Gavin.

Cedric turned back to his troops. The infantry and range had formed their lines. The Dragon Legions were in the front row fol-lowed by Kablisha militia and the Myotis twin swordsmen and whip mistresses, then a second heavy infantry line of Denivan mercenar-ies, Nordice Vikings, and Dwarves. Behind the infantry came the range lines of high Elf and wood Elf rangers surrounded by high Elf battle mages. Given a circling motion from Martha's hand, Cedric turned his attention back to Jonas on the wall.

"So what's it going to be, Cedric? Do these people know what their up against? How many of them really want to die because of a power struggle between two sisters?"

"You really are blind, Jonas, if you think that is what this is about. What about your men? What are they fighting for? Were you promised a share of the spoils? I know what's going to happen: each and every one of them will be sacrificed to Abaddon in his new world. No, Jonas, my warriors know what they are fighting for and that's why we're going to win."

"Commander, we've got him!" announced Gavin.

"Send the Titan bastard into the abyss!" ordered Jonas.

Two catapults snapped back and let loose on Cedric's position. Turning Jericho to his side slightly, the sword master drew Ragnarok from his back. The resulting backswing created a force that split the boulders into a thousand-piece rock shower around him. Snarling and stomping his hooves, Jericho demanded a response. Pushing Ragnarok forward, Cedric screamed, "DOCTOR HEINRICH, TEAR DOWN THAT WALL!"

The hover trains rolled out of the way to reveal the mechanized trebuchets Martha had created. Adopting a crane style, the monstrous siege weapons could be adjusted by computer controls in a matter of seconds. The payload was eighty-kilogram metal spheres. Overly excited at testing out a new toy, Martha shouted, "Fire," as the chainmail bounced up and down on her. The first wave of spheres flew over Cedric's head but fell well short of the intended target on the wall. Turning angrily at their failure, Cedric stared down Martha. The doctor in turn hit Kruger over the head with her clipboard. Relieving herself of her pent up anger, the Titan scientist reprogrammed the trajectory of the shots.

"I guess they have siege weapons after all," noted Gavin.

"If they manage to hit us," taunted Jonas.

"I don't think we want to be here if they figure out how," suggested Gavin.

"Pull back to the city!" ordered Jonas. "Abandon the walls!"

The Acadians sprinted down the stairs as Martha flashed a thumbs up at Cedric.

"Now they're working great!" Martha reassured Cedric.

The trebuchets readjusted with the new program and fired once more. This time they took out the parapet containing one of the catapults. Soldiers ducked for cover to avoid the devastating spheres. Twenty-five payloads smashing into the walls and other objects took their toll on the hastily built construction. Mortar dust and plaster rained down on the inner part of the city. Blindly firing their catapults back at the trebuchets, the marks fell well short. Each shot made it easier for Martha to pick them out geometrically.

"Where the hell did they get trebuchets from?" demanded Roland.

"There were rumors the Titans stole a lot of equipment from the Empire at the Siege of Eagle's Gate," recollected Pytor.

"Is there anything we can do?" questioned Jonas.

The Saints huddled behind some building cover as more spheres penetrated the city.

"Our catapults don't have the range to counter the attack," reported Gavin. "Our spotters can't stay on the wall long enough to calculate an appropriate trajectory."

"We're trapped like rats," observed Jonas. "Suggestions?"

"Meet them in the field," suggested Pytor.

"I don't know. Only a few of them handled this army before," Esteridge reminded his comrades.

"We've got the numbers," determined Jonas.

"Commander, I do not think…" started Gavin.

"We know the military capabilities of the enemy and we've got them five to one," continued Jonas. "We're going to meet them!"

"I strongly recommend that we stick with the original plan!"

"Sir Gavin, are you seriously recommending we allow Cedric to pound us to death with those trebuchets? If we don't take out their siege weapons, we won't last until tomorrow! Attack is the only option. Get to your commands."

The Saints nodded and affirmed, "Yes, Commander."

"ALL SOLDIERS REPORT TO THE POSTERN!" ordered Jonas. "TAKE FORMATIONS ONCE WE GET OUT INTO THE PLAINS!"

From one of the high towers of the Castle, Sharon used her keen eyesight to stare at the battlefield. Shielding himself from the sun's light, Luminas reclined in a coffin, the only piece of furniture in the place saved from the barricade.

"How about an update, darling?" murmured Luminas from the coffin.

"It's a barrage of siege weaponry I've never seen before. The eastern wall is under severe stress. Jonas is mobilizing his troops for an assault."

"If Cedric was planning to storm the walls, he is taking his sweet time."

"They never rush into anything. I'm not surprised they are behaving cautiously."

"It's a little too late to look back, but the Titans certainly prepared for this hour better than we did. Trebuchets are the perfect weapons against these walls."

On top of the Wizards' Tower, Abaddon and Virgus observed the battlefield.

"Jonas, I sure hope you know what you're doing," observed Abaddon.

"We have the superior numbers, my Lord," added Virgus.

"Yes, but Cedric likes to back an opponent into a corner. What you see is what he wants you to do."

"The trebuchets will have the walls down quickly. Even if we are to lose half of our forces, it'd be worth it to take them out."

"I've never been fond of sacrificing my own soldiers. It's the best way to lose a battle. Damn, what are you up to?" Abaddon could feel his wound throbbing as Cedric retreated back towards his men.

That's right, Jonas...do exactly what I want you to do! thought Cedric to himself. As he rejoined his group, Wilhelm and Amuro approached and saluted him. "Okay, Amuro, how are my warriors doing?"

"They're jealous that Martha's getting to have all the fun," quipped Amuro. "Everyone is in position as ordered. Florence has the triage unit up and running. We suffered our first setback; a Legionnaire broke his ankle getting off the train."

"Heck of a way to be the first casualty of the rotation. Jonas has taken the bait, so everyone's going to get their chance."

"Ready the pennants!" ordered Amuro.

The four animal pennants were raised high on the battlefield as Jonas and the defenders took up their position in front of the eastern wall of Verian. Just as predicted, the sun irritated their eyes. Proudly riding to the front, Jonas and the Saints took their command positions.

"All right, you bastard, you got what you wanted," taunted Jonas. "To arms!"

As the rebels drew their weapons, Cedric signaled for the range pennant. The pennant was dropped and Malcolm ran his archers in front of the infantry. Drawing their bows they waited for the order.

"Let them fly!" screamed Malcolm.

Firing the first round, the rebels watched the arrow shower approaching their positon.

"SHIELDS UP!" exclaimed Gavin.

Locking their tower shields together, the rebels deflected the volley. Not rattled by the ineffectiveness of the first flight, Malcolm ordered his troops to reload and fire at will. A steady barrage of arrows kept the rebels pinned down. While protected by their shields, any soldier leaving the center location was picked off by five or six arrows. Tensions flared and complaints about being "sitting ducks" were murmured underneath the protective shields. Jonas observed the area around him and noticed the safety of the east wall behind him.

"Commander Marimon!" exclaimed Gavin trying to get his attention. "What's the true purpose of this barrage? It's as if they want to purposely hold us here."

"As long as we keep the wall behind us they can't flank us with cavalry from the rear," Jonas argued back. "Our pikes are in the front, so they can't take us head on! Trust me, Cedric's setting up a cavalry charge."

Jonas was partially correct. Cedric was attempting to herd them. From the towers Sharon and Abaddon witnessed their armies getting pushed closer and closer together by the barrage. Any soldier on the wings was picked off, forcing them to move to the center.

"Sharon, you're gasping! What do you see?"

"It's strange, Maximilian. Cedric is bombarding our forces with range weaponry but it's not doing any real damage."

"Cedric, that's not like you at all. Where are our forces positioned?"

"Jonas has the pikes to the front."

"If Cedric is carrying the infantry and range units with him, he must be planning an assault with cavalry from either the flanks or the rear. Jonas is going to keep his army with their backs to the wall to negate that advantage."

"There's something else, though; our forces are packed very close together."

"You want them spread out for a cavalry charge, but putting them together would increase the strength of the defense. Sharon, you don't think…?"

Cassandra and Nadia levitated to a flanking position around Jericho.

"I see everything is going according to plan," observed Cassandra.

"It's your time," noted Cedric.

"You do know that if we use this spell now, Nadia and I are going to need the rest of the rotation to recover. We'll be out of the battle."

"Isn't this the spell that killed your uncle?" countered Cedric.

"You need not fear for her or I, Lord Cedric," Nadia reassured him. "There are a few variations of this storm. If we dared use the version Cerwin used, it would kill everyone here."

"All right, then," agreed Cedric. "Bring up the infantry!"

The second pennant fell and Cagius ran his infantry in front of the archers, Cassandra and Nadia. Malcolm and the range continued to fire while Cedric stayed in the front. The two sorceresses chanted and held their staffs above her head. Feeling the tremendous amount of energy from his observation tower, Abaddon dropped back.

"Lord Abaddon?" asked a concerned Virgus.

"It's a high level spell. I knew Cassandra was incredibly powerful, but I never expected this. We have to possess her, Virgus! She will win the war for the Prince."

Streaks of red flares darted across the blue sky as Cassandra and Nadia finished their chanting. Both women ended with "Star Fall," and the rebels were thrown into panic. Seeing the red flares headed directly for their position, Jonas took control.

"Scatter!" ordered Jonas.

The Saints and their commands were on the flanks, so they were in the best position to scatter. Many of Virgus' created army formed a large portion of the shield so they were trapped in formation. The raining hellfire scorched the land and the army trapped on it. Staring in horror, Jonas watched as a large portion of his forces were scarred and scorched from the furious attack. Enraged by the attack, he turned his horse toward Cedric and stared down the Titan prince.

"You okay, Cassie?" asked Cedric.

"I'm fine," responded Cassandra. "We used the weakest version of the spell. I'm sorry we couldn't do more damage."

"Trust me, you've done better than I could have imagined. You made them stupid, and a stupid army is ripe for the slaughter. Load them up, Cagius!"

"Thanks, Commander," quipped Cagius. "I didn't think I'd be able to hold these boys back any longer. Dragon formation! It's time we pay these rebels back for my brother!"

Yelling and thrashing about, the Legion locked their shields into formation. Jonas drew his blade and held it up to his nose in the air, riding up and down along his lines. The Saints placed their weapons in the same position. The remaining troops cheered on their commander, as Malcolm briefly ceased fire.

"Don't lose heart now!" rallied Jonas. "This is the rotation you will tell your children and grandchildren about! This hour we stand up to the fanatics of Titanus and show them the teeth of the lion! For our freedom! Long live Queen Marie! Charge!"

Retreating to safety behind the Dragon Legions, Cedric joined Joshua with the Napolitan Paladins in reserve.

"All right, Cagius!" commanded Cedric. "This is your show now. Keep them at bay!"

"Thank you, Commander."

Cagius whistled and the Legions pushed their shields forward as the rebel army came at them. Malcolm's unit let loose once more as they made up the distance. Spread out, they were easy pickings for the skilled Elf rangers. When the rebels crashed into the first line of Legion shields, they experienced what so many foes had felt before. Unable to gain any ground against the Legion, a new horror emerged. Argus ordered his militia to get their crossbows on the shoulders of the Legionnaires and fire into the rebel front lines. Desperate to avoid the slaughter trenches against the Legion, some of the rebels tried to flank Cagius' position. However, the carefully placed Dwarf and Denivan units under Ethan's command easily cut them down and penned them in the middle with the long arcing swings of battleaxes. Using his patented system, the Napolitan Legate blew his whistle three times and his Legions shifted their weight to better ground. Cagius blew twice more and the front lines tossed back the rebels in one mass shield push. They thrust their spears forward and killed off the front line. Cagius blew the whistle a second time and the Legion snapped back to the original position. Faced with the repeating impenetrable attack, Jonas pulled back his force and spread them out to get around the lines.

"Cecilia has been patient," observed Cedric to Amuro. "Let's give her a reward."

"CAVALRY PENNANT!" shouted a smiling Amuro.

The eagle went from its flying position into a sharp dive. Rocks on the ground trembled and rattled. Knowing what was coming, Gavin got his head on a swivel. Jonas had exhibited tunnel vision towards Cedric's attacking force. None of the rebels noticed the massing of heavy cavalry near the trebuchets. Cecilia and Horace lead the charge in a pincher formation circling around the Dragon Legion infantry shield.

"Pikes to the flank!" desperately exclaimed Gavin.

With most of their spearman lying dead from the meteor strike or from the engagement with the Dragon Legions, no protection remained for the rebel army from the heavy horse. The lucky ones met death by spear, sword, or mace, the unfortunate were trampled into the ground under the power of the mighty horses. Herded like cattle, the Saints found themselves in the middle of a nightmare. Infantry tore them to pieces in the front and the heavy horse cut off their rear retreat.

"On my command!" shouted Cedric. "Break ranks! Free attack!"

Jericho leapt over the Dragon Legions as Cedric cut down soldiers with Ragnarok on either side of them. Carnage ensued as each of the Alliance warriors found themselves in the middle of the battle. Wilhelm threw his spear into one of the soldiers and then stabbed a second in the throat. Abandoning discipline, Cagius fought like a man possessed, stabbing soldiers with his trident and driving his armor shield into others. After he dismounted, Joshua used his sword and shield as a weapon as Valentine used him as a blocker. Ducking in and out behind his larger pupil, he pulled soldiers to the ground and slit their throats. As they made their passes in the rear, Cecilia stabbed a soldier and lifted him in the air as a trophy for the Riders to cheer on, while Horace bashed right through iron helmets with his mace. Even the Elf rangers traded their bows for daggers, leaping into the fray. Malcolm simply used his bow at close range. Saria leapt onto Maiden. As the winged unicorn charged, Amuro sliced on one side while Saria struck with her whip on the other. Finding himself temporarily surrounded by ten rebels, Francis laughed.

"You guys don't have any luck," warned Francis.

Francis put his staff forward. Emitting a blue light from the orb on top, a blinding flash sent the rebels flying in all directions with severe burns. Another soldier charged him with a pike but Francis quickly parried the attack with his staff while lopping his head off with his blade. The once large opposing army found themselves disorganized with their ranks broken. Abandoning the attack, the Saints broke through on horseback with as many of their command they could keep intact. Retreating for the safety of the Castle, through the dirt and blood on his eyes Roland could see Cedric giving the order for the final pennant to drop.

"Now what? What more can they do to us?" demanded Roland.

"Alliance... twelve members... by the Saints, it must be the Tribes!" determined Gavin.

Martha's deception was successful and the light horse hover train had arrived at the western end of the city undetected. Waiting for the order, the Ogle Tanka Un led the charging Wolf Tribe cavalry and battle wolves against the broken and retreating forces. Riding next to Chief Hippolyte with feathers braided into her hair, Colin pushed his fist forward ordering the war-painted light riders to draw weapons and attack.

"Commander Marimon, we can't make the posterns in time!" observed Gavin.

"The world has gone mad," determined Jonas. "Take them head on! We've got to make the city."

Raising her spear to the sky, Hippolyte launched it and caught Sir Pytor in the chest. He staggered his horse forward a few trots before falling over. Watching from the observation tower, Abaddon would have applauded if he still had hands.

"Brilliant!" exclaimed Abaddon. "It was absolutely brilliant! That boy knew what Jonas would do even before the Saint knew it. "

"I can't believe it!" regretted Virgus as he hung his head. "All that work, and they're slaughtered in one battle!"

"It is necessary that we fall back to our secondary plan. Get Marie ready. I don't know if they're coming yet, but we must be ready to meet them."

"Understood."

The collision between the Saints and Tribes was massive. Overcome with elation at the thought of finally taking their revenge against the butcher Marimon, the Tribe fought without mercy. Minerva turned her horse and fired with her new bow. The resulting power caught Esteridge in his temple. The Saint fell dead, but was still ripped to pieces by hungry wolves. Grabbing two wounded soldiers to his steed, Roland and Gavin broke to the side of the attacking forces.

"Jonas! We're leaving!" exclaimed Gavin.

Trapped in the middle of the tribal fray, the desperate pleas of the last two remaining Saints couldn't reach their commander. Jonas broke through in a different direction. Knowing they could not reach them, Roland and Gavin ordered every soldier within earshot to retreat to the city. As the infantry pushed forward, James signaled to his troops to grab the next bit of ground. Coughing uncontrollably, the old general found blood pouring out of his body onto his gauntlet. His time short, he stared at Cagius and Constantine fighting side by side, and then looked to Joshua.

"I thank you for letting me live to see this hour. It's so glorious to know my country is in good hands. My one regret is that Julius wasn't here to see this…"

Falling to his knees, James could feel a woman dragging him to the safety of the Triage unit. He smiled as the last thing in his fading eyes was the compassionate smile of Martha Heinrich.

"You're far too great a man to be trampled in that chaos," said Martha sweetly.

"Never wounded in over ten thousand battles… and cancer eats me alive…"

"You were right, James. I understand why you wanted this dignity. Rest now warrior… you deserve it."

Softly closing his eyes, James serenely drifted into his final sleep. A tearful Florence fell to her knees in front of James.

"Lady Heinrich, the engineers need you to return to the trebuchets, some of the systems are starting to malfunction," reported Florence. "I'll stay with the Legate, it's my duty."

"There is no need, Florence, the Legate is dead."

Burying her head into his chest, Florence let out her final remembrance for the battle-hardened warrior. Unable to remain with him for long, the cleric went about her duties on the living. Riding around the fields for an exit, Jonas found himself on a collision course with a hard-charging Walker. No longer overcome with fear for his life, the Saint Commander gritted his teeth and turned his horse toward him.

"Well, if it isn't Hector Reed's little bastard. You may be one of the greatest social climbers ever."

"Jonas Marimon, I'm here to make you answer for King Stephen."

"Oh, how do you know I killed him?"

"I know the oath you took. While you had no qualms over breaking it, you would have killed any man who dared disobey you!"

"It's a strange little tradition, but you are right. I would never have let another sword touch him, but my own did him in! I never understood why you didn't come in with us, I'd have given you anything."

"Not at the price of my soul! I swore an oath to be Cassandra's Shield Master, and unlike some countrymen I know how to keep my vows!"

"An oath is meaningless, Walker! The only word a Knight has is his sword; still, I should have known it would come to this. You and Reed had such childish notions of honor!"

"For the lion and Queen Cassandra!"

Squeezing his thighs against his steed, Walker broke for his foe. Answering the challenge, Jonas went head on. When they were at arm's length, the two tackled each other from their mounts and went crashing to the ground. Rising again, both men readied swords and shields for combat. They circled each other, searching for a weakness. Impatient, Jonas attacked first, but the Oath shield proved impossible to penetrate with a mere attack. Walker shield-bashed him, but missed with two ensuing slices. Pushing their shields together, both knights refused to give any ground.

Stationing Virgus' remaining forces as cover, Gavin and Roland got more of their men to safety.

"Gavin, we can't wait any longer! The army can still cover us if we retreat now. Maybe we can break through to Jonas."

"Jonas is lost! There's no hope! Make for the posterns."

Reassuming command of the heavy horse, Cedric rallied the Titan Armada. He ordered the wedge formed and prepared to run the remaining stragglers down. Knowing what was coming, Gavin and Roland hit the posterns. Rebels, healthy and injured alike, abandoned their weapons and armor in a desperate attempt to save their skins. Forced to obey an order, Virgus' soldiers pushed forward to meet the charging Titan Armada and certain death.

Pushing each other back, Jonas and Walker found other warriors interrupting their fight. A Myotis sword fighter fearlessly attacked the Saint commander, but met his death. The Order of the Lion Commander easily dispatched a swordsman as well.

"Reed was a great soldier and he trained you well, Walker."

"I'll take that as a compliment, even from a madman like you."

Jonas tapped the back of his shield and a blade emerged from his forearm. Attacking sword first, Walker blocked it, but the second blade ripped into the chain under the Order of the Lion Knight's armpit. Wincing in pain, he was bulled over by the Saint Commander's shield. On the ground, Jonas took the tip of his sword and put it towards Walker's throat.

"Isn't this ironic? It looks like I'm going to get a chance to wipe out your entire family."

Walker saw the spiteful rage in Jonas' eyes.

"Don't look so surprised! It was arranged. Hector Reed's death was required. In the chaos of the Istle Hills, it was easy. Did you really think we were going to sit back and let him create his precious Alliance army? Had I only known then what demon would be unleashed as a result of his death... well, it's too late for regrets now!"

Jonas drew back to strike Walker. As he pushed forward, the Order of the Lion Knight grabbed the blade with his hand. Despite the blood pouring from his palm, adrenaline and rage caused the younger Lord Knight to overpower the Saint and rip the sword from his grasp. He grabbed Jonas and spun him so that Walker wrapped his hands in a neck breaking position. Knowing his death was inevitable, the Saint simply smiled.

"Well done, boy, but if you kill me you'll be just as good as me."

"No... I'll be better... and we'll be better for it!"

"It was worth a shot. Your papa was right...you were better than all of us..."

Walker snapped Jonas' neck. For a man who had wrought misery and death upon his own people and others, it seemed too quick a death. As the Saint fell to the ground, the gold piece Stephen tipped him with bounced from his pockets. Suffering from his wounds and loss of blood, Walker fell to the ground. Alone and with the spirit of death upon him, the shield suddenly found Robespierre putting him on a horse. His half-brother raced Walker back to the Triage unit where Florence went to work on his wounds. The Order of the Lion commander passed out as a white light covered his body.

Meanwhile, the dreaded Titan wedge mowed down the remaining members of Virgus' army and charged for the posterns. Seeing the enemy upon them, Gavin and Roland had no choice. Despite a large number of their forces still trapped outside the city walls, the two Saints sealed the posterns.

"Don't leave us!" screamed a wounded soldier. "Sir Gavin... please help us!"

"I'm sorry," retorted Gavin. "By the Saints, you don't know how sorry I am."

Being pulled away from the posterns as prisoners, some of the soldiers banged on them and tore at the bars until the last moment. Resting his head against the wall, Gavin shed tears for his lost soldiers and comrades even as they cursed him. The sound of the trebuchets barrage resumed once more. The haunting noise was a further reminder of how helpless the rebels were. As he turned to the city, Roland and others were busy comforting the wounded and dying. Soldiers were screaming in agony and it was too much for Sir Gavin to bear. If this wasn't enough, the haughty Sharon had stormed down from the Castle to their positions.

"What are you doing?" Sharon berated Gavin.

"The battle is lost!" determined Gavin. "We cannot fight the Alliance army in the field; any further attack would be worthless."

"The trebuchets are destroying the wall! They will have access into the city!"

"We have no means of stopping their trebuchets! The walls can only hold out as long as they can."

"Rally your cohort and get out there!"

Gavin grabbed Sharon by her cheeks and for a moment she feared he'd snap her neck. Instead, he forced her to stare at the soldiers in the city.

"You want my cohort, Sharon? This is my cohort, this is what I have left! They're dead or dying. We're finished."

Sharon looked on in horror at the remaining forces. Only a fraction of the soldiers could be considered battle ready. Most of the wounded would die before nightfall. Overcome with fear and anger, Sharon returned to the castle to make the report to her husband.

Learning of the injuries to Walker, Cassandra levitated over to the Triage unit. Martha waited for her outside a tent.

"I just heard, Martha," recited Cassandra. "Where is Walker? Is he all right?"

"He's okay, your Highness," Martha reassured Cassandra. "Armor took most of the damage on the first hit, but his own recklessness with his hand caused most of the injuries."

"Recklessness!" countered Robespierre. "Your Highness, Walker's selfless actions killed Jonas Marimon and broke whatever will the rebels had left to fight."

"Everyone has their own assessment of the situation," argued Martha. "Walker is one tough knight and we're all proud of him. Florence has taken over his treatment in the tent over there. When she's finished, I'm sure you can see him."

Knowing it would impossible to breach the posterns, Cedric rode the Armada back to the center of the field. All of the units joined him there, raising their banners in victory and chanting the commander's name. The Titan prince rode around and congratulated his soldiers. When he reached his sister, she winked at him. The siblings embraced and kissed one another. Exhausted and stained in blood, the Alliance army was thrilled that they had few casualties.

"What are your orders, Commander?" asked Amuro sweetly.

"The camp should be established by now. Dismiss the majority of the army and let them rest behind a proper stockade. I want a skeleton crew of our reserves to keep an eye on these trebuchets in case the rebels decide to get heroic. Otherwise, I want our soldiers fed and rested for the second phase."

"Martha signaled me, and based on her calculations, it's going to take into tomorrow to break through those walls," reported Amuro.

"So be it. I must admit, we did more damage than I ever imagined. We need a new strategy to plan for the morrow."

As the Alliance army followed their banners back to the encampment, Abaddon observed them intently from his tower. Staring at the city, he saw a much different sight. Gavin and Roland moved desperately from soldier to soldier trying to save those they could.

"He leaves nothing for chance," commented Abaddon.

"We have no defense against those trebuchets," relayed Virgus. "I doubt Gavin will be able to muster a second charge to take them out."

"It won't be easy for Marie to form an army. We need time, Virgus, and at the rate they're going, Cedric will have us wiped out by tomorrow morning."

In the Alliance triage unit, Walker was lying in a bed. His shoulder and hand were wrapped and he was being given a transfusion. He started to wake slowly.

"Oh God, I died…" stammered Walker slowly.

A loud laugh at his bedside reassured him he was still alive. Florence was washing her hands in a basin beside his bed.

"Don't worry, Knight Commander, you'll be good as new in a few hours," Florence reassured him.

"Is the battle still on?"

"Well, I would say phase one is over. The rebels have withdrawn into the city and we're bombarding the walls right now."

"So they retreated?"

"Are you kidding? When you killed Jonas, the other Saints hightailed it back into the city."

"So I did slay that monster… Stephen, my father, and yet it was only the beginning."

"Florence, is he okay?" shouted Martha from outside the tent.

"He's fine, Martha," replied Florence.

"I've got a VIP who's dying to see him."

Without being announced, Cassandra rushed in with tears in her eyes. It was a position Walker didn't envy, though he appreciated his Queen's compassion. Wordless, the Queen buried her head at his side.

"Your Highness, the man responsible for your father's death has fallen at my hands."

"I don't care anymore, Walker! I couldn't bear the thought of losing you as well. Thank God you're safe."

"WHERE IS HE?" exclaimed Minerva as she pulled back the canvas to the tent. "I hope he's alive so I can kill him!"

"Oh no..." said Walker anxiously.

"Jonathan, what the hell did you do to yourself?" demanded Minerva as her tears ruined her war paint. "You leave me out there in the middle of the battlefield and don't even send Robespierre to tell me you're wounded!"

"You're a soldier, Minerva, and a soldier does their duty. I couldn't have you leave your command to worry about me. Your concerns about me are easily quashed; Florence says I'm fine."

"Good. You just rest up here and leave the rest to me."

"I'll be cleared to return to the fight soon. You can count on it."

"But...you've done enough, Jon!" exuded a surprised Minerva. "I mean, with your wounds, you'll be exempt. Isn't that right, Florence?"

"It's only a recommendation, Minerva. Florence, seriously, can I fight?"

"You know, I really don't want to get involved in a lover's quarrel, unless it has something to do *La Morte Angelus* himself."

Feeling the incredulous stare of Cassandra upon her, Florence hadn't realized she said the last line out loud. Laughing to cover up her error, she stared at Walker and Minerva once more.

"Minerva, Walker is wounded and thus could be exempted. However, he's fine and could get back on the battlefield provided he eats something."

"No problem," responded Walker. "I am the Shield of the Queen, and it is my duty to march with her into Verian to reclaim her throne."

"Well, I've done everything I can, Minerva."

"Steel bellies are so stubborn, but I guess I'll just have to take up a position next to you, so you don't get hurt any worse."

"Like I could ever hold you back, sweetheart," joked Walker. "Well, I guess I'm going to have to be extra careful so I can survive this encounter."

"Why should anything be different now?" questioned Minerva.

"I owe it to the woman I intend to marry."

"Then you did mean it when you gave me the bow!"

"While I was surprised at the custom... my ultimate intentions were realized. It's just a bit sooner than I hoped. I really wanted to wait until this mess was over."

"Well, Captain, I've got your back!" Minerva reassured Walker as she kissed him.

"Well, Walker, Minerva, I'm very happy for you," congratulated Cassandra. "When your sister and I spoke of middle ground between us, I don't think we meant this. Yet, it's good for all of us. Now, Walker, you take care of yourself, because as you said I must have my faithful shield by my side on the morrow."

"Absolutely, your Highness," said Walker, saluting.

A tray of food came in. Cassandra and Florence left to give the two some privacy. Minerva proceeded to feed the hero of the first battle his victory hospital food. All around the triage unit, the encampment was established and properly barricaded. The sound of twenty-five trebuchets smashing against the walls of Verian became the sweetest music in the world to the Alliance. Still, no one in the camp believed that a single victorious battle was the end of this, for the War of Two Queens continued.

Grand Library, Edenia

The Permaneo Eques Ordinares and the Bis Reginum serve
as the embodiments of virtue, but they are not enough alone.
For true salvation will only come when the Denique Refero is
discovered; only then will the mystery of God be revealed to all
of those with hearts of goodwill.

The Legend of the Last Knight, the Edenian Prophecy

Trapped in the library for the second consecutive rotation, Garrett dealt with two constant annoyances. The kobold had assumed if he gathered all four prophecies together, it would be easy to decipher the meaning behind them. However, when he heard the Edenian prophecy, a new slew of questions popped into his mind. His second annoyance resulted from Thomas' inquisitive nature. Garrett wondered if it was wise to have brought the young Titan heir with him in the first place.

"Why are there four prophecies?" asked Thomas.

"I don't know," responded Garrett angrily.

"I thought people like you are supposed to know these things."

"I'm clairvoyant, not a genius."

"I could be home in the safety of Castle Titan receiving regular updates from the front. Instead I've been trapped with you for two rotations in this dusty old library, not to mention the fact that we're no closer to a conclusion than when we started."

"You're not helping."

"Well, how am I supposed to react in this obviously ridiculous situation!"

"Let's go over this again," decided Garrett as he rubbed his temples. "The Elves wrote the prophecy of the Legend of the Last Knight. In a time of darkness, the Elves wrote that a Last Knight would emerge to destroy evil."

"You've been saying that the whole time. In fact, that's probably the clearest prophecy we have."

"Then we have the Kablisha version, which elevates this Last Knight into an actual agent of God. The Titan prophecy diverts to the left flank and starts to talk about a Twice-Blessed Queen, who is a symbol of hope."

"And that brings us to…" added Thomas rhetorically.

"The Edenian Prophecy, which apparently says that it's going to take more than just the Last Knight and Twice-Blessed Queen only. The part that has me hung up involves this *Denique Refero…*"

"What is a *Denique Refero* anyway?"

"It means 'Final Answer' in the old language."

"So… who is supposed to provide this answer? Is it the Queen or the Knight?"

"I don't know, Thomas! I think it's the Queen, most likely!"

"Are we looking for the wrong thing then, Garrett?"

"I don't follow."

"What if there isn't a *Permaneo Eques Ordinares*? What if all of these prophecies revolve around the Queen instead?"

"I never thought of that," said Garrett as he grimaced. "If that's true, then your uncle may be walking into a trap! He truly believes he's that warrior!"

Thomas hit his head on the table.

"What's wrong?" asked a worried Garrett.

"I was really scared leaving my mom and dad. Mom assured me that as long as my uncle was with them, I had nothing to worry about. Now you're telling me he's working off a false prophecy!"

"I'm sorry, Thomas."

Noticing the mood of the two, one of the operatives sat down at the table.

"Prince Thomas, Lord Garrett, we received a transmission from Verian," reported the operative. "Cedric goaded Jonas into a battle. The rebel army was dealt a crushing blow and their numbers have been vastly reduced. The Final Alliance now holds the whole of the Acadian plains, but the battle for Verian itself remains and it will be a difficult battle. Your mom and dad are fine, Prince Thomas. In fact, we suffered very few casualties in the engagement."

Thomas breathed a sigh of relief. "I'm glad they're all right for now."

"Well, it's good, Master Thomas, that you have one less fear this evening. Don't worry, only one path ahead of us leads to the fact your uncle isn't the *Permaneo Eques Ordinares*."

"But can't you see the future, Garrett? Any previews for tomorrow's action?"

"I'm not a seer, I'm a mystic," replied Garrett as he shook his head. "I can see different paths to take, but there is no hope unless someone can bind the soul of Abaddon back to Hell."

"What if we just take Verian for now and worry about that later?"

"Your uncle can win the battle but this war will continue until Abaddon is cast from our world. He will never give up his quest to possess the powers and soul of Cassandra Acadia."

"I don't understand, Garrett. Cassandra is the nicest, sweetest, most caring woman ever! Why does Abaddon think he could ever use her? She'd never join him."

"Thomas, it's difficult to explain. Until you're older, it's best that you understand Cassandra is special. While she shows a certain face to you and all of Terminus Mundus, there's another creature sleeping inside of her."

"That's why my uncle fights so hard for her."

"That's why she cries so much. As with everything in life, it depends on the strength of the individual. Still, I have learned that I'd rather be in a situation where I'm forced to give your uncle a fighting chance. He hates to lose."

"Yeah, but is that going to be enough against Abaddon? Chances are my uncle isn't going to surprise him again."

"I see great things for your future, Prince Rhone. I pray that God is always good to you. I doubt we will solve this mystery this evening. We'll return to the hotel for now. Perhaps a hearty meal and a good night sleep will clarify things in the morning."

"Finally, we haven't eaten anything in hours!"

"You must be starving. Of course, I find it runs in your family..."

Sophia waited for the two and the operatives guarding them. Her cheery disposition made everyone feel less exhausted.

"Ready to head up for the rotation?" asked Sophia.

"Yes, Sophia," affirmed Garrett. "I fear I'm going to have to impose on you tomorrow as well."

"No problem. I'll reserve the room for you again and take you down myself."

"Thank you. Thomas, don't forget the flower."

"You and that stupid flower!"

Thomas grabbed the pot as two operatives helped the kobold onto the platform. As the three grabbed onto the rails, Thomas studied Garrett's face.

"I have one last question," announced Thomas.

"Are you going to ask me about my eyes?" questioned Garrett as if he felt Thomas staring at him.

"Well... it's just... yes."

Garrett sighed and shook his head. "All right."

"What's with the eyes?"

"Let's just say that a blessing can be a curse and a curse can be a blessing."

Final Alliance Encampment, Plains of Verian

Is it lawful for us to pay tribute to the King or not? Recognizing their craftiness he said to them: Show me the currency; whose image does it bear? They replied: the King of Central Acadia. So he said to them: Render to the King what belongs to the King and to God what belongs to God.

The Napolitan Evangelist 20:22-25

A cool evening spring breeze blew through the encampment. In the main tent that was once reserved for King Stephen, Cassandra stood with Cedric and the remainder of the senior officers. A map of Verian was projected as a three-dimensional image on the table.

"It doesn't make any sense," reasoned Christian. "I would have expected some move against the siege weapons but…"

"Could we have wiped out their entire army in one attack?" suggested Cagius.

"No way. Abaddon would never have left himself that vulnerable," determined Cecilia.

"There's something on the other side of those walls that we're missing," said Cedric.

"It doesn't matter. We're only going to be able to enter through a single hole in the wall," said Amuro. "We'll know what we're up against then."

"What if it's worse?" suggested Cassandra.

Everyone turned their attention to the previously silent Queen. The frightened look on her face was enough cause for concern, but the fact Cassandra interrupted a strategy session raised suspicions even further.

"For the last few hours, I've sensed the discipline of conjuration occurring in the city," reported Cassandra. "Someone is dabbling in necromancy, I'm sure of it."

"Cedric, we tore that army to pieces on the field today!" worried Cagius. "I don't feel like fighting them again."

"We'd better order the burial crew to cremate the bodies just to be on the safe side," recommended Christian.

"That's superstitious nonsense!" exclaimed Cassandra. "Conjuration summons fell spirits from the void for a skilled necromancer to bind to physical constructs."

"This doesn't make any sense," interrupted Cecilia. "I know my history. Cerwin sealed the *Libro Mortuorum* away."

"I'm afraid Master Cerwin feared the corruptive influence of the book," recollected Sirius. "The Wizard's Guild agreed to seal it in the deepest vaults of their Tower."

"Well, Abaddon opened it," stated Cedric with a sigh. "All right, if we're fighting fell spirits, we need silver weapons. Hippolyte, I know the tribes use iron, but can you muster up a few?"

"Maybe twenty thousand or so," said Hippolyte thoughtfully. "I need to check with the Dwarves if we can trade for some."

"I propose a single infantry column, no horses," recommended Amuro. "The smaller the better."

"Yes," agreed Cedric. "We will call for best one hundred forty-four thousand warriors we have for this assault. Anyone with a silver weapon should donate it to someone in the attack."

"Very specific, Cedric," commented Christian. "Yet, the sheer size of a force in urban combat isn't going to make a difference. I propose that we leave half of our soldiers in reserve and fortify the rest in Orion."

"I think it's wise," concurred Amuro. "Especially if we're walking into a trap."

Cedric simulated the wall coming down to the east. He used three arrows to represent the army moving into the city and towards the Castle. When the arrows reached the bridge leading to the Wizards' Tower and Castle they stopped.

"Divide and conquer is the strategy," announced Cedric. "I'll lead the main force. Colin and Argus will lead the other two. The main force will hold the enemy army at bay. Colin's team will consist of tribal units; they will take the Castle and protect Doctor Martha Heinrich."

"Martha's coming too?" asked Cecilia.

"She wants to make sure whatever tools Virgus used can't be used against us again. Argus' unit will assault the Wizards' Tower. Make sure you take plenty of runic tokens, you'll need them."

"Right, Cedric," acknowledged Argus.

"Any objections?" asked Cedric.

"Not after this morning, Cedric," teased Amuro. "We never expected to be in position already. So whatever you ask of us, you've got it."

"Make your selections for the detail and order those soldiers to get a lot of rest. We've got one shot at this tomorrow. We must retake Verian while morale is high. Thank for your counsel. Good night and good luck."

As the senior officers left the tent, Cassandra beckoned Cedric to remain behind.

"What's the matter, Cassie?"

"Cedric, you make it sound so easy."

"Easy? Cassie, for all I know, we could marching into the gates of Hell."

"What about Abaddon? I know you've thought about this, and that's why Garrett is in Edenia."

"If he had a new body, he would have appeared already. Still, I think we're in a race against time."

"So who is this new recruit, Duke Francesco Angelino? I don't remember seeing him on any of the lists."

"He's a mercenary who shares our same vision for love and justice. I prefer to leave it at that for now."

"You've been seeking his counsel quite often. What aren't you telling me, Cedric?"

"Imagine being so close to achieving your goals, yet having the one sure baton of victory so far out of reach. It's torture. Francis is a worldly individual and his knowledge even surpasses that of Wilhelm. We need him, Cassie."

"I trust your judgment, even if your reasons sound more like logic puzzles. I'm borrowing a few Knights as an escort. I have something I have to do."

"Be careful."

Cedric rubbed Cassie on her arms as he held her. The two departed the tent as an armed escort of Order of the Lion Knights waited for Cassandra. The young Queen strolled on the plains toward the main gate of the city. In the distance the pounding of the spheres against the wall could be heard and the integrity of the eastern wall had already been significantly compromised. Staring at the top of the main gate, Cassandra noticed a skull with the jester's crown placed on top of it. As she cried hysterically, the Queen used a telekinesis spell to lower the skull from the wall. After a few minutes, the skull reached her. Cassandra knelt in the grass and embraced it to her chest.

"Oh Daddy…"

Hearing the words of her father once more brought her some comfort. *Still quick to cry; that's one part of you that hasn't changed since you were a little girl. Cassie, I want only the best for you and I want you to be happy.*

Snapped back to reality, a demonic furor overtook Cassandra and even her guard grew nervous at the darkness coming from her body.

"I'll do what it takes to bring down those responsible for this, Daddy, and I will do whatever I can to save Marie."

Entering his own tent, the smiling face of Martha Heinrich met Cedric Rhone.

"You wished to see me, my Lord."

"Sit with me for a while, Martha."

The two took a seat. Cedric poured a glass of wine for Martha first and a brandy for himself.

"So, Cedric, while I would love to sit here and pick your brain for a while, I know you had something else in mind."

"I know you intend to march with us tomorrow morning."

"You can't talk me out of this one. I have to make sure Virgus' weapons can't be used against us again."

"Actually, it's comforting to know someone of your talents will be with us. Just make sure you arm yourself with a silver weapon." Cedric took a swig of brandy. "What I was wondering was if you think you could replicate Virgus' tachyon technology."

"Of course. I had to retro-engineer the whole field in order to devise something to stop it."

"How long would it take you to come up with a device that could emit the same tachyon field?"

"No time. It's doesn't require sophisticated equipment and it's not complicated if you're looking at a small area."

"Should the battle go poorly tomorrow, we need to come up with a means of containing our enemies. Even if it bought us just a few rotations, a weapon such as that could be invaluable."

Martha slugged her drink. "My Lord, I'll begin work on it right away."

"Do me one favor and keep it quiet. Morale is hanging by a thread around here."

"I understand. May I ask why you've had this sudden change of heart? After what happened on the field today..."

"I thank you for your time, Martha and I hope we will never have to use the fruits of your labor."

"Very well, your Highness, I bid you good night."

"Wait..." added Cedric as Martha was about to leave. "You've always been good to me and my sister. There have been times over the revolutions when I took your genius for granted. Even trapped in that Kablisha prison, I knew you'd find a way to take that barrier down..."

Stopping dead in her tracks, the doctor was very concerned about the sudden change in Cedric's tone. Tears fell from the corners of her eyes. "Cedric, is everything all right? Please... you and Cecilia are as precious to me as any child of my own body could be... if I can..."

"Certain responsibilities fall on the shoulders of some people. I just wanted to make sure you knew how much I appreciate that genius of yours. After all, I wouldn't be here if it wasn't for you."

The two laughed as a shaky Martha left the tent. In another tent, Wilhelm sat down in his chair reading a book. Nadia was resting on the bed behind him. Wilhelm bent over her and kissed her on the cheek.

"Nadia, my beloved, how are you able to sleep on a night like this?"

A cold wind suddenly blew into the tent and a candle went out. Wilhelm smiled as he rose up and turned to see a mass of ethereal locusts forming into a single entity.

"Hello, Krystos," announced Abaddon.

"Finally figured it out, didn't you? Nothing gets by you, Abaddon."

"You've been a very naughty angel! Playing us for fools while you've been working for the other side—the Prince is very displeased."

"I never really was on your side to begin with. Your Prince is a poor judge of character to think that I would actually betray God."

"Subterfuge, Krystos? I didn't think that was a strongpoint for the angels."

"We change our tactics constantly," said Wilhelm as he stood and put his book down. "When dealing with the Prince of Lies, it becomes quite effective. Well, we've seem to have bought ourselves some time. You haven't figured out a way to reconstruct a physical body yet."

"A temporary nuisance, Krystos, it will all end in due time."

Abaddon stared at Nadia. It nearly broke his heart to see her with Wilhelm. "She was our finest!" exuded Abaddon. "Nadia was beautiful, and you destroyed her!"

"Destroyed, old friend? Don't you mean 'saved'? I've broken the hold her Daddy had on her. She's not coming back to you."

"What's the difference? The time is coming; the Gates will be torn down and Lucifer shall sit on the throne of Heaven, Earth, and Hell."

"Talk is something you do well, Abaddon. I prefer action. Though I must admit, you have a good many people here sworn to prevent such a thing from happening. Guess what, my friend, you brought them together. I don't think you came here to gloat, so what is your purpose?"

"The last time Cedric Rhone and I were together, there was little chance for words. I believe a pre-battle parlay is appropriate."

"Very well. I will see if he will receive you."

"Of course."

Wilhelm poked his head outside his tent and saw no one was coming. Motioning Abaddon to follow, the two crossed into Cedric's command tent. The Titan prince was scribbling away at something on the desk. His mentor poked his head into the tent.

"Cedric, I have someone here who wishes to treat with you."

Hastily putting away the parchment, Cedric stood and put his arms at ease. Abaddon entered the room behind Wilhelm.

"Crown Prince Cedric Rhone," said Abaddon in greeting. "I come on behalf of myself. This has nothing to do with the rebels in Verian."

"I'm not surprised that you would come here," quipped Cedric. "What terms do you wish for my unconditional surrender?"

"For starters, you can turn Cassandra over to me—"

"Oh, that's a deal breaker; and we started off so well. I'd offer you a seat… but you can't sit down. If you don't mind, I can."

Curling his lip at the insult, Abaddon watched Cedric sit down.

"Your wit is as sharp as Ragnarok, Prince Rhone. So you've been hiding out among the Kablisha for five revolutions."

"More like, was incarcerated."

"I thought they had developed a bit of a spine. I know you learned a few tricks from them, but when we meet again, that alone won't make a difference."

"Do you expect me to back down from a challenge?"

"You're good, Cedric, you're very good, but in the end you are a Divikin not a Sentinel. You cannot take down a divine being."

"I did it once before."

"You destroyed a physical body; you were not able to bind my soul. You didn't defeat me, you simply delayed the inevitable. Look at you. I left you in a crumpled heap and you know for sure not one man or woman in this camp could outperform you."

"Well, I guess I should just surrender then. Wilhelm, go tell the camp to pack up, we're going to surrender."

"Of course, sir," said Wilhelm chuckling.

"No, I think I'll cancel my last order," quipped Cedric.

The sound of the tent opening caused Abaddon to turn. Francis stood there with a smile on his face. Abaddon was in genuine shock to see him.

"I knew I felt the Guardian," reasoned Abaddon. "What are you doing here?"

"You know I could ask you the same thing," retorted Francis. "Actually, it's wonderful to see you, Abaddon. Now why don't you crawl back under the rock you came from and leave these people alone!"

"You can't threaten me, Guardian! I am well aware of your extraordinary powers, but you lack to ability to cast me into Hell as well."

"True, but it is only right that I give you a fair warning. You're not so far gone yet, my friend, but if you pursue this madness there's no coming back from it. Repent, Abaddon, God will still take you back, I promise."

"You fools don't have any idea what this is all about, do you?"

Francis was disappointed when Abaddon refused him.

"I know that we have business, Abaddon," said Cedric.

"Of course, I have been authorized by my Prince to make an offer to you."

"There is no price on my soul, Abaddon. I thought I made that quite clear five revolutions ago."

"So you're going to continue to stand up and protect these people. For what? Let's say you win, let's say you get rid of me and everything you've been dreaming comes true. King Cedric takes his position next to Queen Cassandra. These people love you now because they're too scared to fight me. The second I'm gone they'll banish or even kill you. A war like this must have cost you a pretty penny already, there is bound to be an economic disaster from it. Still, you seem to love these people, so the Prince is offering Terminus Mundus in exchange for Cassandra."

"You don't have the power to distribute the realms of creation."

"I am not offering the right to rule. I am offering you their souls. My fiendish friends are quite infuriated by you holding up our chance at revenge. Let me explain what happens after my body is restored. All of my might and power will be directed at you. You will fight with honor and nobility, but you will die in battle. With you out of the way, I will turn Cassandra into her true form. She will become the Succubus Queen to whom no living soul on Terminus Mundus will resist. You were privy to that vision, Cedric, and you know what happened to your Divikin companion who saw her. Because she has an angelic component in her, they are powerless to resist her temptations. One by one they'll submit themselves to their beautiful Demon Queen and to her grandfather through her. Mundus and all of the other realms shall serve Cassandra's will. Then we'll proceed to the other worlds and do the same. This time Lucifer's army will be of God—his own creation fighting for their beloved and beautiful Queen. If the attack originates from God, it cannot be destroyed! Tell him, Guardian!"

"Cedric, it is my duty to speak the truth," Francis informed Cedric. "Abaddon doesn't lie in this matter."

"There is only one man that can prevent the fate of this world," offered Abaddon. "It's in your hands, Cedric. If you were to surrender Cassandra to me willingly, the Prince will spare creation. You've seen the powers my Master has over the temporal realm. He's just made you the most important person in history."

"There is no bond to ensure you would keep your word!" exclaimed an angry Cedric.

"You know that I'm an honest enemy. Give me Cassandra now and I will leave. The fools in that city be damned... they're traitors, anyway. It's these difficult decisions in life that are hardest. Save the girl or the world, Commander—what will you do? Let me show you something to motivate you."

Abaddon held out his hand. Cedric was forced to see a potential future version of his sister. Black armor covered her chest and waist where gold once was. Black lace leggings emerged just above her long, armored black boots. Her fingerless gauntlets held a corrupted version of the Gottin-speer with a green eye dividing the bloody spear tip from the shaft. Adorning her head was a black metal war crown with the same green eye at its center instead of a jewel. Sadistically smiling, her glazed red eyes were filled with lust for battle and destruction. From her back, two purple demon wings spread wide.

"She'll be the Queen's first general!" boasted Abaddon. "The perfect blend of Succubus and Valkyrie with an insatiable appetite for war and destruction. Do you see the blood on her spear? It is from the offering of her firstborn child to the glory of her Succubus Queen. I thought older brothers always sought to protect their little sisters. You seem very eager to sacrifice her to sate your own ego."

Unable to hold back any longer, Cedric took a swing at Abaddon. Expecting the blow to pass through him, the dark angel couldn't believe that the Titan prince actually created a contact. Abaddon staggered as Francis and Wilhelm held their commander back. Noticing the open Bible on Cedric's desk, Abaddon tried the intellectual approach.

"Read your Bible carefully, Cedric. I don't know it all, but I do know of a passage that says, 'Render to the King what belongs to the King and to God what belongs to God.' Cassandra was never meant to be a child of this world. She doesn't belong to you...she belongs to her grandfather."

"No one has the right to own a life!" exclaimed Cedric.

"You try my patience, boy. Make your choice: the girl or the world."

"There is no choice! No matter what I would choose I take the same risk. For now you may inform your Dark Master that I choose Cassandra, and to defend her honor, I will meet you or any dark angel of his choosing on the field of battle. I swear to you right now, Abaddon, you will rue that hour! You think you've defeated me, but you have no idea of the demon you've unleashed! Get the hell out!"

"Then we have nothing more to discuss," reasoned Abaddon. "We will be seeing each other soon."

Abaddon disappeared. Cedric turned to Wilhelm.

"This is the point where I plead with you to tell me that everything he said was a lie," begged Cedric.

"Cedric, think carefully!" said Wilhelm. "Did you bring Argus into that vision?"

"Yes. He begged to come in with me and I watched the way Argus lost control in the presence of Cassandra's demonic nature."

"That was a lesser form of what Cassandra could become, because that is the form you know," explained Francis. "When I was in Hell, I gained far too much insight into Lucifer's plans and I was unfortunately privy to the vision of what the Succubus Queen was intended to be. If Cassandra falls under the sway of her grandfather, it will end all of creation and, quite likely when God is defeated, the end of everything."

"I thought Lucifer would sit on the throne," argued Cedric.

"If God is defeated, he is no longer omnipotent," stated Wilhelm. "If one of the four tenets is broken, the temporal and spiritual realms will be cast into oblivion."

Cedric fell back into his seat and put his hands on his forehead. "I have never suffered such a wound in battle as I have in the last five minutes. What the hell am I going to do now? My God, my God, why have you forsaken me?"

The sentinels stood silent as Cedric buried his head.

"Wilhelm, I would speak with Francis alone, please."

"Cedric, I'm sorry. God, I am so sorry."

"Wilhelm, the fault lies not with you, but with the powers of darkness alone. Please, I need some time."

"Don't lose faith, Commander, we can always pray for a miracle," Wilhelm encouraged Cedric. "Even if it means my own banishment, I will not allow God to forsake you. Not after all of this!"

Wilhelm stepped back and saluted him. Cedric was unable to muster the proper response to answer the salute, and Wilhelm left him.

"I knew Abaddon would try to hurt you, Prince Rhone," said Francis. "Yet, even I couldn't have imagined such cruelty. Why speak with me and not Wilhelm?"

"Wilhelm loves me too much. His compassion is unmatched and he would not allow me to speak of what needs to be said now. This is a time for courage."

"And so you would ask of a Guardian Angel the one boon he is unable to grant?"

"It doesn't matter anymore, Francis. We both know what we're up against and we're losing. I don't have the answers. I can't put up a false front and pretend we're fine. Can you defeat Abaddon?"

"No. Not if his boasts about this body are correct."

"Where would he get this power?"

"From Marie Acadia…her bloodline is of House Orpheus. It's a divine bloodline."

"This isn't one of those pathetic conspiracies of Christ and a consort having a son who would rightfully rule Terminus Mundus."

"No, Prince Rhone, this one is quite real. In the Garden, the seven virtues were present, but contained in the fruit of the Tree of Knowledge were the seven deadly sins, the embodiment of the most powerful fallen angels to serve the court of the Dark Prince. Thus, Leviathan took the form of a serpent and tempted Adam and Eve to eat the fruit. In that moment, all seven deadly sins erupted in their bodies and because of Leviathan's presence, lust dominated the other six. Cain was conceived then and there, the only man born before the Fall of mortals! Thus when Cain killed Abel and was damned by God, a regenerative agent entered his bloodline to prevent him from dying. A power passed unknowingly to his descendants. While they are not long-lived anymore, they heal. Because the bloodline is divine in origin, his power can be used by mortals and divine beings alike."

"He's going to sacrifice Marie so he can live. Why hasn't he done it yet?"

"There must be something else I haven't learned yet. If she is their necromancer, and I believe she is... it must have something to do with that."

"Watching her sister being sacrificed could push Cassie over the edge. It works so perfectly together. Francis, why did you willingly go into Hell?"

"I was ordered."

"No, that doesn't make sense. Other sentinels were better suited than a Guardian Angel. Why did you go?"

"I went because I heard rumors that a creature born of hell invoked God's name to save herself from despair. I always found it interesting that Guardian Angels are often depicted as mean and nasty in artwork. At times, we can be haughty since we're so attentive to detail and often get snippy ordering other choirs around. However, the guardians can't stand to see even one soul suffer. That's why I went down there, and I dare not repeat what I witnessed on my journey. The hardest part was the end, clawed hands reaching through glass that was once sand. I begged them to forsake their despair for the love of God, yet they had lost the ability to comprehend my tongue. As hard as it was, I'd do it an infinite number of times even if I could just save one soul."

Cedric stood from his seat once more and walked over to Francis.

"Now I understand why you're so against this," said Cedric with understanding. "Promise me that you'll make the decision at the appropriate time and place. It's all I have left. If that time comes...I beg you, I can't be so selfish to condemn creation..."

Francis held Cedric in a tight embrace.

"Cedric Rhone, I promise you, when the time comes, I'll take care of it. Now if you don't mind, I'll see if I have any favors left to call in."

"One last thing, Francis...why does the Prince of Darkness want me dead? If Cassandra is this powerful, why wouldn't she turn me as well?"

"There are theories. Most believe that you are this planet's embodiment of faith and thus remain incorruptible before the prince. However, I think it's something entirely different. You are Cassandra's anchor, put here by God. Lucifer knows he can never truly turn her to darkness while you are alive. That's why he wanted you to reject the deal, and even Abaddon didn't figure that one out. Lucifer remains the Dark Sefiroth of Pride, and sometimes pride blinds you to everything else. That's the only reason why I'm reluctant. Contemplate this, Cedric: without you, what happens to her? Good night."

Francis left the tent and Cedric returned to his desk. Not even bothering to pour a glass, Cedric drank his brandy right from the bottle. Pulling out the parchment he used before, the Titan prince made some final changes. Rolling up the paper, he tied it with a band and dropped wax on it. Christian pulled back the tent.

"Cedric, I just saw Francis leave," stated Christian. "He didn't look well, and I don't think it was liquor that disagreed with him."

Sealing the wax with his ring, Cedric sat back in his seat.

"Cedric, why is this night different than any other night? Why do you remain isolated in this tent after the grand victory we've won?"

"Christian, I thank you for your loyal service even after I was considered dead. Your decision to operate in Palacio Magnifico was bold. The others are going to look to you for counsel and advice if this should go badly. This document contains my final orders; you are only to break this seal when I am dead. In it you will find step-by-step instructions on what to do next, and a little something for each of you."

"Cedric, you're not making me feel too comfortable here. I demand you tell me what is going on!"

"This document will explain everything, my friend. With any luck you and I will be using it as fire tinder while sipping a drink and celebrating a glorious victory."

"You're lying to me! Twenty-five revolutions together and you don't think I know? What needs to be done? I'll do it! I owe you that much."

"You can't follow where I'm going, Christian. It will be hard on Cecilia, so make sure you read the part addressed to her first. You're going to need her help with Cassie…"

Cedric stopped himself. He found the reassuring hand on his friend on his shoulder.

"There are some orders in life you don't question," affirmed Christian. "If anything happens to you, I will break this seal and whatever you ask will be obeyed. I couldn't make such a promise five revolutions ago, but I can promise you that now."

"Thank you, Christian."

"Good night, your Highness."

Christian left the tent. Pulling out his rosary beads from his desk, the Titan prince got on his knees, blessed himself, and prayed. "Heavenly Father, give me the strength to endure my Divine Test! If this cup is to come to me, I accept! If this world requires one last sacrifice to save it, I am more than willing…"

Cedric prayed the rosary. In the city, the remaining Acadians under the command of Gavin and Roland grimaced every time they heard another sphere hit the wall. Gavin held the hand of a dying soldier.

"Lord Knight, what are we fighting for? Did I die for nothing…"

"No, soldier… you died for a mad vampire's ambition… I am sorry…" stammered Gavin.

"Lord Knight… please, don't bother to avenge me… why should anyone die for this? Cassandra, Marie… we are all sons of the Lion…"

The soldier died in his arms.

"I'm done," affirmed Gavin.

"Are you deserting?" asked Roland.

"I won't have any more blood on my hands, not for that Fallen Angel's insane plots!"

"We're all this city has left."

"Have you seen what's going on here? Sharon was willing to sacrifice us again all too easily. I'm not going to die for them, Roland… there will always be another battle. This one is lost!"

"You're going over the wall!"

"Yes, and I'm taking anyone who is able and wants to come with me."

"My ambitions do not lie with the pretender Queen either…I agree, I shall not die for them. It's our duty now to save what we can."

The two Saints went from one soldier to the next. Those that were able and those that could be moved were taken through the posterns. Those that could not be moved pleaded to come with them, but they could not be saved. As they moved across the plains at night, Titan operatives and Wood Elf rangers watched them desert.

"Should we take them out?" asked the wood Elf.

"Let them go," ordered the Titan operative. "Our fight is with Abaddon, not them. By the looks of it, they suffered enough already."

Castle Acadia, Verian, the Next Morning

Contrary to old wives' tales, necromancy does not truly involve raising a so-called zombie. Rather, it involves the binding of a fell spirit condemned to hell with a material construct, which is usually made of sinew or bone. This gives it the appearance of a raised creature out of the grave. Nevertheless, the malevolence driving these fell spirits makes them incredibly dangerous and that is why necromancy was banned and its practitioners hunted down by cabals over the revolutions.

On Necromancy, Cerwin Faulkner

The doors of the Castle opened, Queen Marie in her necromancer robe and the clone of Julius walked into the courtyard. The skies were unnaturally dark as a group of wizards provided power for the weather spell. Luminas and Sharon waited for them at the head of the remaining loyal Acadian soldiers. Luminas wore armor similar to Cedric except he wore a full moon as his insignia. His steel sword had bat wings on the handle with red rune stones. Sharon wore light vanadium mail with two sharp daggers on her waist. Her hair was tied back in a gold twist circlet. Kaladra had his remaining Nephilim and Demonkin ready for battle as well.

"I did not expect to see you so early, Luminas," observed Marie.

"Celius had the Wizards' Guild work on a spell to blot out the light of the sun," responded Luminas. "As long as I'm fed, I'll be protected."

"Well, at least that incessant pounding that kept me up half the night will be over soon," commented Marie. "We shall not keep my sister waiting any longer. Come with me."

A cock crowed at the encampment, though the skies remained gray over the plains. In every section of the camp, soldiers awoke from the tents. The one hundred forty-four thousand named from each country readied themselves for the battle with their silver weaponry, tokens, and talismans. The reserves stationed themselves around the trebuchets in a protective shield. They could see the final cracks in the wall about to give way. Still shaken from the events of the night before, Cedric emerged from his tent. Waiting for him and tapping her foot was his twin sister. From behind, he felt Jericho nudging at him with his nose.

"No, old friend, I go somewhere today where you cannot follow," Cedric calmed the mighty beast.

Hugging the face of the horse tightly, he turned to his sister once more. Eyes red from crying, she grabbed him around the waist. Dropping down to her ear, he revealed everything to Cecilia. In the distance, Ethan emerged from his tent to a disturbing sight. He could see the Titan prince whispering something to his beloved sister. At first, the Vanadis pushed away from him and pounded against his chest. Screaming at him in the ancient language, Ethan wondered if he had forbid Cecilia from joining them in battle. Yet, the sword master grabbed her hard once more and whispered something else to her. The sight of his wife bawling and moaning in her sibling's arms left the Denivan knight heartbroken. Finally reconciling what had to be, the two twins calmed down enough to speak to one another.

"Did you sleep well?" asked Cedric, trying to change the subject.

"As good as I can with the sound of twenty-five projectiles smashing against a wall," joked Cecilia as she wiped the tears from her eyes.

"Where's your husband?"

"He's still getting ready. I may have worn him out last night. And what about you?"

"I did the best I could, Cecilia. I just thought…"

"You are placing a lot of pressure on yourself."

"I'm still the one holding this thing together."

"Hey, you've got a great command staff behind you. Don't think you have to put everything on yourself. I know none of us have what it takes to deal with Abaddon, but we can hold our own against these bozos."

Deciding it was safe to approach, Ethan walked up to the two. "Good morning, Commander."

Biting his lower lip, Cedric reached up to the larger knight's shoulder. "You've got a great girl here, Ethan, and a wonderful son," proclaimed Cedric. "I know no matter what they'll be safe in your hands."

Cedric walked over to join his other soldiers standing in front of the trebuchets. Ethan put his arm around Cecilia. "Cecilia, what the hell is going on?"

"I can't now Ethan… I just can't…" stammered Cecilia.

As he approached the warriors, who would journey into the city with him, Cedric took the time to personally greet all of them. Some had ventured on many campaigns with him, others had even opposed him in such campaigns, but there were fresh faces as well. Before he could leave for the front lines, he saw his mother waiting patiently for him. Staring into her mournful eyes, Cedric surmised she had guessed his intentions. As the Titan queen collapsed into her beloved son's arms, a watchful Cecilia's heart broke again. At least this time, she felt her mother had a chance to say goodbye. After kissing her on the forehead, Cedric solemnly marched to the front line where Amuro and Wilhelm paced nervously. Uncharacteristically, the commander pulled Amuro in for a hug. Though the Elf maiden cherished the warm embrace on a cold morning, her empathy picked up that something was horribly wrong.

"I need you this morning, Amuro," demanded Cedric. "Are you with me?"

"Let's go, Cedric!" exclaimed Amuro.

Cedric stared at the target, took out his flask and drank. He passed it to Wilhelm who also took a swig.

"I owe you an answer for your salute, Duke Wilhelm von Angelhardt," said Cedric. "May I say that of all the souls who have been at my side these past thirty-five revolutions, I have been blessed to serve with the greatest warrior this planet has and will ever know. Teacher, friend, brother, we march into the Gates of Hell to save this planet's soul."

The two looked at each, took a deep breath, and nodded. Placing a hand on each other's shoulder, they reaffirmed what must be done. Not wanting her to feel left out, Cedric passed his flask to Amuro.

"I don't know how you could think of drinking anything right now. If I did, I'd throw up."

Cedric took a final swig and put his flask away.

"The weather is unnatural, all of our reports spoke of good weather," observed Cedric.

"I detect the use of some powerful magic," surmised Amuro.

"Maximilian must want his presence to be known," determined Wilhelm.

"Good, we'll take care of everything in one decisive strike," pronounced Cedric. "Martha, when we move forward, order the engineers to disassemble the trebuchets and fall back to the camp. We don't have the manpower to protect the engineers in this battle."

"Yes, Commander," replied Martha with a wink. "Just so you know, everything is taken care of."

"I knew I could count on you. Captain Josephine of the Myotis, please step forward."

Though she found it odd to be called out by the Prime Eagle, she obeyed his order. "What do you ask of me, Commander?" responded Josephine.

"Josephine, I'd like you to meet Doctor Martha Heinrich. She's a wonderful lady and a good friend of mine. You're unit is going to be in charge of her getting to her proper destination. Do you understand?"

"Yes, Commander, she will not be harmed."

"All this protection for little old me? No wonder they say you flatter all the girls."

"All right, we're just about ready to go."

"Not yet, Cedric," interrupted Walker. "Her Highness isn't here yet."

A groan came over the unit. Hopping along the grass trying to get her left boot on, Cassandra raced into position.

"I am so sorry," Cassandra apologized to everyone. "I don't know how, but those trebuchets pounding on the wall had the same effect on me as the night sounds I play to help me sleep."

"Late to the conquest of her own city!" exclaimed Cecilia as she buried her forehead in her hands.

"You ready?" asked Cedric as he pulled Cassandra tightly in his arms.

"No, but I don't think that really is important anymore," Cassandra responded.

"Suit up!"

The chosen warriors closed their helmets and drew their weapons. The snap of the trebuchet was heard once more distracting everyone. A sphere smashed the final partition of the wall. A huge gap opened and Cedric raised his hand.

"Once more into the breach!" cried Cedric.

The army followed the lead of their commander as they marched forward towards the hole in the wall. Upon entering the city, the army was overcome with grief to see what Verian had become. The once beautiful canals were horribly polluted, the buildings were crumbling to the ground, and debris was everywhere. On one of the larger main strips, Marie was waiting for them at the head of the army that had joined her in the courtyard. Cedric raised his arm causing his army to stop. Cassandra walked to the front but stared in disbelief at her sister.

"Marie? No…this can't be…"

"Greetings, dear sister, I guess it's time that I properly welcomed you home."

"There's not enough of them to hurt you anymore! Come quickly! We can protect you!"

"Why would I leave them?"

"Are you possessed or something? They've been using and abusing you these past five revolutions!"

"Used, dear sister. I'm not the one marching on my homeland to fulfill the insane rantings of a religious fanatic. If anything, you need to join me and pay the proper homage to the true Queen of Central Acadia."

"Yes, my dear Cassandra, the rightful heir now sits on the throne of Central Acadia," added Luminas. "You will end your illegal rebellion against the crown and ask your followers to swear the proper fealty."

"I will not until you and your followers answer for your crimes, Maximilian Luminas," proclaimed Cassandra.

"Sister, I do not want to fight you, but if your army does not lay down their weapons immediately I will be forced to attack."

"Attack me? Marie, they murdered our father! Can you not see…unless…oh God, no!" Cassandra saw the haziness in her sister's eyes and the darkness corrupting her soul. "Please tell me you didn't read that book!" cried Cassandra.

"Yes, Cassandra!" exalted Marie. "The *Libro Mortuorum* should have never been denied to me. I have been granted great powers."

"Are you in league with Abaddon?"

"Lord Abaddon has performed many great services for me. He helped me to realize that I was not a weak Princess anymore. I had powers within me, powers stronger than you could ever imagine. A proper Queen, powerful and deadly, has the power to rebuild what the war criminal Cedric Rhone destroyed."

"I don't want to fight you, Marie, but I cannot in good conscience end my rebellion against you. Someone with those powers cannot sit on a noble throne. I'm so sorry."

"I knew it. I knew you were only interested in claiming the power for yourself. You always wanted it! You left me to die, Cassandra!"

"I'm sorry, Marie, I shouldn't have left you behind! I don't care if I was under the influence of Abaddon or not! I beg you to cast away that book and come back to us! Please, we can end this madness together."

"It had to come to this anyway. There could only be one ruler of Central Acadia. In the end, Father probably would have chosen you and there would have been a war. As the challenger, you have presented your army first. Now allow me to present mine."

Marie held her staff up and began to let out an eerie purple glow. The fears of the Alliance senior officers were about to be confirmed.

"It is my time!" exclaimed Marie. "I summon from the depths of Tartarus all of the Forces of Hell! Bring forth to me the army of Fell Spirits that we may destroy the invaders of my beloved homeland."

Skeletal and decayed flesh pulled itself from the grounds and canals. Emitting blood-curdling screams, skeletons and wraiths formed ranks in front of Marie.

"What is that magic?" asked Huskal.

"The darkest form of all magic, the ability to bring forth the tormented of hell itself," answered Francis. "Central Acadia is littered with tormented souls whose vengeance and anger has manifested itself in the creatures you see before you."

"My Army of the Damned has risen to defend my crown," pronounced Marie. "Now all I need is for someone to lead them. Come forward, my beloved Commander, and led my army to victory."

Julius stepped forward armed in his Dark Paladin gear. He had his new sword drawn and his spiked shield ready for battle.

"Cagius, is this another abomination?" wondered Constantine. "It looks so much like your brother, but…"

"Dad, you don't think she raised him as well…?" pondered Cagius in response.

"No, it's a trick," Martha informed them. "You said the soldiers in the other army looked like Julius, but there were differences. The first time you clone someone, a perfect clone can be created. Virgus theorized this and I guess he actually did it."

"It makes sense. How else could they have programmed that tactical data into the army, if they didn't have someone to lead them?"

Seeing horrors brought to light was difficult for even the bravest of the Alliance warriors to accept. Abaddon and Virgus watched from the back of the command with smiles on their faces.

"They're beginning to crack. Cedric, you know there's only one way out of this…surrender her to me," murmured Abaddon. "You have one last chance."

Lifting Ragnarok to his eyes, his army witnessed Cedric muttering a prayer under his lips. Bellowing out a loud cry, he charged for the undead legions.

"FOR GOD, ALLIANCE, AND QUEEN CASSANDRA!"

"The Hero rises once more. Let that be your undoing," said Abaddon as the smile swept away from his face.

Wilhelm and Francis screamed and immediately took off after them. Cecilia was not to be outdone and she went next into the fray. The action had the effect Cedric had intended. By not allowing his army to think about what was going on, it was easier for them to enter the fray. Echoing his sentiments and cry, the warriors were on the undead creatures before they could react. The Titan prince led by cutting the head off of the first skeleton he could find. His friends and comrades followed suit. Sliding down the ruins of a bridge, Cassandra put her staff in the air.

"Let's shed some light on this situation," said the Queen, chanting.

Bursting with a solar flare, the staff repealed the unnatural darkness covering the city. Knowing something was wrong, the Acadian Wizards fought back against the spell.

"Celius, stop her!" ordered Marie.

"Impossible!" exclaimed Celius as he joined his fellow Wizards.

Even with all of their combined powers, the Guild was no match for Cassandra. Everything Cerwin had predicted was coming true. The raven-haired Queen truly had the magical ability to shatter the false wizards. Encouraged by Nadia, Cassandra screamed out a loud cry.

"We can't stop her!" determined Celius.

Maximilian watched as the sun started to break through.

"Marie, I can't stay here!" yelled Luminas. "I'll fall back to the palace with the Demonkin. Hold their forces at bay."

"Fine, you pathetic vampire," retorted Marie. "I guess we'll have to rely on my summoned army then. Take command, Julius, and destroy the Alliance!"

"With pleasure, your Highness!" said the clone as he drew his weapon.

As they watched the two armies split, Cedric enacted his plan. The Alliance pushed through the initial melee to seize the strategic bridge just in front of the Castle and Guild. Luminas and Kaladra raced for the safety of the Castle, while Celius and his wizards fortified themselves in safety of the Guild Tower. With the bridge taken, only twenty to thirty enemies could advance on the warriors at a time.

"WE CONTROL THE NORTH BRIDGE!" announced Cedric. "Colin, execute plan Rhone Delta Omega!"

"Cedric, no matter what comes…" stammered Colin, "we've got this!"

The two men gripped their fists together, before Colin lead his unit of the selected tribal warriors along with Josephine's escort of Martha. Turning to Argus next, Cedric nodded.

"Take your Kablisha Warriors, go with them and make sure the job gets done right."

"Won't you need me here?"

"We can handle the likes of this, get going!"

"Cedric, stay safe!" exclaimed Argus. "I mean it."

Argus went with Mesmara, Quinn, and the remainder of his forces, leaving the four countries of the original Alliance along with the Titan Vassals to hold the bridge. Julius stared at the chosen warriors taking defensive positions.

"Let's show them what we're made of," shouted the clone.

The echoing haunt of Julius' favorite cry hit a nerve with the remaining soldiers. It was only the sheer will and fortitude of their commander that kept them together. Not wanting him to be too exposed, Cecilia and Christian shoved Cedric to the middle of the pack. Though he tried to fight through to the front, Francis held him place. As the Titan prince stared down the incoming army, he issued final orders.

"We make our stand here at this bridge, in order to give our comrades the time they need to gain the advantage. This small area gives our skilled fighters the tactical advantage over their numbers. Malcolm and Rosa, you've got the archers, shower them with silver and fire arrows. Those in the melee, fifteen minutes on, tag out, fall back, and let your partners take over. Warriors of the Alliance, are you with me?"

"We are with you!" shouted everyone. "Hail Cedric Rhone!"

Malcolm and Rosa led their archers in a barrage. The fire arrows had a berserk effect on the undead. They mindlessly ran into their own troops igniting a greater conflagration on the bridge. Seeing the effectiveness, Nadia and Amuro hit one fire spell after another in tandem to keep the fell spirits off of their troops. As Cassandra moved to join them, Nadia held her up.

"Save your magic well, Cassandra," ordered Nadia. "You'll need it to confront your sister."

"How?" questioned the Queen.

"I think you know the spell. Prepare yourself and be ready."

Rushing to the back of the formation, Cassandra summoned the Book of Rune. Leafing through the text, she came to the desired spell. Closing her eyes, she meditated in preparation to cast it. Burning skeleton warriors and wraiths mindlessly wormed their way through the fire. The front lines of the Alliance army engaged them and the defining battle of the War of Two Queens began. Sabers and blades sharpened, the sword wielders separated the heads of their foes from their decrypted bodies. Titan knights led by Horace and Samuel simply smashed the bony skulls into pieces. Cecilia ordered the Valkyries to draw swords in their off-hand. The two-weapon combinations led to arcing attacks that drove the flanking enemies into the center. Waiting for them was the bulkhead strong force of Legionnaires led by Cagius, his father, Marcus Polonius and Joshua. Shields forward, they bashed into the skeletons allowing Elf battle mages the chance to use their fire spells.

In the chaotic retreat, Sharon found herself cut off against the rubble of a collapsed building with two Acadians serving as an escort. Seeing Cassandra in a vulnerable position behind the troop lines, she ordered her guard to capture her. As the halberdiers closed on the Queen's position, Civilia peeled off from her fighting position. Parrying the first halberd attack with her bow, the Titan Queen hit the soldier with a jumping sweep kick to his head. Stunned for the time being, she attacked the other guard slicing first at the hole in his armor behind his knee and finally loping his head off. Still trying to recover, the first guard found Civilia tossing him into one of the Verian canals. With his armor on, he simply sunk to the bottom and drowned. Suddenly alone, Sharon stared into the eyes of the Matriarch of Destruction. Though she had always been frightened of the power Civilia wielded, nothing could have prepared her for this moment.

"Well, look what we have here," taunted Civilia as she replaced her bow. "I didn't expect it would take five revolutions for you to pick my glove. You always wanted to put me in my place, Sharon. Well, now you've got the chance."

"I am a high born Elf!" exclaimed Sharon. "I'm about to show you that I am not without my own powers."

Sharon drew her blades and came at Civilia. The more experienced Titan Queen effortlessly parried the attacks of the false Queen of Central Acadia. Rearing back the Matriarch of Destruction struck Sharon's face so hard it drew blood down her right cheek. Horrified, the high Elf dropped back and felt the large abrasion adorning her formerly perfect cheek.

"My face! You bitch, you scarred my beautiful face."

"You are still quite beautiful, Sharon, certainly more beautiful than I could ever hope to be. Yet, your heart is black and twisted. I think it's fitting that I am the one that gets to pass judgment on you. After all, you killed the man I loved!"

"You don't understand! He treated me like garbage!"

"Because you intentionally hurt him by sleeping with anyone you could. Luminas just happened to be the most powerful rung on the ladder. I have my sources, and as far as I'm concerned, you murdered both Stephen and Penelope."

Realizing that she didn't stand a chance against the seasoned warrior Queen, Sharon fell to her knees.

"I beg you for your mercy."

Secretly, the twisted high elf put her hands behind her back and silently chanted for a ball of fire to materialize in her hands. The haughty Civilia put one hand on her left hip and laughed.

"Mercy? Did you show mercy to Penelope when you watched her get raped to death by Jonas? Did you show mercy to your own daughter when you intentionally handed her over to Abaddon? No, you are incapable of that emotion! How I would love to make a Jezebel like you suffer for what you've done, but I love Cassandra too much. Your death will be quick and painless."

"You should learn to be more careful around cornered creatures, Civilia! I'll send you to your God!"

The high Elf brought her hands forth and shouted, "Firestorm" to complete her chant. The wall hit Civilia head on and for a moment in the smoke and flame, the Titan Queen could not be accounted for. Laughing maniacally at her clever deception, Sharon pointed her finger at the fiery ruin.

"I've done it!" taunted Sharon. "I've incinerated the Matriarch of Destruction!"

As the smoke from the fire cleared, all Sharon could see was the glistening blue light of a magic shield protecting Civilia. Holding an amulet tied to her hip in her left hand, the Titan Queen offered a malicious smile.

"Did you honestly think I trusted you for a second? I wouldn't have earned the honor of the title Matriarch of Destruction if I fell for such cheap tricks."

"A firestorm should have burned you to cinder!"

"You may be a high born Elf, but your magic talents are lacking. You were no match for the natural powers of a Divikin. Especially when backed up by powerful magic defense tokens."

"You'll find I am not so easily humiliated."

Relying on her daggers once more, Sharon pressed the attack against a defensive Titan Queen. The high Elf was more agile and swifter than the stronger but slower Civilia. The two had enough skill to hold each other off for some time. Realizing she had to regain the upper hand, Civilia pressed her saber into Sharon's weapon. She added a second hand to the flat part of the saber to generate more power. At this range, the high Elf was no match for the veteran light armor knight. Fear appeared in Sharon's eyes as tears streamed down her face.

"It wasn't supposed to end like this!" cried Sharon. "How can it end for me here and now?"

"You could never defeat me, Sharon," taunted Civilia. "You failed as a Queen, and more importantly, as a mother! Those are my greatest strengths!"

Sharon jumped back one last time. She lost her balance when she tried to come forward at Civilia because of a loose stone. The Titan Queen slashed and in one clean stroke cut through the vanadium armor on the chest. The spiteful she-elf gasped as blood trickled out of her mouth and down the front of her body.

"Why?" begged Sharon, falling back against the stone wall.

Civilia showed no remorse. "Why what?" demanded Civilia. "I do not need to justify my actions after the crimes you committed."

"No... why didn't you marry Stephen... you loved him..."

"The first time, it was the choice of my father," explained the Titan Queen as she nodded her head. "I could not carry on the Rhone legacy and take the name of another family. I had a duty to my father and Stephen understood that. When he came back to me, I could no longer accept his love. I had two beautiful children by then. There would have been issues for the throne had I borne a child for Stephen. Thus I sacrificed my happiness and my love—something an ugly and selfish person like you could never understand."

Choking up the last of her blood, Sharon fell over dead. As Civilia moved to rejoin the battle, she could see the sympathy and tears in the eyes of Cassandra. In spite of the bitterness that poisoned that high Elf's soul, she was still Cassandra's mother. The true Acadian Queen was an orphan of war, and from that hour forward, the Matriarch of Destruction treated her as her own. Determined not to let the same fate befall her sister, Cassandra closed the Book of Rune and approached Walker. The Order of the Lion Commander was getting his last seconds of respite before tagging back in.

"Walker," ordered Cassandra. "I need a path cleared to reach my sister. Get me to the edge of the bridge; I'll do the rest with a levitation spell."

"Of course, your Highness."

Looking around, Walker found Valentine and Joshua ready to rejoin the fight. Nodding at the two, the Napolitan warriors eagerly volunteered for the duty. As the warriors moved to tag in, Walker and Joshua set their shields into a charging formation. Busting through the lines, two shield-bearing knights knocked fifteen skeletons and wraiths into the canals. Using the larger men as a boost, Valentine leapt into another group of soldiers. As others moved to cover his escape, Cassandra ran to the edge of the bridge. Casting a levitation spell, she floated on the air to the other side of the canal. Marie leapt onto the second story of a collapsed building, holding the high ground against her more powerful sister.

"You've never behaved like this before," pleaded Cassandra. "Marie, there's still time to end this madness."

"Stop trying to confuse me, Cassie. I know what I must do to preserve my country and this throne," retorted her sister. "Lord Julius and I are more than a match for you and your Knight!"

"Marie, you were there. You saw Julius die fighting Abaddon."

"Yes, but I've become stronger now, sister. My magic was powerful enough to restore his life and Abaddon paid his penance for his sins. The way I perceive it, this was your fault, anyway! Your cowardly fiancée wouldn't lift a finger to save you. Had he been there, Abaddon might have left you in endless sorrow instead of me!"

Black energy surrounded Marie. It didn't harm her physically but instead bore deep into her mind. As she watched the madness pervert her younger sister's soul further, Cassandra lowered her staff and shouted, "Dispel." Circle after circle washed over Marie's body, despite initial success, the overpowering voice and influence of Abaddon penetrated the impressionable younger sister's mind.

"You would listen to this deceiver, Marie?" whispered Abaddon. "She would do anything to claim what was rightfully yours! Do not give into her lies! You can only trust in me."

"Of course, Lord Abaddon," agreed Marie aloud.

Lifting her hate-filled eyes at her older sister, Marie stared at the teary Cassandra. "Even in death, my Julius would have never abandoned me!"

"Marie, I hid it from you for your own good and the good of our country. He never loved you. He loved my handmaiden Felicia. They conceived a son together long before you ever knew him."

"NO! I was his chosen wife! There was no other woman."

"By God, I tried to subtly dissuade you! Why would I lie to you about it now?"

"Look at how he defends me now. He's given up his country and his family to save me. I could think of no greater love!"

"Abaddon's poisoned your mind. Just look at what you've become!"

"Cassandra, I've had enough of you! You left me in Verian and never once thought to rescue me. I was the sacrifice so you could consolidate your power without challenge. I was missing, sister, and you didn't give a damn!"

"You'll never know how many nights I cried myself to sleep thinking of what abuse you were suffering. Marie, if there was anything I could have done, I promise you I would have saved you."

Raising her flail above her head, Marie leapt at her older sister. As she swung wildly, Cassandra used her superior agility to stay out of her way. Unwilling to attack, the raven-haired Queen was at a disadvantage. Finally walloped by her younger sister, Cassandra staggered back against the wall holding pieces of her broken vanadium chest armor. A sick smile crossed Marie's face.

"You won't even fight for Verian!" Marie berated her. "We'll settle this here and now! Let's see if you have what it takes to claim this throne, or if Father was right in his judgment."

"I'm holding back because I'm afraid I'll hurt you. However, if this is the only way to save your soul, I'll do it."

"Then we'll be even!"

Charging herself in white light, Marie chanted and pushed her staff forward. A white light went towards Cassandra, who twirled her staff and let loose a dark blast.

As the powers of holiness and darkness met in the middle, a massive explosion took place. Shielding their eyes from the explosive aftermath, Marie and Cassandra both smiled.

"We're evenly matched!" surmised Marie.

"Then whoever has the stronger will is going to win this fight."

"I assure you that will be me."

The younger sister went after the older aggressively with her mace and flail. Refusing to attack her sister physically, Cassandra stayed on the defensive. Yet, a soft chant emerged from the raven-haired maiden's lips as she built towards a stronger spell. On the bridge, Christian watched the enemy army using the dilapidated stones and buildings to cross the canals at a different point.

"Cedric, they've got us flanked on the left," reported Christian.

Dropping back further to a command position, Cedric watched carefully. He looked down at his pocket watch and nodded approvingly.

"We're going to be all right," Cedric reassured Christian.

"Cedric, we can't take them on from both sides! At least let me reposition our troops!"

"It's not necessary."

Just as the fell army screamed and prepared to charge, a huge hole in the ground opened up before them. Keiko popped out of the ground first with a smile beaming across her face. Unleashing her missile attack on the enemy first, it stunned the fell troops. Rumblings emerged from the hole and the thirteenth army finally arrived. Alia Drathan's spider-drawn chariot led the assault of Dark Elves riding giant spiders into battle.

"Dark Elves!" exclaimed Amuro. "How many battalions did Abaddon call in?"

Putting her sword in a defensive stance, the Elf marshal was shocked to see the spider cavalry charge the fell army instead of the Alliance defensive position.

"We fight for Prince Cedric Rhone!" announced Alia.

The eight-legged monsters overwhelmed the smaller skeleton and wraith warriors. Using the dilapidated terrain to their advantage, the spiders ran up crumbling buildings and rubble as Drow swordsmen sliced their heads off from above.

"I don't believe it," stated Amuro as she stared at Cedric. "What did you do?"

"I dispatched Keiko before the battle to negotiate with the Dark Elves about joining us in battle against Abaddon. After promising to answer my call when summoned, Alia Drathan needed little coaxing."

Seeing the new army approach, Julius pulled back his armies to devise a new strategy. Cassandra fired a blast at a building. The collapsed rubble divided her and her sister from the main battle for the time being. While the quick respite occupied the Alliance soldiers in Verian, Colin and the Tribal army had stormed Castle Acadia. Since all of their defenses had gone to the outer walls, Kaladra and the makeshift army of Demonkin and Acadians were all that stood in the way of absolute victory. The massive Nephilim stood at the end of the main hall with his army gathered behind him. Knowing there would be no mercy, they had sworn to fight to the death. The Ogle Tanka Un and his forces stared them down as they entered the main hall. The Chief of Chiefs stood next to her chosen consort.

"What is the word Ogle Tanka Un?" asked Hippolyte.

"Cedric has given us the honor of sacking this Castle," commanded Colin.

"Well, let's not let our generous Commander's present go to waste," said Minerva with a laugh.

"Tribe of the Wolf and our brave allies!" exclaimed Hippolyte as she raised her spear in the air. "Today we avenge Chieftain Aramas' death! Death to Maximillian Luminas! Death to the Rebels!"

Nodding to Colin, the Ogle Tanka Un's fur cape flapped through the slight breeze in the collapsed castle walls. Fearlessly leading the charge, Kaladra and his army met them head on. The first wave was intense as bodies flew from the collision of the two reckless armed forces. Colin and Kaladra went right for one another, each trying to use their strength to their advantage. Leaping into the fight, Hippolyte drove her spear into the throat of an Acadian knight as Stryker tore at a goblin behind her. Josephine used her whip to snag a Nephilim around his neck and slice his throat with the edge of it. Huskal hacked away with his sword while Minerva managed to run and shoot at the same time.

The scene at the Wizards' Tower was much different. The Kablisha militia led by Quinn rammed at the door of the tower while Mesmara cast fire and holy spells on the door. On the other side, the wizards worked desperately to keep the door sealed magically. Celius nervously paced around his throne, tapping his staff against the ground. Figuring Argus had loaded the Kablisha up with magic resistant charms, the Master Mage had no idea what his comrades would do when the doors came crashing down. Mesmara's voice echoed louder in the main halls as the first splinters in the ancient door formed. A last chant and yell of "holy beam!" from the Kablisha maiden opened a five-meter hole in the door. Crossbowmen rushed in and fired on the wizards sealing the door. Killed immediately or left on the floor to die slowly and painfully, wizards were abandoned by their own for the center spire. Five revolutions ago, Abaddon had first meet them there and here would come the culmination of all of Celius' plans. The Alliance with darkness had failed the wizards. In their desperate attempt to wrest power from King Stephen Acadia, they had destroyed their Guild forever. The approaching Kablisha army grew louder by the second.

"Master Celius, what are we going to do?" demanded a wizard nervously.

"The Ancients are at our doorstep, and no matter how many spells we place on the door they use their magic to break through!" exclaimed a second wizard.

Celius looked around at his frightened comrades. The sound of magic on the door outside the room and blood-curdling screams suggested the Kablisha were drawing near. Celius resigned himself to the fact that this was the end.

"Master, please!" exclaimed the second wizard. "I don't want to die here!"

"I will not forget your sacrifice," retorted Celius.

Celius held his staff up in the air. All of the wizards and witches in the room began to scream as he started to suck their magic from them.

"But Master… why…" stammered a powerless wizard.

"I need all of your magic so I can escape this death trap," demanded Celius. "Do not worry, my fellow comrades, for I shall continue the battle against these foes. Farewell!" The Master Wizard finished chanting a spell, cried some crocodile tears, and disappeared in a flash of light.

The first breaks of magic and sheer power against the door of the central spire arrived.

"What do we do now?" wondered a powerless wizard. "Celius has abandoned us and we're trapped in this room without the use of magic."

Mesmara shattered the door with her magic. Argus led Quinn and the others into the room with swords drawn. They stared down their pathetic foes.

"We die…" stated the wizards in resignation.

"No mercy!" ordered Argus. "Kill them to the last, and rid Central Acadia of their taint!"

For the sins they committed against Terminus Mundus, the slaughter was quick. The Kablisha warriors attacked any wizard or witch they could find and struck them down with swords. Some of the wizards decided to fight with their hands or staffs, but most accepted their fate and stood there like lambs at the slaughter. Deserted by their leader, many felt there was no need to fight anymore. When the massacre was over, Argus turned to his kin.

"We search these halls and destroy any weapon or chimera the Guild has left behind. Do not be afraid to use any purification spells when necessary!"

The Kablisha warriors nodded and went about their work.

"Cedric, please hold out just a little longer…we have to be sure!" begged Argus as he joined the others.

Inside the Castle Acadia, the original chaos caused by the initial charge had led to a series of brawls between the warriors. Fighting in every hall and room, it was not possible to bark out commands. Finishing off a Myotis tribe swordsman, Kaladra returned his attention to Colin. The Ogle Tanka Un had just managed to take down an ogre of his own. Finally given enough space, the hulking Nephilim retreated to the throne room. Lifting his sword to his eyes, he challenged Colin to single combat.

"Challenge accepted, but beware, for you draw your sword against death himself!" offered Colin as he entered the throne room.

"En garde!"

Kaladra charged and swung but Colin blocked the first attack. The Nephilim was stunned by the command and speed that a warrior of Colin's size had. He expected to use his giant's strength to overpower him, but the Ogle Tanka Un proved more than a match. A swing of Deathbringer and the Nephilim was on the defensive.

Contorting her body to avoid combat whenever possible, Martha delicately waded through the waves of attack. Josephine was true to her word and kept the doctor well protected. The Titan scientist was not without her own defenses as she used a dagger when the enemy got too close. Reaching the lower stairs at last, the Titan scientist gathered the Myotis whip mistress and her team.

"Josephine, get me down to the basement," ordered Martha.

"No problem, doc!" retorted the whip mistress.

Signaling to her whip battalion, the arcing strikes of their combined weapons opened a path for Martha and Josephine. They fled the chaos of battle for the lower levels as Hippolyte and Minerva fought in an empty room. The younger covered her older sister with her bow as the Wolf Tribe Chief examined their surroundings.

"I know this place," recollected Hippolyte. "Walker took us this way to meet Count Luminas the first time."

"So you think the vampire's hiding out in his old office?" questioned a smiling Minerva.

"I'd want to be on safe ground if I knew what was coming after me."

"So you want to take matters into our own hands?"

"Luminas gave the order to kill Grandpa, and we owe it to him to avenge his death."

"I'm with you, sis."

"Let's go!"

Thrusting her spear through an Acadian Knight, Hippolyte took to the opposite door. Minerva cleared the passage with bow drawn as the sisters raced down the hall and two sets of stairs. The empty and quiet hallways were a direct contrast to the chaos reigning above them. All they could make out were some rays of sunshine peeking out of Luminas' office. Running into the room, Minerva covered the corners as Hippolyte moved to the center of the room. Bathed in light, the Wolf Tribe Chief was not sorry to see the trophies of her people no longer present in the formerly pristine and ornate office.

"I don't like this," said Hippolyte cautiously.

"He can't be here if the shades aren't drawn," reasoned Minerva. "He'd fry like firewood!"

"Well, it was a good idea. He must have retreated deep into the basement or dungeons."

An otherworldly force suddenly slammed the door shut. As Minerva pointed her bow around the room, Hippolyte turned to cover the door, but no one was there.

"Now what?" wondered Minerva out loud.

Automatically, the shades rolled down on both windows. Cloaked in darkness, the sisters went back-to-back as some candles at the north end of the room mysteriously went ablaze. Maximilian's voice echoed through the whole room.

"You girls should have known better... never cross a vampire!" proclaimed Luminas.

"He could be anywhere," warned Hippolyte.

"We've still got numbers on him," Minerva said encouragingly.

Hearing the chant of flame, the girls spotted the bat-winged sword of Luminas. As it burst into flames, Luminas made himself visible.

"Did you think that Cedric Rhone was the only sword master in the Western Plains?" boasted Luminas. "I can hold light and darkness in my heart as well."

"There's no light left in you, Maximilian Luminas!" shouted Hippolyte angrily.

The vampire swung and sent out a track of fire at the two girls. Hippolyte and Minerva rolled out of the way. As she got out her roll, the younger archer fired an arrow. Luminas deflected it with his sword, but felt a burning on his fist.

"A silver weapon. You children have learned much in five short revolutions. However, for two hundred revolutions I have served as advisor to the Kings of Central Acadia and honed my skills accordingly. I was tired of serving an inferior race, the time of the Nephilim had come."

"You're no Nephilim," retorted Minerva. "Wilhelm said you're nothing more than a Demonkin."

"I've been promised much, child. Imagine what Cedric was promised for delivering Cassandra to Abaddon."

"As if," countered Hippolyte. "You killed our grandfather!"

"Such are the costs of war!"

"Why him?"

"Who else was there? Renard? Posha? No, I needed hostages and I knew that Aramas would do anything to keep his precious granddaughters safe during the negotiations. So I suggested that he send them here where they would be perfectly safe. After those two rich boys appeared to be killed by your tribe, I was going to have my pretty little hostages executed in a beautiful ceremony. It would have enflamed your armies to march against Central Acadia and the

Alliance would have had no choice but to answer. Abaddon would have had everything he wanted and I would have claimed power. But that Titan Bastard was one step ahead of me and ruined my coup."

"Then Cecilia was right... it was you all along..." stammered Hippolyte.

"No other would have had the competence to create such a brilliant scheme. Actually, I should thank you girls for granting me a rare opportunity."

Maximillian stared hungrily at the two girls and licked his lips. They noticed his eyes becoming bloodshot and that some of his body began to contort into a wolf shape.

"I may not be known to drink human blood. I have long satisfied my hunger on the blood of swine and bovine, but that was simply out of appearance and necessity. For me, human blood is a delicacy that should be savored like the Acadians savor their wine. Once in a while, I would feast on a young girl, never taking too much, I never wanted any competition for food and disposing of a body is a hassle."

"I'm nobody's dinner!" challenged Hippolyte as she gritted her teeth.

"I've got your scent now," proclaimed Maximilian as his face twisted in ecstasy. "Virgin blood is the most wonderful feast of all. Sharon used to let me feed on her, but it never tastes the same once a maiden has been spoiled."

"I'm tired of the monologue," quipped Minerva.

She fired another arrow, but Luminas caught it. Shooting bats from his cloak distracted the archer, as Hippolyte went forward with her spear. The vampire deflected each of her thrusts, as Minerva tried to fire through the bat cloud. Even when she got a shot off, the cape of the Count formed a metal shield to block her arrows.

"Damn!" cursed Minerva. "They're not getting through."

Luminas laughed as he knocked away each of Hippolyte's thrusts.

"Maybe if you were faster you might be able to strike me," taunted Luminas.

"I'm trying to kill you!" exclaimed Hippolyte.

"Eye for an eye! Tribal law! Aramas must be proud as he watches the final tracks of his lineage avenge his death!"

"It's more than simple revenge!"

"I respected your grandfather because what he wanted was peace, yet you chose the path that will result in one meaninglessly battle after another."

"We're fighting for life, not death!"

"That's rich! What life do you speak of? That two-bit assassin the Titans try to pass off as a noble? Haven't you given any thought as to what is going to happen after this? You know Cedric is going to seize all the power for himself."

"Shut up! The Prince of Titanus is a good man."

"The Prince of Titanus is a psycho! Do you know what the Divikin believe him to be? They think he is the incarnation of some holy warrior, and the worst is that he believes it! They will erect him as a god-emperor of Terminus Mundus. Those who do not worship and obey his commands will be struck down! He will break your wills and your way of life. Everything Aramas wanted will be ground into dust."

"DECEIVER!"

"Are you trying to convince yourself? You knew you couldn't trust me the second you saw my eyes in this room. Yet, the Prime Eagle charms you as he waits for just the right moment to dig his talons into you back!"

"Says you, who would have had me executed!" challenged Hippolyte behind her laughs. "I have no reason to trust you."

"Cedric still speaks of the Tribes bending the knee, doesn't he? Do you think he'll allow any individual nation to survive? The Titan Prince will bring every province in the west into his new Empire. No nation or tribe will be immune and all will serve his will. That is the reason I rebelled against the King, because I saw the events that are coming. Cassandra means nothing to you. Join with me, we'll give Abaddon his prize and together we'll maintain the status quo. Independence for both the tribes and Central Acadia! We can destroy Cedric Rhone together."

"Cedric Rhone is the blood brother of the Wolf Tribe and we honor our brethren. In the short time I've been on Terminus Mundus, he's done more for me than any other member of the Alliance."

"So be it! If you will not listen to reason, I shall not allow you to function of your own will."

Upstairs, Colin and Kaladra fought their duel. Stunned by the speed, power, and weapon handling of the Ogle Tanka Un, the Nephilim Commander used every ounce of his brute force to gain an advantage. Baiting his foe, the Lunar Falcon darted around the giant slicing at both of his thighs. His foe fell to his knees, unable to stand. Despite all of the giant's efforts to hit him, the assassin stayed just out of his reach. Exhausted, the Nephilim finally accepted his fate. Spinning one-eighty Colin unleashed such a blow that the head of Kaladra was lopped clear off. The last of the Nephilim that haunted Terminus Mundus had finally met his fate. The appearance of Abaddon was supposed to usher in a new golden age for the ancient conquerors, yet it had led to their absolute destruction. Returning to the main hall, the tribes had finally won the battle of the Castle. The last Acadian soldiers had yielded while the Demonkin were either dead or in retreat. Quickly scanning the room, the Ogle Tanka Un noticed that the girls were missing.

"Where's Hippolyte and Minerva?" demanded Colin.

"We were separated in the chaos," reported Huskal. "We'll begin the search immediately."

"Hippolyte! What are you up to?"

In Maximilian's chamber, the vampire performed a back flip to retreat from Hippolyte's spear. Pupils glowing red, the girls felt a fog overtaking them. They lowered their weapons and swayed back and forth.

"Haven't you heard of the ancient tribal magic, young ladies? I possess the discipline of domination and can assert temporary control over an individual's mind. I've heard that Cedric knows a spell that could permanently break your will, but I've never seen him try to use it. What a foolish waste of his powers."

Strutting to Hippolyte, the vampire focused all of his attention on her. The Wolf Tribe Chief was held enthralled by his power.

"Especially when it can turn an enemy into an ally," boasted Luminas.

Brushing her brown hair away from her neck, Hippolyte watched helplessly as Luminas bore his fangs. Sinking his teeth in her neck, the vampire was overwhelmed with the taste and pleasure of human blood. However, this caused him to lose control over Minerva. The sight of her sister in the clutches of the Count was too much. Minerva drew a silver arrow and stuck it into Luminas' throat. Writhing in pain from the assault, Maximilian covered his bleeding throat and dropped back. As the archer readied a second shot, Hippolyte mindlessly walked into the way.

"Get out of the way, sister."

Terror filled Minerva's eyes and heart when she noticed her sister had the same red eyes as Luminas, and an evil smile crossed her face.

"Well, little sister, that is going to be a problem," blurted out Luminas. "You see, Hippolyte is now my thrall and she's going to do whatever I command of her. But first I'm going to need you to come to me."

Minerva felt her mind being overridden by Luminas' control again. She had one last bit of control of her right hand to expose a crucifix from under her cloak. Shielding his eyes, Luminas lost control of his spell.

"That's impossible...a mere relic is not enough to counter my power..." gargled Luminas through the blood.

"No, but when combined with faith it's a powerful weapon against your kind. I've seen so much in the past five revolutions that I can't explain…so I believe in what the Titans and others are fighting for."

"Well, I may not be able to control you but I still have your sister. Hippolyte!"

"Yes, Master Luminas," answered Hippolyte meekly.

"Subdue your sister, but don't kill her! I need her blood to heal this wound!"

"Yes, Master!"

Hippolyte reached down and picked up her spear. Minerva gasped, terrified.

"Sis, I know you're under his control, but you've got to fight him. Just long enough for me to take him down."

Hippolyte came at her spear first. Minerva leapt back on her tiptoes in order to avoid the coming attacks. She intermittently tried to get a shot off at Luminas but he continued to deflect it with his cape. The archer maintained her composure despite her sister's wild assaults.

I can't hit him, thought Minerva to herself. *Sis is never this wild or slow… she's his marionette! Maybe…*

Taking advantage of her sister's awkward attacks, Minerva jumped on a table. The archer begged her sister's forgiveness as she kicked her in the face. Throwing her fur cape on Hippolyte, the spear fighter tried to claw it off. Licking her lips, Minerva struck a match on her thigh and lit up one of her arrows. Raising his sword to his eyes, Luminas defended himself.

"A fire arrow, this should be interesting…" choked out Luminas.

Minerva had her bow set on Luminas but at the last second, she titled her bow up and fired. Maximilian laughed at her incompetence, but the archer simply stood there triumphantly.

"That wasn't even close, Minerva! I must have had you under my control after all."

"I wasn't aiming for you!" taunted Minerva.

"What?"

Luminas looked up and saw the shade covering the window engulfed in flames. Sunlight burst into the room and Luminas found his skin roasting. Crying out in searing pain, the vampire ran to the dark corner of the room. With the advantage, Minerva lit a second arrow and burned the other shade. With nowhere left to hide, Maximilian crawled into the last area not shining with light.

"YOU BITCH!" cried Luminas as he huddled into a ball.

Minerva reached into her quiver and took out an arrow.

"Your tribal stone heads can't pierce my skin," taunted Luminas.

"No, but silver arrows will!" countered Minerva.

Throwing his cape over his body, the vampire protected himself as Minerva reached deep inside of her to awaken the power of her new bow. The silver arrow burned through the cape shield and found Luminas' heart. Paralyzed by the arrow, the Count lost his hold over Hippolyte. The wolf chief finally tossed away Minerva's cape and was relieved to have her free will restored. Not wasting any time, she took Gungir and drove it into Maximilian's viscera.

"For my grandfather!" yelled Hippolyte.

"Nice try, but there's not enough silver in that weapon to kill a vampire!" taunted Luminas. "Your sister's arrow may have me paralyzed for now, but I will escape."

"Who said that was my main attack?" offered a smiling Hippolyte. "I just wanted to pin you into the wall so you couldn't get away."

Hippolyte pulled out a dagger in the shape of a cross from the back of her belt.

"My fiancée gave this to me to protect myself against the undead. It's a pure silver dagger blessed by Bishop Arthur Langley of Titanus himself."

Luminas looked on in fear. Paralyzed and pinned, he accepted his fate.

"You must understand that your grandfather…it had to be him…I would have never killed him but for that reason."

"Nice try, Count Luminas, but I am so going to enjoy this."

"I'll die knowing… Cedric will fall to Abaddon…all of you will join me in hell," stammered Luminas.

Driving the blessed dagger into Luminas' throat, Hippolyte screamed and cut until the vampire's head was completely severed from his body. Every last moment of the silver digging into his flesh was agony for the traitorous vampire. The wolf tribe chief grabbed the head and tossed it into the purifying fires of Primus' rays. The sisters retrieved their weapons from the headless body and then dragged it into the light. The ashes of Maximilian Luminas dispersed throughout the room. Crying, the long journey of the Wolf Tribe sisters was finally over and the long-awaited embraced they shared was in memory of their beloved grandfather.

"Great shot, Minerva!" said a grateful Hippolyte.

"I thought I was going to lose you," said Minerva through her sniffles. "I don't think I can go back, Hippolyte. The Wolf Tribe is going to be yours, and it's better that way."

"I understand, Minerva. One thing I learned over these revolutions is that we have to be true to our destinies, but this was one thing that had to be done together. Grandfather, this was for you!"

"He would have wanted us to do this together. He's got to be so proud."

Colin kicked down the door to the room with Huskal and other tribal soldiers in tow. A sense of relief overtook him as he spotted Luminas' empty armor and weapon in a pile of ashes.

"I guess I had no reason to be worried…though when you're the Chief of the Tribe Hippolyte, you shouldn't wander off in the middle of a battle," scolded Colin. "It's damaging for morale."

"I figured taking out the head would make destroying the body easier," retorted Hippolyte.

"Then I guess we were both thinking the same thing," Colin agreed with her.

Hippolyte noticed Nephilim blood on Colin's sword. "Kaladra?"

"He did not survive his dance with death."

"Good!"

"We're securing the Castle as we speak and taking account of the final prisoners," reported Colin. "We're waiting for final confirmation from Martha and Josephine before we can rejoin Cedric in Verian."

"Then let's finish the job," announced Hippolyte.

In the basement below, Martha held a small computer against the wall. A single metal door caught her eyes and quietly the doctor approached it. Examining the readings she anticipated, she nodded her head.

"Josephine, cover the door," ordered Martha. "I'll call you in when I need you."

"I'm not sure that's good idea, Doctor," countered Josephine. "Commander Rhone gave me very specific orders."

"Well, I won't tell you that he'd want me to do this because he certainly wouldn't. But Josephine, this is the man who raised me and I know what horrors he's capable of. I've got to make sure first."

Reluctantly, Josephine allowed Martha to enter the lab alone. Closing the door behind the doctor, the unit covered the room. As the Titan scientist entered, the blue cloning vats were the first thing to catch her attention. Staring in horror, tears formed in her eyes.

"A beautiful site, isn't it, Martha?" lectured Virgus. "I see it brings tears to your eyes."

Martha looked up at one of the catwalks and saw Virgus.

"How could you?" challenged Martha. "This is against everything you taught me! What about ethics?"

"Ethics? Was it ethical to inject nanite machines into the broken body of a baby girl left in the Titan highlands to die? Everything you are, everything you have achieved, was because I experimented on you."

"I was hardly in a position to give consent, Doctor."

"No, you weren't. Yet, in the orphanage and then the Academy you did everything to cultivate the tremendous gift I gave you. Ceaselessly, breaking every glass ceiling erected above you. Face it, Martha, I was closest thing you had to a father, and I couldn't have been more proud."

"For that I could forgive you, but why did you butcher those people in Titan Academy?"

"Now you have a self-professed love for the poor and vagrants. I was tired, Martha. I was an old man who should have been killed in a laboratory fire. Look what you had to do to me just so I would survive. I couldn't start from scratch again. I couldn't wait for revolutions on end. As a scientist you must appreciate that…"

"Never with human beings!"

"Really? And how is this different than that little service you performed for Queen Civilia?"

"I paid for my sins before God in the form of excommunication. Yet you abandoned it all for the sake of darkness."

"There is nothing left here for you, Martha. I have already taken all of the necessary data. You'll find the computer banks stripped and loaded with viruses. I remained because I knew you'd come here. You were my finest student and I loved you. You shared the same passion for knowledge and the desire to push the envelope beyond simple theories. I should have known that one I was so fond of would betray me."

"I won't pretend that I don't appreciate the superhuman intelligence and eternal beauty as a result of the nanites. You were more than that to me. The stipends you secured for me in the orphanage, the exemption to enter the Academy, and the promotion to personal assistant. It brought me no joy to stand before the board as your accuser." Martha fell to her knees and cried. "I could never allow something like this perversion... chimera after chimera... this isn't science anymore... its madness."

"It pains me to see how closed-minded you've become. You should have never gone into politics, Martha, it has ruined you." Virgus closed his eyes and smiled. "Our time has come to an end, and I fear that I must depart. Perhaps you would like to take a look at that last blinking computer on the right side. Then you will finally realize how hopeless this crusade is against the might and malice of Abaddon. Farewell, Martha, perhaps we will have the chance to have one of our long conversations by the fire once more."

Virgus disappeared into a tube that was waiting for him behind the catwalk. The tube became a high-speed elevator that whisked him to the ground level and safely away from Heinrich. Curiosity getting the better of her, Martha ran to the computer. Typing at a rapid pace, she brought up all of Virgus' recent experiments and theories. Her eyes widened as she examined what was on the screen and unleashed a blood-curdling scream. Busting the door down, Josephine and her brigade arrived.

"Doctor Heinrich, are you all right?" called out Josephine.

Still shaking, Martha set a single charge where the computer was. Josephine put her hand to her shoulder, but there was no acknowledgment.

"Doctor? What's happening? What are you doing?"

"I just can't bring myself to trust my old Professor. This will destroy everything in this room. You've got to get me to Cedric quickly, a surprise is coming neither of us anticipated."

"What do you mean by 'surprise'?"

"I mean the end of this battle—possibly everything if we don't reach him quickly."

Sprinting out of the room, the device Martha placed on the wall fired off a shockwave. All of the computers in the room short-circuited and caused a fire. The cloning vats began to boil over and spilled out on the floor. The conflagration spread through the whole basement and Castle Acadia went up in flames.

Grand Library of Edenia, Palacio Magnifico

Actually, I'm quite good at puzzles...

Prince Thomas to Queen Cassandra

Patience lost after three rotations of searching, Garrett paced back and forth in the lower levels of the library. Having lost his patience a rotation ago, Thomas hung off the edge of his chair. Nervously, Sophia watched the young boy and prayed he didn't fall and hurt himself.

"Blessed with the visions of a thousand prophecies, and I can't see my way through this damned riddle!" cursed Garrett.

"A riddle?" questioned Thomas.

"What kind of sick joke did the Divikin and Elves come up with? It's like they intentionally came up with four stories just to drive me crazy centuries later."

"I have a feeling they weren't that vindictive."

"I know, young Master Thomas, but the time has come to start thinking outside the box."

The young Titan prince took the four prophecies out on the table again.

"I think we determined they're not in succession of one another," reasoned Garrett.

Thomas played around with the pieces and placed them in a different order. Moving them from one spot to the next finally gave him something to do.

"Maybe it's a puzzle…"

"A puzzle?"

"Yeah…Margrave Dennis has them all over his study in Deniva. He taught me a great trick to determine where the pieces go. First, I aim for the corner pieces and try to build a border. It gets easier from that point."

Listening to the sound of Thomas playing with the copies of the prophecy gave Garrett an idea. "I am a fool!" Garrett berated himself.

"I don't follow," said Thomas.

"Maybe they aren't exactly a puzzle, Thomas, but they certainly aren't linear. The prophecies are meant to be read as one, but like the scriptures written from different perspectives—they overlap, my young friend."

"So there isn't a particular order that the events are supposed to occur," reasoned Sophia.

"Yes, rather the Lord revealed different parts of the prophecy to the descendants of the Sentinels and his Chosen people so all races of goodwill would stand together at the time Lucifer's agents entered this world. It's impossible to predict which recorder was more correct than another, because they all saw the same vision. The *Permaneo Eques Ordinares* is the embodiment of faith and the *Bis Reginum* is the embodiment of hope. Titanus and the Elves had opposite prophecies revealed to them."

"Okay," deduced Thomas. "So we got faith and hope, what comes next?"

"The *Denique Refero* is discovered, and the only question is by whom. If we've got faith and hope it has to be the embodiment of charity, the union of people of goodwill coming to a single goal."

"If we figure out who determines this final answer, then the Knight of God will appear."

"Camael may come to save us yet. We must hurry, Thomas, and send word to our allies!"

The three gathered the papers and books on the table and desk with a newfound sense of hope.

"Don't forget the plant!" Garrett scolded Thomas.

"You and the plant!" As he grabbed the plant, the young Titan prince noticed the buds opening. "Hey, Garrett, this thing looks like it's about to bloom."

"Get the radio down here immediately," Garrett ordered. "Thomas, Sophia, stay where you are!"

The two operatives made for the platform to retrieve the equipment. Thomas and Sophia stared intently at the plant.

"Thomas, the second the plant opens, I need to know the color."

CITY OF VERIAN

Locusts came out of the smoke onto the land and they were given the same power as scorpions of the Earth. During that time people will seek death but will not find it and they will long to die but death will escape them. The appearance of the locusts was like that of horses ready for battle. On their heads they wore what looked like crowns of gold; their faces like human faces and they had hair like women's hair. Their teeth were like lion's teeth and they had chests like iron breastplates. The sound of their wings was like the sound of many horse-drawn chariots racing into battle. They had tails like scorpions with stingers.

The Scriptures of the Christ, the Gloria 9:1-12

As the sun reached the noon point of the sky, Cedric continued to lead his forces against the legions of undead. Disappointed repeatedly that they were unable to gain the Alliance positions, the clone of Julius ordered his troops back once more. Alia and her spider cavalry prevented any from flanking the positions. With no hope of commanding his army to victory, the doppelganger left his skeletons and wraiths to die.

"Wilhelm, any sign of Abaddon?" asked Cedric.

"His presence is everywhere, Cedric," reported Wilhelm. "I cannot nail him down nor tell when he will choose to appear."

"Something's wrong, we've been beating them back for hours," added Cecilia. "Colin and Argus have both reported their successes. This should be over!"

"Cedric, my spotters have Marie on the retreat to the main gate area," Christian inserted himself into the report. "Cassandra's intent on chasing her down."

Shouts and screams from the rear distracted the warriors as Josephine hurried Martha through the crowd. One look at the scientist's face was all the Titan Prince needed. Doctor Heinrich grabbed Cedric by his arms and took two deep breaths.

"Your Excellency," started Martha. "Marie's death is the key to Abaddon's resurrection. Virgus has figured out a way to use her blood to regenerate his body. They've theorized it will be enough to push Cassandra over the edge and revert her into her succubus form."

"If Cassandra chased her sister down to the front gate, you can bet that's where Abaddon is going to appear," surmised Cedric. "All divisions, all commanders, we're charging. We've got to see to the safety of both women."

The commanders of the individual fighting units passed the word to their troops. Cedric took the front with Ragnarok high in the air. Inspiring his warriors into battle, they followed him over the bridge. Alia and her spider cavalry led the way, trampling the first rows of troops, before the eight-legged monsters retreated to the safety of the crumbling buildings. Spears, swords, and maces glistening in the sun made contact with the bleached and crumbling bones of the undead army. Weakened by her own duel, the false queen's quickly depleting magic well no longer allowed her to summon more reinforcements. As the coalition pushed forward, Marie turned to attack her sister at the barred main gate of the city. Cassandra continued to avoid all of Marie's wild and angry swings.

"It wasn't supposed to happen like this!" exclaimed Marie. "My magic is superior. How can I possess the power to raise the dead and not be able to defeat you?"

Cassandra finally retaliated against Marie with her rod. The two sisters pressed their staffs into one another seeking firmer ground.

"The creature before you, Marie, is a perversion of science, not Julius!" argued Cassandra. "Abaddon has been using you, and this fake Julius is just another level of his control!"

"Control? I command Abaddon...he gives me whatever I want..."

"At what price, Marie?"

"He gave me the world I always wanted, Cassandra. I had my crown, I had my lover, and I didn't have to worry about you!"

Feeling horrified by her sister's statement, the true Queen would not let it pass. "What does that mean?" demanded Cassandra.

"I couldn't stand always being compared to you. You had everything, Cassandra! Everyone loved you so much and complimented you on being so smart and beautiful. The only thing I could count on was that the crown would pass to me."

"Trust me, Marie, I didn't have everything."

"Did you ever see how our father looked at the two of us? You were always his favorite. I sought his attention time and time again, yet he never dared to educate and discuss the things with me that he did with you. I was relegated to second status even though I was the true Acadian and you were a mere half-breed. He looked at me like a child... like a doll. I hated it! And because of that I hated you!"

Cassandra closed her eyes and cried. When she opened her red eyes, the older sister pitied the younger. "You always seemed so happy and you always made me feel better when I was hurt. I remember when they told me you were born; I made a list in my diary of all the wonderful things I was going to do for my younger sister. Why didn't you tell me you harbored these feelings? I would have helped you...I never wanted to hurt you, Marie!"

"SHUT UP! I'm tired of your excuses, Cassandra! You seem to have no shortage of them."

"Sister, please, there is no need to continue this. Join with us against Abaddon! Cedric has the power to purge the darkness consuming you!"

As Marie shook her head, the dark aura surrounding her body grew wider. Feeling the negative powers affecting her, Cassandra jumped back and threw the flail away. The older sister took a few breaths to restore herself as a determined look crossed the pretender Queen.

"No, I will not kneel to you," asserted Marie. "Not after our father promised the throne to me."

Marie created a ball of dark energy in her hand. She chanted, "curse," and threw it at Cassandra. The true Queen's eyes opened when she recognized it was the same magic Abaddon used on her five revolutions ago. Twirling her staff and slamming it into the ground, a magic shield formed around her body. Barely raised in time, the initial curse wormed its way through Cassandra's powers. The true Queen could feel the corruption of Abaddon's influence and power coursing in her veins.

"Whether by your own will or mine, you will join me, sister," taunted Marie.

Resisting the power with all of her might, Cassandra threw her staff forward and dispelled Marie's curse with an echoing shout.

"How could you stop my trump card like this!" demanded an astonished Marie.

"You may be a conjurer of basic spells and summons," explained a determined Cassandra. "But I am warning you that you are about to match magic against a Rune Mistress. You are not capable of understanding what spells I can use against you! Surrender now and return to the light, or else I will unleash the full force of my magic against you and end this."

"Just keep talking yourself up, Cassandra, it doesn't matter to me," laughed Marie. "I can conjure an infinite number of minions. I summon the forces of darkness! DEMONS, COME FORTH!"

Raising her bone staff into the air before crashing it against the stone pavement, the younger sister called two demons from the void to aid her.

"Now, my pretties, destroy my dear sister."

Despite watching two demons flying towards her, Cassandra never batted an eye. Evoking her ice assault, the two creatures froze in place just moments before striking the raven-haired Queen with their talons. Two swift strikes from her staff and all that remained of her foes were shards of melting ice.

"Marie, I will no longer allow your powers to harm my people nor will I let the corruption of that book control you! I am the Queen of Central Acadia and I will restore the throne to its glory."

Radiating with flashes of red, blue, yellow, and green light, Cassandra levitated a meter off the ground. Her hair and cloak blew in a new wind swirling around her.

"More tricks!" responded Marie.

"Do not assume that I am a mere magician of simple tricks, Marie!"

The Staff of Rune floated in front of Cassandra with the orb on the rod level with her heart. Desperate to head off this new assault, the blonde-haired pretender fired every piece of dark and light magic in her repertoire. However, nothing penetrated the shield.

"Marie, you will no longer be able to use your magic to harm others! I evoke the true power of the four elements; lend me your might and strength!"

Four balls containing the powers of the four elements surrounded Cassandra's body with fire and water above her shoulders and wind and earth at her legs. The fire went into her staff first and turned it red. Water came next turning it blue, then wind which turned it green. Earth came last turning it yellow briefly. The combined elements shined a white light causing Marie to shield her eyes. Shouting the last words in the ancient Elvish, the blast left Cassandra's staff. The bone staff of the younger sister was completely consumed in the power. The necromancer held onto the weapon as long as she could, but the burning sensation in her hands finally caused her to drop it. Exploding, the raised army engaged with the Final Alliance fell listlessly to the ground. Without a power source to maintain their presence on Terminus Mundus, the Battle for Verian and the War of the Two Queens had seemingly come to an end. As her army faded into the dust, the blonde-haired pretender desperately read from the *Libro Mortuorum* in an attempt to bring them back. When the raven-haired sister landed, she snatched the foul tome away from her.

"Marie..." cried Cassandra as she held out her hand to her sister. "Marie, I'm sorry. I didn't want to do that but I had no choice. The war is over, your army is wasted away...your powers are broken forever."

"Luminas promised... my armies..." shouted a heartbroken Marie.

"It doesn't matter anymore. Nothing matters except the fact we're still sisters!"

Cedric and his army approached the tender scene as Marie's aura faded away. Her eyes were calm again as she reached for her sister's hand.

"Cassie?" asked Marie as if leaving a fog.

"It's all right, Marie. I'm here now and you don't have to worry about being alone anymore."

"Alone, Cassandra?" shouted the voice of Julius' clone. "Your sister was never alone."

Swooping in too quickly for Cassandra to stop him, the clone scooped Marie away from her. An aura of darkness swept through the Final Alliance army causing them slight pain. Recognizing the attack, the Titan Prince rushed forward.

"Show yourself, Abaddon!" demanded Cedric.

"All these noble heroics and sacrifice!" taunted Abaddon's voice. "What battle have you truly won while I'm still here?"

The clone of Julius made Marie look at him. "It isn't over yet, dearest," he encouraged her. "As long as we have each other."

"No... this isn't right..." reasoned Marie. "If my other minions have perished, you should..."

"I guess you finally figured it out, dummy."

Quickly and brutally, the clone bored his dagger deep into Marie's abdomen. Screaming in agony, a darkness overtook Cassandra. As Cedric rushed to her, Joshua jumped over the rubble of a building. Enraged at the monster with the face of his father, the young Paladin beat him repeatedly with his shield.

"A Paladin is the shining star in the sea of darkness!" exclaimed Joshua. "You are the manifestation of the darkness that dares to take the face of one of the noblest knights to ever walk Mundus. Father, I avenge you in this hour and leave my hate to die with this abomination."

Drawing Excalibur high in the air, Joshua decapitated the clone in one perfect swipe. Expecting ridicule and a lecture from Valentine, the young Paladin received only an appreciative hand on his back.

"Now it's behind you," offered Valentine. "Be ready to take the next step and you will be greater than your father ever was."

Marie clutched her stomach and crawled to Cassandra. Just as the two sisters were about to reach each other, a plague of ethereal locusts swarmed into Marie's stomach and tore at her body and soul. Gathering the sustenance they needed in seconds, the plague retreated to the ruins of the old Titan Canton.

"All divisions!" shouted Cedric. "All commanders! Full retreat!"

The Final Alliance stood dumbfounded as Cedric blessed himself and readied his sword. Colin and Argus had just rejoined the battle with their commands and witnessed the chaotic retreat of their Alliance.

"Oh my God," exclaimed Argus. "I can feel him again! Abaddon walks this world once more."

Overcome with grief and terror, the Kablisha looked to the calm Prince Cedric Rhone for strength. In turn, the commander sought the support of Francis and Wilhelm; the incarnate angels nodded and readied for battle.

"Holy Father, pray for us!" chanted Cedric.

In the Titan Canton, Abaddon's body took shape. No longer transparent, the dark angel turned the pristine blue skies of Terminus Mundus to black and the three moons bore a blood red color that frightened all of the planet's inhabitants to their very cores.

"One to shed salvation's light, one as black as darkest night!" shouted Wilhelm as he unlatched his cape.

The two-color wings of Wilhelm emerged once more. Francis threw off of his battle coat and a single wing formed on his right side.

"Can you stop this transformation?" questioned Cedric.

"Holy War may be the only chance we've got," argued Wilhelm.

"If he drew in those regenerative powers, it won't work!" explained Francis. "We must save everything we've got for what's coming."

Even with the Alliance soldiers falling back, many rushed to Cedric's aid in defiance of his orders.

"We are with you, your Excellency," Horace informed Cedric. "It doesn't matter what demons we face."

"Any martial or spell craft is no longer of any use here! Please, Horace, this is embarrassing enough already... RETREAT! There may be a time shortly when each and every man and woman here is going to have to sacrifice their lives to stop Abaddon!"

A stern look from his mother would not sway the sword master. It was a heartfelt regret between the two that brought the even the coldest heart to tears. One last embrace between mother and son was all that was needed before she would leave him to destiny. Though they hated to obey, Civilia's courage forced the Final Alliance into retreat at the eastern wall of the city. Finally reaching her dying sister, the tears fell from Cassandra's eyes onto the cheeks of Marie.

"By the Saints, Cassie... what have I done... I didn't..."

Stung by the regret of her younger sister for a situation she had no control over, the raven-haired Queen cried harder. "Marie, hang on... we have clerics back at the encampment that can help you. He used you! He used you like a puppet! Damn him! Damn him to hell!"

"Cassie... I don't... I don't want to die..."

"You can't die, Marie! You're only the family I have left."

The darkness erupted around Cassandra. The trained eyes of Walker and Cecilia could already see demon wings emerging from her back and horns from the sides of her temple. The emotional loss of her last family member was overtaking her capacity to reason. With her brother distracted by the coming of Abaddon, the desperate Vanadis went to help her friend.

"Cecilia!" ordered Cassandra. "You've got to help me get my sister to Florence now!"

"I'm sorry, Cassie," apologized a tearful Cecilia. "It's too late. Abaddon ripped her apart, body and soul."

"I won't let her die!"

"We can't restore the lives that have been lost, Cassie. I'm sorry... she doesn't deserve it, but she is going to die!"

Cassandra swiftly brought her hand from her dying sister to Cecilia's forearm. Like a parasite, the Titan princess felt an infection brewing inside of her. Insatiable blood lust and service to her Dark Queen flooded her mind as a malicious smile covered her face. As the golden armor on her left arm faded to black, only the thoughts of protecting her young son kept Cecilia from falling to the powers of darkness. Frightened by the power brewing inside Cassandra, she staggered back two steps, and readied her spear to strike down the Queen. Looking to her brother for comfort, Cedric stood powerless as Abaddon laughed from his perch at the Titan Canton.

"Cedric Rhone, I have allowed you to live long enough to see what the creature you love will become. Let your last sight be how she brings ruin to all you hold dear."

Watching her sister turn more and more demonic, Marie accepted her fate, but wouldn't allow it to happen to her beloved sibling as well. Mustering the last of her strength, she pulled Cassandra's forehead to her own. With a gentle kiss from Marie, the darkness washing over the raven-haired sorceress waned.

"No, Cassie. I won't let him hurt you like he hurt me. You have to protect Central Acadia and you have to be there for Cedric. He's going to need all of the help he can get."

"Cassandra!" shouted Cedric.

The shock of the anger in Cedric's voice and sorrow invading his eyes shocked the Queen back to reality. As her storm receded, the embarrassment of what she almost allowed herself to become overwhelmed Cassandra. Reduced to tears because of her behavior, her reason returned and the raven-haired maiden mourned for her sweet sister.

"I will do what you say, Marie... but don't you dare go to your grave believing that this was your fault."

"Thank you, sister... I would have loved to have been with you... but I'm glad I was given a chance to see you with my own eyes again. Take care of Cedric, sis... you are each other's anchor!"

Her weak body finally gave out, and Cassandra held her dead sister close to her heart. Robespierre and the other Knights of the Order of the Lion offered to take the body with them. The robes around Abaddon's body disintegrated. Cedric gripped his chest as Abaddon's wound was blazing in front of him.

"Do you see this wound you inflicted on me, Cedric Rhone? It is a wound that will never heal! I believe you have a matching one! It was fated before this battle began that you and I would be forever linked in this combat."

A corrupted version of his original mail formed over Abaddon's body. Human skulls cried in agony on the shoulder plates of the armor and sharpened bone projections emerged from the dark angel's forearm and shin plates. The feathers on his bony wings grew larger than they had ever been. The great helm adorned with ram's horns only exposed his glowing red eyes and smiling white teeth. His old swords having been broken last time, Abaddon armed himself with a massive ball and chain powered by his overwhelming strength. Attached to the ball and chain on the other side was a sharp curved blade.

"The influence of the powers of the *Libro Mortuorum* and the essence of a necromancer have merged with Abaddon," surmised Francis. "By God, there's no turning back for him now, Cedric, his soul is truly lost."

"Wondrous powers!" evoked Abaddon. "I should have done this a long time ago. So, Cedric, you send your army fleeing while you stand once again ready to die for love. It's a shame that soon they will all be serving Cassandra; a heroic end like yours should be worthy of song. Behold the fifth trumpet!"

Manifesting a great horn in his right hand, a thunderous blow echoed across the planet. No ear was immune to its deafening sound. From the heavens above, a star fell to the earth and exploded inside of Verian. A great gateway opened and the barrier between creation and the sixth plane of hell was shattered. As the believers witnessed this new plague, the prophecies of the Gloria became real before them. The Army of the Locust King as described in the scriptures emerged from the smoking abyss, hell-bent on serving their sovereign to the death. Knowing his comrades needed more time to retreat, the Alliance Commander looked to his two angelic companions. Nadia flew forward to join them, adorned in her succubus form. Wilhelm tossed his paramour his ivory spear. Gripping her magic staff in her right hand and the spear in her left, the daughter of the Prince was ready to sacrifice herself for all Creation. She balanced herself with her wings as the four waited for the inevitable.

"Thank you, Nadia," Cedric said encouragingly.

"There is no need for thanks, Prince Rhone," returned Nadia. "Know your courage and compassion even makes the demons believe."

The dauntless act of courage even took Abaddon by surprise, but the dark angel took pleasure in the fact his four most formidable foes would soon meet their end. In the mist of the chaos, a ringing started to sound. Cecilia stared at her spear and it shook in her hands.

"Why is the Gottin-speer shaking?"

The same sound began to emerge from the weapons of other warriors: Argus, Christian, Colin, Cagius, Joshua, Valentine, Amuro, Malcolm, Walker, Hippolyte, Minerva, and Ethan.

"Uncle, what's going on?" demanded Mesmara as she noticed the effect of her uncle's weapon.

"These weapons are made from the ore in Lion's Peak," concluded Argus. "The ancient scrolls foretold that such an ore has the power to destroy the creatures of Hell. Warriors of Mundus carrying the weapons crafted in the deep of Lion's Peak, you are the only ones of this planet with the power to join the divine warriors and kill this invading army!"

Minerva stared at her bow and then to Walker. "Thanks, Jon, for the wonderful gift."

Walker laughed and readied his weapons.

"I for one am certainly not going to let my brother have all the fun!" exclaimed Cecilia as a heroic smile crossed her face.

"If he is going to fight Abaddon, he certainly can't waste his time on those things," reasoned Cagius.

Argus turned to Mesmara and Quinn. "You know what you have to do," ordered Argus. "Quinn, if I don't survive this…you will receive the mantle of leadership for our people. Take care of them and marry my niece! That's an order!"

"Of course, Argus," responded Quinn.

With a tearful goodbye, Mesmara kissed her uncle. As warriors carrying the weapons charged to the position of the last four defenders of creation, the two Kablisha warriors cleared Martha's position at the base of the eastern wall. With the Final Alliance in full retreat, the Titan scientist had no choice. Placing her faith in the order of Cedric Rhone, she activated her version of the tachyon barrier. The same shield that had imprisoned the west for five long revolutions was the only thing penning in the Army of the Locust King and Abaddon's wrath. Taking no chances, Horace issued orders.

"Set a picket line here on the eastern plains. Find anything we can use to stockade the area. Reform the ranks and call up everyone from the encampment. This is our last stand!"

Inspired by the courage and sacrifice of their strongest warriors, no one in the camp allowed themselves to be thought of as lesser. Rushing forward with everything they could manage, the picket lines were formed. Wagons, carts, and heavy equipment were brought in to be used as a stockade against incoming troops. The five fusion trains fired their engines in case a hasty retreat was needed. Martha rejoined her siege engineers and prepared to fire her trebuchets once more. Silently, Civilia stared at the city.

"This is all I can do for now, your Highness," advised Horace.

"May their Guardian Angels protect them," prayed Civilia.

As the Army of the Locust King converged on Cedric's position, Christian and Colin jumped in front of him. The Titan prince was silent as Deathbringer and the Ornihalcum daggers brought death to the foes in front of him.

"Cedric, we're giving you a chance to get Abaddon," offered Christian. "We'll handle these foes."

Turning back to Wilhelm and Francis, the encouragement of the two incarnate angels was all the sword master needed to continue. Ragnarok put behind him, the Titan prince charged his hated foe. Members of the Army of the Locust King blocked his path. Arrows from Malcolm and Minerva helped clear the way while Amuro unleashed a barrage of earthquake spells to send the locusts back to Hell. As another armed swordsman approached his flank, Cecilia's Gottin-speer slipped into its ribs.

"We ran last time, brother…no one is leaving you behind again!"

She tipped her spear to her helmet in a quick salute, and Cedric moved on. Three more enemies were all that stood between the Titan prince and the ruins of the Canton. He heard a chant of magic that concluded with the Elvish word for "death" behind him. Three black and purple triangles appeared under the enemies. In an instant they were all killed. Cedric looked back at Cassandra, who had a surprised look on her face.

"I didn't expect that to actually work," quipped Cassandra. "I guess my magic and class level is much higher than I thought. Listen, Cedric, I may not carry a legendary weapon but I have the divine power to protect my people."

"You okay, Cassie? No homicidal tendencies or delusions of world control?"

Cassandra winked at Cedric and blew him a kiss. "Go get him, baby!"

Ripping Ragnarok from his back, Cedric walked purposely towards Abaddon. The Dark Angel whipped the mace and chain of his weapon above his head.

"You are nothing more than a Divikin with the strategic genius to exploit the one weapon I couldn't predict," taunted Abaddon. "Here you stand the hero in this final dramatic confrontation."

Assuming a side position, Cedric brought Ragnarok up with two hands to the level of his eyes.

"You don't really think you can win a second time," Abaddon continued. "Had I not been so reckless with you last time, I would never have lost. It shouldn't have come to this; you could have taken my offer and lived."

"There is no greater love than to lay down one's life for the sake of his friends."

"Those words still haunt me," said Abaddon chuckling. "This time I'm the challenger, so the first blow is mine!"

Abaddon swung the ball forward on his chain, but Cedric raised Ragnarok at the last second to deflect the blow. The dark angel opened his wings and flew towards the Titan prince. On Cedric in a split second, Abaddon shoulder-blocked him into a wall.

"Damn, he's fast," cursed Cedric.

Another set of blows came in the form of both mace and sword, but Cedric parried them all away.

"I see that the Kablisha have improved your blocking abilities. I wonder how long you can keep this up!"

Abaddon attacked Cedric at close range again. Crossing the mace and sword against Ragnarok, the dark angel pushed hard into the sword master. Abaddon could make out the grinding of teeth and smell the heavy perspiration falling from his foe.

"Getting tired yet, Rhone?" gloated Abaddon. "Maybe you should have taken more care than to start two battles before you fought this penultimate one. You don't even have the speed to get in one attack. What hope is there?"

Abaddon looked down at Cedric and noticed him holding his blade with one hand.

"You bastard!" cursed Abaddon.

Bringing his glowing left hand forward, Cedric shouted, "Holy War!" The ensuing explosion in Abaddon's midsection sent the Dark Angel hurtling into a stone wall. Armor disintegrated from the impact of the blast and the bloody right side of Abaddon confirmed he had two broken ribs. Not wasting a moment, Cedric ripped a dagger from his boot and rammed it into Abaddon's stomach. Managing to push the sword master back with one hand, the dark angel tried but couldn't remove the dagger. In an attempt to regain the advantage, the fallen flailed his wings. The wind blew Cedric back as his boots scraped the ground. Coughing up some blood, Abaddon wiped it from his lips with a smile.

"Well done!" congratulated Abaddon. "Such an ability is only known to angels and is supposed to be beyond the Divikin. Why am I given this great honor?"

"Only a fool would think they could duel someone the same way twice." Cedric returned his sword to a fighting position.

"You just used your most powerful spell, Cedric Rhone. You won't be able to use that spell again for another rotation. It was a gamble, but certainly worth it. These broken ribs will be a bit of a nuisance for the rest of the fight. You've won round one, but let's see what the second round has to offer!"

Abaddon clashed his sword and mace together to discharge his hell power on Cedric. Even with his shield up, the Titan prince was blown back, but the magical discharge no longer had an effect on his body. Disappointed at the failure of his attack to register, the dark angel pondered his next move.

"So this is the warrior I was denied the opportunity to fight the first time because of my meddling with Cassandra," observed Abaddon. "Purely amazing…"

Abaddon flew towards Cedric with sword forward. Readying his defenses for a bulrush, the sword master was shocked to see Abaddon fly vertical before reaching him. Spinning the mace and chain above his head, the dark angel brought it down with such a force it shattered the right pauldron of the Master plate. Though there was no visible wound, Cedric could feel a bruise developing from a displaced fracture.

"I must thank the blacksmiths of the Kablisha for their fine craftsmanship, or else the whole shoulder might be broken."

"Oh well, at least you're defenseless there now."

Calling forward his wind saber powers, the sword master forced the dark angel to land. On the defensive now, Abaddon found himself at the mercy of a flurry attack. The size and power of Ragnarok still proved a difficulty for Abaddon. When he was knocked off balance, Cedric sliced his sword across the exposed portion of Abaddon's body. Yelping like a wounded animal, the fallen felt the holy saber magic in the sword digging into his insides.

"It works both ways, Abaddon!" taunted Cedric. "When you took on a part of Marie's soul, you took on the corruption as well. Last time, I couldn't use my saber magic to this effectiveness, but now the powers of light will torture you just as your hellish brew poisoned me."

"I don't believe this! How can I, an angel gifted with such powers, be humbled by the likes of you? Now I remember the name of your blade!"

"Crafted in the fires of Lion's Peak by the Dwarves and blessed by the powers of an Angel."

"So Krystos gave you the sword named after the Great War!"

"Yes, ironically I didn't know I would be using it to end it!"

Cedric swung and Abaddon blocked his attack. Swinging his mace, the dark angel struck the Titan prince in the left arm. Pieces of armor broke off the Master plate once more and even part of the Paladin gauntlet was damaged. While the battle continued, the bearers of the legendary weapons found it impossible to continue their battles individually. Already the Army of the Locust King closed in on the barrier of the eastern wall, the first waves striking the tachyons in rapid succession. The bonds were severing quickly and if the bombardment kept up, the barrier would fall.

"Rally to me!" ordered Cagius.

As the warriors fell back to the eastern position, Francis got ahead of the field. Whipping his body in a circle, silver projectiles flew from his wings. These holy and unstoppable daggers struck the enemy army in their necks. Burning them to ashes, it bought time for the bearers to get into place. They lined up, melee and spear fighters in the front, magic users and archers to their rear. Watching the seemingly endless horde come at them, they contemplated their end.

"I've never served with finer friends," Amuro encouraged the warriors with her.

"Fight as long as you can!" commanded Francis. "You need not fear for your lives, for if any of your life forces are in danger I'll teleport you out of here. While I can't kill every single one of these foes alone, I can grant each of you a tremendous gift."

Raising his staff to the heavens, a divine white and gold light shone through the apocalyptic colors above them. A halo appeared over each of the bearers and ran down the length of their bodies as if they were being scanned. A silver and blue glowing shield surrounded each of the warriors.

"This is awesome!" exclaimed a laughing Valentine. "I feel invincible!"

"Yeah, like I can take on anything," added Minerva.

"It is a divine protection spell that Guardian Angels use to shield their charges," explained Francis. "It will help repel the crafts of these creatures. Fight well, my friends! God is with us!"

Nervously awaiting their charging foes, the warriors put forward their weapons. Minerva and Malcolm released a barrage. Through the powers of their bows, a single shot multiplied into a hundred. Those in the front lines of the Locust King army fell over dead or tore at the wounds in their heads and neck.

"Hold the line!" shouted Cagius.

As they approached the melee line, the Army of Locust King found spears, swords, and one huge axe waiting for them. Cagius, Cecilia, and Hippolyte held the flanks, their spears glowing in incomprehensible light. Dozens of foes fell from one thrust. Walker and Joshua formed their defensive line in the center as Ethan buried his axe into the ground. The ensuing fault shift sent groups into hell. Bolstered by celestial strength, Colin assaulted entire battalions, while the increased speed let Christian, Argus and Valentine cut through foes as if they were on horseback. Amuro used magic through Enhancer as though she were a high class magus. The divine warriors were all over the field, assisting the bearers as best they could. Through it all, Cassandra stood at the shield to serve as the last line of defense. Any foe that foolishly passed the line met her death spell. However, the Queen was terribly distracted as she could see Cedric and Abaddon battling on top of a ruined building close to her. Abaddon unleashed a new flurry through his dual weapons as the Titan prince desperately blocked one attack after another. The strain on Ragnarok was growing as the ball and chain of the dark angel's weapon pounded on it.

"Cedric!" cried Cassandra.

Cedric blocked Abaddon's attack but the strength of the angel knocked him over. The sword master swept the legs out from under the angel and tried to quickly get to his feet. Abaddon used his wings for balance and beat him to the punch. The dark angel struck the sword master on his exposed shoulder and drove his blade through deeply. Screaming in pain, Cedric ripped the blade from his shoulder thanks in part to the power of the Paladin gauntlets. As he rose to a kneeling position, Abaddon whipped the ball and chain above his head.

"You disappoint me, Cedric. From the way you began I expected more of a fight from you," taunted Abaddon.

Unleashing the mace attack, Cedric crossed the gauntlets to create a defensive shield. Frustrated that the Titan prince had deflected the first attack, the fallen angel struck repeatedly. Despite the shield, the sword master visibly felt each blow. Bloody cuts formed on his face and body and every effort made to attack was met with resistance. One last whip and swing by the dark angel shattered the shield of the Paladin gauntlets. Hurtling to the ground, Cedric landed behind the defensive line of his friends and mentor. He coughed up blood upon impact, and was further mocked with the hellish laugh of the fallen descending to the ground. Overcome with grief, Cassandra stared at Cedric's breaking body.

"I can't..." cried Cassandra loudly. Falling to her knees, despair and darkness enveloped the Queen. Cedric felt it happening and rallied himself to his feet.

"Cassie... never forget... what I told you," stammered Cedric. "You must believe in the charity in all of creation."

As the Locust King army moved to take her, Cecilia jumped to Cassandra's defense. Killing the first two foes with her spear, the Vanadis grabbed one of their swords and struck the third in the neck.

"Don't kneel in the middle of a battlefield, Cassie!" scolded Cecilia. "You won't find salvation, only death."

"I wanted to believe in him," recited a monotone Cassandra. "Everything that he did... he made me believe that he could overcome this moment. And now... what hope is there against the powers of darkness? Perhaps I can still barter to save his life!"

"Don't you dare! My brother would despise you for all eternity if you dared give yourself to the darkness for him."

"But how can you still fight? Why do you not despair?"

"I can still be ruthless if you let me!" laughed Cecilia. "And I still believe in my brother!"

Barely staggering into a fighting position, Cedric coughed up more blood. Abaddon simply waited for him. Though bleeding heavily from his own wounds, the dark angel was in far better condition to finish the battle.

"Cedric, you can't hold out any longer," boasted Abaddon. "It's over, I won! The Divine Beings will always triumph. God was incorrect in having us share the glory of the angels with you lesser creatures. Behold your friends!"

Briefly moving his eyes, the Titan prince saw the despair enveloping Cassandra. The same cloud befell his other friends as their eyes and resolve weakened in the face of his imminent defeat. The only thing holding them together was the magic and divinity of Francis and Wilhelm. If Cedric fell, though, the two incarnates would certainly be next and with the condition Cassandra was in, the succubus Queen would be more than a match for the desperate sentinels.

"Look at their faces, Cedric," observed Abaddon as he readied his blade. "They had all of their hope in you and you could not deliver for them. They expected you to be their savior. It must hurt knowing that you let everyone down! How can you fight? No one believes in you anymore. It would be better if you lay down and died."

Putting his sword back to the level of his weary eyes, the determined sword master would not be intimidated.

"I can still fight, Abaddon. I still believe in myself… I will keep fighting even if no one else believes in me. That's why your sin was so terrible… you gave in to despair."

"You were an honorable opponent and your faith was unwavering among these scattering sheep. I would enjoy letting you suffer, but I will not repeat the same mistake again."

"Have at you!" shouted Cedric.

Fearlessly charging into battle, Cedric swung Ragnarok with all his might. Abaddon met the attack with his blade and mace. As they pushed their weapons into one another, auras ignited around the two combatants. Abaddon's was purple, while silver light surrounded the Titan prince. Pressing with further magic, the ground broke apart beneath the two as both blades went red-hot. After a few seconds, the red-hot gave way to white-hot. The power exerted by the Titan prince and dark angel was too much and this final press would decide the battle. It was in that moment the unthinkable happened. Ragnarok shattered and Abaddon's blade found its way through. It cleaved through the Rising Moon Helmet, and Cedric was thrown back and landed on his left knee. Cassandra observed a trickle of blood running down the forehead of the Divikin she loved. Breathing heavily, the blood rolled past his left eye. Still clutching the handle and the part of Ragnarok that remained intact, the Titan prince raised his eyes to his shocked friends. Buying them precious seconds to react to what happened, Wilhelm and Francis nodded at each other. Unleashing a double "holy war," they cleared the streets temporarily of all of the Locust King army. However, with Abaddon at full power, another wave prepared to descend. Cassandra went to run to Cedric, but Cecilia held her at the direction of her brother's free hand.

"Cedric, please… it's my choice to save you!" stammered Cassandra. "I can't watch you die."

They expected a plea, they expected sorrow, but what they didn't expect was for Cedric to calmly raise his eyes to all of them. Across his face they observed a smile, a smile Cecilia hadn't seen since her brother was a young, innocent boy when they played together. In the midst of the chaos and apocalypse that surrounded them, it made everyone feel happy.

"Don't be afraid," Cedric encouraged them. "I will make the demons go away!"

"NO!" retorted Cecilia as she realized her brother's meaning.

Wilhelm flew full force at Abaddon and barreled him over with an attack. Francis took his staff and twirled it above his head. Striking the ground, magic circles appeared underneath all of the bearers. In a flash of light, they were safely teleported to the defensive positions outside of the barrier.

"How long do you need, Francis?" asked Cedric.

"Give me a few minutes. God, I can't believe we have to do this, but a promise is a promise!"

"Wilhelm doesn't have a few minutes!"

Beating Abaddon with his shield to gain separation, Wilhelm found his attacks slowing down. Gripping his left hand tightly, the dark angel accelerated the flow of poison from the wings of the sentinel into his body.

"I'm going to enjoy this, traitor," proclaimed an elated Abaddon.

Cedric watched as Locust King soldiers descended on his position. Still bearing half of a sword, and knowing Francis needed more time, a moment of divine inspiration enlightened the Titan prince.

"I reject Satan!" exclaimed Cedric as he drove his broken sword through his first foe. "And all his evil works! And all his empty promises!"

Cedric cut through three more soldiers. "I believe in God, the Father Almighty, the Lord of all creation! I believe in Jesus Christ, his only Son, our Lord, who died for our sins and rose again to the right of hand of the Father! I believe in the Holy Ghost, the Mother Church, all the Saints, and the resurrection of the dead!"

Two soldiers descended upon him. The first soldier attempted to strike Cedric with his scorpion tail, but the sword master carefully grabbed it below the poisoned tip. Summoning his strength, he jabbed the stinger in the neck of the second soldier.

"I believe in the faith, hope, and charity of every citizen of Terminus Mundus!" Grabbing the tail of the now twitching second soldier, Cedric shoved the poison tip into the throat of the first one to attack him. As both of his foes lay dying from the poison, the Titan prince spit his blood at both of them. "And I'll give everything for the right of all creation to embrace their own destiny without the influence of the forces of darkness!"

Wilhelm wouldn't give in despite his suffering. The ball and chain attack from the dark angel broke his tower shield into pieces. A mighty thrust from his blade and Abaddon broke the armor around Wilhelm's heart. Collapsing to his knees, the sentinel clutched his bleeding wound. Nadia stopped what she was doing and held him tightly in a final embrace.

"Say your last goodbyes to this wretched traitor, Nadia!" mocked Abaddon. "When you see him again in Hell, the lost souls will have ripped his body to pieces again and again for time eternal. Once your father is through with you, you will beg for my protection!"

Outside the city, the warriors were still in shock at the sudden appearance of their strongest. Cassandra stood there as the walking dead. She didn't respond to anyone or anything. Cecilia was on her knees in tears, and only her husband's warm embrace from behind gave her any comfort.

"What the hell just happened?" asked Colin.

"They teleported us out," explained Christian. "Cedric's going to sacrifice himself to bind Abaddon."

"We should have known better," added Cagius. "Why him? Why does our best have to give his life to save us?"

"IT'S NOT HIS LIFE!" exclaimed Cecilia in a deafening scream. "He's going to ignite his very soul!"

The sudden revelation of the plan caught everyone by surprise and Cassandra shook from her stupor. "What do you mean *ignite his soul*!" demanded Cassandra.

"Francis and Cedric knew there was a forbidden taboo that could be used in lieu of a binding spell. If my brother ignites his soul at the levels of power he is now, Abaddon will be cast into hell. However, in the process, his soul is going to be erased from creation. He won't go to Heaven, but oblivion instead. Everything that he is and was will be erased, even our memories of him. The only people who will know he ever existed would be God and the angels themselves!"

"No!" exclaimed Cassandra. "I will be damned before I let that happen."

"Your Highness, there is nothing we can do," offered Argus. "The prophecies were all lies. The Knight of God will not appear. Cedric is doing the only thing he can to save us all."

"Don't you all understand!" Cassandra scolded. "I forced his hand with my foolish statements back there. I promised to stand with him, but I was willing to give into despair. I was ready to turn over my soul, but his faith..."

It was as if the last word of her sentence sparked something in Cassandra's very soul.

"His faith…my hope…"

The darkness that had surrounded the Queen since the battle began was suddenly shattered around her. Replacing it was a beaming golden light, which caused the warriors surrounding her to briefly cover their eyes.

In Our Hour of Darkness, When Evil Infests Our World, When Courage

is No Longer a Shield, When the Hearts of the Bravest Lie Broken, the

Last Knight Shall Take up His Sword and the Prayers of the World,

And Inherit the Power to Destroy Evil.

"That's it!" revealed Cassandra as she turned to her audience. "The *Denique Refero* Garrett transmitted to us. Five revolutions ago, Cedric was ready, but I wasn't!"

"So then Cedric really was the *Permaneo Eques Ordinares?*" asked Argus.

"No, Cedric is and always has been the Last Knight, he took up his sword but he lacked what he needed to finish the job. He needs the prayers of this world as well. He tried to tell me Christmas night in Deniva. Faith and Hope only take us so far if we don't have Charity as well… I will not fail you my love!"

Argus witnessed the two silhouettes of wings emerge from Cassandra's back. One demonic, one angelic, but it didn't matter because the child of two celestial realms loved Cedric Rhone and neither Heaven nor Hell could pull her one way or the other. Dropping to her knees safely in the Acadian plains, Cassandra closed her eyes and prayed.

"God the Father, Jesus Christ, the Holy Ghost, the Blessed Virgin, the Heavenly Choirs, the Communion of Saints... in fact, I don't care who among you hears my prayers, I need your help! I pray... I pray for the people of Terminus Mundus... I submit myself to you so that you may give Cedric Rhone the power to deliver us from evil that corrupts our souls."

"The prayers of this world... why not?" determined Cecilia as she joined in the prayer.

Soon all of the warriors followed the example of the Acadian Queen. The Christians invoked similar prayers as the Elves lead by Amuro sought the aid of the Divine Father. The Napolitan warriors and Dwarves invoked the pagan gods of old, as the Tribes turned to the spirits.

"Please, Cedric, I beg that you hear me," continued Cassandra. "Your faith became an inspiration to us all and gave me the hope to carry on the fight against this darkness. I need you to feel this charity that flows through all of us. Here we came together to make the ultimate sacrifice to drive out Abaddon and restore light to these lands. It's been a terrible journey, but one you're not making alone this time. Cedric, I pray to see you in your glory!"

The sound of trumpets blasting could be heard in Verian and the plains. Everyone started to look at one another wondering what was going on. Briefly distracted by the crackling across a radio, Martha flipped it on to hear Thomas and Garrett laughing and screaming.

"Garrett, is that you?"

"Oh Martha, it's marvelous! A sight to be seen, for sure."

"I don't understand! What's going on there?"

"Aunt Martha, the poppy is white!"

In the ruins of Verian, Abaddon crossed over Wilhelm's lifeless body as Francis finished his spell. A glowing magic circle dripping with blood manifested itself in front of him. Cedric spread his arms wide as Abaddon approached.

"So this was your plan all along!" recounted a nervous Abaddon. "Cedric Rhone, you never cease to amaze me. Not only were willing to accept oblivion, but here you convinced a guardian angel to aid you."

"I promised my friends I'd make the demons go away," replied Cedric. "This is all I have left. What can I say, Abaddon, but you beat me."

"Before you invoke it, Guardian, you may want to know one little side effect. That spell will weaken the divine barrier surrounding the temporal and celestial worlds. It may send me back, but it might also allow the Prince to enter creation!"

"It's a gamble I have to take," retorted Francis.

Just as Francis was about to strike the circle with his staff, he stopped. Listening to the breeze he heard the blasts of celestial trumpets. Not wasting a moment, the guardian immediately ended his spell. Dismayed, Cedric wondered what possessed Francis to betray him.

"I guess it was too high of an ante," mocked Abaddon. "With your sword destroyed, the dual blade is worthless and you have no divine power to invoke in your state. A quick death will suffice for us both. I salute you, Cedric Rhone, but you will die."

Flying at full speed, Abaddon struck for Cedric's heart. Puffing his chest in final defiance, the Titan prince felt the atmosphere changing around him. An unnatural haze formed as if his body was smoking, yet no fire ignited. Just as Abaddon's blade reached Cedric's body, golden light protected him from the blow. Both the dark angel and the sword master were equally surprised, but as the light faded a mighty, green and black wing covered him.

"My Lord and my God," invoked Francis.

Nadia gently lifted Wilhelm's head. Elation befell the dying sentinel as the divine plan of God was revealed to him.

"Wilhelm, is it... can it be..." wondered Nadia.

"Lord Camael felt he dishonored God when his soldiers betrayed the Lord," lectured Wilhelm. "Thus he sealed his soul away until the time when it was needed again. The Kablisha could have searched until the Second Coming, but Lord Camael's wings would remain broken. However, if the Queen of Central Acadia, the embodiment of hope, convinced her people to pray..."

"He would awaken!" finished Nadia.

"My mission is fulfilled. I have lived long enough to see my friend and my Duke once more. We all have to make sacrifices as angels when we fall and his was the greatest of all."

As Wilhelm slipped away into final sleep, a cloud of dust blew from Cedric's feet and the air around him was instantly purified. The smell of blood and death gave way to that of lilies. Brought back from beyond, Wilhelm cried aloud as he found his chest wound instantly healed. Leaping to his feet and stretching his arms wide, the poison in his wings dissipated. The four dark green wings of the Powers Choir protruded from his back and shoulders once more. Powers awakened within the loyal shield-bearer of the Powers Choirs he hadn't felt for epochs and once more Krystos readied himself for battle. Francis was not immune to powers growing around Cedric either. The ring of his right hand exploded in light and the second wing that was missing from his back was replaced as he ascended into his true form as Teman. Finally, the light touched Nadia. The horns on her head shed to the ground and were replaced with a burning halo. The succubus wings grew white feathers as the divine cleansing purified her. No longer a daughter of the Prince, she joined the choirs of angels. The black leather making up her outfit was washed white in lamb's blood and streams of white lace now covered her exposed skin.

"It can't be!" shouted Abaddon in defiance.

Frightened by everything around him, he pounded on Cedric with mace and blade. In response, three more identical wings formed out of Cedric's shoulders and arms. The four dark green wings formed a protective cocoon to further the metamorphosis.

"I will rid this world of your plague and save those I love!" promised Cedric from the cocoon.

Krystos, Nadia, and Teman formed a Triad together as they stood before the doorway for the Army of the Locust King. Willed forward by their nervous leader, Abaddon's slaves were still ready to invade Terminus Mundus.

"It feels good to have divine powers coursing through these veins again," stated Krystos.

"I guess with the weakened barrier, some rules can be bent slightly," offered Teman. "By the way, Nadia, you look adorable as an angel."

"Wait, I've got to try something… Our Father, who art in Heaven… this is amazing, I can finally say it out loud and it doesn't come out backwards!"

"That's my gal," Krystos complimented her. "Well, we still have about a million enemies to deal with."

"Shouldn't be a problem anymore," reiterated Teman. "God gave us an opportunity to be ourselves again, so let's have some fun!"

The Triad readied their weapons and charged at their foes. Teman and Nadia unleashed bombs of holy energy as Krystos unleashed wave attacks from Devilslayer. The combined divine powers of the three overwhelmed whole divisions. Invaders were blasted out of existence the moment they entered Terminus Mundus.

Outside the city, the Alliance warriors watched as the black clouds and red sky gave way to the radiant sunshine of Primus. Golden light covered the city and plains.

"Argus, what's going on?" demanded Walker.

"We have found our Final Answer!" exalted Argus. "The wings are no longer broken. It is the love of the Last Knight and the Twice-blessed Queen that have saved us."

"Then I saw another mighty angel come down from heaven wrapped in a cloud with a halo around his head; his face was like the sun and his feet were like pillars of fire," recited Mesmara with a smile. "He placed his right foot on the sea and his left foot on the land and when he cried out it was like the loud voice as a lion roars. Then the angel I saw standing on the sea and on the land raised his right hand to heaven and swore by the one who lives forever and ever who created heaven and earth and sea and all that is in them."

As the divine triad tore his army to pieces, Abaddon nervously treaded away. As he slinked back the winged cocoon opened and waves of green-black feathers heralded the arrival of the fallen angel's judge. Before him was Camael Incarnate, bearing the body and persona of Cedric Rhone, but the armor and powers of Duke Camael of the Powers Choir. Folding the wings over his body like a cloak, the incarnate raised his long-brimmed hat ever so slightly to stare at Abaddon with his own eyes. Though still bearing Cedric's brown color, a circle of blood surrounded them. Grasping a newly forged Ragnarok in his right hand, the shield and scorpion tail combination was in his left hand.

"You can't be...it's not possible," disbelieved Abaddon. "You're not a Divikin! YOU'RE A SEFIROTH!"

Laughing, the incarnate slowly removed his hat and placed it on the ground. The giant halo was around his head, and like the prophecy, his face gave off a radiating light. His boots were engulfed by flames but not consumed, and every fallen Locust King soldier he stepped on was reduced to ash. A seventh and final trumpet blasted and when the incarnate spoke two voices echoed against one another representing Cedric and Camael.

"There shall be no further delay. At the time when you hear the seventh angel blow his trumpet, the mysterious plan of God shall be fulfilled as he promised to his servants and the prophets. The time has come to purge Creation of the King of the Abyss."

"Duke Camael, but the rules... an angel of your power..."

"My physical body in this world is the Crown Prince Cedric Rhone. You are correct that no Sefiroth may enter creation, but since we share the same soul, I may take this Incarnate form. My mission is from the Lord God and I fear your fall is complete!"

"I don't fear you, not after all this time serving the Prince!"

"Then I shall finish what I should have at the beginning of time."

Opening his wings, the incarnate took the sky. Expecting the winged angel of death attack, Abaddon raised rocks around him to defend himself. Instead, the incarnate swiped his sword in the form of a cross of fire and shouted, "Cross of Salvation." The fiery cross enveloped the area around Abaddon. Trying to summon magic to shield himself, the dark angel faltered. As the full brunt of the attack hit him, his wings burned to ashes. The doorway allowing the Army of the Locust King to enter Mundus was sealed. The divine triad was slightly upset as they were having too much fun killing all of them. Desperately trying to gain the advantage once more, Abaddon tried to summon his dark powers. Terrified by these new attacks, the fallen could invoke no spell.

"How can you do all of this?" demanded Abaddon.

"The fires of purification eliminate all of your magical abilities. When the lamb was slaughtered for original sin, new powers awakened in the Sefiroth!"

"There's no salvation left for his soul, Duke Camael," offered Teman. "I'm sorry, but you must banish him to hell."

The Incarnate landed and readied his sword and shield. Abaddon got his weapons ready as well.

"I will not suffer the same embarrassment at your hands," cried Abaddon defiantly.

"Abaddon, I will lead you into the Promised Land!"

The two screamed and charged. They struck each other in the middle as the attacks of their swords and shields gave off tremendous energy bolts. In moments it was the fallen who was drained. Off-balance and driven back by the overpowering might of Camael Incarnate's blows, the dark angel lost his footing. The opening allowed for a strike from the scorpion's tail on the shield. The incarnate shattered Abaddon's armor and his left arm in the process. Unable to wield the ball and chain anymore, the dark angel let it fall to the ground. Barely holding onto his single blade, Abaddon fell to his knees and lowered his eyes.

"Lord of the Powers Choir and Sefiroth of God, hear my final plea. I understand that my acts cannot be forgiven. Prove to me that you are both an Angel of Death and an Angel of Mercy."

The Incarnate stood silent and held his sword in a striking position.

"Let me go…let me go and I shall swear a pact to serve you…"

"Lord Abaddon, what will I have to bind you to this pact?"

"My word as an angel…better an honest enemy than a false friend, eh, my Lord?"

"I am sorry, but after you damned yourself by sacrificing the soul of an innocent against her will, you painted a black mark on your soul that cannot be purged by any craft I possess. Abaddon, you have been judged."

"If you will not accept my gracious offer, then you will die, Duke Camael."

Abaddon sprung from his kneeling position and rammed the incarnate with all his might. The dark angel tried to cleave his foe in his midsection, but his opponent caught the sword in between his arms and wings. Swinging his scorpion tail once more, the Sefiroth held Abaddon in place. Ragnarok found its way into the same wound on the dark angel's chest. Armor cracking and falling to the ground, the incarnate released his dying opponent and pulled his sword out. Gasping for air and defiant to the end, Abaddon held out his bloody palm.

"It's your move!"

The incarnate locked his sword and shield into a single standard and buried it in the ground in front of him. Raising his hands to the heavens, he closed his eyes and prayed.

"By the Hand of God, source of all faith, hope, and charity…"

As he spoke the words, all of his body glowed in gold and white light. A binding circle appeared below Abaddon and held him in place.

"Duke Camael…please, don't send me back…I beg you, don't send me back there. I'm a failure. If I go there…the Prince warned me and I have no army left… I'll be cast out!"

"Bestow unto my unworthy hands the power…"

"You don't know what it's like…we have no hope, only despair…you wouldn't wish it upon your worst enemy…HAVE MERCY!"

As the Incarnate opened his eyes, Abaddon could sense sorrow over the imminent events.

"To become the final arbiter of creation…"

The ground opened below Abaddon, but he remained afloat. The smell of fire and brimstone was unmistakable and screams of torture could be heard.

"In the name of mercy, Camael… don't send me there! I'll do anything! I AM YOUR SERVANT!"

"Let the fools who stand against your glory repent or suffer eternal damnation!" the Incarnate continued his prayer. "Hand of God, judgment!"

As he thrust his hands forward, white light covered Abaddon. As if he was magnetized, the dark angel found himself being pulled into the fires below. Grasping for anything to keep him above ground, lost souls emerged from the wall. They jumped and clawed at Abaddon, biting his flesh. Still the dark angel would not let go. A vast maelstrom rose from the pits with thousands of lost souls spinning eternally in the torrent. The dragon face of Leviathan, the Dark Sefiroth of Lust, was at the center of this unnatural disaster. Opening his mouth, he sucked Abaddon down into the pits. No longer able to hold his grip, the dark angel slipped into the deep circles of Hell, but not before unveiling one cryptic warning: "Play the prophet, Camael! Read the Gloria carefully, for there will come a time when I can be released. You haven't heard the last of Abaddon—I will return!"

As the cries and screams of the dark angel who had tormented the souls of Terminus Mundus grew silent, the ground closed. The gateway into Hell was sealed and the Divine Triad rejoined Camael Incarnate. Overcome with joy at seeing each other face to face again, Krystos and Camael embraced each other tightly.

"My Lord, I am glad that your honor has been regained and that the vessel provided for you was so worthy," rejoiced Krystos. "You were right, I saw you and I did not recognize you."

"I don't think that's entirely true, old friend," retorted the Incarnate. "I highly doubt you would have put me through such rigorous training and opportunities if you didn't believe who I truly was. The duties of a sentinel belong to you no longer, loyal Krystos. God has freed you of your poison. As for you, Lady Nadia…"

Nadia knelt before the Incarnate with tears in her eyes.

"I thank you for helping me complete my mission and for taking care of the Twice-Blessed when she needed you most. Your time of penance is over, you have proven your soul worthy of entering the Gates of Heaven. No longer shall you be condemned to your fate in hell. When you and Krystos wish, you may return at any time."

The two stared at one another for the first time without the burden of fate and prophecy. Grabbing onto each tightly, Krystos pulled Nadia to his heart.

"Please accept our apologies, Lord Camael," apologized Nadia. "I think we might wait a little longer."

Krystos reverted back into his form as Duke Wilhelm von Angelhardt and Nadia reverted to her form as well.

"There's a lot of catching up to do," said Wilhelm. "Besides, I have a feeling our daughter is going to need us more than ever."

"I understand," replied the Incarnate. "It was an honor to fight with each of you. Farewell, my friends."

"But Lord Camael," questioned Nadia. "What will happen to Lord Cedric?"

"I'm sorry. As we share the same body and soul in this incarnation, I am not permitted to remain in creation like this."

The single statement cut the two harder than any weapon Abaddon had used against them. Nadia and Wilhelm had expected their Lord to end this transfiguration, but the incarnate was speaking of ascension.

"No," retorted Wilhelm. "You can't leave these people yet. There's so much you have left to do."

Camael Incarnate bowed his head as he took his hat from the ground again.

"You know, one of the grand duties of the Guardian Angels is to serve as an advocate," offered Teman. "I have my duties to return to in my own end of the Universe, but I have enough time to make a good case for an old friend."

"I appreciate it," replied Camael Incarnate. "Perhaps together it may be enough, but please prepare everyone for the worst. I fear I cannot go back."

"What are we going to do if Abaddon's prophecy was correct?" asked Nadia. "What if evil returns?"

"If darkness returns and my services are needed, this form will return as well. The Nephilim cast into Hell, the demonkin on the run, and those that brought ruin upon this land have faced final justice. The people of Terminus Mundus need not fear the Prince any longer. I will make the demons go away!"

As Wilhelm and Nadia stood watching, Camael Incarnate and Teman disappeared. Silently, the two remaining behind wondered how they would break this news to the others and regretted for a moment not joining them back in Heaven. Outside of the city, a giant, full rainbow made its way across the sky.

"Just as in the story of the flood," recounted Amuro. "The covenant of Adonai and the people of Terminus Mundus is renewed once more."

"I don't think we need the barrier any longer, Martha," suggested Christian.

"I don't know, Vice-Marshal DeVries, his Excellency left specific orders…" replied Martha.

Reaching into his cloak, Christian pulled out the scroll Cedric gave him. Breaking the seal he prepared to read it. "I have his final orders here, Doctor Heinrich. Please drop the barrier."

Pushing a button on her controller once more, the barrier dissipated. Since they were not swarmed by the forces of darkness, everyone assumed Abaddon had been defeated. But what should have brought them joy, was meet instead with inconsolable fear. Desperately seeking answers, Cassandra turned to Cecilia for comfort. When the Titan princess shook her head and buried her tears in

Ethan's arms and chest, the Queen knew her worst nightmares were confirmed. Everyone removed their helmets and bowed their heads.

"I don't understand," said Cassandra mournfully. "I really thought... I thought we couldn't remember him but... I'm so sorry, Cedric... I'm so sorry I failed you..."

Finding the strong arms of Civilia around her, Cassandra let her emotions go. The Matriarch of Destruction shed her own tears as well.

"Duke Wilhelm and Lady Nadia approach!" shouted one of the guards.

No longer impeded by the barrier, the two divine beings returned to the camp. As soon as she saw Nadia, Cassandra rushed into her arms. Trembling with fear and tears, the newly saved angel could not offer her daughter any comfort. Knowing they would not have left Cedric behind, everyone came to the realization that their leader and friend was truly gone.

"Wilhelm, what happened?" asked Argus.

"Abaddon is gone, cast into Hell... he haunts our world no longer," explained Wilhelm.

"To hell with that! What happened to my brother!?" demanded Cecilia.

"Your Excellency, Cedric did not ignite his soul and as such is not damned to oblivion," offered Nadia. Freeing every one of their worst fears, Nadia continued. "However, a great sacrifice was necessary for your brother to defeat Abaddon. Thus he received his eternal reward after the battle was over."

Failing to sense her brother despite her desperate attempts, Cecilia accepted what Nadia said.

"After all this... after everything Cedric did for us..." cried Amuro. "How could the story end like this?"

"What's going to happen to us now?" reasoned Argus. "He brought all of us together and he held us together through all of this."

Disappointed at the wallowing of the elves and divikin, Cagius stepped forward. Though merely a mortal human, he wouldn't allow the same dark thoughts to touch him. "Well I for one am not going to let his sacrifice go to waste. You think Cedric Rhone would want us to be wallowing and crying over his death? He'd be begging us to drink a toast to the hero of the past who bravely burns the path for the soldiers of the future. Let the bards compose songs and epic poems about the mighty Prince of Titanus, because when we face our darkest times, we should reflect on a hero who will make the demons go away."

The words of the Napolitan Prince were not enough because the grief surrounding his comrades was too great. A reassuring pat on his shoulder by Horace Irvine proved the Titan War Master appreciated his noble comments about their fallen friend.

"It's getting late," announced Civilia. "We must tend to our own and we shall return to the safety of Fort Orion for now. There is much still to be done."

There was no joy or plans to celebrate such a grand victory with a proper feast. Resigned to the fact they had kin and countrymen waiting for their safe return, the Final Alliance army trudged to the hover trains to take them home. Nadia aided the numb Cassandra on her way back as Ethan did the same for his wife. As if refusing to leave, Christian silently read through Cedric's final orders. Rosa grabbed him around the waist and read the parchment as well.

"Do you want to say anything about them?" asked Rosa as tears came to her eyes.

"There's something in here for everyone. We spoke about this inevitability, but he knew what was going to happen here and he wanted us to live no longer threatened by this darkness."

"It's really over, isn't it? There'll never be anyone like him again. My heart breaks for Cassandra, I hope some rotation she'll come to terms with the sacrifice he made for her."

"It wasn't just for her, Rosa, he gave this final gift to all of us. Our destiny is ours again and the Prince and his wretched minions can't take that from us anymore."

"Let the others go Christian, I want to wait here with you just a little longer…"

Inspired by their conversation, the outcast Elves stared at the ruins of the smoldering city. Through her tears, Rosa's keen eye sight caught a shadow making its way from the ruins of the battle. Believing it to be a mirage or wishful thinking at first, she moved from Christian's embrace to get a better view. Not knowing what Rosa was doing, Christian followed his lover until she was two hundred meters from the hole in the eastern wall. Elated, the exiled She-elf watched as he emerged from the broken wall. Armor broken, helmet cleaved and using Ragnarok as a cane, Cedric staggered out of the city. Joined now by Christian, neither outcast could believe their own eyes. Whether it was a specter or a mirage, they were not sure until the Titan prince pulled his flask from his cloak and drank the last of his brandy. Sighing to find he had already finished the last of it, Cedric Rhone continued on.

"That's him, Rosa!" cried an elated Christian.

"Cedric Rhone is alive!" shouted Rosa at the top of her lungs.

The two outcast elves just fell to their knees praising God for the miracle. Every warrior in the Final Alliance army turned and saw their commander staggering towards them. Cassandra and Cecilia took off and even though Vanadis sprinted much faster, she let the Queen jump into her brother's arms first. Barely able to catch her due to his wounds and exhaustion, the Titan prince was on the receiving end of many profuse kisses. Cecilia embraced her brother on one side while a hustling Civilia did so on the other. Joined by Christian and Rosa from behind, Cedric lost the strength to stand. He slipped to the ground as his friends and family covered him in a warm embrace. Overcome with joy that their commander was alive, the others came up to him one by one. Assisted to his feet and supported by Ethan and Joshua, Amuro grabbed Cedric by the waist and put her head and tears to his heart. She found herself rudely shoved out of the way by Florence who insisted she tend his wounds immediately and privately.

"Soldiers of the Final Alliance!" ordered Horace. "Pay homage to Terminus Mundus' greatest hero!"

In a single motion everyone knelt before Cedric and offered their weapons in salute. After returning their salute with his own, Ethan and Joshua put the sword master on their shoulders and paraded him about the dancing and singing Alliance officers. Saria led the warriors in a canticle of victory just like in the ancient scriptures and Martha ordered the trebuchets to fire confetti among the troops. All of the warriors were screaming, "victory!" For one rotation in the West no one cared about race, creed, politics, class, or old rivalries, they were just seeking out someone to celebrate with. Argus simply stood with his arms crossed against his chest, a wide smile beaming across his face.

"Well, Uncle, what do you think of him now?" teased Mesmara.

"Yeah, you've got to admit, he's pretty amazing," quipped Quinn.

"I feel embarrassed to say this, but my knowledge of the ancient language isn't great," offered Argus. "I know his name means "war leader" in the unified, but what does *Cedric* mean in the ancient language?"

"I believe it's roughly translated as 'Hero of Terminus Mundus,'" offered Mesmara.

"Then God bless his mother because she knew all along," prayed Argus.

Thrusting a fist in the air in victory, Cedric shouted to his comrades. "The Acadian Revenge is over! I'm tired and thirsty so let's go home."

Setting Cedric to the ground, the troops happily boarded the hover trains back for Fort Orion. Wrapping her arms around his neck, Cecilia gave her brother a big kiss before leaving to get on the train. Alone now with the Queen on the grassy plains, Cassandra cried tears of joy as she stared at her love.

"Your Highness, Verian is yours and it will never be taken from you again," promised Cedric.

"To hell with Verian! Promise me you'll never be taken from me again."

Cassandra grabbed Cedric tightly as a wave of white feathers showered down from the heavens upon the two. Cedric raised his head to the sky and he watched a golden portal closing behind him.

"Thank you, Teman, and know that if you ever wish to return, you'll always have a home on Terminus Mundus. Good luck in your adventures and may I live to return the favor."

In his mind, he could hear the Guardian say, *That's the beauty of it, you'll never have to.*

Archangel Basilica, Rhinegard, Christmas Day

Our lead story tonight involves the announcement of the Wedding Date of Queen Cassandra Acadia of Central Acadia and Prince Cedric Rhone of Titanus. The Wedding and Coronation will be set for Christmas afternoon. While this is quite an unusual date, there are rumors that mitigating factors were stipulated too in announcing it. We have not been graced with a region-wide Wedding Ceremony in a long time and no doubt Queen Civilia Rhone will spare no expense.

Alliance News Organization on the Wedding Announcement,
Seven Rotations after the defeat of Abaddon

Through the sheer dedication of thousands of Titan workers, the overnight and morning snowfall was cleared from the streets. The first snowfall in Rhinegard in over two hundred revolutions would have caused a lesser Queen to delay such a grand ceremony. Yet, Civilia was determined to make sure this long-awaited ceremony finally occurred. Christmas decorations and Nativity scenes were on display throughout the city and were placed prominently at the Basilica.

The unexpected weather had not drawn away the populace. Citizens of all four kingdoms lined the streets waving banners and shields in the air. Children were lifted on the shoulders of their parents, and everyone wanted to catch a glimpse of the beautiful Acadian Queen when she arrived. Sixteen white horses drew a large crystal carriage surrounded by ten Order of the Lion Knights. The lead rider carried the banner of House Acadia while the two flanking the carriage bore the flags of Central Acadia and the Order standard. Seated in the carriage for all to see was Queen Cassandra herself. The Denivan seamstresses had finalized their masterpiece just eight rotations before the ceremony. While the dress was still a traditional white, the talented artisans took the time to sew the House Acadia coat of arms all over the dress. The lion's eyes in the coat of arms were adorned with diamonds while garnets were stitched down the seams of the gown to give it a rosy hue. White lace covered the Queen's arms and neck and a white lace veil was draped over her face. Since her coronation was finally going to be made official, her raven hair was set without her normal crown. In Cassandra's arms was a bouquet of white roses and red poppies. However, the Queen made sure to place the single white poppy in Garrett's possession in the direct middle of the bouquet. Distracted by the sounds of her name being screamed, the dutiful Cassandra waved to every citizen she could.

"Queen Cassandra Acadia is now passing into the upper district of Rhinegard," reported the on-scene correspondent of ANO. "As you can imagine security has forced some of these people to arrive almost twelve to fifteen hours ahead of time to reach these prime positions. We are experiencing a first in the history of the west. Never before has there been a wedding and a dual coronation. We've checked with some of our fashion experts and some have dared to say that the Queen's gown is the most expensive ever made. It will go on display in the Titan Museum of Art immediately after the wedding and remain there until the Museum of Verian is repaired."

At the steps of Basilica, Knights and Valkyries in ceremonial armor and weapons stood guard. In the center was Cecilia wearing a red gown with gold trim around her hem and neckline with her Valkyrie crown proudly on display. Ethan stood next to her in a black tuxedo with matching black cloak. Popping up and down on her heels to stay warm, the Vanadis pulled her black fur wrap tightly around her chest. Adding to her annoyance, her husband was humming and slapping his thigh in rhythm to one of the songs he had heard from Francis.

"Will you stop singing that ridiculous song!" ordered Cecilia. "I wish Duke Angelino never brought it up."

"I'm sorry, it's catchy. Boy, you look like you're freezing."

"Two hundred revolutions and no snow in Rhinegard. Yet, on the rotation of my brother's wedding, we get this. I'm telling you, Ethan, it's a sign."

"I thought you were done with the whole 'Cassandra is evil incarnate' thing."

"I'm not saying he shouldn't marry her, I'm just saying it's a sign."

"It made for a fun game this morning at least!"

"I'm sure it did. Alas, all of the production it took to make me look this good denied me the opportunity to play in the snow. Come on, Cassandra, hurry up and get that carriage here before I freeze to death!"

Photographers flashed thousands of bulbs at once as the carriage stopped at the steps of the Basilica. A red carpet was rolled down to the carriage as two footmen rushed to the glass door. After opening the door, they assisted the Queen down a set of wooden steps. Her white heels clicking loudly against the wood, Cassandra posed for three shots before finally walking to Cecilia's position. Keiko swooped in behind the Queen dressed in white silk and lace. She grabbed Cassandra's train carefully as she walked along. Cheeks becoming visibly rosy in the cold weather, the raven-haired maiden moved as fast as her dress allowed her.

"It's freezing, Cecilia!" commented Cassandra. "What happened? I thought you said it didn't snow here!"

"At first I was ready to blame you!" countered Cecilia. "All of your talk about a white Christmas. You're over two hours late!"

"The crowds were larger than we expected and the weather…"

The three moved inside quickly as the soldiers outside individually cleared some of the reporters and photographers into a special box in the Basilica.

"I appreciate the tradition of the bride and groom not seeing each other before the wedding," started Cecilia. "Of course, I didn't think you'd take it to the point where you stayed the full rotation at Wilhelm's plantation in the Heartlands rather than in Castle Titan."

"It's bad luck!" exclaimed Cassandra.

"It already snowed! How much worse could our luck get? My brother is about to pace himself through the floor in the back of the church. I don't think there's enough brandy in Rhinegard to calm him down."

"What's he afraid of, that I was going to transform into a succubus Queen and fly down into Hell?"

"As a matter of fact, he confided in me that he dreamed just that last night."

"Poor Cedric. Cecilia, I'm afraid I have to ask one more favor of you."

"Another favor?"

"I've discussed this thoroughly with Walker and I think it would be appropriate if..."

"I understand, your Highness. Consider it done."

Dropping her fur wrap with one of the well-dressed servants, Cecilia walked down the long aisle while Cassandra waited in the church foyer. Amuro and Saria greeted her, wearing matching blue and gold dresses. Not wanting to ruin the preparations of hours of work, they air-kissed one another. Amuro took Cassandra's hand.

"Getting excited yet?" asked Amuro.

"When we got delayed, my stomach felt so bad I thought I was going to ruin my dress and the carriage," commented Cassandra. "But I made it, and I've been waiting for this moment for so long..."

"Well, as one of your best friends, even though you picked Cecilia over me as your Maid of Honor, it's my duty to tell you it's not too late to call it off."

Crestfallen even at the suggestion, the Queen's normally porcelain complexion went ghost white. As she staggered back a few steps, the two Elf sisters managed to catch her.

"That was so mean, Amuro!" pouted Saria. "She has enough on her mind."

"It was important, Saria, that she has all of her options available. Trust me, this girl is ready to go."

As Cassandra regained her composure, Rosa and Hippolyte took up their positions with the bridesmaids. Rosa's gown was green and gold to honor the wood Elves. Hippolyte felt confined in her silver and gold dress. Part of her wanted to rip the ruffles right off of the sleeves, and break the slit all the way up to her hip. However, the Wolf Tribe Chief did not want to insult her hosts. Her break of tradition was that she wore a wolf's tooth necklace rather than traditional jewelry.

"It's a shame that Cedric demanded Colin to be in his party," observed Rosa. "I'm sure your sister would have much preferred to wear a dress like that."

"It's only for one rotation, right?" questioned Hippolyte rhetorically. "I guess I can make one sacrifice after everything Prince Cedric has done for us recently."

The honor guard had taken position on either side of the central pews, dressed in ceremonial white military jackets, black pants, and black boots. Each wore a blue cape attached to their jackets by a gold chain. A golden rapier was present at each of their sides and their hands had white gloves on them. Spying the whole congregation for any last signs of trouble, Horace commanded the honor guard at the front of the church. The Titan War Master made sure everything was perfect from the selection of each individual to cutting off even the smallest string that flawed the uniform. The first row of pews were reserved for the wedding party, and the next two rows were reserved for the Rhone family on the right side and the Acadia and Fenidor families on the left side. Banners were stationed at each pew for every individual nation and tribe, so the main dignitaries from each family had a place to sit. Even King Richard Archibald and his wife Elizabeth attended the ceremony with Saladin of the Chinotal Empire. Sultan Khan wouldn't be caught dead at the occasion, but for protocol's sake he sent a delegation. Due to the nature of the coronation ceremony, many of the rulers still had to process into the church. Praying on the Rhone side of the pew, Wilhelm sat next to a weeping Nadia and Martha Heinrich. The gentle tapping of Cecilia's gloved hand on his shoulder roused his attention.

"Oh, your Highness, is anything wrong?" asked a startled Wilhelm.

"I'm sorry, Wilhelm, but your presence is required immediately in the foyer. It is the wish of the future Queen that with Stephen deceased, her 'father' walks her down the aisle."

"I don't think it's a good idea to broadcast such a thing."

Wilhelm felt a finger jabbing him in his ribs. "Will you just go do it?" demanded Nadia.

"You had something to do with this, didn't you?"

"I will not deny my daughter her one wish at her wedding. Besides, you're the only one worthy to give Cassandra to Cedric."

Wilhelm looked down the long aisle and saw Cassandra standing there. She was following Keiko's instructions for deep breathing routines to calm herself.

"I guess I owe her…"

"Come on! It's late enough as it is and my brother will never forgive us if we keep him waiting any longer."

Standing, to Nadia's delight, Wilhelm started the long walk to the foyer of the Basilica with Cecilia on his flank. From a door on the side, a smiling Christian nodded his head. Dressed in the same black tuxedo as Ethan, he turned to Cedric, who was sipping the last of his brandy in the back of the room. Cedric wore the same tuxedo he had worn the night of the victory ball in Verian.

"You owe me one round, Cedric, he's going to walk her down the aisle," observed Christian.

"A good bet to lose," quipped Cedric. "Best we make our grand entrance, you've got a hike ahead of you."

"Just one last thing before we go. I broke the seal on your orders when I saw the rainbow, I really thought then…"

"That was a reasonable decision."

"I read what you wrote to me. Thank you, it was very touching."

"Hey, you've always been there for me. I always counted on you to question my orders when they needed questioning and followed when they needed to be obeyed. It'll be formally announced soon, but you might as well know Cassandra and I have consented to name you Chancellor of the Alliance."

"Pulling me out of the field, Cedric? Don't you think that's dangerous?"

"You've done the dirty work long enough. If you and Rosa are really going to settle down and have a family, it should be done in the safety of the Royal Court."

"I thought the groom was supposed to get the presents at the wedding. Your Excellency, I graciously accept."

Hugging Cedric one last time in thanks, Christian whispered a last "good luck" into his friend's ear. The Nightblade left the room and headed to the foyer to join the wedding party. The Titan prince left the room and walked straight for the altar. He took a moment to stare at the magnificent mural behind the altar.

"This is the rotation that the Lord has made, let us rejoice and be glad," prayed Cedric.

The Titan prince snapped to attention and turned to face the back of the Basilica, arms at ease. The parties were gathered and ready. Pipes bellowing with entrance music, Horace still managed to shout his orders loud enough for everyone to hear.

"Honor Guard, middle face!"

The honor guard turned in one swift motion so that all of their back heels clicked on the ground at the same time. Staring at their counterparts across the aisle, they waited for their commander's next order.

"Raise arms!"

In a fluid motion, they all drew their weapons from back to front so that it looked as if one began to draw as soon as the one behind had their sword drawn out. Bringing their rapiers to the level of their eyes, the ceremonial procession began. The first to come down the aisle was a group of altar servers lead by Thomas carrying the crucifix, though at times it seemed the weight was going to tip him right over. After the servers came two priests carrying large velvet pillows. On the left pillow was Cassandra's crown and a silver scepter adorned with a white gold and diamond ornament on top. On the right pillow was the Titan ceremonial crown of King Frederick the Great. The circlet of gold was adorned with fifteen diadems representing the provinces of Titanus. Under the reign of Robert Rhone, it was adapted so that the diadems met at a gold cross on top of the crown. The piece of jewelry had never been worn, as the more important symbol of office was the silver-plated mace sitting next to it. The mace had been adorned with Cedric's personal crest that he used in the Acadian Revenge to mark his victory. Officiating the ceremony was both Archbishop Langley and Bishop Wulf. They were attended personally by Father Michael Giovanello.

The next groups to process were the rulers of each of the eleven nations that had taken part in the Final Alliance. Since certain rulers were in the wedding party, Minerva marched for her sister, Gerard marched for Rosa, Argus marched for Wulf, and Alistair Fenidor marched for Evengard. The old codger of an Elf ranger uncharacteristically smiled for once. They arrived in order: Napolitan, Evengard, Deniva, Wolf Tribe, Myotis Tribe, Syrus Clan, Nordice Vikings, Dark Elves, Kablisha, Wood Elves, and Dwarves. After they had taken their places, Samuel marched the banner of House Rhone down the aisle and Civilia was escorted by Joshua. Despite being dressed in the horse blanket she hated, the Matriarch of Destruction proudly processed down the aisle as the mother of the groom. On her right hand was a corsage with a single white poppy in the middle of red ones and she carried her own silver mace down the aisle as the symbol of her office.

The wedding party was the last group to process. The organist altered her music for each couple as they made the final approach to the first row of pews. Christian and Rosa went first. When they reached the front, Christian went straight to the altar while Rosa took her seat. The next couple was Colin and Hippolyte. To honor the Wolf Tribe and maintain his station as Ogle Tanka Un, the assassin wore his cape. Cagius and Saria were next, followed by Amuro and Malcolm. The last two to process were Ethan and Cecilia. As Christian had done before, Cecilia went to the altar while Ethan took his seat. With Cedric waiting for them, both his sister and best friend offered him final encouragement and thanks before everyone faced the back of the church.

As the organist reached her crescendo for the bridal march, Walker stepped forward holding the banner of House Acadia.

"Present arms," ordered Horace.

Raising their swords to form an arch, the Honor Guard waited for Cassandra's arrival. A blinding flash of photographic light overtook the entire Basilica as Cassandra marched down the aisle with Wilhelm escorting her. Keiko carefully fluttered behind him keeping the train up. The tears from the eyes of the little sylph watered the floor of the Basilica. Outside the church, the streets of Rhinegard cheered and celebrated her march via huge screens despite the bitterly cold weather. All across the west, every citizen was glued to a television set. Savoring every moment of the long journey, Cassandra did her best to hold back her tears. After what seemed like an eternity, they finally reached the altar. Using the utmost care, Wilhelm pulled back Cassandra's veil. The sight of her shinning green eyes brought comfort and hope to the sentinel's heart. Embracing him tightly, Cassandra kissed him.

"Thank you, Daddy."

Horace ordered the honor guard to return to their places and each took their place in the aisle.

"Duke Wilhelm von Angelhardt, you stand before us in place of the late King Stephen Acadia, do you consent to give Queen Cassandra Acadia's hand in marriage?" Arthur began the ceremony.

"I do."

Walking over to Cedric, the mentor and ward embraced once more. "She's yours now, Cedric. Take care of her."

The haunting final words of King Stephen resonated in the Titan prince's mind.

Wilhelm genuflected and took his place next to Nadia. She cried and hugged him tightly.

"Jesus Christ, Nadia, no one died!"

"You keep speaking like that in a church, and they'll give you back your black wings."

"*In nomine Patris, et Fillii, et Spiritus Sancti*, amen!" continued Arthur. "We are gathered here today to celebrate the marriage and formal coronation of Queen Cassandra Acadia and King Cedric Rhone. As Archbishop of Titanus and Shepherd of the Faith, it is my duty and privilege to perform both of these ceremonies."

Taking Cassandra's hand, Cedric saw the Queen beaming brightly at her soon-to-be husband. Cedric assisted her as the two knelt before the Bishop. Receiving chrism from one of the servers, the Archbishop dipped his finger and anointed Cedric and Cassandra.

"As sovereigns of your lands, it is your solemn duty to rule in accordance with the Natural Law. Since you would have no power except which is given to you by the Lord God, may the Heavenly Father guide you that you may rule with wisdom, and temper justice with mercy."

The priests brought the velvet pillows forward. Bishop Wulf blessed the crown of Cassandra while Arthur performed a similar blessing on Cedric's mace. When they finished, each Bishop took the symbol of authority and brought it to the kneeling rulers.

"Cassandra Acadia, Queen of Central Acadia, daughter of the King of Justice, Stephen Acadia, as per your traditions, I place this crown upon your head," prayed Bishop Wulf. "May it symbolize your authority to lead the people of this Alliance with grace."

"Cedric Rhone, Prince of Titanus, son of the Matriarch of Destruction Queen Civilia Rhone, as per your traditions, I give to you this mace," offered Bishop Arthur. "May it symbolize your authority to lead the people of this Alliance with strength."

Reverently, Cedric received his mace, as Cecilia and Keiko aided Cassandra with properly setting her crown above the wedding veil.

"Please rise," continued Arthur.

Cedric and Cassandra stood. Bishop Wulf sprinkled the two rulers with holy water as the rulers turned to face the congregation.

"In the name of the Holy Father and before the leaders of the Kingdoms of the Western Alliance, I coronate thee Queen Cassandra Acadia and King Cedric Rhone," pronounced Arthur. "*Vivat Rex, Vive Le Reine.*"

The entire congregation and everyone across the west echoed the statement, "*Vivat Rex, Vive Le Reine!*"

"Please be seated, for Archbishop Langely and I would like to say a few words before we continue with the bonds of matrimony," requested Bishop Wulf.

The congregation was seated as the two Bishops stood side by side.

"This is a magnificent rotation for many reasons," started Wulf. "As many in this congregation know, today is Christmas, the celebration of the birth of Lord Jesus Christ. We also honor Cedric Rhone and Cassandra Acadia. I've come to know them over these past revolutions and may I say that they are two of the most exceptional individuals I have had the privilege to meet."

"At times, the last five revolutions for us has been surreal," explained Arthur. "We were tested beyond the limits of what those in creation would ever expect. Nothing was tested more than the love these two individuals have for one another. It would have been easy for either of them to give up in the face of the circumstances thrust on them. Yet, they persevered and together they delivered us from the darkness. They are a beaming example of Hope and Faith that every citizen of Terminus Mundus should emulate."

"This is truly a rotation that the Lord has made," prayed Bishop Wulf. "Let us rejoice and be glad. Cedric Rhone and Cassandra Acadia, I wish you the best and may you continue to lean on one another through the challenges and changes you will face."

"We will now continue with the sacrament of matrimony," offered Arthur as he beckoned the congregation to stand. "Please bring the rings forward."

Christian and Cecilia each presented a silver wedding band marked with the diamond of Central Acadia and the opal of Titanus. Arthur blessed the rings with holy water and made the Sign of the Cross over them.

"Cassandra Acadia, do you take Cedric Rhone to be your lawfully wedded husband, in sickness and in health, in good times and in bad, for richer or for poorer, until death do you part?"

"I do."

"Cedric Rhone, do you take Cassandra Acadia to be your lawfully wedded wife, in sickness and in health, in good times and in bad, for richer or for poorer, until death do you part?"

"I do."

In the crowd, a loudly crying Florence nudged Mesmara in the ribs. "Don't I get a chance to object to this union?" demanded Florence.

"Not in this ceremony, Florence," answered an annoyed Mesmara.

"Rats!" screamed Florence as she cried harder. "I should have stayed a nun!"

Arthur picked up the first ring. "Cedric, please repeat after me." Arthur gave him the ring. Cedric placed it on Cassandra's finger.

"With this ring, I thee wed..." started Arthur.

"With this ring, I thee wed..." repeated Cedric.

"May it serve as our eternal bond in the eyes of man and God."

"May it serve as our eternal bond in the eyes of man and God."

Arthur handed Cassandra the other ring. She placed it on Cedric's finger.

"Cassandra, repeat after me. With this ring, I thee wed…"

"With this ring, I thee wed…"

"May it serve as our eternal bond in the eyes of man and God."

"May it serve as our eternal bond in the eyes of man and God."

"Princess Cecilia Rhone, Lord Christian DeVries, you have been chosen to bear witness to this holy sacrament," stated Bishop Wulf. "Do you honor this responsibility in the eyes of God and man?"

Both witnesses answered, "I do" simultaneously.

"Then before God and man I pronounce Cedric Rhone and Cassandra Acadia man and wife," pronounced Arthur with a beaming smile. "You've been waiting all this time, your Excellency. You may kiss your bride."

To the sound of deafening applause, Cedric put his hands on either side of Cassandra's face and kissed her. After a good ten seconds, they broke and turned back to the Bishops.

"This is a great hour for our land. May we ask the Holy Father to bless your reign and your marriage," blessed Bishop Wulf. "As promised to our father in faith, may your descendants be as numerous as the stars in the sky and may the scholars preserve your grand deeds. Go forth, *in nomine Patris, et Fillii, et Spiritus Sancti*, amen!"

Wulf made the sign of the cross as the congregation in unison yelled, "Alleluia! Alleluia! Thanks be to God! Alleluia! Alleluia!"

All that was left was the final formality. Cedric and Cassandra recessed down the aisle as husband and wife for the first time. A love that had been tested by the powers of darkness was finally consummated in a most fitting ceremony. As Horace ordered the Honor Guard to arms again, they passed under the golden swords and the Titan king grabbed the Acadian Queen around her shoulder. The massive hordes outside the Basilica snapped every photo and video they could as the two entered the carriage again. The chants of *Vivat Rex, Vive le Reine* resonated throughout the west. The carriage took the two to the Castle for the wedding reception. Martha had a special train built in the underground so the principal delegates of each nation could slip out of the Basilica for the party.

Two hours after the ceremony was complete, the courtyard of Castle Titan was flooded with press and citizens. Ten stories high on the main balcony, the new royal family emerged. Cedric and Cassandra waved from the center. On their right were Civilia, Wilhelm, Nadia, Ethan, and Cecilia. To their left were Rosa, Christian, Amuro, Malcolm, and Keiko. In a single motion, each member threw confetti down onto the people before formally posing for their first shot. After posing for about ten minutes, they returned to the massive celebration going on inside the Castle ballroom. Other coronation parties were being celebrated all over the western plains ranging from a lavish ball to just a bunch of friends having a good time in a local pub. Cedric and Cassandra had touched so many lives it felt that everyone should be celebrating and this Christmas night was a night to remember.

While the others hurried down the staircase to their positions, Cedric and Cassandra took their position at the top of the velvet staircase. The music was interrupted and Walker took his place on a podium on the right side of the staircase.

"Majesties of the Alliance Kingdoms, Chiefs of the Tribes, Margrave of Deniva, and Lords and Ladies of the Outer Realms, allow me to present for the first time together, King Cedric Rhone of Titanus and Queen Cassandra Acadia of Central Acadia."

A thunderous round of applause and whistles reached the couple as they paraded down the stairs. They continued until they reached the podium where Walker stood. The couple took their place on the pedestal as Christian and Cecilia stepped forward. Servants carrying silver trays passed out sparkling wine to everyone gathered in the room.

"I have been given the privilege of offering the first toast to the new sovereigns of our lands," started Christian. "Today is a great rotation for many reasons. I remember back a revolution ago when many of us were sitting together at a Christmas celebration, boasting that we'd all be celebrating a wedding in the halls of Castle Titan. It seems so long ago, because of all that has happened since then. The traitors have been overthrown and brought to justice. Cassandra, it is a testament to your strength that you were able to overcome all of the hardship that befell you because of Abaddon's actions. It is clear to me now why Cedric told me the rotation of the jousting tournament that you were the girl he was going to marry."

There was a lot of fawning and sighing in the room.

"Cedric Rhone, the knight who seems to have the power to defy fate. You held together the most ambitious coalition ever attempted and when it seemed like all was lost…you spit right in the eye of the devil. No person in the West, let alone this room, can ever repay you for what you've done. From the time we were little kids playing as crusaders together, I didn't realize that my friend and I would have to win the greatest crusade of all. God bless you and our great land."

Everyone took a drink and said, "Here, here." Cecilia stepped forward and there was a sense of foreboding concerning the nature of her toast.

"As Christian recounted, I remember Cassandra's Quize well. I remember the tournament where I became the first woman to ever make the final four… thank you very much. At the conclusion of that tournament, my brother had the option of crowning the Queen of Love and Beauty—a crown I demanded from him, but he passed me over for a young, beautiful, raven-haired maiden. And I hated her for that alone!"

Everyone laughed with Cecilia as she played it up.

"The next time I saw her at a ball I had my insults ready and then came pretty close to stabbing her as well. Cassandra, I had always fashioned myself as the perfect maiden, and, who are we kidding, I still do. However, my brother saw something in you and the suffering we pulled ourselves through made me see that something as well. You are the worthy wife for the greatest hero in the history of my planet and I am proud to have you as more than a sister-in-law, but as an equal. I lament for your loses over these past five revolutions and on behalf of my family we gladly welcome you with open arms."

Cassandra had been good the whole rotation, but Cecilia's heartfelt sincerity finally put her over the top. Bawling uncontrollably, she clutched her Maid of Honor tightly and cried on her shoulder.

"Careful, dear," teased Cecilia. "The crying comes the rotation after the wedding. As for my beloved brother, Cedric..."

Cedric stared at Cecilia expecting the worst, but she smiled with a tearful glint in her eyes.

"You always promised your baby sister that you'd make the demons go away. I know you hate it, so let me say on behalf of everyone, thank you!"

Instead of applause, the men and women in the room bowed and curtsied in front of the Titan king.

"Enough hero worshipping, this is supposed to be a party," requested Cedric. "And now as per Titan custom, it is my duty and honor to escort my lovely wife onto the dance floor and have our first dance as a married couple. That's only if she's managed to empty all the tears out of her eyes. Maestro, if you please..."

Extending her hand out to her husband, the Queen allowed the Titan king to take her to the dance floor. Cedric had selected a traditional Titan waltz for the wedding song with a lead violin soloist playing above the rest. As the dance consisted solely of turns and changing steps, it was an obvious performance of the superior dance skills of the bride and groom. During one of the steps, Cassandra pulled close to Cedric.

"Cedric, I love you."

"I love you too, Cassie."

"Since we're this happy now, you don't suppose some demon from below is going to break through the floor this second and start a new holy war?"

"Don't worry, we'll kill him first."

"The destiny of these lands is in our own hands now."

"Are you nervous, Cassie?"

"Part of me…but knowing you are with me brings me comfort. We will do this together."

"Even with our friends, we will experience difficult times. The economic indicators are bad… we're about to have a recession here in Titanus. The financial markets don't look promising…not to mention the dilapidated infrastructure."

"War is a terrible thing. My beautiful city is a wasteland…. and the finances…"

"Peace is as difficult a thing as war… but we'll do this…"

As a second song played, Civilia came to dance with Cedric while Wilhelm took Cassandra's hand. The other couples soon joined them as well.

The plague that had covered the Western Plains had been eradicated. The traitors vanquished, the Demonkin broken, and the Fallen Angel that led the people of Terminus Mundus astray would be tormented in the fires of Hell. Thirteen nations of people lived in peace for the first time in countless revolutions. King Cedric and Queen Cassandra Rhone had taken their place as stewards of the Western Alliance. Changes and challenges awaited all of the heroes as they anticipate the new disasters just on the horizon. The Acadians had their Revenge, but the Saga of Terminus Mundus was far from over…

EPILOGUE

GRAVIUS COUNTRY ESTATE, NAPOLITAN

The laws of the Acadian succession shall be agnatic-cognatic primogeniture. As such, any son born of the King's bloodline has the right to inherit the Central Acadian throne before his sisters. Only in the absence of a son shall a daughter be considered.

On Acadian Succession, Marquis Nicholas Acadia

Gavin and Roland stood around a television watching the events of the rotation. Despite their rebellion, the Acadians could not pull themselves away from the ascension of an Acadian to the throne.

"She does look beautiful," commented Roland.

"Yes," returned Gavin. "Makes you wonder why we bet on the wrong horse."

"It seemed a great idea at the time. It was nice of Norville Warrington to give us a place to hide out for a while."

"Warrington never gives anything for free. We're getting called into service, I know it."

"Shall we drink to the Acadian Queen?"

"It is proper."

The two raised their glasses and said *Vive le Reine.* After slugging down the booze, they heard the door to the room opening. On high alert, the two went for their weapons, but they dropped them quickly when Norville entered.

"Gentlemen, come now," Norville calmed them down. "You have the assurances and pledge of Matthias Gravius that you have sanctuary here."

"We'll take our own chances," countered Gavin. "Ever since Cedric promoted him, Valentine has been very effective at hunting rebels."

"Valentine won't be a problem much longer, he's heading to court with Cedric," Norville assured them. "With DeVries promoted to Chancellor, a new head of spy operations will be needed."

"Why so generous, Norville?" asked Roland. "You must have a reason for keeping us here."

"I've come across sensitive information. There have always been rumors, but a source has informed me that Stephen had another child."

"Nothing the Saints have ever heard of," added Gavin.

"Considering that butcher Marimon's track record, I'm not surprised," scolded Norville. "A source within the Empire has confirmed that there is a teenager living in the Imperial capital who is about five revolutions younger than the late Marie. Apparently he's shacked up with some powerful merchant's family. The boy had a physical recently, and Stephen's DNA was matched to him."

"Was this done by the source as well?" asked Gavin.

"Yes."

"It's a little too coincidental that an Imperial would be so magnanimous to the rebels," considered Roland. "Aren't they still furious with us for Deniva?"

"The Sultan is, but he's getting old," noted Norville. "Saladin cannot keep all of the Sultanate advisors in line anymore and many of them are jousting for power. While we can't do anything with the teenager yet, this particular advisor promised us aid if we were to take up arms against Cedric and Cassandra."

"If we do so, we need more than a single DNA test," said Gavin. "It's a very serious charge to claim Cassandra violated the succession laws, especially in light of Stephen's abdication."

"Stephen seemed to be under great stress at the moment with Jonas' sword over his head," responded Norville. "I can make it work, if this source is correct."

"Just who is so eager to see Cedric disposed of?" inquired Roland.

"Ivar Rhone," answered Norville. "The exiled brother of Civilia!"

We hope you enjoyed *The Acadian Revenge*
Book 3 of *The Saga of Terminus Mundus* series by
Michael Mazzaro.

For additional titles by this author and others, including
Book 1, *The Legend of the Last Knight*, and Book 2,
The Denivan Exile, please visit our website and online
catalog at:
http://www.signalmanpublishing.com